The Tudjina

Mirrors in
Black & White

Linda Keres Carter

ISBN-13: 978-1530658053
ISBN-10: 1530658055

Pronunciation Guide

j	as in y̲es
c	ts sound as in ma̲t̲s̲
č	as in c̲h̲urch
ć	as in t̲u̲ne
đ	as in G̲eor̲g̲e
ž	as in plea̲s̲ure
r	as in register, or dirt, lightly trilled, used as both consonant and vowel/consonant.

To Nada Ljubic, my dear friend in Belgrade, many thanks for an incredible gift — knowledge of the origins I'd sensed all along, that were the most important thing in my life all along. Without your encouragement and tireless patience with countless questions, this story could not have been written.

"The worst thing you can do to a people is take away their memory of themselves." – Randall Robinson

". . . the people who do this thing – who practice racism – are bereft. There's something distorted about the psyche. It's a huge waste and it's a corruption and a distortion. It's like a profound neurosis that nobody examines for what it is. It feels crazy. It *is* crazy. And it has just as much of a deleterious effect on white people, possibly equal to what it does to black people." – Toni Morrison

American racism is the perversion of the Post Traumatic Slave Syndrome[1] of the runaway slaves *of Europe.* – Linda Keres Carter

---

[1] Joy DeGruy, Ph.D., *Post Traumatic Slave Syndrome,* Joy deGruy Publications, 2005

"I *love* people from persecuted minorities. We're the bomb. We have superhuman powers. We *have to*. My loyalty knows no bounds and I'd go through any kind of difficulties on our behalf. I've even been known to *put up with us.*

"America wants to tell me it's impossible for me to define 'my own' across the Great Divide (of race). Kiss my ass America."

– Leslie, 2018

Chapter 1
The Throwback

A Match Made in Serbian Heaven, 1976

Jovanka, recently recruited as a Guardian Angel, was lithely dancing the *kolo* in Serbian Heaven when she heard about the American brother who was destined to rescue her Goddaughter, Leslie, from the *Tudina*. As she danced, a floret of tiny red flowers bounced furiously at the end of her waist-length braid of shiny, blue-black hair. More red flowers danced along the bottom of her black apron. Above them, on the body of the apron, rows of gold coins jangled a high-pitched percussion along with the music.

During her lifetime on earth, at a time when even the leather to make a pair of shoes was hard to come by, there had never been any coins to adorn her apron. But God in His Heaven is always the most indulgent to those of His children who gave their lives defending their own, whose lines are now extinct, with no children left on earth to pray for their heavenly repose.

The many coins on her apron in Heaven were pure, solid gold. There were so many, that after dancing for hours her waist would be chafed from the weight of them. She had added an embroidered set of black suspenders to support them more comfortably.

There were smaller gold coins suspended from her headband as well, with strings of tiny, sparkling beads cascading above her ears. If these touches were reminiscent of harem girls, that was a fact no one *ever* mentioned, it being too humiliating to reflect on how many of their girls had been stolen and sold into the slavery of harems. The coins, a gift from God, and the beads accented her large, light brown eyes, flecked with gold, fringed dramatically with dark lashes and brows.

Her genie shoes, braided tan leather uppers culminating in a curved up-spout at the toe, suggested that she could take flight, as she danced more in mid-air than on the floor. She moved like a graceful child with the complexity of movement typical of a strong, kinetic intelligence.

The kolo is highly aerobic. It's danced in a circle with a basic pattern of three bouncy steps in place, followed by three steps to the right. With each step, the dancer stands uncommonly erect and skips upward as high as possible. The music is loud and primely rhythmic in the style of Central European peasants, heavy on a muscularly-belted accordion.

Jovanka's group danced a complex choreography. This included a Kossack-style step the young men would do, crouching down and then leaping upward with a strong front kick. Since they were in Heaven, however, where gravity has less effect, particularly on spirits such as they, their Kossack kicks, starting from a crouched position, sent them over five feet into the air. It was quite impressive.

All the girls, and all the boys in Jovanka's circle, or *kolo*, were from the *Krajina*, the No-Man's-Land that defined the border between the Middle

East and Western Europe for three centuries. That was no accident. It was an act of will. Theirs.

During their lifetimes on earth, most had been the Keepers of the Gate, or Grenzers, runaway slaves resisting the onslaught of their Turkish enslavers to the East, who still held in peonage slavery their brothers and sisters on the Eastern side of the border, in colonized Serbia. The rest were from the generations following that enslavement, when their status had slipped to that of vermin, and had died defending their helpless ones.

They were all dressed with impeccable consistency, the girls with their black skirts, gold coins and floral embroidery, the boys in matching vests and fez. Each one was either quite beautiful or at the very least, extremely interesting.

She was just finishing the dance, scarcely winded, when a much older soul, a shipwrecked sailor by the name of Dušan, told her about his many greats grandson, Daniel, the American brother who was destined to rescue Jovanka's Goddaughter, Leslie.

Dušan stood well above six feet, well-muscled for someone who still moved like a cat. He had a broad jaw and heavy brow accented by dramatically arched eyebrows and warm, dark eyes he worked like a rakish magician – an extraordinarily handsome fellow.

He had lived on earth during an era when there were still a few seaports in the Balkans launching ships that sailed even to China, actualizing themselves across the planet. His ship had floundered in a hurricane off the Outer Banks of what became North Carolina, thirty years after Contact, in 1522AD. Kindly locals took him in, and he lived a long life among them, leaving behind many beloved descendants of color.

He had to shout to be heard above the din, "I hear you're trying to find a Balkan scholar in America. Have I got the genius for you!" He motioned toward the door and the two made their way out of the boisterous hall.

He then told her about his great-great-great-great-great-grandson, Daniel. "I mean really great," he said, "A real gem. You gotta see this guy."

"You think he can understand my Goddaughter Leslie?"

"What needs to be understood?"

"She doesn't know she's a Krajina Serb, or what's been happening to us. She has been told she is a Croat," she said, then bitterly, "though none have taken her family in." She lowered her voice dramatically and leaned towards him. "She is a victim of cultural genocide, *kulturna genocida*, lost in the *Tuđina*."

"My God!' said the sailor, crossing himself with three fingers. "What a cruelty. To live without knowing you're a Serb! How can the world possibly make any sense?"

But then he tapped her on the shoulder with a thought, "Ah, but you know. Daniel is obsessed with the subject." He pronounced the word "obsessed" with reverence.

Jovanka continued with her explanation, "Yes, she is a total throwback. A beautiful sight to see. All she knows is who seems familiar, the people there the most like us, and that's who she loves, of course – the *Amerikanac* she has, as they say, assimilated to. Thank God." She crossed herself. "We are so proud. But the other *Amerikanac* are persecuting her for it, for choosing the Kingdom of Heaven. Of *course*, she's depressed.

"What we need is someone to rescue her and bring our family back to life in the world, at long last. We will never be extinct, never. Only dormant, waiting for spring," she said, then flinging her arms out fervently, "to sprout!"

"And he's the one to get it sprouting, eh?" he nudged her with a wink and a loud guffaw of lusty laughter. "Well, let me tell you about this boy. This is what I've had to do on the in-law's side, over in the Chowan Spirit World.

"Over there it's very strict," he went on. "You must look after your children for seven whole generations, and all your decisions, while you lived, were supposed to be for a whole seven generations out. And they say the bond is the strongest with the last of the seven generations. So, the wife was after me to keep up with all that and now I'm glad I did because that boy hears everything I say, I swear. And he's looking for me! He doesn't realize that's what he's doing, but that's just making him look all the harder!"

"Yes, I would love to meet your wife," Jovanka said. "I absolutely adore extinct people. They are my favorite. We need to stick together, you know, and be as noisy as possible . . . the noisiest of ghosts."

"Please don't teach my wife to be as noisy as a *Srpkinja*," he teased, referring to female Serbs.

Jovanka laughed very loudly, slapped at his hand and fairly shouted, "And I shall learn from her secrets on how to keep in line such a rude fellow as yourself!" Several people turned their heads in her direction, distracted by all the commotion.

"How could anyone say such a thing about me?" he asked.

"Anyone who's made your acquaintance," she countered.

3

"Yes, sister, I see what it will be like to be in a family with you," he said.

"So, tell me about this genius child of yours," she asked.

"He is a very special young man. Ever since he was a little boy he always followed me whenever I led him out a little further than he wanted to go. I taught him how to cross many a narrow gangplank. That came in handy later when he started admiring what The Turk did to us!"

"God forbid!" cried Jovanka, crossing herself.

"But I just had to knock a few books in his path and he got the picture right away and straightened right up. Why does your girl need for him to be black, *crni?*" he asked. "Unusual request coming from America. I should know, most of my descendants are considered *crni*."

"Those are the people she listens to," Jovanka replied. "She's mistaken them for us. They are the most like us. Don't you see? She doesn't know who she is, but she *feels* it." She pounded her heart with her hand.

"Interesting. I can see how that would happen . . . No one knows better than me how much they are like us. They've been living through what *we*'ve been living through." He felt a sour burn in his stomach, which he knew was entirely his imagination, since, naturally, being a ghost, angel or no angel, what a ridiculous idea, whoever came up with that? *Gospodi pomiluj.* Obviously, he had no stomach to burn, but it burned nevertheless, as did his words. "It didn't matter where I was, the same things were happening to the same kinds of people."

Jovanka crossed herself and spoke reverently, "Yes, they are God's favorites, too."

Dušan burst out laughing, amused with Jovanka's 'humility.' "But they don't like themselves nearly as much as we do," he said, and laughed some more, knowing it was harmlessly going over her head that he was laughing at her. With affection.

"But they *must*," she said, her face stricken with concern. Though she'd been in Heaven thirty-five years she still had the earnestness of an eighteen-year-old. "How have they managed without liking themselves?"

Dušan laughed again and crossed his arms in front of himself, "I don't know, but I certainly enjoy watching," he said.

Jovanka continued her explanation. "So that's what's going on. She has been told she's a Croat and knows nothing about us. All she's been told is that Croats are better than Serbs. But being a natural Serb, she can't *stand* people who think they're better."

4

Dušan's brain exploded with a carousel of images from Leslie's life, just like that. 'So, You did have mercy on me, *Gospode*,' he thought, grateful for the quick backfill, then took Jovanka's hand.

"Actually, this is perfect!" he said, shaking her hand warmly. "Your girl is just the one for my boy. I can see you will soon be my new sister. Come, let me buy you some *šjlivovica*. Let's go make a toast to the happiness of our beautiful children."

They made their way to the church bar to buy their plum brandy. Some of the neighboring heavens thought it scandalous that a church should have a bar, but those in Serbian heaven thought it very good sense. Nobody's going to get foolishly drunk at a church bar. No, they are just going to imbibe a bit of convivial spirits as they ought and leave it at that.

Warmed by the brandy, Jovanka and Dušan sang several songs with the lively group singing in the church bar.

"So, my sister, *moja sestra,*" he said. "When can we start on this adventure?"

"The sooner the better," she replied.

"Well, then, let's go!" he said, jumping up enthusiastically. "We can catch him in his lecture hall."

"His what?"

"He's an assistant professor."

"Oh!" said Jovanka, smiling broadly, her eyebrows raised, impressed. "Good deal!"

"Let's go," he repeated.

"No, no, I have to change. I want to wear something else."

He laughed good-naturedly. "Once a woman, always a woman."

"Why thank you," she said.

"But why should it matter what you wear? Hardly anyone ever sees us."

"It's not about being seen. It's about the total experience. Come on with me. I have just the thing for you to wear."

"Me?"

"Yes, I have a plan."

She took him to the little cottage she shared with her husband, Srđa. He was not so dashing a figure as Dušan. He had light brown hair and stood at an average height. He had about him an air of good-natured brilliance. He loved history and had used his knowledge to appoint the simple home with all the trimmings of a 19th-century Serbian peasant cottage, including a rough stone floor, rough-hewn furniture and fragrant

5

dried herbs hanging from the rafters under the steeply pitched roof that gave the tiny room the vaulted feeling of a chapel.

A raised firepit was in the center, used for warmth and cooking, directly above a vent in the center of the roof. It was more decorative than functional, since, in Serbian Heaven, it was never cold, and no one was ever truly hungry. Just thinking would produce whatever dish that was a sentimental favorite, without any beast ever being slaughtered.

Jovanka took his hand and faced Dušan, "My Srđa was one of only 30 people, out of the 40,000 in our district, who had a college education," she boasted, pronouncing the last words distinctly. "You have no idea how much my vocabulary has improved since meeting him. He absolutely delights me with words."

"Nice to meet you," said Srđa, "don't mind my wife, she never brags about herself. Just me. It's terribly embarrassing."

"The love of my life," she explained to Dušan. "*And* my after-life." Then she addressed Srđa. "Dušan thinks he has just the boy for our Leslie. He's going to take me to him." She was unbraiding her hair. "Do you want to come, baby? We're about to run down there."

"All right then," he said. "Do I have to change as well?"

"Well no, I think these will fit Dušan better."

She gave Dušan some clothes while on the way to change hers. When she came out she was resplendent in a lovely flower child outfit, with a paisley top, jeans with gargantuan bell bottoms, enormous sunglasses, and platform shoes. She wore a headband with a large, perky pink plastic flower in the middle of her forehead. Srđa was amused.

She inspected Dušan's attire. "You make a great hippie," she said.

"Yes, I must admit, this does suit me," he said of his own get-up, a flowered shirt with wide lapels he had only buttoned to mid-chest so as to reveal his manly chest hair. He already had long hair on his head.

"Ready?" she said.

"Certainly, let's go." Dušan took her hand and she held Srđa's as they all three stood shoulder-to-shoulder. He turned to look at them to be sure they were on his wavelength since they had quite a distance to go on that basis alone.

He nodded as they took a step forward and stepped into university commons bustling with young people hurrying in many directions between stately oaks and old Gothic architecture. It was the University of Chicago. The year was 1976.

Jovanka was delighted. It was a glorious autumn day, a pleasant breeze rustled the golden leaves of the oaks. "What a beautiful square," she said.

"I always dreamed of going to college. Now you see why I wanted to dress like the natives. Today I am a college girl."

"And I am a 400-year-old college boy," Dušan said.

"I used to crash lectures here in the thirties," said Srđa. "Jovanka failed to mention that much of my college education was acquired on the sly."

"Really," said Dušan. "What a good idea. Is the place changed much?"

"The place is the same, but the people look entirely different."

They were, in fact, in a throng of 'natives' dressed as they were, tie-dyed tee shirts colorfully competing with the golden foliage. Big hair was everywhere. Big Afros, big Jew-fros, big curly jumbles of unkempt hair, long, straight hair wafting in the breeze. Some were dressed conservatively, but here the Silent Majority was clearly a minority.

Dušan escorted them to a lecture on Islamic history in one of the old Gothic halls. It was filled with young people, black and brown, just one blue-eyed blonde boy sat in the front. He was a Bosniak boy whose uncle and aunt from Sarajevo had made the acquaintance of Malcolm X while in Mecca. They were quite sure it was them he had referred to in his autobiography – the blue-eyed blondes who had convicted him of the humanity of Europeans.

The three ghosts wandered down to the front of the class and surveyed it. Dušan whispered to Jovanka, "Why am I whispering? No one can hear us. I always forget." So quite loudly he asked her to see if she could guess which one was Daniel, although in those days he was still known by the name Hakim he had taken on several years earlier while exploring Islam.

She surveyed the assemblage of bright, handsome young people, then closed her eyes. She spread her hands in front of her.

Srđa chuckled. "Her Geiger counter," he mumbled to Dušan.

"Her what?" he asked, lost.

"I'm sorry. I forgot that's not your era."

After surveying the crowd Jovanka looked toward Dušan and pointed at an average-looking brother of average height, with broad shoulders, unequivocally brown skin he was clearly very comfortable in, an oval face with high cheekbones, his haircut a 'natural,' meaning his own natural, nappy hair, closely cut, and very bright eyes. He exuded the air of someone concerned with seeing, not being seen. Dušan smiled broadly and nodded. Jovanka excitedly chased up the aisle and sat down next to Hakim (aka Daniel).

The professor, a black American in a fez, was finishing up his lecture. "So, in conclusion, during that period of history when Jews were being burned or driven into the ocean in an Inquisition, the Islamic empires exercised a degree of religious tolerance unknown elsewhere, free of persecution and forced conversion. Any questions?"

"Except, of course," muttered Jovanka, "when they were stealing our eight-year-old boys."

Hakim raised his hand. When the professor saw it he almost hid a frown as he acknowledged Hakim. "Yes, Daniel?"

There were several gasps from people who understood the relationship between the two men and knew that the professor's sudden use of Hakim's Christian name, Daniel, heralded the professor's decrial of Daniel's fall from the blessings of Islam. At least insofar as it existed on his department floor.

"What is your estimation of the practice of the blood levy?"

"The what?" the professor squinted.

"The Ottoman practice of stealing the best and the brightest of non-Muslim children, every fifth eight-year-old boy, inducing their conversions to Islam and impressing them into eventual military service for the Empire."

Most of the students had turned in their seats to stare and/or glare at Daniel, intoxicated by the scandalous unfolding of scholastic heresy. At least in that department.

Daniel pressed forward. "It's estimated that 3.5 million boys were stolen in Serbia alone during its 530-year occupation. They were trained as *janissaries,* in other words, goons, who enforced a brutal, enslaving police state onto their Serbian parent population. There are even anecdotes of parents who were driven mad by the practice and would cut off some of their son's fingers to make them defective and prevent them from being stolen. The *janissaries* were the base population of the present-day Moslems of Bosnia, the Bosniaks." The blonde boy in the front row winced angrily.

Jovanka was beside herself. She threw her arm across him and planted a big kiss on his cheek.

He then shifted in his seat, closer to her, and leaned onto that cheek with his hand.

"I love this guy!" she shouted down to Dušan, who was watching bemusedly. "You're right. He's perfect. My hero!"

Jovanka was in Seventh Generation Heaven.

8

She followed the newly re-Christened Daniel home, with Dušan and Srđa tagging along behind.

They followed Daniel on to his apartment. His girlfriend was already there. Dismayed, Jovanka regrouped, settling in to observe.

The girlfriend's name was Tina, a tiny, bright-eyed, nutmeg-colored girl with a cherubic innocence to her face, haloed by a perfect circle of fluffy hair. She chatted with Daniel in her soft, high-pitched voice as she made two grilled cheese sandwiches on the tiny apartment stove.

They fell silent as they began eating.

Jovanka was about to place her hand on Tina's shoulder, to discover what Tina was thinking, when Dušan pulled her into the living room.

"You're right," she said. "I can't meddle."

"Don't worry, you don't have to," he said.

"What do you mean?"

"There is a situation brewing here. You will see. There are some things, like a boil on your butt, that can only come to a head."

"Oh, why did you have to bring up that image?" she said, laughing.

Joining in her laughter, he teased. "Why, have you had one?"

"No, but my husband did."

"And you're the one who had to pop it?" Dušan asked.

She fell out onto the couch, laughing, and forgot all about her anxiety concerning Tina.

* * *

Daniel had an appointment the next day with the professor he was assisting, the same man Daniel had clashed with the day before in the lecture hall.

"What is this shit?" Professor X asked.

The door into the cluttered office was ajar. Professor X stomped over to it and shut it.

Dušan, Daniel's Guardian Angel, always enjoyed walking straight through shut doors and, nonchalantly, did so. He settled down into a side chair to witness the exchange.

The Professor picked up a stapled document and waved it at Daniel. "Abuses of the Moorish and Ottoman Empires?"

"Yeah?" said Daniel.

"You'll do well," said the professor. "Playing right into The Man's hands." He threw the paper down onto the desk in front of Daniel.

"I'm not playing paddy cake with anybody," Daniel replied. "Equality is a bit more nuanced than anybody's party line – it has to be about both power *and* powerless*ness*. That's how I feel, and I don't care which set of thought police are trying to push me. Are my arguments defended properly, or aren't they? That's the only issue you are authorized to address. Whatever chunk of truth has come to my attention that I want to investigate is entirely my business.

"So, are they?" Daniel pressed.

"Are they what?"

"Are my arguments well defended?"

"I haven't read them yet."

"Ah, I see. Those are the kind of academic standards we have around here." Daniel picked the paper up and handed it back to the professor. "Hope you enjoy." He left the office. The professor tossed the paper onto a credenza already stacked with papers. It slid onto the floor, crumpled, where he left it.

Dušan stuck around until the professor left. He'd spotted a fez on the bookshelf he wanted to check out. He tried it on and looked at his reflection. He took it off and read the Aramaic.

"'Believers are like brothers.' Well, brother, you took something of ours, so I will take something of yours." He put the fez on his head and left with it. It looked good on him. Fortunately, he remembered to transition it into his realm just before the department secretary would have seen it sauntering down the hall by itself.

* * *

Daniel and Tina were eating subs in a small, hole-in-the-wall shop on Seminary Street. It had started life as somebody's front lawn. The deli bar was on the long front porch, a customer stepped up three steps to make his order, then sat at one of the tiny bistro tables in what was once part of the front lawn.

Daniel stuffed his mouth with some fries. "What pisses me off," he said, "is that I actually feel guilty applying for that grant."

"Why, baby?" she asked.

"It's not because I care what anybody would say about me. It's that, even though he's an ass, I still understand all the work he's done and why.

I don't want to harm that. But this concept I'm exploring is very important. It's the idea the great ones always understood and is why they're the ones who have always progressed the struggle the furthest.

"The trick is not in getting the white folks to see *our* humanity. It's to see *theirs*. When you can do that, that's when you're free and the world changes. And that's why this work fascinates me."

"Wow, baby, that's deep." She looked into his eyes and smiled. She touched his hand, then reached for some fries. "He's really not an ass," she went on. "Neither are you. And he does think you're talented. He said so just the other day."

"But you do understand the deal, don't you?" Daniel asked. "Wilkerson is the head of the Manson grants. The same racist ass who good ol' Ralph X had to fight like crazy to get his dissertation accepted, and then fight again to get the Islamic Department instituted."

"I understand," she said and touched his hand.

Later that week Daniel got a letter from the University stating that his position as a teaching assistant had been terminated.

* * *

"What the hell is this?" Daniel demanded as he burst into the professor's office. He was brandishing the termination letter in his hand but had a whole new 'what the hell' on his face once he'd opened the door.

Tina was sitting in Ralph X's lap.

Daniel was in a rage. Too angry for words. Too angry to dare any action, except one. He completed the application for the Manson Grant with an immense sense of pleasure.

As soon as he dropped it into the mail chute, he started thinking about Tina. His sprite was gone. His sweet little sprite was gone. He woke up dreaming about her, turning to the empty side of the bed, only remembering that it was empty when he opened his eyes.

She had no idea what she was getting herself into. He thought of his mom, how emaciated she became in the end, how removed from the world, lost in a sea of depression. Her greatest sin in life was that of loving selflessly someone who betrayed her relentlessly.

Just like his mom, Tina was headed for nothing but disaster with a man like Ralph. He had to warn her. He called her and asked her to meet him at the cafe on Lincoln.

11

It was an odd, triangle shaped building that sat at the juncture of three angled roads. They sat at the table in the front that gave them a view of three streets at once.

"Whether you want to be with me or not, I need to warn you about a jerk like that," he said. "You're the one who will be hurt. It won't even occur to him to take *any* kind of responsibility."

Tina's girlish face remained impassive. "Daniel I'm really sorry I did you like this. I really do care about you, but I'm just not in love with you. And you're wrong about Ralph. He does love me. I'm sure of that. Daniel, look at me, he's not your father. This is not the same situation. I'm really touched that you're concerned about me when you have every right to be hating on me. You're a great, great guy. I know there's somebody out there looking for you. I'm sure of it. It just isn't me."

Several weeks later Daniel received word that he was the recipient of the largest grant in the history of the Manson Endowment Fund.

* * *

There Are No Accidents

Jovanka was following Daniel through a University hallway. She'd been working on the timing for several days. They passed by a tall young man with light brown hair whose name was Nikola. Jovanka knocked a book from the pile Nikola was carrying into Daniel's path.

"I'm so sorry . . . *Žao mi je.*" Nikola said as the two young men reached for the book. "I'm so clumsy," he laughed, "too much *šljivovica* last night!"

Daniel noticed the book's cover, written in Cyrillic. "What kind of Cyrillic is that?" he asked. "Russian?"

"*Ne,*" Nikola replied. "*Srpske.*"

"You can read Serbian? No kidding!"

"I would be in sorry shape, *brate,* if I couldn't," Nikola smiled.

"I have a grant to write a dissertation on the Ottoman occupation of the Balkans. There's money for translations. Maybe you'd be interested."

"I'm always interested in money, *moj brat.* I'm always interested in that topic, as well."

"Well, whoever said there are no accidents?" Daniel said as he headed in Nikola's direction.

Jovanka threw her arms across both their shoulders and kissed them on their cheeks. "Not when I'm around!" she cried with glee. Daniel touched his cheek absently.

"So, you're post-grad?" Daniel asked.

"*Da.* Yes."

"Did you get your undergrad here?"

"No, not here."

"Where?"

"Howard University," Nikola replied.

"Really," said Daniel, surprised Nikola would go to a historically black college. "Why'd you choose Howard?"

Nikola threw his arm across Daniel's shoulder, "Just between you and me, *brata*," he said, speaking confidentially, "I feel more comfortable around black *Amerikanac* than white. You are the more familiar. We two are like mirrors, but I'm not telling you anything you won't see for yourself, as you write your dissertation. And I will help. *Rado.* Gladly."

"Fascinating," said Daniel.

"Oh," said Jovanka mischievously, "you will be much more fascinated by the time I'm done with you."

Daniel smiled.

"I take it 'brata' means 'brother,' he asked, and Nikola nodded. "You must have picked up the habit of calling people that at Howard."

Nikola burst into laughter. "Go to Serbia, *brata*, and find out for yourself."

* * *

Srđa had been doing a lot of thinking about a conversation he had with Daniel, while the young man was sleeping. That's an important Guardian Angel technique — talking to the living in their dreams. He was hoping to talk to Dušan about the conversation, but first, he had to locate the rascal. Availing himself of the latest Guardian technology, which is always forty or fifty years ahead of that on earth, he had to focus his attention for an unusually long period of time, over 25 seconds, before the search bar in his head brought up Dušan's location on maps.angels.God. He flew on out, enjoying the transcontinental scenery beneath him. He liked traveling at the same height and speed as the big jetliners.

It was an unusually clear night, just city lights and starlight, all across the country. Then there it was, floating in a Caribbean bay —a 16th-

century galleon. Where else to find Dušan? Except how in the world did he come up with a 16th-century galleon?

By then it was sunrise — a breathtaking view of the tropical paradise — the sky and water gloriously aglow in reds, oranges and golds. He could see Dušan perched on the railing along the bow of the ship, fishing. "Of course," thought Srđa, "The perfect time of day for him to have the place to himself, before all the tourists take over."

* * *

From the bow of the ship, Dušan squinted into the distance. He could swear he saw someone off a ways swoop very calmly downwards, as if he was falling to earth, feet first, but slowed up at the end as if a parachute had caught him. Except there was no damn parachute. Then the dude landed on the water, as gracefully as a cat lands on all fours. He headed straight towards Dušan, on the water. Yes, walking on the water, calm as can be, as if the cat did it every day.

"Zadravo, brate!" Dušan called out to Srđa when he stopped about ten feet away from the ship, and ten feet down from where Dušan sat, who said to him, "Now that was one fine, purely Serbian entrance."

Srđa looked up at him and smiled wryly. "You don't think any of the other Guardians could master the technique?"

"No damn way, and if you can get your sorry ass on up here, I got a pole here with your name on it."

A fine, heavy-duty rod and reel suddenly materialized to his left. Srđa's eyes lit up at the seductive object. With absolutely no exertion whatsoever, he lightly skipped the ten feet up and sat on the railing as casually as he'd sit on a sofa in a parlor.

"What a treat!" he exclaimed.

Dušan handed him a small shrimp to use for bait.

Srđa observed the small creature writhing in his hand. "Poor thing," he said.

Dušan shook his head. "What are you looking for me to do, man, bait your damn hook for you?"

"No," said Srđa, smiling at Dušan's teasing. "I can bait my own hook." If he was to serve as a Guardian, he had to live on earth's terms and inure himself once again to the sufferings of all the creatures in God's creation. "I do my best thinking while fishing." He fell quiet, deep in thought. After a moment, he looked toward Dušan, "You know, your speech patterns remind me of black Americans."

"Well, where the hell do you think I've been for the last 400 years? How many black Americans do you think there are, average Joe Blow on the street, who can say that? Huh? I've been around them longer than they have. But why did you get me to say 'them?' There is no 'them.' There's just 'us.'"

"You're quite right. My apologies. I did not intend it that way. I meant it as a compliment, rather to say that you have managed, in all that time, to hang onto the accent of your mother tongue, but it has the quality of conscious intent to it, revealing it's the other, American accent -- that my statement implied was an acquisition -- is your more natural state, which you are perfectly correct, is the only possible result of 400 years' usage.

"You know, that is the damned longest sentence I have ever heard. How do you do that? Personally, I couldn't hold a thought that long."

Srđa chuckled, then digressed. "I misspoke when I said I do my best thinking while fishing. Lately, it has been during my chats with your very great grandson. That boy's thinking is revolutionary!"

"Of course," said Dušan, picking his teeth with the same dagger he used to cut up bait. "I've seen it coming for centuries."

Srđa continued on, excited, "And his grandfather is quite interesting too. How well do you know him?"

"I know him very well, *of course*," said Dušan. "He's my child too. They are on my straight paternal line. They don't know it, but their real name is Kraljević."

"Really!" said Srđa, bemused. "Sons of the King."

"Yes," said Dušan. "They are Serbian princes. Can't you tell?"

"Yes," replied Srđa. "Now that you mention it, I *can* tell. They do certainly have a penchant for the Kingdom of Heaven. It appears they have both always been perfectly certain they would choose to be *exactly* who they are."

"Exactly," said Dušan. "And that's really something. To have no choice on who you must be, and to *still* choose it. I've always admired the hell out of that.

"It's not like it's been for us," he went on, "Every one of us *was choosing* to be a slave, to be a man and stand with his own, the slaves, no matter *how* hard it was. All any one of us had to do was convert to Islam and we'd be a free man, that and a slave driver to our own. Here it was the opposite torment."

"Yes," replied Srđa. "You're right, they *are* both torments. Either you have no choice, or the choice is ridiculous."

Dušan guffawed. "*Very* ridiculous choice. You decide to be a man and stand with your own, who are constantly running all kinds of crazy shit, so you're asking yourself, 'What in the hell am I doing paying all these dues just to be with *these* crazy people?' And then when the Turk gets around to ramming that pole up your butt," he said, referring to impalement, "you're *really* asking yourself that question."

Srđa laughed, "But people under such duress are always a bit crazy."

"Of course, everybody knows that, that's why you're always putting up with their mess. Why they're so easy to love and so easy to drive you insane. And why that girl of yours is putting up with so much crazy shit from that boyfriend of hers. Same principle. She's got the Serbian 'put-up-with' gene in her DNA."

Srđa asked, "How'd your descendants come to lose track of their name?"

Dušan jerked his pole at a nibble, but nothing came of it. He replied, "My son, the one Donald descends from, knew his name, of course, but he was known in his village by his mother's clan name, as was the custom. His son was a guide for the English while doing espionage work on the English for the clan at the same time. The English also knew him by his clan name.

"This grandson married a brave Diolan girl who'd escaped from the English. You should have seen that fiery beauty. She glowed like velvet. He was crazy about her. But then their world fell apart. Their firstborn son, Thomas, was stolen at the age of eight by some slave traders."

Srđa instantly noted the irony that the British slave traders had unknowingly duplicated the Ottoman practice of stealing eight-year-old boys. "Such Turks!" he exclaimed.

Dušan continued. "He died trying to rescue Thomas. But the Diolan mother survived. She became an archer and hid out in the treetops. The English told horror stories about her."

The two men laughed.

"By then I was in the Chowan Spirit World and, of course, Serbian Heaven as well, and got completely hooked on the Chowan custom of watching over my descendants. I was with that boy Thomas every day of his difficult life."

He looked earnestly to Srđa, stricken. "It was worse here, you know. Here you had the equivalent of the Turk right up in your face," he put his hand several inches from his own. "Every day, barking at your every move. Can you imagine that? The sheer torment?"

His eyes were intense, angry. "We might use the word 'mother fucker' a lot ourselves, but there were no *Hajduk* in the hills here, taking revenge, kicking the mother fucker's ass. Here the outrages happened all the time, unavenged."

"I've thought about that, too," Srđa said, also moved.

"Though there were, of course, spontaneous revenges, but they met with instant death." Dušan pressed on, becoming indignant. "No revenge! No defense!"

"It's intrinsic," said Srđa. When you look so different from the free people, guerrilla warfare becomes impossible."

"Huh?" asked Dušan.

"Think about it," replied Srđa. "We have always been so superb at our guerrilla warfare because we could easily pretend to be simple peons, or we could dress up like Bosniaks and spy on them. And then there were those few stolen *janissary* boys who defected from The Turk and brought with them all their soldiering skills. We were pushed straight into armed resistance. Here it was the opposite extreme. The exact opposite. Only a non-violent resistance could be pursued."

"That's what my Thomas stumbled into," Dušan said. He got quiet for a spell. "Thomas watches over Daniel, too, you know. A true prince. And now he's a saint who looks after all *his* children, and he adopts them like crazy. He was #1 Busiest Guardian three decades in a row."

"Must have been before my time. I hadn't heard," Srđa said.

Dušan snapped his fingers and a widescreen viewer appeared with a collage of Dušan's male heirs that link straight to Daniel. Srđa studied on them, starting from the left. He pointed at the first one, "That must be your son. He looks so much like you."

"Yes, he was, of all my sons, the one who looked the most like me."

"You had more?"

"I had many more."

"How many?"

"Twenty-six."

"Sons? That's just the sons? I won't ask about the daughters."

Dušan looked genuinely sheepish, bearing a big grin with his head down. "Best not," he said. Then he looked up at the viewer again. "Look

17

at that handsome lad next to him. That's Thomas, the one I was just talking about."

Dušan's grandson, Thomas, was one-fourth Serbian, one-fourth Chowan, and one-half Diolan. He had Dušan's best features, his expressive eyebrows, his height and physicality, though more sharply defined. He had that African trait that lacked an extra layer of fat, right under the skin. That extra layer of fat became widespread elsewhere during the Ice Age. He had his Chowan grandmother's thick, lustrous black hair, though deeply curled.

And from his two Diolan grandparents he had a gently rounded bone structure that caught up meticulously with the delicacy of expression he'd inherited from his Chowan grandmother. His skin was exactly in the middle range of tones. It had a Sienna cast to it and still much of the glow his Diolan mother had possessed.

Then the photo of him came to life and stepped outside of the frame.

"Hello, sir," said the young man, extending his hand to Srđa.

"Thomas," said Dušan, "This is Srđa Mrkalja, a dear friend of mine."

"My pleasure," said Srđa. "I've been so eager to learn more about your family. Honored to know all of you, actually."

"The honor is mine, sir," Thomas replied. "I see Grandfather has been talking about me, so I thought I might step in. As you can see, my appearance was rather unusual for the time and place. Throughout my life, people would stop and stare at me. Though no matter where I was, they would see enough of the familiar in me to know I was not entirely a stranger. If they nonetheless started to challenge me, I'd start preaching to them from the Holy Book. In my youth, there was a neutered old man on the plantation they tried to enslave me on, who talked about it nonstop. 'Confess and ye shall be forgiven,' I would preach. Keep in mind it was just something I was toying with to keep people from bothering me.

"I'll never forget the time I stopped a very drunken sailor in the street and said that to him. The sailor looked at me with the most guilt-stricken look a soul can express and began weeping in great sobs. There were a few onlookers watching quietly. Then the sailor began to confess the voyages he'd taken part in, bringing slaves to the New World. He'd been just a boy at the start and had no idea what he was getting into. The horrors were too much for him. Seeing that beautiful girl he fancied debauched. That was the worst of it."

Dušan interjected proudly, "Later in his life, the sailor wrote a song about it. Something about how amazing grace is. Some Americans don't know it, but they got a lot of their religious zeal from saints like my grandson."

"You do me honor, Grandfather," Thomas said, bowing slightly.

"Oh, stop with all that noble crap. The first Serbian king in 500 years was a pig farmer who couldn't read or write. That's *our* kind of class. Our favorite kind, actually."

Thomas resumed his narration, "At first I was just throwing scripture at them because I'd noticed how glassy-eyed people get when you preach at them like that. Once glassy-eyed, they tended to leave me alone. It worked quite well. I added more to the act, that's all it was to me at the time. The more I did it, the more powerful I realized it was and how much I could get away with because of it.

"Then one fine day I realized the reason it worked was because it *is* real. It is powerful, and it is *real*.

"Some people thought it was my undoing, but they had it completely wrong. I got the biggest prize of all. The one that never ends." He smiled inwardly, as if contemplating bliss, and disappeared as quickly as he'd appeared. Only the static image on the screen was left.

Srđa watched after him, "What became of him?"

"Crucified. Technically, whipped to death, but crucified nonetheless. He helped some people escape, then refused to whip some others."

Srđa was quiet with that thought, deeply moved. "That *is* a saint's death. I can see why you're so proud."

Srđa felt a nibble and jerked up on his pole. A struggle ensued as he reeled in his catch. A fine ocean trout was on the line. "A beauty," he said. "What do you do with the catch? Let them go?"

"No," Dušan said. "Leave it on the deck there. I'll put it on the porch of an old woman in town everybody thinks is insane. She never questions finding them, knows exactly where they're coming from. She's another one of my children."

"Good idea," Srđa replied.

"And you thought I was just indulging myself. I try be out here every morning feeding that poor child of mine."

Dušan snapped his fingers. A bit of sage dropped from out of nowhere into his hand. He snapped his fingers again and a flame appeared on the tip of his finger. He lit the sage and smudged the gasping fish with the smoke. He placed his hand on it and said a Chowan prayer. "Thank you, sister, for the gift of your life." The fish stopped gasping as her fish spirit slipped back into the water to the spot where she'd laid her eggs.

"So, then what happened to the generations following Thomas?" Srđa asked.

Dušan replied, "A fine line of holy men. What they call preachers here. Like at home, when holy men assumed leadership after The Turk killed off, or bought off, all our rulers. I'll have you know, my boys contributed to the strategy that led to the War of Liberation here, what they call their Civil War. The world's first unarmed warriors. It took 1800 years since The Christ had called for the strategy, but a nation, a slave nation, finally pulled it off."

Srđa smiled introspectively and added. "Hats off."

"Yeah, that was pretty slick," Dušan smiled, poking Srđa in the side with his elbow. "They got the white *Americanots* to fight their war of freedom *for them!*" He laughed. "Watching that was delicious."

"Yes," said Srđa, laughing, "It is kind of hard imagining us inducing the Turks to fight a war with each other over whether or not they should be nicer to us." The two Guardians laughed heartily.

Dušan tried to snag another nibble, "So, what is it my boy said that's got you so enthused?"

* * *

Daniel was half awake at first light. His room faced the east. Bright sunlight dazzled around the edges of the window shade. He drifted back to sleep. His grandfather sat on the other side of the bed.

"What you still doing in that bed, boy?" his grandfather demanded. "The sun's been up ten minutes already. How you expect to get your chores done, lolly-gaggin' in bed like that, half a day?

"I'm up," Daniel replied, then snored lightly.

"Now what were we talking about yesterday? Boy, you listening to me?" Granddad put on his dream-hearing earbuds, official Guardian issue.

"Of course, Granddad, I always listen to you." Daniel was now deeply asleep, his eyes darting around behind his eyelids.

"Okay, then, now that I have your full attention, this is the secret that my great granddad passed on to me. He was one of the greats. I don't care how hard you try to top him, you never will. Just keep your humility about that, you hear me?

"Yes, grandad," Daniel replied, speaking fully inside his dream since Grandad was now in there with him. "But you told me this when I was eight-years-old. I'm grown now. Did you forget?"

There was a knock at the bedroom door. It was Srđa. On Dušan's suggestion, he had made a visit to Black Baptist Heaven, to look up some of Daniel's more recent family and pay his respects. Daniel's granddad had, of course, invited him to stop by anytime. "Don't even think about waiting for an invitation. Just stop on by."

"Hope I'm not intruding, Reverend," Srđa said.

"Oh, not at all, sir." Reverend Edmonds replied, who had slipped out from inside Daniel's mind and back into the room to greet Srđa. *"Please, come on in."*

"Thank you so much," replied Srđa.

Rev. Edmonds turned to his grandson. "Daniel, this gentleman, Mr. Srđa, has come all the way from Consolidated Heaven to meet you."

Daniel mumbled in his sleep, just the end was intelligible, ". . . meet you."

The Reverend continued with his introduction, "He is himself from a very persecuted minority of long-standing which is having a terrible time. Horrible violence, worse than anything we've had to deal with. Not on that scale. You remember Greenwood? The Tulsa Race Riot? They just went through a spell where *every* town was Greenwood. All at once. *Everywhere*. To live through five hundred years of Jim-Crow style slavery, I mean a *harsh* version, just to end up exterminated like vermin. The unthinkable. Actually, it's those people you're so interested in — Serbians."

Daniel thrashed about in the bed a bit, alarmed, as if he were dreaming that the family's three-year-old had just run into the road. He let out an odd, garbled sound that sounded something like "Huh?"

"See?" the Reverend said, elbowing Srđa. The two were still standing at the side of the bed, looking at Daniel. "I told you he was *obsessed.*"

"Yes, yes, I've heard. We're *so* grateful for his interest, though I have to say, we were just commenting on how much worse you all have had it on your end."

"I appreciate that sentiment, sir," said the Reverend. "But holocausts on that scale must be respected as such. If you and your children still have the gift of life, there's always hope for another day."

"Well," said Srđa, "I guess we'll just have to agree to disagree. We think *you've* had it worse, and you think *we've* had it worse."

Two symphonic notes, ending in a major key tectonic up note sounded from above. The two Guardians looked up, amused at the acknowledgment from on high regarding their angelic behavior, competing in a *proper* manner over who's had it worse.

"Well, it is expected of us at this point, isn't it, Reverend?" smiled Srđa.

"It is indeed, sir," replied the Reverend.

"But, as I was saying," Srđa went on, "we *very* much appreciate your interest. We're Europe's best-kept secret, or more properly, it's worst secret, best kept."

"Anyway, Daniel," the Reverend continued, directing his voice at Daniel. "He's understandably obsessed with finding alternative strategies. And he knows quite well that's all we've been talking about for the last 400 years, give or take a few."

Then the Reverend whispered to Srđa, "We won't mention anything about your plans for him to marry your Goddaughter."

"No, that would seem entirely presumptuous," Srđa concurred.

"I'm sure she's a lovely girl," the Reverend went on, "but no point being premature."

He turned his attention back to Daniel. "So, I told him he was more than welcome to jump right in. And I'm telling you, it will be an honor to share with him."

Daniel was no longer struggling to talk out loud to Srđa. He was speaking within his dream. "Hello there." He smiled.

The Reverend gave Srđa a pair of the dream-hearing earbuds.

Once fully inside Daniel's dream, Srđa could see Daniel, not as a mumbling sleeper, rather he appeared to Srđa wide-awake, alive with ideas, sitting up on the bed, very excited to be addressing him.

"So glad to meet you!" Daniel said.

"That feeling is certainly mutual," Srđa replied. "Your grandfather has been telling me about your interest in my people. I'm so happy to hear that. How is it you happened to become interested in us? Not a common occurrence in this country."

"I only know this in my dreams. If you asked me when I was wide-awake, I'd be dumb as a rock, but I actually have a distant ancestor from there. He used to play with me when I was little, and he still comes and chats with me now and then, but only when I'm dreaming. Don't recall any of it when I'm awake, but he's certainly had his influence, I'm sure."

"Ah yes," Srđa exclaimed. "Those are the conversations that can be the most influential." He winked in the Reverend's direction. "They have a word for it now — subliminal."

"In my day, we'd say it came from spirit. I like that idea better."

"In truth," Srđa said to Daniel. "You can't have only one ancestor of a certain type. If you have one, you have thousands along that line. But keep in mind, being of Serbian descent is like homeopathic remedies. The more diluted the tincture, the more powerful it is." He laughed.

"Are you going to give away all our secrets?" announced a deep voice that appeared in the room a few seconds before the speaker. It was Dušan.

"There you are," Daniel said. "Long time, no see."

"Not true, you nit," Dušan replied. "I dropped in on your dream just last week. You just don't remember shit."

Daniel smiled at Srđa. "That's me, the 'nit who doesn't remember shit.'" Then he turned back to Dušan, "What were we talking about last week?"

Dušan continued, "We were talking about how important it is to believe in what you have to do. A man must do that. We had to believe that it was God's intention to allow us to be beaten and enslaved so badly. He was saving us from having to become those nasty people who abuse others like that. At the end of the day, *we* are the people who will prevail, but only if we refuse to become nasty abusers ourselves. I mean, just look at those English. They were everybody's bitch for centuries and what did they do with it? How did they despoil the glories they might have achieved from all that? They turned around and became the biggest colonizers of all time! What a disgrace!"

Daniel's eyes danced amusedly at Dušan's words. "In other words," he explained to Srđa, "Civilization is trying to raise itself to a higher level. To go up a notch. Being part of a persecuted minority is," he switched into a voice of comic earnestness, "a *Mission from God!*"

"What's the matter, boy?" asked the Reverend. "Are you afraid of a direct confrontation with the Almighty? You always have to make it, what's the word?"

"I have to secularize it? I just think that it's useful to translate."

"Oh, that's the way you define your "ministry?" he said, mimicking quotation marks with his hands.

"We don't need to call it that, at all," Daniel replied gently.

"I'm sure we don't."

"I thought you came here to visit because of who I am, not because of who I'm not," Daniel chided good-naturedly.

The elder gentleman deferred, "So, what have you been thinking about lately?"

"Remember what you used to tell me about the way to conquer evil? When I told you that I realized that the cowboys weren't on my side? My side was more like the Indian side. And you told me that it takes the strongest kind of man to win when in such a position?

"Sometimes I wonder what that means," he went on. "Our world has changed some since the Sixties, but it's the Seventies now and we've still got such a long way to go. So, what's the next step? If we have made progress in making the dominant culture see that we are their equals, then the next step is for us to see that they are *ours*.

"I've been in lecture halls where I am often the only black person in that room and I look around and there's an impulse to feel intimidated, out-of-place. And it makes no sense. Ninety-five percent of those people, all white, have ancestors who, within the last hundred years, were escaping slavery, peonage slavery of some sort, to some degree. We're not opposites, we're not light years apart, they're on the same damn continuum my ancestors occupied. So, why is it I can't look at this mass of people and feel that? Why can't I feel that camaraderie? That commonality?

"I know damn well, even though they were sold an illusion that that heritage does not affect them, that it does. I can see from my own family how long that kind of generational distress persists.

"There's just one reason, one word for it – racism – that creates an illusion of polarity on that subject. So, if I want to effect agency on the situation, what do I do to reverse that illusion? How do I see who they *really* are behind the American whitewash? How do I begin to rout out this illusory polarity of superiority/inferiority? How do I train myself to see them for who they really are? And that's why I've become so interested in Serbs," Daniel said.

"Why?" asked Srđa.

"Because it's the absolute easiest place to start."

* * *

24

Srđa Helps Leslie with Her Diatribe
on Racism, Chicago, 1976

Srđa was very encouraged at the likelihood that Daniel could respond to his Goddaughter, Leslie, who needed rescuing from the Tuđina. If nothing else, they should certainly be fine friends. But for the moment, the question was how their little band of Guardians was to bring the two together. He contemplated that as he and Jovanka hung out with her in her apartment.

He never could quite put his finger on what it was that made Leslie look so different from Jovanka. Something was missing. Biologically they were first cousins, one generation removed, and feature by feature they might have been twins, but there was some ineffable essence that was lacking in Leslie. Where Jovanka glowed, Leslie flattened sadly. He prayed Jovanka was right and her matchmaking would do Leslie some good.

Srđa and Jovanka were both lounging on Leslie's bed, relaxing as best they could in the din of noise coming from Leslie's ancient black Underwood typewriter. Srđa loved writing with her. Other than when she was dreaming, that was the time it was easiest to talk to her.

He liked the juxtaposition of the newly-sanded hardwood floors, which seemed to glow with the sunshine captured a century earlier when the oaks the wood came from lived, and the crumpled old plaster walls. The walls were bordered by ornate moldings lurking under the many layers of paint that had accumulated over the decades. He was observing the dentil crown molding on the other side of the room, like a long row of teeth smiling down at him from ten feet above. Leslie's clattering on the keyboard abruptly stopped. He got up to read where she was stuck.

A fundamental problem was obvious. Under the title, where her name should have been, was her boyfriend's name instead – Reggie Wilson. She was pretending she was him! When in the world was she ever going to just be her own self?

Srđa understood why she was doing it – understood all she'd been through that made it plain no one was in the least interested in what she really thought, only in their presumptions. Nor was anyone interested in how she felt about the way the world was persecuting her for being with her black boyfriend. He'd overheard her say the day before that no one ever seemed to have a clue where she was coming from. Of course, that was the problem. Neither did she. Literally.

She was most of the way down the page, describing an incident she'd recently come home talking about – one of many incidents she often regaled her boyfriend with. She described them as the "Things White People Say When They Think There Are Only White People in the Room."

"Bob Pirotelli," she had written, "the president of Pirotelli Management, the largest apartment management company in the city of Chicago, may have officially stated to the city's mayor earlier this spring that 'I am deeply committed to fair housing practices in our beloved city,' but recently told his own personnel, 'do the best you can to keep those porch monkeys off our porches."

Srđa thought of a rejoinder and laughed. He then whispered into Leslie's ear. She laughed as well and then resumed her typing.

"I'm not sure," she wrote, "why Mr. Pirotelli would ridicule other people as ape-like. I've seen Mr. Pirotelli roll up his sleeves. His arms are as furry as any primates; while mine, on the other hand, are perfectly smooth, *human*."

This was the same furry-armed creature who'd just fired Leslie when he found out who that smooth-armed human being was to her, the one whose point-of-view she was assuming.

Srđa sighed. Had he made a mistake, all those years ago when she was just a little kid he encouraged to see the world this way? He'd thought it would help her recover and defend her own identity, but all she was doing was defending someone else's, someone who would never do the same for her.

But no, he needed to stop doubting himself. There had been no other way. Even without his interference, she and her father were clearly responding to America's racism in a way that connected them to the European form of racism that was consuming their own family, the family they knew nothing about. It was how they talked about themselves. Anyone could see it. Well, anyone like him, anyway.

It all started when Leslie, all on her own, had discovered her imaginary friend, King Martin.

* * *

All in the Family,
Chicago, 1958

The Family Civil Rights Debates began in 1958 when Leslie was six years old. She won every one of them.

She met her debate mentor, King Martin, on the swing set. Her dad, Archie, had made the swing set out of galvanized pipes. It was a homely contraption, but he'd sunk the pipes deep into the ground and then set them in concrete. Swing as hard as she might, it would never tip over. "Not like that crap next door," her father had pointed out. It was the first lesson he was to give her on how to "Polish" something up, referring to the nationality. That's when you make something that looks like jack-legged hell but works like crazy. It's real.

Jovanka and Srđa were there. The two of them loved hanging out on earth on bright sunny days. Srđa liked to play with his goddaughter, the little big-eyed girl who sat on the swing seat pretending her legs were helicopter blades while she churned excitedly through the air. She made a loud whirring noise. Then she backed up as far as she could and ran forward till the seat slid up under her butt and propelled her high into the air.

She was swinging very high when she turned around towards Srđa, who was pretending to push her. "Who are you?" she asked. "Oh, I know you, I saw you on the news. Swing me hard. I like to go way up high."

Jovanka clapped her hands with joy at the recognition. "Who does she think you are?" she asked Srđa.

"I have no idea," he said.

"That's what Auntie Myrna told us, remember?" Jovanka asked. "Look for the ones who imagine they're hearing or seeing you. They might imagine you're a goat, or a saint, and everything in between."

"Yes," answered Srđa. "I remember. Fascinating. I am very eager to find out who she thinks I am."

"Well, I don't want you getting upset if it turns out she thinks you're the family dog," said Jovanka.

Srđa laughed. "I think she'll have more imagination than that. I think she's already understanding a lot."

"That's your girl," said Jovanka. "Of course, she does."

* * *

27

Srđa loved a good-hearted woman. Leslie's mom, Deloris, a principled woman who principally favored pastels had a fair, Germanic complexion and look, though her own mother had favored the mixed-blooded people, commonly referred to as "pioneers" in the Midwest, who had originated in the Upper South. One of Deloris' earliest memories was an argument she'd overheard between her parents when her dad had said to her mom, "Shut up, ya old squaw."

No one knew it except Dušan, but she was distantly related, through her maternal line, to his wife's tribe. Deloris was similarly soft-spoken. She noticed Leslie fingering with fascination the satin of an old bridesmaid's dress unearthed in a closet she was cleaning out.

"That's the dress I wore when your Auntie Babe got married," she explained to the girl. "Do you want to wear it?"

"Yes, yes!" the girl responded with excited joy as only six-year-olds can express it.

Deloris got out her pinking shears and cut the dress down to the girl's height. Leslie ran from the house with glee.

Srđa followed her as she ran to the house next door.

The neighbor girl, Betty, looked jealous when she saw it and badgered her mom for a similar dress stored away in a dusty box that would see the light of day one last time.

It was the first few weeks of spring. Dandelions were blooming in profusion. The girls made themselves huge bouquets. Leslie hesitated for a moment, then helped herself to a few of her mom's tulips.

Srđa wished he'd had time to warn her, but it was too late.

"Who told you to pick those?' her dad, Archie, said, poking his head from under the hood of her mom's car, as the girls scampered by. "Huh? I'm talking to you!" the swarthy man insisted. He had dark, full, arched eyebrows that were very useful when he wanted to look angry. Betty disappeared behind the hedge, heading home.

He lumbered over to Leslie, bow-legged, and towered over her like a grizzly bear.

"Nobody," she said, looking up at him. "Mom won't mind."

"Well, I mind," he said. "You're not supposed to pick those flowers. You're supposed to leave them alone. You didn't know that?"

Srđa recognized that crumpled-up look he was always seeing on her face when confronted by her father. She made no reply.

"You mean you didn't know that?" he demanded. "What's the matter, you stupid?"

"No!" she defended.

"Well, what are you doing, picking flowers and you didn't ask first? You think we spend money and plant flowers just to have a bunch of stupid kids picking them? What kind of stupid crap is that?"

Srđa had counted three 'stupids' already. He knew she had at least three more to endure. There were strict grammatical rules in their language attached to the use of this word that had apparently carried over to the family's current usage. If used once it must be used at least six more times in the same paragraph before the subject could be changed.

"Huh? I'm asking you something," demanded Archie of Leslie.

"What?"

"What kind of stupid crap is that?" There it was again, in his tone of voice – that tone of contempt and scorn that made her gut lurch and her body tense, wanting to bolt.

"I don't know!" she defended mightily.

"You're supposed to ask before you do something stupid like that. Do you hear me? Huh? Do you hear me?"

Every question mark pounded his point further that she was a disgusting, stupid little thing. "Yes!" she said. She had heard it so many times already that there was no doubt in her mind that that was what he really thought of her. That's all she was to him.

"All right, then. Don't let me catch you picking stupid flowers again." Leslie gasped as her father grabbed her wilting bouquet and tossed it into the garbage full of greasy oil cans. So much for her ever being a beautiful princess bride! Of course, not her! She burst into tears of grief and ran into the house.

Jovanka had witnessed the whole exchange as well. She pressed her face into Archie's and shouted at the top of her voice, "Shut up!"

Archie blinked.

"Why do you talk to her like that?" she shouted again. He looked down and began wiping oil from the grille of the car.

"The Tuđina has got him," Srđa said. "He's brainwashed. He thinks we're what the Croat Ustaša – what they call Klanners here, say we are – worthless trash."

"And now he's brainwashing Leslie," Jovanka moaned. "I hate this!"

"And then, of course, there's the tradition," he went on. "If the best and brightest of our children are always being stolen, of course you have to run them down."

"I don't see any child-stealing Turks around here," she replied, still annoyed.

"Of course not, but old traditions die hard."

"No excuse," she said. "No excuse."

* * *

Leslie threw herself onto her bed and cried.

Srđa's heart went out to the poor girl, her all-important bride play betrayed by her very own father.

Then she angrily took off the dress and threw it into the corner.

Then something miraculous happened. He went to pick up the dress, and it actually moved in his hands. He realized it was because she could *see* him! She was engaged enough in his dimension that he could act as a poltergeist. That had never happened to him before. He folded it and offered it to her.

Leslie looked up at him. "Oh, there you are," she said with a nonchalant familiarity. "That dress looks stupid. Betty's is much nicer than mine."

"I really like this dress on you," he said. "Please take care of it."

"He's the one who's stupid," she sniffled, referring to her father, Archie.

"Shush now," Srđa said, sitting next to her and patting her hand, "nobody's stupid."

Her mom walked in, "Who are you talking to, honey?" she asked.

"My new friend, King Martin," Leslie said.

Deloris looked around the room, then laughed a little, like she thought that was funny. "Oh, I see, another 'special' friend. Why don't you ask him to come to dinner?"

"Oh, he comes all the time," Leslie explained, "during the news."

* * *

It was after dinner when Srđa found out who Leslie thought he was.

She was painting a model of a Baltimore Oriole set up on the coffee table when the news came on. Her dad was in the room, too.

There he was, on TV, outside a hospital. The Cronkite man said, "Today, the Rev. Dr. Martin Luther King left the hospital after being stabbed several weeks ago in the sternum by what is believed to be a mentally ill woman at his book signing."

They showed a picture of him sitting calmly in a chair with the hilt of a letter opener sticking out of his chest while a lady wiped at his hand.

Cronkite continued, "The blade lodged just a fraction of an inch from his aorta. Doctors had to operate for several hours to remove it. He is on his way to a full recovery."

The Reverend said into the microphone, "I am not angry with this woman. I believe she just needs help."

"Damn spooks," her dad, Archie, said, commenting on the newscast. He was not referring to ghosts. "They'll knife ya' for twenty bucks."

Srđa slipped next to the girl and prompted her, "Why does he think he's better behaved when he gets mad over a few flowers?"

Leslie nodded her head fervently.

Srđa whispered something more, something good for her to tell her dad.

She rinsed her brush and marched over to Archie. Her eyes were flashing in anger by the time she got in front of him, her fists balled up at her sides.

She shouted at him, "You think good is bad and beautiful is ugly and, and" she stammered, crying, "and smart is stupid!" A tear raced down her cheek.

Her father's jaw dropped, and he gasped, not in shock, but in absolute, unadulterated awe.

Srđa continued whispering to her excitedly, "Look, look, you got him. Now he knows *just* how smart you are!"

"I'll show *you* who's stupid!" she shouted at her dad and ran from the room in tears.

* * *

"Well," said Srđa, who Leslie called King Martin. "I guess you've got his number now."

"What number?" the girl asked.

"What he wants you to do to make him proud."

"He's not proud of me," she pouted.

"Oh yes he is," Srđa said. "I saw that look in his eyes. You amazed him."

She shook her head. "He only thinks that when I talk like you."

"You don't talk like me," Srđa said. "I could never talk like you."

She yawned and settled her head onto the pillow. "You know what mommy did? This morning she came and picked me up out of bed while I was still 'sleep so I could see Mighty Mouse and the windows were open and I could hear all the birdies singing."

"Your mommy is nice. I like her," he said.

"So do I, and I like you, King Martin," she said sleepily, as he tucked her covers up under her chin. "You and Mighty Mouse."

"You get some sleep now," he said. "I'm sure your daddy's going to give you lots of opportunities to make him proud."

After Leslie had fallen asleep Srđa, *aka* King Martin, turned to Jovanka with joy.

"She's done it!" he said. "She's done it! She's figured out who she is and how to undo the brainwashing! And your cousin, her father, is going to help her. Of all people."

"No, come on," said Jovanka.

"You saw the look on his face when she said that," he said. "She's got his number. You just wait and see. Somewhere underneath all that contemptuous betrayal, he knows who he is – he *feels* who he is."

* * *

Uncle Joe Moves In

Uncle Joe was creepy. He moved into the basement when Leslie was seven.

He was her dad's brother and never talked to nobody. Even so, he was real noisy, partly because everything he did, he did real loud. He moved real slow and clumsy with loud steps and was always bumping into everything. And then there was all the clatter with her dad putting a bathroom and an old kitchen sink down there, putting in all those pipes and putting up a wall to make a bedroom. He even painted all the concrete on the walls and floor, so it wouldn't be so dusty.

Uncle Joe came up to the kitchen, now and then, when he ran out of the food he had down there. He'd wait till mid-morning, or mid-afternoon when nobody was around. If Leslie happened to be there he ran her out of there with his scowl. Her mom explained that he was all crippled up with arthritis and hurt a lot, so that's what made him look so mean. But Leslie wasn't buying it.

She started to dread dinner time when her mom made her go down there with Uncle Joe's dinner. She had to take him his plate. Down to The Dungeon. Since she had to carry the plate she couldn't go fast down the stairs. That was the worst part. She imagined tendrils of carnivorous vines growing up through the open stair treads, snatching at her feet.

She'd put the plate on the card table, then knock loudly on his door. Then she'd run as fast as she could up the stairs, so the Man-Eating Dungeon Vines couldn't get her.

Jovanka tried to help poor old Joe. She'd watch TV with him and laugh at the game shows, trying to cheer him up but he'd get up and turn it off. Then she'd chatter away. Just pleasant small talk to take his mind off things, but he'd turn his back to her and put a pillow over his ears.

Deloris tried doing the same thing, but it didn't work for her either.

Srđa couldn't think of anything to help either, though he knew the problem wasn't arthritis. Joe was glad he had it. It gave him an excuse to excuse himself from the world, which he had no faith in whatsoever.

"Why in the world would a Krajina Serb be feeling like that?" Srđa asked bitterly. "Especially one who's been raised by a Croat who thinks his half-Serb son is a worthless good for nothing?"

Of course, the reason the Croats hated Serbs so much, that Srđa would readily tell anyone who'd listen, was because they'd been through virtually identical crap for centuries, enslaved to the Austro-Hungarians. In Srđa's college days in the thirties, sneaking in on classes at the University of Chicago, he delved deep into the history of the American South. He recognized the 'poor white trash' KKK mentality in an instant.

He laughed out loud at the recognition. Right there in the middle of a lecture hall that got everyone turning to stare at him. He couldn't help it.

'Poor white trash' American racists were too funny. They were just like Croatians. At a critical point, at the beginning of the 20th century, when Croatians' Old-World peonage captivity had finally ended, they used their new-found freedom to pursue their long-coveted fantasy of being superior Aryans themselves. The Serbs marooned in their lands could readily be cast as their opposites, the despised 'Others.' Croatians could then hate themselves with complete abandon by way of hating Serbs. And if it was his own half-Serb son Joe's father saw as a throwback Serb, so much the better. Or worse, depending on your point of view.

From then on out Srđa was hooked on the history of American slavery, both before and after the American Civil War. It was a mirror to his own country's unfolding history. Those po' white trash KKKroatians sucking up to Hitler like total fools. Didn't they know they were Slavs, and Hitler hated Slavs as much as he hated Jews? The fools.

Frederick Douglass was Srđa's favorite American. Srđa stumbled upon him on a dark, cold afternoon in a library, when he was feeling particularly homesick, lost in the Tuđina, thinking of how beautiful home was and longing for her, feeling sick with guilt at his abandonment of her. Every report from home was revealing the deepening threat of Aryan supremacists. It had been fifty years since the extermination of the Serbs had been called for, and that talk was gaining ground mightily. What was he doing, so far away?

"In thinking of America, I sometimes find myself admiring her bright blue sky — her grand old woods — her fertile fields — her beautiful rivers — her mighty lakes, and star-crowned mountains. But my rapture is soon checked, my joy is soon turned to mourning. When I remember that all is cursed with the infernal actions of slaveholding, robbery and wrong — when I remember that with the waters of her noblest rivers, the tears of my brethren are borne to the ocean, disregarded and forgotten, and that her most fertile fields drink daily of the warm blood of my outraged sisters, I am filled with unutterable loathing."

Something in Srđa snapped, the truth was unavoidable. He had no business indulging himself with university stacks in a privileged country. It was time he went home to stand with his own. It was time to choose the Kingdom of Heaven.

* * *

Ketchup Hair, Greensboro 1960

Leslie was eight. She was advancing considerably in her skill level at winning debates with Archie.

Her ghostly Godfather, Srđa, was quite proud of the progress she was making. Her young mind was developing just as it ought, considering who she really was.

They were in the car driving to Wisconsin for the state fair when the news came on about the black college kids in Greensboro sitting at the lunch counter. Leslie saw a scene of it on the news the night before. One of the girls had ketchup in her hair. A young white guy with greasy hair was standing behind her with the ketchup bottle and a big smirk on his face. She was miserable, but she just left it on there, looking brave and scared.

"Damn jigaboos," her dad said. "Pushing their way in where they're not wanted."

Leslie wondered how in the world he could be so stupid. Then she imagined King Martin waving his finger at her, admonishing her not to call anyone stupid. She had reached an age when she understood that she was just imagining his visits, he really didn't know her at all, but that did not diminish her enjoyment of the daydreams.

Srđa and Jovanka still relished them as well.

"Is your shoulder still bothering you?" Deloris asked Archie.

"Yeah, it's still biting me," he said.

The next thing Leslie imagined King Martin saying to her shocked her.

"No!" she said out loud.

"What?" asked Deloris.

"Nothing," she replied and sulked.

But King Martin wouldn't stop insisting.

Very reluctantly, Leslie sat up behind her dad and started rubbing his left shoulder. After a while, she got into it and worked hard at softening the spasmed muscle.

Deloris smiled at Leslie and then Archie did the unthinkable. "Thank you," he said.

Before Leslie sat back she pulled herself closer to his ear and she said, "Everybody deserves to be wanted."

She sat back and caught him looking in the rear-view mirror at her with another fleeting millisecond of pure awe.

He still had no comeback. Yet again, he gave her the last word. Once again, he let her win.

* * * *

The Slav Mentality

Leslie developed her treatise on the Slav Mentality at the age of fourteen. She had mercifully passed the worst of puberty, the changes of which had thoroughly devastated the miniscule self-esteem that Archie was hobbling at every turn. It was only in their Great Debates that her sense of herself as an emerging young woman of considerable acumen was being reinforced. In that, Archie never failed her.

He was continuing almost daily to instigate another debate on racism he would as consistently as inexplicably allow her to win.

Even Jovanka was starting to understand him. The guy had two souls at war in him. His Croatian soul was spewing out all the bigot talk, and his Serbian Krajina soul was slipping goodies to Leslie for ripping it to shreds. Made sense to Jovanka.

Leslie had learned the derivation of the word 'slave.'

A book, courtesy of Srđa, literally fell off the library shelf right in front of her.

She had been waiting for an opportunity to share it with Archie. She knew it would knock him speechless.

The occasion and motivation occurred on a day, like every other day, when the brainwashed part of his psyche found another excuse to harangue her on her stupidity.

She rode her bike, a Royal Blue Huffy racer, into the driveway. Her dad bought it for her twelfth birthday. It was a special bike, a thin, lightweight racer that was way ahead of what the other kids had. The front fender was damaged, so he got it for a song and hammered out the dent. She was ready to roll with her beautiful new bike, even if the delicate frame slid around a bit on the gravel roads of Bridgeview, Illinois.

"Hey, come here," Archie ordered. "You see this?"

"What?" she asked with dread on her face. Her stomach lurched and burned at the tone in his voice, knowing she was in for it.

"What do you mean, what?" her father challenged, looking at her rear tire.

"The tire's low?" she asked. A muscle in the back of her neck spasmed with a sharp pain as if a man-eating vine had bitten into it.

He looked at her like she was the stupidest thing on two legs. "Yeah, the tire's low. What are you doing, riding around on a tire like that?"

Some man-eating vine tendrils started creeping over her shoulders, getting ready to strangle her. She was, of course, aware that this was just an old childhood fantasy, but they liked to sprout up in her imagination nonetheless. She loved reading up on psychology and was trying to analyze her fixation on the vines.

She'd identified what it was, a certain tone of voice, that always brought them on. It wasn't so much the statement, "What are you doing, riding around on a tire like that?" It was the WAY he said it. He took each word and spit them at her with total contempt. The statement and the tone didn't match at all. That's what threw her. If the statement had been, "Why are you such a disgusting subhuman?" the tone of voice would have matched.

She heard it every day, when she let the screen door slam behind her, or she spilled the milk. All those trifling things, the screen door and the spilled milk and the bike tire were all worth *way* more than she was. The tone of his voice told her that.

She shook her head defiantly, trying to dislodge the vines, knowing there was no rational counterpoint to the contempt. She tried anyway. "*I* didn't *know!* It must have just happened!"

The disgust continued to rise in his voice. "Well, you're supposed to know! You're supposed to stay on top of that stuff!" Archie continued stepping towards her. She saw the man-eating vines cascading menacingly from his fingertips. "You can't just be riding around without looking all the time to make sure your tires are good!"

Leslie looked up at her dad with sheer, smart-ass incredulity. She had learned that impudent insolence, in his view, had at least some value in countering total contempt.

"You hear me?" he demanded.

Both of their voices had already risen to a loud enough volume to have the neighbors wondering who was getting ready to kill who.

"Okay!" she said. "I'll fix the tire!"

"You're supposed to fix the stupid tire *before* you ride on it, not *after!*"

"All right, I'll fix the stupid tire!"

"It's too late now!" he said.

"It's not too late! It's fine! I'll patch the stupid inner tube! It'll be fine!"

"You know what happens when you start riding on the rims?" he harped on. A drop of his spit carried with his shouting. It hit her cheek. She wiped it away, turned her back to him and marched away with the bike. "Do you? They're ruined! You might as well throw the damn thing out if you have to replace the stupid rear wheel!"

"All right!" Leslie said, raising her voice even louder as she entered the garage. She'd show him who was stupid and contemptible.

She disassembled the wheel, found the leak in the inner tube, patched it and re-adjusted the *derailleur* before dinner. Archie, in fact, had a daughter who could do all that without any instruction from anyone, just by eavesdropping on what he taught the neighbor kid who he was always just *so* nice to, as if anyone in the world was better than her contemptible self. Leslie stepped back and admired her work. "How stupid is that?" she muttered.

Deloris called Leslie in for dinner twice. Leslie had to get the grease off her hands with her dad's Goop, so it took a while.

"What took you so long?" chided Deloris. "Uncle Joe's dinner is cold already."

Leslie let out a big sigh at the prospects of her daily trip to The Dungeon. "Why don't you make him come upstairs?" she whined for the thousandth time. In fact, Uncle Joe hadn't been up from the basement in several years. It had been months since she'd even seen him. Though only seven years older than her dad, he already seemed decrepit to her. He obviously hated being seen, as much as she hated seeing him. Sometimes she could hear him scurrying like a mouse into his room, then the sound of his door closing, whenever she started her trip down the stairs through her homicidal, if imaginary, man-eating vines.

She'd hear her parents wondering what was going to happen. The last time they tried to take him to the doctor was a disaster. He wouldn't go. He just grabbed onto the bedframe, shaking like a leaf, and panting like he was suffocating. Leslie saw the tail end of it and ran back up the stairs, terrified.

They didn't know *what* they were going to do about him.

Srđa witnessed the scene, too, and broke down in tears over it. "We held off an entire invading subcontinent for *350 years!*" he cried. "A bunch of runaway slaves. Like the world's never seen! And this is what we've been reduced to, momma. The world has never hated us as much as we now hate ourselves. That's the only "refuge" we've found! Self-destruction. I can't take it."

That made Jovanka cry too. "Maybe we can make room for him up top a little early," she said, pointing towards the sky, "so we can take care of him. Poor guy." She cried some more.

So, Uncle Joe was still down there and couldn't even get to the doctor. Deloris worried about it and got a nurse to come and take his vitals. Then when she pursued it further all she got was talk about commitment. Archie pitched a fit. "I ain't putting nobody in my family in no loony bin!" It stalled out there.

Everything settled back into the routine Uncle Joe could manage. Deloris knew he'd start breaking out in a cold sweat if Leslie didn't hurry up doing her part. It had to be Leslie bringing the plate or he wouldn't be able to eat. Everything in his day had to unfold like clockwork or he'd start to panic.

"Young lady," she commanded. "Get your butt down there or I'm going to paddle it!"

Leslie knew that was an idle threat. She hadn't been spanked in a decade, so she let out another huge sigh and made her way down into The

Dungeon. As usual, she ran back up the stairs, aware that it wasn't just her routine, but his too now, and she had to do her part.

She finally sat down at the dinner table. They were having chuck steak for dinner. Archie was a real red meat eater, like the next Great Famine was impending, and he was going to load up like there was no tomorrow, at least when it came to the meat rations. He got very intense, his mouth shining with grease, cutting the finest little vein of meat away from the fat, holding onto the fatty rind with one hand, while wielding the knife in the other. After he ate the sliver he rubbed his hands together, rubbing the grease into them.

Leslie had watched a scene with her mother in the movie, "Broken Arrow" when Cochise rubs the bear grease into his arms and tells Jimmy Stewart that it's good for the skin. She told her mom, "See, it's a good idea!"

"Sure, if you want to smell like a bear," Deloris quipped. Leslie wondered if her mom was tired of her dad smelling like a steer.

The evening news was playing as usual.

Srđa always enjoyed news broadcasts, so he and Jovanka were present. He considered being dead no excuse to lose track of current events.

Two young black men from the Chicago Freedom Movement were being interviewed.

Jovanka noticed something. "Look, love, aren't they just like our brave *Krajina* boys? Just look at all that beautiful anger!"

"Oh, you like that?" Srđa said teasingly.

She cut him a flirtatious glance. "Sometimes, baby, it's the most interesting thing in the world," and she kissed him.

"Let the brother speak," one of the young men said, stepping forward and interrupting his friend. "We had to live through the worst America has dished out. We were slaves for 300 years!"

"You'd think they're still slaves," Archie quipped, "sitting around expecting other people to feed them."

"Oh," Leslie scoffed loudly. "That's a total *nonsequitur*." She absolutely loved dropping Latin on Archie since he had no clue what any of it meant and was all the more impressed as a result. "If they're slaves, they're not the ones sitting around waiting to be fed! It's the slave *masters* who are sitting around waiting to be fed."

But then she remembered – the word 'slave.' That's right! She was waiting for a chance to whip this one on him. "Do you know the derivation of the word 'slave?' Do you know where the word came from?" She always threw in some vocabulary augmentation for free.

"Oh, here she goes!" said Srđa. "I told you this one was coming."

Archie looked at Leslie with feigned indifference, pretending he was only half hearing her, which meant he was all ears. She proceeded with the sassy self-confidence Archie was as inadvertently as fastidiously grooming in her on these occasions.

"Back in Roman times, they needed people to work their wheat plantations, so they'd stage raids to the east and bring back some Slavs, I mean slaves, to do the work.

"I guess we must have made really excellent Slavs, I mean, slaves, to get such preferential treatment." She looked at him for a reaction. He was looking at his plate, which she knew meant he was hanging onto every word she had to say.

"It was probably us, in particular, the Romans were picking on since we were among the barbarians coming after them when the time was right.

"But then the Moslems took over and cut off that route, so Europeans had to start going south to get the really good slaves. So, I guess," she said with a giggle, "if it weren't for those Moslems, we would have been picking all that cotton."

Srđa commented to Jovanka. "Wait till she finds out what those Moslems had us picking."

"Which brings us to the Slav Mentality," she went on. Of course, Archie didn't know that she was playing on Prince Malcolm's "Slave Mentality."

"See, you got a bunch of stupid serfs running around, doing all the stupid stuff. It doesn't matter how smart they are, or how good they could be at doing things, you need all the stupid stuff done, so they're *it*," her heart was beating fast and she felt sweat on her forehead. "So, to keep them doing all the stupid stuff you've got to convince them how stupid they are, which is easy, since they can't use five words in a row without throwing the stupid 'stupid' word in there."

Her voice had risen loudly, angrily. "Of course, they don't know that's the reason they're doing stupid stuff, because they're just brainwashing themselves with all the stupid words all the time, and are too stupid to figure out what they're doing to their stupid selves!" She slammed her fist on the table and glared deep into her dad's eyes, "AND to their stupid kids!"

There it was, that involuntary eye contact for just a hot second of a response. She had hit that nerve, only this time it wasn't just the 'awe' nerve. This time, as his eyes met hers, mixed in there, there was a flash of honest-to-goodness *remorse!* It shot through her as if she were a lightning rod.

Being Archie's little girl, that was as good as it was going to get. She knew full well that she had, in that moment, achieved *The Ultimate*. She had vanquished Archie. He no longer defined her. She had confronted his abuse, and he'd acknowledged it. She was free of him.

She drew in a deep breath of gratification, got up from the table and walked away, throwing her fork dramatically into the sink as she left, daring to utter *The Ultimate* in the beat immediately behind the tinkle of the fork into the sink.

"Fork you!"

∗ ∗ ∗

Chapter 2
The Jolt

He Looks All the Way In

It was time. Time for Leslie to go off on her own into the world for the first time. She was sixteen and her parents were sending her off to an art camp for the summer, all by herself.

Leslie took a train from the Chicago suburbs to Kansas University for the summer camp. She had won an art scholarship. It must have impressed her dad. As she got onto the train and turned to say goodbye he said, "Make it count, Leslie, make it count."

It was the first time Leslie was leaving home on her own -- other than those stowaways, Srđa and Jovanka, who were hiding in the baggage compartment, cuddled up together in total contentment. Leslie was traveling by train to a strange city and finding her way to the University all by herself. It felt very good and she wasn't afraid at all, just excited, till it happened.

All the kids were assembling in a large hall for an orientation. She was sitting high up in a balcony seat. About five rows down from her there were four or five black guys sitting. One of them was standing facing her direction, looking up into the crowd, as if looking for someone. He was dressed oddly, mostly the hippie stuff that was *de rigeur,* but with a few streetish elements, like a gray fedora.

It was kind of cool, though, because it was an understated, forties-style Humphrey Bogart kind of hat, not some tacky, superfly mess. Peeking out from under his hat was some long, fluffy hair. She wasn't thinking he was cute or anything, she just thought he looked different, and with him surveying everyone, he *was* kind of commanding everyone's attention. Then it happened.

He *looked* at her. He had enormous eyes, that commanded absolute attention. He grabbed onto hers and would not let them go.

And *he looked all the way in!*

Panicked, she broke the spell and glanced away. How could that audacious hooligan do that to her? Zap her with that high-voltage jolt of attraction, for which she was, by her own father's inadvertent hand, perfectly wired, and fling her across that horrifying color line? She slouched down in her seat, hyperventilating with the panic. Her heart was pounding.

"What's going on?" demanded Jovanka, alarmed at Leslie's fright. She and Srđa were sitting behind her.

"What a terrifying line to cross!" he said. "Don't you remember what happened to that boy in her neighborhood just twelve years ago, on her third birthday? They were born just a half a mile apart. Though it might as well have been the other side of the moon."

"What boy?" she asked.

"That boy, Emmett Till. It's like what happened to your cousin, Marko. Remember him?"

"Of course, I remember Marko!" she replied loudly, with anger. "He was the first to go in '41. They broke into his house in the middle of the night and shot him for marrying a Croatian woman, then shot their 14-year-old daughter for being the product of an impure union. Then they shot his sister just for being Serb but left his wife alive so she could remember that day for the rest of her life." She calmed herself. "So, what happened to that boy?"

"He was just a normal, occasionally foolish 14-year-old boy. What 14-year-old boy isn't occasionally foolish? He was visiting his cousins in Mississipi, showing off for them, and whistled at a white lady. It *was* a rather rude thing to do. But he'd scolded his cousins the day before for giving in to a bully, so he wanted to show them how to be bold. He should have gotten some punishment, maybe grounded for the weekend.

"Did he ever get grounded! He's still in that ground after what those *Ustaša* did to him. They found that child's mutilated body floating in the river."

Jovanka shook her head and sighed bitterly.

"He's become quite famous in his martyrdom." Srđa continued. "His mother, Mamie, was even bolder. She insisted his mutilated, rotting corpse be displayed in an open coffin."

"Good for her!" said Jovanka.

Srđa went on. "Thousands of people came to see it and it made headlines all over the world. So poor Emmett became the Patron Saint of 14-year-old boys everywhere, dying for their right to be natural and normal, even if they're black boys growing up in the South. It was the beginning of the Civil Rights Movement. They should have named Leslie's school 'Emmett Till Junior High.'"

"So that's why those kids acted so strangely around her?" asked Jovanka.

"Exactly," Srđa replied. "They were shunning the white kids over Emmett."

* * *

Emmet Till Junior High

Most of the white kids in Argo Summit school district had never even heard about Emmett. On the ten-year anniversary of his death, news of him was again all over the media. Leslie had, of course, interpreted the story for her father, who had, as usual, left-handedly expected, and received, a thorough report on the subject. But Leslie knew nothing about where Emmett had been born.

Leslie interpreted the aloofness of her black classmates as a Jim Crow-type obsequiousness. Seventh grade was the first "integrated" class in the district, though it was hardly that. The school kept the children separate by way of a 'grade' tracking. The 'A' class, the one Leslie was in, was nearly all white, the 'C' class nearly all black and Hispanic, with varying degrees of ethnicity in the class in between.

There was only one black boy, Howard, in the "A" class Leslie was in. For two years she was assigned to sit behind him. He never once spoke to her. He never once even looked her in the face. If he were to drop a pencil and she picked it up for him, he wouldn't even say 'thank you.'

In fact, there were only two black kids in the whole school who'd ever looked her in the eye. There was her friend, Alfredda, the only black girl in the 'A' class and there was Carolyn, a bully, who wanted to beat Leslie up. All the other kids would just pass her by, not noticing her, not wanting to be noticed – especially the boys.

Howard was the only boy in the school with better grades than Leslie. And that's how she spent her puberty – ensconced in a tight, double helix of covalent energy that swirled in a four-foot radius where those two bright children sat.

The two silences, Howard's silence and her grandmother's silence about the genocide ravaging her people into oblivion – were screaming the terms of Leslie's future.

* * *

Argo Corn Starch

Thirteen-year-old Carolyn was one of the only two black kids to ever look Leslie in the eye. Carolyn had issues. She was a rangy, dark-skinned black girl whose long limbs always seemed at odds with each other. She was constantly making a lot of noise and trouble. She often had white powder around her mouth. That was because she ate Argo laundry starch. The Argo corn starch plant sat in the middle of the district, belching into the air the foul, sweet stench of fermented corn.

Leslie saw Carolyn eating it. She kept it in her gym locker and would dip her fingers into the box, grab a handful and stuff it into her mouth, in between whatever loud thing she was saying, in so alien a dialect that Leslie often found it unintelligible. Carolyn made Leslie think of those two urchins in Dickens' *Christmas Carol*. Ignorance and want.

Leslie had gotten on Carolyn's bad side one day in class when Leslie was talking to another girl, walking in Carolyn's direction. Leslie was complaining about the teacher, frowning, when her eyes inadvertently met Carolyn's.

Leslie went into the locker room and Carolyn followed, grabbed Leslie's shoulder and pulled her around into her face.

"You was talkin' about me!" the girl hollered.

"No, I wasn't!" Leslie responded, afraid of what crazy thing this girl might do.

Carolyn shoved her. "How you like it if a beat you up?"

Leslie looked Carolyn in the eye, touched her arm and addressed her just as loudly. "Carolyn, I was *not* talking about you! I was talking about Miss Brown making us do all those stupid push-ups for talking too much!"

Carolyn retreated. For a while.

The next week, Carolyn waltzed into the bathroom part of the locker room with the toilets, the sinks, and the mirrors, where the white girls from the "A" class did their hair and whatever makeup their mothers allowed them.

There was another big mirror in the main room where the other girls combed their hair. Nobody had said anything dictating who was to go where. That's just where everybody went. Carolyn waltzed into the white girls' room, and grabbed Leslie's hairbrush from out of her hand, in mid-stroke.

"Let me see your hairbrush," she said, though she didn't want to just see it. She took the brush, dominated the center of the mirror and brushed her own hair – a very bold girl.

Leslie was appalled. She was a pubescent girl with straight, flimsy, thin, flat hair that by afternoon would be an ugly, stringy mess plastered to her skull with all the oils her scalp was mercilessly pumping out. The prospect of the pomade Carolyn was voluntarily plastering her hair down with – so that it could look just as bad, in Leslie's opinion – getting brushed into her own hair, was horrifying. And, of course, there was also the issue that she was being bullied.

Leslie went home, pulled her brush out of her purse and told her mom what had happened. She didn't realize Archie was in the doorway. "Throw it away!" he said.

That remark instantly clarified the issue for her.

She knew full well what Carolyn was up to, what she was trying to make Leslie do. She remembered the story a girl in the neighborhood, Denise, had told her about the colored girl – the word 'black' did not yet exist as an option – who'd worked at the Dairy Queen. But she didn't call her a colored girl, she called her a nigger girl. Some customer had insulted her, so she put a wad of her hair in the bottom of a milkshake. And Denise didn't just fake retching at the thought of how disgusting it was to have hair in your food, this was a special kind of disgusting – to have *nigger* hair in your food, it was clear from Denise's histrionics that would be *ten times* more disgusting.

Leslie knew that contempt intimately. It was that all-too-familiar, shrill, gut-wrenching noise of disgust Archie commonly expressed towards her, his only child. That's what Carolyn was trying to tempt Leslie to surrender to. That special kind of disgust that relegated some people to a state of perpetual worthlessness.

Srđa was there, coaxing her on. This was a critical moment! She couldn't lose her resolve, or she would be lost forever! Trapped in The Dungeon with Uncle Joe, vanquished as a disgusting subhuman forever!

"Come on, my girl, you can do it! Don't let the Ustaša win. You know what you have to do!"

Leslie went into the bathroom, filled the sink with hot water and shampoo, and washed the pomade out of her brush.

She used it for another four years.

* * *

Back in Kansas

But at last, Leslie was sixteen years old on a college campus for a summer camp, on her own after that long train ride all by herself. At last, she was free from Archie's regime of contempt. She was free for a whole summer from him and that Bigot Belt wherein he held her in contemptible subjugation.

There at the summer camp, in that auditorium for their indoctrination, way up in the balcony, she sat, hardly hearing a word the camp administrator was saying, remembering instead the way her life had flashed before her eyes when that rude black boy had looked her in the eye.

The course that had been charted for her, that Archie had led her along step-by-inadvertent-step, that she was already way too far along, was taking her somewhere terrifying she had not anticipated. There was no way she could possibly deny that boy's jolt, out of hand, not without losing *The Ultimate* -- that victory she'd won armed with the rhetoric of the Slav Mentality, that forced Archie to acknowledge how he'd sabotaged her – that one supreme victory that made life on earth, instead of The Dungeon – possible!

Her fate was sealed. Her future flashed before her eyes, instantly, enormously, frighteningly difficult.

There she was, hurtling towards that No-Man's-Land between the Great Divide of Race in America, as if it were her homeland.

* * *

She Might As Well Get to It

Leslie's new roommate was Cindy Goldstein. Cindy thought that boy who'd just jolted Leslie and precipitated her imminent expulsion from the white race was the epitome of coolness. She even knew his name – William.

Cindy was a petite Jewish girl from Newton, Iowa who went to New York City every summer and was infinitely more sophisticated than Leslie was. She knew Leslie was brighter than she was, she talked about it even, but she also knew Leslie's pollack provincialism neutralized that in their personal dynamics. Leslie was no threat.

She lorded it over Leslie like the Princess she was, chiding Leslie's pollack ignorance, and filling her in on all the intricate fine points in conforming with the Flower Children -- the wild and free, tuned in, let-it-be, radical iconoclasts and revolutionaries.

Such things as exactly how long one's bell-bottoms are supposed to be, the precise degree of makeup one should wear so as to appear not to be wearing any makeup. The correct brand of blue jeans, ("Oh God, not K-Mart!") and just exactly how worn they should appear, *etc, etc.* Who was cool. Who was not.

In public, Leslie was far too uncool for Cindy to acknowledge, but in the evenings in their room, she loved to chat and she talked and talked about the exclusive clique to which she belonged.

And Cindy talked about William all the time. Everybody loved him. His father was the editor of the black newspaper in Phoenix, had been in the Movement for years. William was at the very epicenter of the cool, hippie kids. They all looked to him to interpret their counter-culture and give it meaning.

He was just so special, she extolled. He was a wise soul, a natural born leader who cared about everyone else, had no ego, had transcended all that and knew *the way.* Apparently, the "in-crowd" had just designated Leslie's 'tormentor' the Dali Lama of Kansas.

By coincidence, that for once Jovanka had nothing to do with, Leslie's lockermate, Jim McDaniels, was also his roommate. Then Jim got thrown out of the summer camp because he'd put up a sign in his room, "SDS Headquarters and Campus Barber Shop," referring to the radical, controversial *Students for a Democratic Society.* Leslie ran into him just as he was cleaning out his locker. He seemed amused by it. He was just joking around, for chrissakes, he explained, but the admins made a big deal about it and now they were sending him home. "Bye, lockermate," he said and gave her a big hug.

In Jim's defense, William wrote a Letter to the Editor in the Kansas University Summer Camp newspaper protesting Jim's expulsion. He used a word to describe the administration's attitude that was new to her, that immediately intrigued her.

She ran over to the ass head's room – that's what they called the college girl who supervised their floor – and pleaded for a dictionary, as excited as if she were cashing in a winning lottery ticket.

She was delighted. It was just the word she was looking for!

Chauvinism! It was the word *chauvinism!*

Leslie was in love.

This was a big deal getting a new word from a boy. She was the class nerd who everybody tittered at because she used big words, at least ever since her parents had moved to Pollack Hills so she wouldn't have to go to high school with the coloreds.

She used big words because she liked them, but then when she saw that people thought it was weird to use big words, she had to expand her vocabulary even further to find less objectionable synonyms, and then heighten her abilities to edit everything on the fly. She still wasn't all that good at it, so she got picked on readily.

They had a very sexist caste system at her high school. Girls who wanted dates deliberately kept their grades down because boys never dated girls with better grades than them, so if you had a high GPA, what choices would you have? And multi-syllabic girls? Forget about it! Nobody had ever asked Leslie out.

But William gave her a word! And such a word! Such a transcendent word! She'd had a crush on Brian Danley for two years because he used the word 'precarious,' while goofing around, standing on a chair in French class, but this word was so much better! She already knew what 'precarious' meant, but this was a whole new, glorious word! It didn't just define a concept, it defined part of the worldview she was acquiring that would shape her future.

She sat down on her bed, letting the glories of this new word sink in, while brushing her hair pleasurably, savoring the feel of the brush on her scalp.

It was a special brush. The package it came in had advertised that the end of each bristle was rounded so that it would stimulate the scalp without scratching it. Leslie was giving it a good workout when it broke in half. She looked at the two pieces for a moment and wondered if she could find rounded bristles again. She tossed Carolyn's hairbrush, as she called it, into the wastebasket.

Her initial terror at William's intrusion into her world had vanished as soon as Cindy started talking about him. What became obvious was that he was exactly what she, and all the counter-culture kids there wanted black people to be. Perfect. Transcendent. A beacon to a Brave New World, leading them all away from that corrupt Establishment their conservative parents lived within.

Her attitude concerning her fate had thus shifted from dread to an excited resolve as this part of the equation beckoned. 'Since I know I'm going to have a hard life,' she thought playfully, "I might as well get to it!'

She skipped happily out from her room and joined her friends. It was a Friday night and there was a band playing that evening. The mood was very festive, and all the kids were out on the commons, cruising. The four of them were on their way to the dance, passing the boys' dorm. There was a group of a dozen or so hippie boys, with their shoulder-length hair, milling around on the steps. Then a tall, elegantly graceful boy in their midst, with a 35mm camera around his neck, turned in the girls' direction. It was *him!*

Her expression must have let the cat out of the bag. He looked stunned at first, then delighted, and beamed at her. He raised his camera to his eye, and she immediately ducked her head, embarrassed with delight. All the boys laughed. By then the girls had passed them and she turned back around. "Can I have a print?" she asked. They all laughed again, egging the two of them on.

She couldn't believe it. This was the smartest, cutest, most popular boy she'd ever liked, and he was flattered that she felt that way. She could have cried!

Later on, at the dance, she looked for him. It was pretty empty at first when they got there, but it filled up rapidly. She was half-listening to her friends' conversation, which was kind of drifting since they were all doing more cruising than talking. A crowd of people shifted and there he stood – and he was *looking at her!*

Then she did something that perfectly fulfilled every prophecy Archie had ever made about her stupidity. Even as she did it she knew the enormity of the error, but there was no stopping the reflex.

She turned to look over her shoulder to see who he must *really* be looking at.

When she turned back, the sea of people had filled in again and he'd vanished from sight.

Days passed, and nothing happened, except in that inner world in which she lived, where she delighted in the possibility of seeing him. They'd often pass on the sidewalk during lunch break. He'd smile and tip his hat. She'd happily accept the gesture, amazed at her own good fortune. Neither of them spoke.

* * *

Uncle Joe's Demise

Deloris had worried that Leslie's leaving for six weeks was going to be hard on Uncle Joe. He and Leslie might act like they barely tolerated each other, but Deloris knew better. She was well aware that he could only eat his dinner when Leslie brought it. It brought a tear to her eye to think how much he loved the girl, even if he had no idea that's how he felt.

Sure enough, now that Leslie was absent, his dinner plates were going untouched. Her counter-tactic was to leave more food in his little pantry, cans of tuna and Vienna sausage, more boxes of cereal, things like that which didn't need cooking.

In fact, every time Deloris brought him his plate, knocked gently on his door and spoke to him, he would begin hyperventilating at the break in the routine that comprised his confinement. After several weeks of this, his heart – with undiagnosed valve problems, since he couldn't make it to a doctor's office – gave out. Archie heard a clatter and went to find his brother Joe on the floor, already gone.

Deloris didn't know what to do about Leslie. She didn't want her to miss out on her camp, so she made up a story that she'd gone downstairs with his plate and found him fading fast and he told her to make sure to tell Leslie to finish up her camp. He didn't want her to miss out on his account.

That made Leslie cry because she knew her mom was lying. Uncle Joe would never say nothing like that about nobody. That was his legacy, double, even triple negatives. It was impossible to think of him without using them herself. It made her cry over what a pathetic family she had.

That night she had a dream that Archie smashed her bike up and locked her in The Dungeon.

Srđa and Jovanka, on the other hand, were overjoyed to have Uncle Joe to themselves. They'd been there when he collapsed and Jovanka had reached for his hand, "Joey!" she said. "Joey, come on, let's go home!"

What emerged from the old man's twisted carcass was the bright-eyed boy of eight he'd been just before his old man had locked him in a closet for three days, as his father had done before him, with nothing but a bucket and a pitcher of water, for being such a stupid, worthless thing.

"Yay!" said Joey, jumping up and doing cartwheels around the room, with a big happy smile. "Let's get out of here. I can't wait!"

* * *

Mud-Colored Gold

Leslie couldn't stand spending time in her room unless Mindy was there. And if Mindy went out, Leslie tried to be in the vicinity. Mindy hung out with people who hung out with William.

But Mindy was nowhere to be found, off somewhere the cool people went that Leslie knew nothing about. She was killing time in the dorm room lounge, reading a magazine. She turned to a page with pictures of young people with big Afros and upraised fists and a banner with a catchy new phrase Leslie'd heard once or twice before that summer, "Black is Beautiful!"

The first thing that flashed in Leslie's mind when she saw that phrase was her grandma. There was a baffling enigma the old lady had laid on her about the insecure interchangeability of ugliness and beauty. The old woman always wore the dowdiest house dresses in the world and the ugliest, thickest glasses. It's as if her grandma got up every day and figured out what she could wear that would make her look as ugly as possible. Her shoes were also ridiculously ugly. Those high-top, black pumps with the laces like a man's shoes. Old lady shoes. Could anything possibly make a woman's ankle look thicker or less attractive?

Sheesh, Leslie thought, immigrant people were the un-coolest people in the world. Except, of course, Jewish immigrants. They were cool. Oppressed people were always very cool. All that beautiful anger. People with those kinds of problems were the most important people in the world to her.

But not the pollacks. They were just stupid bigots. Usually pretty ugly and not very bright. Leslie knew that's why Cindy thought she was so uncool.

Leslie's grandma had to have been one of the meekest people on earth. Leslie felt as sorry for her as she felt grateful for the old woman's unqualified affection. Kata had been dead for several years already. Leslie was fourteen, on the way home from Sunday School when she found out that her grandma had gone to the hospital.

Auntie Babe told her what happened. Grandma was an extraordinarily fastidious person who lived in dread that she would lay dead in her apartment for weeks before anyone smelled what had happened. No, she would not leave the world that way. So, when she felt her lungs giving out under the strain of her enlarged heart she first unlocked the front door, then called for an ambulance. She was gone before they arrived, but they had no trouble getting in and finding her children's phone numbers on the dresser.

When Leslie heard her grandma was in the hospital she sent a prayer up to God that she'd do anything at all in the world if He would spare her grandma. How could she possibly live without her? But it was too late. Grandma was already gone. Neatly, with no embarrassment. No mess.

Leslie remembered her grandma's accent – well-formed English sentences relentlessly self-effacing. The two were in the back seat of the big two-tone green '54 Chrysler. Leslie was eight years old. She smelled the scent of her grandma's favorite hand lotion, Jergen's Cherry Almond. She always used it. Leslie asked for some and her grandma poured it first into her own hand, then massaged it tenderly into Leslie's. She sat, stroking the child's hand in recognition. "You have the pretty hands," Kata said. "Not like mine. My hands are ugly."

Puzzled, Leslie looked at her grandma. Her hands were, in fact, a replica of her grandmother's. They were small, feminine, almost dainty hands, with nails shaped like fans, nails with small ridges in them that increased with age. A lifetime as a charwoman had not erased that femininity. They were still the same girlish hands.

The girl turned her questioning eyes intently onto her grandmother. "And you have the pretty, gold-colored eyes. Not like mine," Kata said. "Mine are mud-colored."

Little Leslie was even more astonished. She stared into her grandmother's eyes, which were precisely the same large, warm, expressive, hazel eyes. If Leslie was ever complimented, it was over her eyes. Leslie remembered her astonishment. It was the most important, baffling thing her grandmother ever told her. Even at that young age, she knew that gold could turn into mud in their family for the same reason, whatever that reason was, that they had a Dungeon full of man-eating vines.

But sixteen-year-old Leslie was now an almost-emancipated girl all by herself in Kansas, sitting in a college dorm lounge reading a magazine. She admired the certainty of the upraised fists in the magazine article and the amazingly fluffy 3D hair that had sprung energetically into life, transformed from that greasy mess Carolyn had tried to gross her out with. Who knew hiding under that tortured mess was something so interesting and full of life? Not to mention all that kinetic energy. At least *somebody* was figuring out who they really were.

Leslie had a hobby of collecting Stupid White People Artifacts. She kept them in an old Dr. Kildare folder, with a photo of Richard

Chamberlain dressed up like a doctor. She'd had a big crush on him a few years earlier.

One of the 'artifacts' was an illustration that showed how, in a well-formed, good-looking profile a line could be drawn from the tip of the nose to the chin, with the lower lip falling right along that line. How racist, she had thought. There was absolutely no aesthetic reason why a curved line instead of a straight line couldn't be perfectly interesting and nice looking.

It was even more racist since it was in a plastic surgery brochure, not a racist publication. Just blind, ignorant racism.

Archie's training of his prodigy, as meticulous as it was inadvertent, relentlessly reinforced the point that all racial truth could be calibrated precisely to its exact polar opposite -- in other words, whatever he or any other racist said, the opposite was The Truth.

Identifying that point 180 degrees from his contemptuous racism had never once, in all her childhood, failed to earn her father's approval in the form of The Last Word in one of their Great Civil Rights Debates at hand. He always gave her that Last Word. He only ever gave it to her, of all the people on Earth, but it was only on that subject. It was clearly supremely important. That's what he had taught her.

So, if racists saw black people as ugly, then the truth had to lie 180 degrees in the opposite direction. But up until that summer, her thoughts about racial aesthetics had been only theoretical.

* * *

We Land on the Moon, July 19th, 1969, and Phoenix Rises

"I knew I'd find you here," fussed Jovanka as she approached Srđa. She knew from her internal homing frequencies -- latest update from the geek angels -- that he was in this row of books in the university stacks, but for the life of her, or afterlife, she had no idea which one. "Will you come out now? I need you to see this."

A thin wisp of ether emanated from one of the tomes on the top shelf. Srđa was reconstituting himself from a microstate. This technique allowed him to attain a size so small he could squeeze into the space between the pages in a book. The words would then be viewable at a gargantuan size, and he could cascade through the pages at break-neck speed. To him, it was like a roller coaster ride across the big screen at a movie theater. An absolute favorite pastime.

"What's wrong, my love?" he asked. She looked worried.

"The boy Leslie has a crush on is being stalked."

"Really? By whom?

"The police."

"The police are after that sweet boy? Why in the world?"

"You tell me," she said, then added acerbically, "maybe they think he's a Serb." She pulled his hand. With that contact, they instantly reappeared outside the dorm buildings. A squad car was parked near the intersection. Two officers were inside.

"I've been watching them all evening," she said. "Everywhere he goes, all those kids go, and everywhere they go, these *policia* go. But before that, this afternoon, when he was all alone, already they were following him."

"A popular guy," said Srđa. "Actually, he's quite surprised by all this. He thinks he's shy. I was eavesdropping while he talked to himself just this afternoon."

"Then why are the police bothering him?"

"That's what I was just reading. Lawrence, Kansas has a terrible history of pogroms against the blacks, and here he is acting perfectly comfortable around white people. It's making them very nervous. They think he must be a trouble-maker. That's why all those kids are following him around too. It's a whole new world for them. They are completely unused to a normal world in which black and white people are comfortable around each other. They find it quite thrilling."

"Well, don't ask me about a normal world," said Jovanka. "I'm from the Krajina. Should we send in for some of the boys?"

"Sure, why not? They'd probably enjoy the excursion if nothing else."

The two of them approached Leslie.

She was walking past one of the big dorm buildings. She heard a lot of cheering and laughter. She headed in that direction. She walked past a cop car at the corner, then followed the sound to the right. Downhill a bit, a big, happy crowd was watching and applauding something going on in the grass. She approached the commotion.

It was *William,* wrestling in the grass with a long-haired white boy, both laughing more than they were wrestling. William pinned the boy down. The whole crowd laughed and applauded. The round was over.

William picked up his shirt from the grass and threw it over his shoulder. He headed straight towards Leslie, the whole crowd following him.

He looked up in her direction and looked into her eyes. He beamed at her as if she were the one person he most wanted to see. The shirtless boy sparkling in the golden sunlight.

She'd never seen anything more beautiful.

He was tall and slender, with an extended grace to his movement. His skin was a warm brown, wet with sweat and shining gloriously. On the cusp of a beautiful child and a handsome man, his face fulfilled every aesthetic rule, but there was nothing European in its form. Instead, it was a compilation of rounded lines, not a harsh angle anywhere. It was an African aesthetic, flaunting emphatically every stupid plastic surgery brochure ever printed.

He passed her by, the crowd still following. 'My Phoenix,' she thought, 'rising right in front of my eyes. My alchemist, turning mud into gold.'

"Oh, will you listen to that," observed Jovanka. "She's got it bad."

Someone called to him and he walked up the hill, the whole crowd still following him and his friends over to the bridge that spanned the freeway.

Everyone was talking about the impending Moon Walk. Cindy was there with her boyfriend, a short, curly-headed Jewish boy with the same round, wire-rimmed glasses, who matched her perfectly. They were talking to William.

"Oh Leslie, come here!" Cindy called out. Leslie was astonished how easy it was to just smile and walk over to them. He was smiling back. She was finally going to get to talk to him!

"This is my roommate, Leslie," Cindy told William. "She was Jim's locker-mate." Apparently, Cindy was no longer embarrassed to be seen with Leslie since she'd tipped Leslie off on how to curl her unfashionably short hair into a Jew-fro look.

"So that's your name," he said. "I'm William Johnson."

"I know," she said. 'Oh, why did I say that?' she thought. 'I sound like a groupie.'

She watched his face. He didn't take it that way. "Thank you," he said. Leslie realized he must be enjoying how much all these white kids thought he was super cool. Why not? After three hundred and fifty years of persecution, he certainly had it coming.

Srda, reading her mind, laughed. "But he's only been here seventeen!"

"What camp are you in?" William asked.

"Art camp," she said.

Cindy jumped back in, "Oh you should see the collage she did. Fetuses and spaceships and all kinds of shit."

"Cool," he said. "Sounds like *2001*."

"Yeah," she said. "I was in a *Space Odyssey* kind of mood." Leslie was astonished how calm she felt. "Oh, I wanted to thank you."

"For what?"

"You gave me a word."

"A word? How did I give you a word?"

"That letter to the editor you wrote about Jim."

"Oh, that. What word did I give you?"

"Chauvinism," she said. "I'll never forget you gave me that."

"Never?"

"Nope. Twenty lifetimes from now I'll still remember."

He laughed.

A curly-headed intellectual-looking boy interrupted. "William, listen to this, man. Tomorrow, when they land on the moon, it's estimated that one-fifth of the people on the planet, 600 million damn people will be watching the same thing at the same time."

'Oh damn,' she thought. 'Already I've lost him.'

William turned back to her. "What do you think of that?"

He was bringing her back in! "Sounds like 600 million people will all be watching the same Pepsi commercial at the same time," she said. "There probably won't be any left on the shelves the day after."

"Wish I had Pepsi stock," he said. "Where are you from?"

"Chicago. I hear you're from Phoenix."

"Who told you that?"

"Cindy." She looked to Cindy, who was chatting with another girl. Leslie leaned in to whisper to William, "She talks about you all the time."

A squad car had approached. The cops got out of it and went straight for William.

"Oh God," Jovanka moaned. "This must be the most subversive thing he's done all day, talking to Leslie."

William looked over at Cindy and smiled. "Cindy talks about me all the time?" he asked.

"Yes, you're famous," Leslie replied confidingly.

One of the cops inserted himself directly in front of William. Leslie had to give way.

"Young man, we need to see your camp ID."

Leslie got a bad vibe from the cop. The way he said, 'young man' was forced, as if what he really wanted to say was, "boy."

William fumbled around on his shirt for it, but it was gone. "It must be in the grass over there," he said. "I must have lost it wrestling."

"I'm afraid you're going to have to come with us."

"But we know him," said one of the boys. Another joined in.

The cop took William by the arm and pulled him towards the squad car. He followed along compliantly. To Leslie, he seemed admirably calm, brave. She left the boys behind and marched up to the cops, "He's in the summer camp with us," she said loudly. "We know him!"

"Get back," another cop glared, taking a step towards her. She stood watching in disbelief as they drove away with him, her hero, her Phoenix.

But before they drove off, six Grenzer angels, young men who had been brave border guards holding off invading Imperialists for 350 years, piled into the car with them. Just for good measure, Jovanka thought.

"You think they're gonna brutalize him?" the curly-headed boy asked.

"No," Cindy said confidently. "His father is too famous. Too much publicity."

The group started to dissipate, now that its nucleus had vanished.

Leslie stood on the bridge for a while, watching the traffic whiz by underneath. The rarefied world she'd just experienced -- a place where something as natural and simple as talking to a boy she had a crush on could be a part of her life -- dissipated and she knew it was her fault.

She wasn't ready for it. She didn't know where to begin. She wanted someone to tell her, but the cops had just taken him away, as if on cue. And as the sunlight vanished, the gold that had just gloriously manifested itself into her world reverted to mud.

She walked to the far side of the bridge. The dark, deserted road on that side seemed to go nowhere. She thought of her grandma. In all her life, Gramma never got to see anything *but* mud. Leslie's eyes began to tear up. Her lungs felt empty of oxygen and she took in a deep breath, then a long sigh.

She thought of that glittering boy. It *could* be done. It *was* possible to defeat the contempt and be beautiful again. And crowds of people would gather around you, thrilled to see the transformation, dazzled by your sparkle. She smiled while a lump formed in her throat. A tear raced down her cheek.

Maybe someday that would happen to her, too. Maybe someday she could be a Phoenix and not be that contemptible kind of ugly, that had nothing to do with how you looked.

"Yes, *moja draga kuma*, my dear Goddaughter," Srđa whispered in her ear, "it *will* happen to you."

"Yes," added Jovanka, who sat behind her, her arms encircling Leslie. "You are already wonderful."

* * *

She was writing in her journal a few days later when she noticed something. Her handwriting had changed. She was enamored with e.e. cummings and realized she'd begun doing cursive more in a printing style, *sans* capitalization, that was getting more and more connected in her own ways. It happened while she was writing some poems.

> you
> an enigma
> i don't know you at all,
> only my own concept of you.
> what if it is not
> the same person as you?
>   - - -
>
> the laughter rings down the hall.
> eager, anticipating laughter
> and hurried planning.
> im lonely.
> oh god, im lonely.
>   - - -
>
> soft, brown, smiling honesty
> awkward, graceful, rambling sweetness
> you Captivate this soul
> with your Self.
> but you will not take me, this unclaimed captive.
>   - - -
>
> soft, brown, smiling honesty
> awkward, graceful, rambling sweetness
> loving all you see,
> your blindness to its shortfalls
> comprises the beauty of you.
> mature innocence,

you are much too fine for me.

* * *

That Notorious White Girl
Who Lets Black Boys Touch Her

Shortly after the cops hauled William away as soon as she finally got her chance to talk to him, she was in the cafeteria at lunch when he passed by her. He was wearing a white sailor's tunic and was, in her opinion, absolutely adorable in it. He gave her his beautiful smile and tipped his hat to her. Her daily salute she lived for.

"Look at that," the homely girl across from her sniggered, following him with her eyes, one leg propped up on a chair, in a cast. She was large-boned, with a big, round, pasty face and tiny features huddled up in the middle. "They caught him," she said, lowering her voice with disgust. "And what he was doing to that girl! Of course, she's getting expelled."

So that's why he'd never pursued her. He already had a girl. Cindy filled Leslie in on it.

"That's his girlfriend," Cindy explained. "The one in the picture with him. The picture that went with the article he wrote about Jim."

Leslie had already clipped the article, the one where William used the word 'chauvinism' that made her fall in love. The other girl wasn't as pretty as him but had a grounded air about her that hinted at a character possessed with enough sense not to have looked away from him at the critical instant the way Leslie had at that dance.

On most evenings, Cindy would head out with a quilt. All the couples at camp would find their way to a wooded area with lots of bushes to find a little privacy. Apparently, some of the cops or security people had followed William and his girl out there, waited for a while, and then caught them in whatever activity they were up to that would be sufficiently embarrassing to cause a fuss.

Of course, there were lots of couples out there, *in delecti,* like Cindy and her boyfriend, but seeing as how they were both alike as two peas in a pod, nobody was concerned about them. It was just William they were after, and whatever white girl had the audacity to let him touch her.

William was, of course, their main target, but his dad was too influential and had intimidated them with threats of media exposure, so they went after his girl, that notorious white girl who let a black boy touch her.

Sure enough, the next day all the hippie kids, about a hundred of them, sat on the front lawn of the girl's dorm in solidarity, waiting with William's girl for her dad to arrive. He pulled up in a big, conservative sedan, got out of his car, and smiling, walked over to her. William was sitting next to her. She turned to him, gave him a discrete kiss goodbye, and left with her dad, like it was no big deal.

It seemed to Leslie that the girl's dad was on his daughter's side. She wouldn't be going through the kind of ordeal Leslie imagined for herself when the day came, as she knew it would, when she would be that notorious white girl who let a black guy touch her.

Camp was about over by then. The last time she saw William was when she was on the bus to the train station. He was on the curb by himself, surrounded by some luggage. He looked up at her. She remembered what her mom said about how, if it's darker in a room than it is outside, you can't see in, so she knew he couldn't see her. She looked away, saddened as the bus pulled away.

She glanced back at him. He looked crestfallen.

She told her mom some about her summer. "And I met a really nice boy," she said, not elaborating any further.

"Good, her mom said. "You should meet more boys like that."

* * *

She wrote one more poem about that summer.

Au Revoir, Mon Amour, Merci

the beautiful ones
  have left me forever
those I could have loved
  and do love.
Leaving regret for the unsaid
  words and affection
But joy in finding their existence
The bittersweet
  trauma

        of
        birth

The ecstasy of beginning life
The death of leaving the womb
                * * *

Black Militant Krajina Srpkinja

Leslie returned to Polish Hills High a changed girl. Once she was home
she gave herself a permanent – a Jew-fro permanent. Everybody realized
she was the school's First Hippie. She took up the guitar and sang "A
Bridge over Troubled Water," which was her ode to William, at the Talent
Show. She came onto the stage and sat down on the floor of the stage.
People gasped at the break from convention, but that was the only way
she knew how to hold a guitar. She had to be sitting on the floor. In bare
feet.

Her voice was a low alto and she was not able to stay in tune singing
harmony, so she did not go far in any choir, but if she had a good accom-
paniment she could sing a melody sufficiently on-key, and was quite good
at being expressive. Some of the notes she hit even sounded pleasant.
That was the high point of the year.

She'd returned to her crush on Brian Danley, which had become a major embarrassment. She painted a picture of him from the school yearbook and asked her art teacher to submit it to the art contest anony-
mously. He'd looked embarrassed and asked her if it was erotic art.

She laughed and said no. But then the day of the exhibit arrived and
her painting was displayed. She hadn't wanted anyone to see it! And she
hadn't gotten anything more than an honorable mention. All that excruciating embarrassment for nothing!

And then Brian Danley showed up, drunk or high or something! He
spoke to her. Incoherent nonsense about Led Zeppelin. Then he walked
away. The only time, out of a two and half year crush, that he spoke to
her and it was in front of this smarmy watercolor of his yearbook picture
she'd painted that everyone was already gossiping about, and all he could
say was that Led Zeppelin smoked pulp.

It was a relief for Leslie to be a rarified school outcast. Pollack Hills
was populated with a huge flock of South Side Chicago White Flighters –
people who had sold their homes at a huge loss the moment anyone black

bought a house on that block. Their racism was blistering. The jokes. The endless nigger jokes that Leslie's brain shredded on contact.

It was unbearable.

She had been raised, in Archie's Inadvertent and Covert School of Anti-Racism, to ridicule jokes like that into pulp, Led Zeppelin smoked pulp. But she would only make herself the subject of endless ridicule *en masse* if she took them all on at once in the real world. She learned that very early on.

She was a freshman when they moved. Back in the Argo School District, there was a silently outraged black Community, a sullen Hispanic community, a fringe of working-class whites, with a liberal Middle Class in between. Other than her dad's broken records on the subject, nobody talked about race. Nobody talked about black people. Not even the black people were talking.

But all that changed abruptly when she got to Pollack Hills. Her first instinct was to switch into Smart Ass mode. What a mistake.

They were in the commons for lunch. She had sat down at an empty table by herself and five greaser boys invaded and claimed the turf for themselves. There were only two social classes at this new school. At Emmett Till Junior High there had been four.

At ETJH the black kids had their Black Bottom Class, the Hispanic kids had their Bottom Variant Class, there was the Low Class Stupid class of white kids and then there were the First-Class White kids. Leslie had been born into the Low Class Stupid class but had risen by way of her talent and intelligence to the very top of First Class White.

Up until the fifth grade, her status as Low-Class Stupid had been enforced by Mary Cumby, who had called her Leslie Jerky Bitch, making fun of her last name, Jerkovich. The Really Cool Girl in class was Nola Brewster, who had really good grades and was very beautiful, with long, honey blonde hair. Her best friend was Mary Cumby. One day at recess Leslie had responded to Mary's chanting "Jerky bitch, jerky bitch, jerky bitch" at her with a name of her own. It only took one word to change her status forever. She responded back by calling Mary, "Mary Crummy." Everyone laughed and Mary retreated in shame, never to taunt Leslie again.

Immediately Nola invited Leslie over and they became best friends. Then over the summer before Junior High, something happened. Nola's father molested her. By seventh grade, she had been transformed. She ratted up her beautiful hair into a dirty, matted beehive, wore way too much makeup and was going out with a Mexican boy. Her status was that of Class Skank. The lowest of the low. That left the #1 spot open for Leslie.

From there on out, Leslie had the best grades for a girl in the school. She was a recognized artist ever since Mr. Ginalik put a poster she'd painted of the ocean floor up on his desk so he could admire it, praising her to the class. And then she played a piano solo of *Claire de Lune* at graduation. Nola nodded to her with pride as she left the piano and Leslie was touched at the spirit of the girl to still see her with pride instead of the resentment she eminently deserved.

So, at ETJH, that's what mattered. Good grades, reasonable good looks, and talent made you cool. If you were white, that is.

The problem of boy availability was already present, since boys did not date girls with better grades, no matter how cool they were, and there was only one boy who had better grades than her – Howard – who had never spoken to her even though they'd sat next to each other for two years. That was, of course, merciful for Leslie since, at 13, she was entirely too juvenile to have handled the sheer terror of crossing that horrific abyss.

At Pollack Hills High, however, there were only two classes, both white – the working-class Greasers, and the college-bound Straights. Greasers ruled. The ancient, anti-intellectual tradition of Eastern European peasants was reigning in full force.

"Why do niggers stink? the biggest of the greaser boys sharing Leslie's lunch table asked. The other boys laughed already, anticipating the punch line.

"So blind people can hate them too." The boys all broke into raucous laughter.

"What about stupid people?" Leslie asked.

"What about 'em?"

"Why do stupid people hate them?" She used the pronoun since the only non-slanderous words available at that time were Negro or colored, both of which words annoyed her. She had planned to end with the punch line, "stupid people finally get a chance to feel like they're better than somebody," but she never got the opening. Archie was not there playing the fall guy.

"They don't need anything since only stupid people don't hate them," the boy retorted.

"And how do you gauge stupidity?" she asked.

"Gauge? What kind of stupid word is that?" he asked.

At Polish Hills High using advanced vocabulary was seen as grossly nerdy stupidity.

66

"Let's put you in the gauge cage," he went on. The other boys broke into more frivolity that ended with them all chanting "Gauge cage, gauge cage, gauge cage," at her. Everyone in the room turned to stare. Then the tall boy scooped up a bit of chocolate pudding with his spoon and catapulted it at her.

She wiped it from her blouse, her left tit to be exact, grabbed her tray and left. He was able to catapult another spoonful of pudding onto her ass before she could get out of range. They never even got written up.

The "gauge cage" taunt had followed her through most of that year, reverberating down the hallway whenever she'd pass those creeps.

But her Jew-fro as a Senior established her as the pioneer of an entirely new class, the Hippies. Even kids who had no interest in counterculture knew it was the new Cool Thing and were in awe.

The Jew-fro delighted her. Finally, she had a very cool, very superior method of asserting her oddness that would account for the stony silence she was giving everyone, in a way that would not be challenged. It was the perfect visual statement to get those racist, greaser creeps to shut the hell up when she was in the room without having to say a word.

Needless to say, still no one had asked her out.

Since it was her last year in high school she had to write a term paper for civics class. Everyone had to pass it to graduate. She never liked to try really hard at anything. She could get mostly A's and B's without really any effort at all, outside reading something she enjoyed reading anyway.

She didn't try to do her best, though, because of a strong expectation, as irrational as it was powerful, that if she tried to do her best it wouldn't amount to anything. That's what Archie had taught her during the rest of the day when she was no longer his darling prodigy, but just that stupid punk kid of his.

As Srđa often tried explaining to Leslie in her sleep, their internalized racism, using the European usage of the word 'racism,' which Americans would dismiss as nothing more than a transient class difference, was dominating their lives – squashing it to a pulp. A big problem. A really big problem for all of them. "We've become what the people hating us say we are," he would say. "Pulp."

But as luck, or Jovanka, would have it, Leslie was assigned to write about the 13th, 14th and 15th Amendments to the Constitution – the ones that supposedly set black slaves free and allegedly gave them their civil rights. Leslie actually used the library, filled out tons of index cards with facts and wrote a really impassioned paper, with that snotty, sassy, pissed-off tone that Archie had nurtured in her so diligently.

Her favorite quote was from Lincoln himself "there is a physical difference between the white and black races which I believe will forever forbid the two races living together on terms of social and political equality." She got particularly snotty in her scathing indictment of his racist hypocrisy. That quote was not commonly spoken of at that time, except among left-leaning black scholars. And then, of course, there was Leslie.

The rest of her approach to the subject was to quote the wording of the Amendments and then demonstrate how abysmally the country had failed to fulfill them.

She was sure she had an A+. It was the best class work she'd ever done. But she didn't get an A. She got a D+.

A grade that low had never happened to her before, except for that time at Emmett Till Junior High when Carolyn stole her gym suit and Ms. Brown gave her an F for the quarter for not dressing out for a week. It wasn't until a week later that someone tipped Leslie off and told her to check Carolyn's locker. It was easy to check since Carolyn couldn't afford a lock. And easy to recognize. Leslie had embroidered her initials, and Carolyn had not done a very good job of pulling out the stitches.

Ms. Brown was the first black teacher at ETJH, just out of the military. Leslie really admired her, but Ms. Brown didn't like Leslie because of her contact lens. Leslie was becoming so near-sighted the eye doctor talked her mom into putting her into hard contact lenses that would prevent her from becoming, he threatened, legally blind.

Her mom worked the graveyard shift at SOS soap pad factory, in packing, so they'd always have money for emergencies like this. One of Leslie's earliest memories was of her mom wrapping her fingers with surgical tape so that incompetently cut steel wool wouldn't cut her fingers, grabbing steel wool pads all night.

Leslie thought she'd lost one of the lenses during gym when it had wandered up into her eyelid. Ms. Brown had the whole class down on their knees looking for it.

She let Leslie know how spoiled she was to be in contact lens at only thirteen. "Must be nice," she said to another lady, right in front of Leslie. "Having enough money to be in contacts at only thirteen." Leslie saw the look on Ms. Brown's face. That caused her to flash on Ms. Brown's fantasy of the wealthy home Leslie lived in, the rich, little white girl with a grand piano in the parlor and a chubby black maid in the kitchen with a black uniform and a lacy white apron.

Now, four years later, her civics teacher didn't make any notice at all that she had way more footnotes than required with quotes, facts and dates, and twice the required length. All it said was, "D+". There was only one comment, written concisely on the bottom of the cover page, he intended as a criticism.

"You have the bias of a Black Militant."

It was true. Archie had inadvertently raised her to be a Black Militant. Nobody ever even noticed. Except, of course, her civics teacher.

And of course, her dad and mom noticed. They knew what he had done by the time she hit ETJH, and that's why they had moved to an all-white high school, and as fate would have it, Leslie was spared the danger of getting caught up, as she surely would have been, in the Argo High School Race Riot, September 1968. Had she been there, surely others like Carolyn would have responded to what a magnet Leslie was to their angst.

But 'Black Militant' was only the American translation of the concept. Archie had accomplished something remarkable with his daughter, as intensely as unwittingly, purely on Serbian instinct. By whatever psychological mechanisms there might be that could preserve a traumatized, endangered identity, or by whatever forces in the Universe, like Jovanka and Srda, might be haunting them, he had managed to raise her to be a *Krajina Srpkinja*, in all her glory.

* * *

The Last Great Debate #2,467

And so it came to pass, on Christmas Break, 1970, that their very curious family custom came to a close. This was a few weeks before Leslie was to meet Reggie Wilson, the boyfriend whose name she was to use while writing her diatribe on the racism at Pirotelli Real Estate Management.

This was to be Leslie and her dad's last Great Debate, #2,467. That was her score, versus his, which was zero. It went out with a whimper instead of a bang. She couldn't do it anymore.

The news was on the TV while they ate dinner. A story was playing about some anti-war protest comprised mainly of black university students.

"Damn jigaboos need to love it or leave it," he said.

'How tiresome,' she thought, 'all I'm going to hear are worn-out cliches.' Fortunately, there was that quote from Malcolm X she could throw at him quick and easy.

"Why in the world would they love it, dad?" she said. "That makes no sense. They didn't ask to come here. They got kidnapped. They didn't land on Plymouth Rock. Plymouth Rock landed on them."

Okay, he really liked that one. Already a blessed silence, following that stunned look of pure admiration for her, which she was taking entirely for granted. There was very little that Malcolm X had to say that didn't get an immediate, awed silence from Archie. Malcolm was that old confounded bigot's favorite. She got up and walked away from the table after dutifully giving him his fix one last time.

Just having to listen to him was just too gruesome. She never did live under that roof again, not after what happened the next semester.

* * *

Chapter 3
Coming of Age

Finding Reggie Wilson

She found Reggie Wilson in The Grille, the campus snack shop. It was the beginning of the second semester at the incredibly small, largely Jewish, Shimer college. In 1970 it had 90 students, nestled into a sweet little campus in the rolling hills of Western Illinois. It was inhabited about ninety percent by hippie, radical, pothead freaks.

He was holding court in The Grille. Plate glass lined one wall, a short order grill on the opposite. The fragrance of deep fried potatoes danced with the sweet smell of ketchup. Her stomach growled.

He had it. That Phoenix-like beauty, like William. In some ways, he was even prettier. A disarming boyishness. Tall and slender with an elegant grace to his movement. She forgot about ordering fries and sat down, listening.

He sat debating six white kids at once. Six to one.

He was the only black student at the school. A first.

One of the resident Zionists had engaged him in a pissing contest on whose shit was worse.

"I don't care what you say," said the Zionist, "no matter how bad it is here, the only mass graves associated with American Slavery are at places like Gettysburg, full of white guys, not black. And however bad things are, if you're surviving, you're surviving."

"What Jews have been killed here?" Reggie countered. "I don't see anything but a bunch of people doing quite well, thank you very much."

There was a pause as the Jewish guy had trouble thinking of a comeback.

Reggie took advantage of the silence to further his point. "No, you all came here very willingly, while we were kidnapped and dehumanized for centuries. *We didn't land on Plymouth Rock. It landed on us!.*"

He picked up his paper plate, along with The Last Word, dumped it and left them all in a dramatic exit.

She watched after him. She had, for the first time in her life, encountered a peer – someone who thought a great deal about the subject of racism, with the same perspective and was quite capable of getting the last word on the subject.

* * *

Srđa and Jovanka's Sideline Critique

"Well, what do you think, momma?" Srđa asked Jovanka. They were sitting in the booth alongside Leslie while she ate the fries she finally remembered to order.

"I'm not so sure about him," she replied.

"He's brave enough," he said.

"For himself," she said. "But how brave will he be for her?"

* * *

Reggie's Commitment

Evening came – a Saturday Night. Leslie was just looking for some-place to hang out. There was an open dorm policy. Boys could hang out in the girl dorms and *vice versa*.

Leslie "just happened" to wander into a room full of other kids.

Reggie's room.

The obligatory joint was being passed around.

The music was loud, "The Last Poets." Everybody was kind of in a stoned-out stupor, listening to the music.

There he was, again holding court, presiding over the turntable.

Behind a pair of sunglasses, he was reciting along with the nascent rap.

> When the revolution comes,
> Jesus Christ will be standing
> on the corner of Lennox and 125th,
> waiting to catch the first taxi out of Harlem,
> When the revolution comes,
> when the revolution comes

He looked over the top of his glasses and met her gaze.

"There she is!" he said.

He was flirting!

"Who?" she said, sassily, looking behind her, this time only feigning doubt.

"You!" he replied, setting the sunglasses down.

"You don't know me," she countered.

"That's not my fault," he said, "The Man's never let you past my door before."

73

Just the question she'd been dying to ask. "Well, if *he's* the man, what does that make you?" she said with just the right amount of snarky flirtation.

Everybody cracked up.

He surveyed her for a moment, smiling, his dark eyes twinkling.

"You calling me a boy?"

"You want me to call you a girl?" she sassed. "I thought *I* was the girl."

"Well, then, girl," he said, changing the album. "Come here and dance with me."

It was a sultry Motown song. He pulled her towards him. She needed that proximity in order to tell him what she had to say.

"You know," she said quietly, once she was at his ear, "this is a pretty well-read crowd. You really should cite Malcolm if you're going to quote him. Somebody might call you on it."

He leaned back for a sec' to look her in the eye.

"Oh, somebody might, huh? When did I quote Malcolm?"

"This afternoon, in The Grille," she said.

"Oh," he said, smiling. "I knew you were listening."

"Well, I might," she said. "If you had anything original to say."

"That's cold."

"No, I'm not cold. I'm just waiting. You have every opportunity to prove yourself."

"I have every opportunity, eh?"

By 2 AM the last of the other kids had finally left. Leslie sighed with relief. They had been talking for the better part of two hours, mostly about him and why it was important for the black man in America to establish his own place of worship and his own independent community. He had recently converted to the Nation of Islam himself. She had read Malcolm X's autobiography years earlier at fourteen. Obviously, it had helped her develop her Slav Mentality treatise that had wrested The Ultimate from her dad, so she was, of course, as fond of Malcolm as Archie was. And Reggie.

Reggie wasn't saying much that he hadn't gotten out of the same book, but it was all too complicated for Leslie to explain why she'd devoured it herself at fourteen, so she was unable to speak very freely about her own perspective on it. It was almost like she was pretending to hear it for the first time and act really interested as of it all made such good sense.

It was frustrating. All the white kids in the room made her all the more reticent to speak freely so that added to the frustration. But she was at least back in the realm of her home life growing up, where, being Archie's little girl, there was very little ever discussed except the issue of racism.

They were sitting, still talking, turned towards one another on one of the dorm beds, pushed up under the padded bolster that made it like a couch.

"I never should have come here," he said. "This place is going to mess me up."

He'd become tense. It spread to her and she felt dismayed. He wasn't sighing relief to have her to himself.

"Why?"

"Because of the commitment I made to Elijah," he said, referring to the head of the Nation of Islam, Elijah Muhammad.

"When?" she asked.

"Last summer," he replied.

"Where?"

"At the Chicago temple."

"Have you ever seen Malcolm?"

"Yeah."

"Really? What was he like?"

"Dynamite."

"What was he talking about?"

"I don't know," he said with some impatience, "inferiority complexes. Why are you so interested in Malcolm?"

"Why shouldn't I be?" she asked.

"You're white," he said.

Now how would he know her dad had raised her to be a Black Militant? She sure didn't know how to explain it. How often was that coming out of the Bigot Belt?

"How do you know what *that* means?" she asked.

"I know what it means."

"You don't know what it means for me," she countered. "I don't even know, so, how would you?"

"I should give you *carte blanche*, huh?"

She laughed. "Good one!" she said. "Yeah," she went on, reaching under the hair at the back of her neck and combing it upwards with her fingers, "give me lots of that."

"What baffles you about it?" he asked.

She felt encouraged. He wanted to understand her. "Well, what's the stereotype? Somebody privileged who thinks they're better than other people. I spend too much time trying to make myself feel as good as the people around me."

"Why?" he asked.

"Hell if I know. Just some bullshit running around in my family." He moved his arm onto the bolster behind her. 'Yes,' she thought. 'You're too far away.'

"Listen, I was trying to tell you something," he said. "I made a commitment not to be messing with white women."

"Then don't," she said. Don't think I'm white, she thought, knowing that was a sentiment impossible to utter in American English.

"I wouldn't except for one thing."

"What's that?"

He leaned towards her, finally close enough, and kissed her. She felt enormous relief with this proof that he did want her.

The floodgates opened and she wanted more and more proof. She could feel it wasn't just her sliding backward, pulling him, that he was moving towards her, synchronously. He wanted her! He really, really wanted her!

"That," he said, out of breath. "The way they kiss back."

"They?" she whispered, breathless herself, her arms still around his neck, slouched most of the way down the bolster. *"They* all kiss you back like that!?"

"You have a point," he said.

"I have a lot more," she said.

* * *

Sideline Critique Continued

"This time and place is ridiculous," Jovanka said. They had resumed their places in The Grille. "This is not a good environment for Leslie."

"Why?"

"It's too free, this free love thing. If a girl gives her love, it's a gift that should be protected, respected, but here that will not happen. This has just happened way too fast."

"Seems to me you were rather quick on the draw in your time," Srđa remarked.

"Oh, there's no comparison," she said. "You had proven yourself completely. There was no doubt you would readily die for me," she said. "It hasn't even occurred to that boy that's even required of him. He's just thinking of himself."

"Give him time," he said.

"This is all out of order. I don't like it at all."

* * *

Keep Instead of Borrow

The dorm beds were singles, not twins. Narrow as hell. More than comfortable, Leslie was comforted, cuddled up with him when she woke the next morning. And he *was* beautiful. The slightest detail delighted her. The way the neat curves of his small ears dovetailed into his head, those graceful, elegant hands. And that face, my god that boy was cute! And that lamb's wool! She'd been so curious. It was so soft! Incredible!

She imagined the layout of a black and white photo, rich mid-tone gradients throughout and a beautiful girl with a big thick, fluffy Afro, looking down shyly with a mysterious smile as if seeing the catch line at the bottom, "Lamb's wool."

'Johnson's Products should put me on their payroll,' she thought, laughing to herself, 'writing Afro Sheen commercials!'

"You're tickling me," he said, his eyes still closed, smiling, swatting her hand away from the hair she was twirling.

"No," she said. "That's not tickling. *This* is tickling."

"Stop," he said, sitting up. "I'm starving."

"So am I."

"Come on, we can still make breakfast," he said. "I need me a BIG stack of pancakes."

"Oh, damn," she said. "I don't want to wear that to the cafeteria." The night before she'd worn a 'granny dress' a long, ankle-length dress with a high, laced Victorian collar that she'd made. It was popular at the time. She would have felt self-conscious wearing it, proclaiming to the world that she hadn't gone home the night before. "If I go change I'll miss breakfast."

"Here, baby," he said. "Wear this." He threw her a pair of his bell bottoms and a maroon button-down, short-sleeve plaid shirt. She was a bit broad in the beam and was skeptical they would fit, but they did, after rolling a cuff into the jeans.

"You look good in that," he said.

She threw her arms around his neck and kissed him. "Thank you," she beamed.

"Yeah, why don't you keep them for a while?"

She hadn't heard it put that way before, and liked the sound of it – the word 'keep' instead of 'borrow' – intimated a greater generosity.

She wore those clothes like a flag. She felt like he'd laid claim to her and she liked belonging there very much.

* * *

Brown on Rice

It was a chilly night to be sitting on a Commons bench in the early evening with the Quonset hut behind them, watching big flakes of snow fall silently, but they weren't cold. At least she wasn't. He was straddled behind her, wrapping around her like an afghan. They were in a giggly mood.

"Life's funny," he said. "Yesterday, there I was watching you over there, that evil-looking white girl with the big eyes and the big legs, looking to squash me like a bug, and here we are now, like white on rice."

That was a novel analogy for her and she laughed. "Am I supposed to visualize you as a plateful or just a grain?" she asked.

"Actually," he said, "In this position, you'd be the rice. Like brown on rice, I guess it should go." He shook his head. "Nah," he said, "that don't sound right."

"No, but it is more nutritious," she said.

"True that,' he said. They were still giggling.

"What do you mean, evil?" she asked. "You were just pissing me off, ripping off that quote."

"You're a stickler for quoting people, huh?

"Hell no," she said. "You can rip off Richard Nixon all you want."

* * *

Ripping off Richard Nixon

It was open mike night in The Grille. A New Men's guy did a great James Taylor everybody loved. And when he was done, Reggie grabbed the mike.

"Well folks," he began, "this is dedicated to my lady, Leslie," he said, motioning towards her. He took the black beret he had on his head off and held it modestly in front of his chest with his left hand. He held up his right hand and made a V sign and shook his head as if he had jowls. Half the audience laughed in recognition of his mimicry of Richard Nixon.

"And that's about it," he said, launching into the routine. "That's what we have and that's what we owe. It isn't very much," he said, gesturing towards her again, "but Pat and I have the satisfaction that every dime that we've got is honestly ours."

'He's a damn good mimic!' she thought.

"I should say this -- that Pat doesn't have a mink coat. But she does have a respectable Republican cloth coat. And I always tell her," and here he broke character completely and went totally salacious ghetto, speaking to her, "baby, you'd look damn fine in anything!" He had the room.

"One other thing I probably should tell you because if we don't they'll probably be saying this about me too, we did get something – a gift – after the election. It was a little cocker spaniel dog that a supporter sent all the way from Texas, black and white spotted. And our little girl – Tricia, who's kind of black and white spotted herself, named it Checkers. And you know, the kids, like all kids, love that damn dog and I just want to say this right now, that regardless of what they say about it, we're gonna keep that damn dog, yeah!"

Then he took a few steps over, squared off in front of the table where Danny Cohen was sitting. Leslie had been practically living with Danny the semester before, though they'd never been lovers, well, except that once, and that just confirmed there was zero chemistry. But there was a great friendship. He was so damn chatty. That's what she was learning about Jews, now that, thank God, nearly all the white people she knew were Jewish. They were gorgeously chatty -- a groaning table of words, well-crafted, witty, thoughtful, intellectually provocative. 'The world has to be out of its mind trying to get rid of these people. It's like getting rid of gold. Gold stein.' That was her thinking concerning Jews.

And Danny's satire was the most mellowing source of raucous laughter available to her, and she reveled in it. It's was very black humor, literally. He'd spent a summer in a literacy program in St. Louis, mentoring kids in the ghetto. By the end of the summer, he was fed the hell up with liberals.

He was a long-haired, prototypically Jewish-looking guy doing a routine ridiculing redneck racists. He was constantly saying outrageously bigoted things she hadn't heard since two weeks earlier when she was home. But with him, she could fall out with a big belly laugh instead of girding her loins to whip out some rhetoric to silence the unendurable tripe she had to listen to from Archie. She found it cathartic.

That was her home away from home her first semester in college – living in a quad at New Men's dorm with Danny and his outrageously cute roommates, the Olson brothers, on the other side of the quad. The name "New Men's" was intended as temporary, but there was something about naming a building full of 18-year old males "New Men's" that seemed appropriate and the name stuck. The two long-haired, bearded boys looked so prototypically Scandinavian they took turns wearing a Viking helmet. It definitely flattered them.

The whole time there was a hoot for Leslie. She was a free, unattached spirit living in an entirely male environment, safely, happily, having a ball. She liked them. Boys. New men. She really liked them.

So that was the backstory as Reggie squared off to Danny in The Grille, at the close of his monologue. Reggie must have heard of Danny's bigot routine, maybe he'd caught wind of where she'd spent the last semester. He put his black beret and sunglasses back on, raised his arm in a fist and shouted, "Black Power!" Everybody howled.

"Well," he said when he sat back down next to her. "Was that better? Do you approve of that one?"

She grabbed him by the chin and kissed him. "With all my heart," she said, totally blown away he would make such a gesture for her, feeling like the luckiest girl there that she was with such a beautiful guy, and she was *his* girl.

* * *

Deeper into the Tudina

Leslie and Reggie were sitting on the floor of his room, just relaxing, talking. It was a weeknight, so things weren't all high energy party-time like the weekend. It was quiet, and she had him entirely to herself. He was sitting across from her, his back on the opposite dorm bed. His foot was on her lap, while she massaged it. He had a mellow Marvin Gaye album on the turntable.

"My mom used to do that when I was sick," he said.

"I'm pretending I know reflexology points," she said.

"You're hitting 'em, baby, you're hitting 'em," he said.

She laughed.

"Reflexology is African, you know," he said.

"Really?"

"Yes, it's documented back, like, 3,000 years, to the Egyptians."

"Interesting," she said. "I didn't know that." Hard to believe, but somehow she missed that one during her years at her dad's Inadvertent School of African American Studies.

Then she dropped her foot in his lap. "What's good for the gander is good for the goose."

"What's this?" he said, affecting a face like her foot was funky.

"Oh, come on now. There's foot parity here," she argued. "My foot is not funky. It's sweet as can be."

Gingerly he sniffed, then smiled. "You'll do," he said and started rubbing her foot.

"So, your momma took good care of you when you were sick?" she asked.

"Yeah, moms is cool."

"And dad?"

"Pops split three years ago, thank god."

"Oh yeah? What was he up to?"

"Just an ass. I mean, it's not like he was beating on anybody, but the way that mouth of his would get going, you'd almost wish for a whuppin' instead."

"I know what you mean," she said. No wonder, she thought, thinking of her own dad and understanding more deeply why she related to Reggie so strongly. They had the same kind of fathers. And felt the same way about them.

"But it's cool," he said. "I understand it now." He sat up, withdrew his foot, dropped hers and crossed his legs and arms.

"It's not his fault. He just got raised on the Slave Mentality Brother Malcolm talks about.

Then he said the unthinkable. "It's not something you can understand." Her heart started beating fast while her mood plummeted.

"You live with a privilege that protects you from all that," he went on. "But when you've got a situation where you've got assholes controlling you, brainwashing you with what a worthless piece of shit you are, keeping you from an education, keeping you from any opportunities so you live in poverty, after a while you start to believe it, and you pass that worthless feeling onto your children. That's what you people did to us."

Her mind was racing, trying to remember the treatise she had done for her dad on the Slav Mentality that she'd borrowed from Malcolm. The Ultimate victory she'd won with Archie concerning his berating of her was at stake, in danger of being relegated into oblivion. "I might understand more than you think," was all she could manage.

Leslie searched Reggie's face, trying to see how she could communicate how well she knew that subject matter and how important it was to her. But she stopped short telling him about Archie. She was too ashamed of him. She had not told Reggie her dad was a disgusting bigot. He'd *never* understand that.

"You might understand intellectually," he said. "But you can't know what it's like. You can't experience that. It's not the same."

Except every day of my childhood, she thought, but she failed to say that. "The same thing happened in Slavic cultures. Serfs internalized a very poor self-image they passed on to their children," she countered.

"*But you's white now, baby!*" he proclaimed, throwing his arms out in a large gesture.

And in that moment, it vanished – the key element intrinsic in the privilege of being white – the ability to simply be a person living one's life. Suddenly, she was no longer just a person, instead, she was a *white* person, trapped in that assigned identity whether that stereotype fit her or not. She knew exactly what that stereotype was, what that word meant to him and that there was no space in it for *her*, who she really was. She crashed into a hopeless head space. He was never going to know who she really was.

All the deplorable adjectives embodied in that word came crashing in on her. Corrupt people who make other people feel worthless – the way her father made her feel worthless because *he* felt worthless. She knew that's all people like him were. If she didn't know that, then she knew nothing. If she was not the opposite of him, she was nothing. *She* was worthless. She lost her thunder, was lost far deeper into the *Tuđina* than she'd ever been before.

"A lot of people have parents who are verbally abusive," she said.

"Well, yeah, but I mean, it's not in the context of the psychological damage done systematically to generations of a family just so they can be exploited."

"Wouldn't that make it easier?"

"Easier?" he was sounding annoyed.

"Easier to make sense of. Easier to attribute to something else, not just your own innate inferiority. You're just hopelessly screwed up people because you're hopelessly screwed up, worthless people."

"Who's worthless?" he asked.

"Whoever's treating their children like that," she said. "You can forgive your father because you understand what was wrong with him. So, you can move on." Her eyes were starting to water and she blinked it away. "If you couldn't explain it you might still just be hating him, and you'd be worse off."

"Okay," he said, skeptically. "So white people have it worse because they can't blame racists for their problems?"

"I don't know," she said. "Some do."

She defiantly pulled his foot back to her lap and aggressively worked those points in between the joints. He sighed deeply and relaxed into it.

So, there it was. Her new role in life. He was upstaging her secret, if improbable, life as a Black Militant, and now what she had dreaded was happening. She was going to be stuck playing a white girl! A role that had absolutely nothing to do with any kind of karma natural to her. Its only relevance lay in how he felt like stereotyping her, so he could be more important. His problems were more important. She had to forget about hers. They were nothing.

He didn't fool her for a minute. She knew why he was saying all that. Why he wanted it to be true. Because he *wanted* to be more important and dump all the un-importance on her. She was from Bigot Belt. She knew *exactly* what she was seeing.

All her youthful idealism was dashed. Everybody does it. Everybody stereotypes. Everybody objectifies. Everybody scapegoats. Everybody does it, all the time. She'd progressed nowhere. She was never going to escape yet another iteration of Archie, whom she was never going to stop caring about, or going to great lengths to respond to, though her ability to do so seemed altogether compromised.

She pretended to yawn. In a minute, he yawned too.

"I gotta pee," he said and headed down the hall.

She got into the bed and faced the wall. She pretended she was asleep when he got back. He spooned around her -- the only way they could both fit on the bed. In a few minutes, she heard his breathing slow as he fell asleep. She lay awake and silently, without changing her breathing, cried, no sign of it, except the hot tears falling across her face onto the pillow. She felt envious and inferior.

There was a huge inequality between them. She knew to the *nth* degree every possible way he could be stereotyped and despised them all, would go to any length to defy them, would militantly edit all she said to be sure she never said anything that might evoke any of them, even if she meant the exact opposite by it. She'd spent her childhood studying on all that. But not only had he no idea who she was, and wasn't, but it was of no concern at all to him to indulge himself in stereotyping her in whatever way gratified him.

In his sleep, he moved a bit and his arm fell across hers. She moved her hand up under his hand. Reflexively, he clasped it and cuddled closer.

She cried some more, fearing he could never love her as much as she already loved him. She knew him way better than he would ever know her, ever want to know her. She feared that he didn't, and he wouldn't ever, love her at all.

* * *

More Sideline Critique

Jovanka and Srđa were on the flat roof of the dorm. Jovanka was pacing angrily.

"See, I told you. He's never going to help her find herself. 'Well, yeah, you don't know anything about being exploited for generations.' How many generations come along in 600 years, huh? You think all that just goes away because somebody puts a new label on you? Huh? Why do you think she likes *you*, you *fool?*" She stopped ranting at the imagined Reggie and entreated Srđa, "Why can't she just find out who she is? Why is she just stuck dancing around the edges of her life like this? Can't you just drop some books on her like you do?"

"No one knows about us here," he replied. "The few books that exist are in libraries she's never been in. But it's more than that, momma. It's what they're calling 'lack of effect.' The people who survive what we've been through can't feel anything, except worthless. It's just too much. She really does need this device to work through. When she gets to the point where she can assert herself with someone like him she'll be where she needs to be."

Jovanka sighed. "I don't know. She was coming along so nicely with her father, but now, I don't know. I have to find someone for her who's been in those libraries."

* * *

Reggie's Aura

By the end of February, the relationship had become a moot point for another reason. Reggie was getting popular with the other girls. At first, they hadn't known what to make of him, but his bold rhetoric, striking good looks and aggressive manner suggested something. Why wouldn't all that attention tempt an 18-year-old boy?

84

He started begging off at times when he and Leslie would usually be together, and when they were, he was acting differently, as was she. Her insecurities had gotten the best of her, and she wasn't funny and flirtatious anymore.

He never went with anybody publicly, the way he had always done with her. She never saw him with any particular girl. She didn't know if that was them or him making it so clandestine. Likely them. She just heard the rumors. He was making his way down the floor above hers.

One Saturday night, when everybody else was partying, she had nowhere to go. She was sitting forlornly in her own room in the women's dorm when she spotted something in the hamper. Reggie's shirt. She pulled it out and held it in front of her. His aura was inside it. She could see him in it. There was that space where his neck intersected with his collar that always made her want to slip her hand between the two – just that little gesture and she could be so close.

It made her cry and she held it to her as if she could hug it. She thought, 'I'm never going to give this back. I'm never going to wash that aura out, and I'm never going to give it back.' She didn't have the nerve to wear it anymore, but she was going to keep it forever. But then she thought, 'If I tell him to come by and get it, he'll have to come and see me! He'll have to come and see me!'

So, the next day she washed the shirt and pants and approached him in the cafeteria. "Oh, I have those clothes of yours," she said. "If you get a chance, next time you're in my dorm, why don't you stop by for them?"

He did so right away. He came knocking, a pair of sunglasses on, even though he was indoors at night. Probably high. He wandered in, said a few things, then took the clothes and split.

Not only had her plan failed but she didn't even have his aura anymore.

She felt an emptiness that kept her staring at nothing. She shook her head, not sure how much time had passed that she had been doing nothing, just staring. No, it wasn't emptiness, she realized. It was grief.

She fell asleep. When she woke up she started fantasizing about wearing Reggie's clothes.

In the fantasy, she sits down across from him in the cafeteria, and they chat a bit. He's taking in the fact that she's wearing his clothes, flaunting them, all cute and sassy. Then she pretends to suddenly remember what she's wearing.

"Oh, I'm sorry, do you want these clothes back?" she says, then starts unbuttoning half of the buttons. Everybody at the table, all male, is eagerly taking in the evening's theatrical offering their little student body is famous for.

"No, no, baby," he says laughing, "go ahead and keep your shirt on. You don't have to give it back, I gave it to you. You can keep it."

"Oh, thank you," she says as he reaches over and hurriedly re-buttons the shirt, while she brings her chest up to be easier to reach. "I just love this outfit. And there's something of mine I gave you that *you* can keep," she goes on.

"What's that?"

She reaches across the table for his hand and pulls it towards her again while she leans in still closer, to be easier to reach and a bit more conspicuous. She puts his hand on her chest, where we all pledge allegiance.

"This," she says. "And I don't care who knows it."

But she didn't have the clothes anymore, it was just a fantasy.

* * *

Her Soul Takes Residence
Back in Her Body

Eventually, all the carousing got to him. He called her one Sunday morning, telling her he was sick. His stomach was messed up.

She told him she had some herbal tea that was good for that and went flying over there.

So, she tended to the sick Reggie, her love. Her wandering love.

"I've been doing too much shit," he said, sipping his tea.

"I know," she said. "Turn over." She straddled his back and started massaging it.

"I've got to settle down a little."

She leaned next to his ear, and whispered, "Yeah, I'd like that."

"That feels so good," he said, as she kneaded his shoulders.

Eventually, he turned onto his back, kissed her and made love to her. Again, it felt like they were two halves of a whole on that tiny, comforting bed. She cuddled next to him.

He stroked her face and looked at her tenderly. "You're all right," he said. Then he had a thought. "Except now and then you're a little off."

"What do you mean?" she asked.

"Oh, just now and then," he said.

"What?"

"Like when you gave me back those clothes," he said. "Like they weren't good enough for you. It's like you didn't want anything of mine."

She bolted upright and faced him, as stunned as if he'd just nonchalantly punched her in the face. She knew what he meant by that. She knew *exactly* what that meant. Forget all about the auras and allegiances of her own consciousness. They had no reality anywhere. *She* had no reality. He'd *never* perceive any of that. He couldn't. *He thought she was a racist!* That was all he could see in her. That's all he *wanted* to see. She was just a *thing* to him.

"Do you have any idea what you're saying to me?" she demanded in a bitter staccato. "Or are you just having a good time?"

"What are you talking about?" he blinked.

"Oh, forget it," she said. "What's the point? You loaned me those clothes!"

"No, I gave them to you."

"I didn't know that!" she said. "You said I could keep them *for a while.*"

She started crying angrily and felt her soul, which had been wandering elsewhere for weeks, take residence back where it belonged.

She went on. "How could you sleep with someone you thought felt that way about you? What are you doing with me if you think I'm that obscene, that disgusting? You have no idea who I am, and it doesn't matter to you at all. If that's what you think I am what are you doing with me? What is wrong with you!?"

He looked at her as if he'd never seen her before, the way her father used to. "I'm sorry," he said. "I'm sorry. I didn't mean it like that. I wasn't thinking. It was just me, feeling insecure. I get like that."

"Don't ever call me that."

"Call you what?"

"Racist."

"I didn't call you racist."

"Oh *yes,* you did! I know what words mean. You don't understand. You don't know what they're like."

"Who?"

"Racists. You don't know what I've been through with those people. They're such lost, dishonest fools who hate themselves and lash out at everyone around them. They're going nowhere. They're about nothing.

"They're doing nothing. They're saying nothing. They live these incredibly small lives and obsessively talk about people they think they're better than, when they are so determinedly, willfully nothing. I just sink into this depression when I'm around them. It's like an imitation of life. People passing for white."

"What do you mean?" he asked. "They *are* white."

"That's what *you* think. That's what everybody wants you to think. But they're passing. They've left their authentic selves somewhere, and are just shadows." She was becoming more agitated, even more animated as she spoke. "That's how it feels to me. That's how I feel when I'm around them, like some evil thing is trying to strangle the life from me." Her voice broke. "I'm allergic to those people. I can't be around them. If I give in to them," she broke into tears, "I'll be nothing at all."

She searched his face, looking for some indication that he heard what she was saying. "You just think I'm crazy," she said.

He broke into laughter and grabbed her hand. "No, baby, not crazy, I know exactly what you're talking about."

He smiled and pulled her to him. He circled his arms around her. More tears were welling in her eyes at the prospect that he was accepting her.

"Help me," she whispered. "Don't leave me alone. I've been so alone."

For several days afterward, she felt lightened and robust, like she could take on the world.

Leslie went to his room to see him. He was wasted again.

Seth and Marilyn were there. Reggie had been hanging out lately with Seth, whom Leslie liked. His full beard made him seem older, wiser. There was something kind in his intelligent eyes. Marilyn was his girlfriend. She was an incredibly beautiful girl with yards and yards of naturally curly, honey-blonde hair. She was very petite, which seemed to Leslie like a marker for a superior femininity.

Something was up. There was a very ugly tension between Marilyn and Reggie. Marilyn seemed chagrined, embarrassed, like she'd been taken to task, though Seth still seemed very gentle in his demeanor.

Reggie was flying high on a dark, nasty cloud, wearing his beret and sunglasses. High again. Drunk. He'd put a big poster up on the wall and was writing on it, laughing derisively.

It read, "The Hole is Greater than the Sum of its Parts."

He fell out on the bed, laughing, motioning for Leslie to read it.

"What's the matter?" he said, his words slurring. "Don't you get it?"

"I get it," she said. "Whether I want to or not."

"Well, man," Seth looked to Reggie, then Leslie and stood suddenly, "I better go hit those books."

"Okay man," Reggie said, standing up and grasping his wrist, then his hand in a handshake. "Thanks for the weed."

"No problem." As he headed for the door, Marilyn followed behind him, head down. After they'd left, Reggie sprawled out onto the bed.

Leslie sat down in front of him, her back to him. "I have a word for you," she said, craning her neck to speak to him.

"What's that?"

"Chauvinism." She savored the secret irony of comparing him to William.

"Tch," he said, smacking her back lightly.

The bed felt cramped. She got up.

"My head's hurting," she said.

"So is mine!" he said, laughing.

"I'm going back to my room and take a nap."

"Take a nap here, baby," he said, pulling the sheet back and winking sloppily.

"No, there's not enough room there," she said, kicking the bed frame. "I'm going back to my room." She left and stayed away from him all week.

Then she remembered the joyful feeling she'd felt for days after he'd listened to her and let her cry. She was slipping back into that sewer of depression. She went over to his room. He wasn't there. She tried again the next day and the next. And then she heard someone mouthing the same old rumors about his movements, canvassing the women's dorm.

A big weekend came. A band arrived, friends of his. It was four Mexican guys and his best friend, Andre, a big guy who played the congas. They did a lot of Santana music.

She ran into Reggie in The Grille eating fries.

"Hey," she said, sitting down across from him in the booth. "How are you?"

"Pretty good, pretty good," he said.

"Yeah?" she said, sitting down across from him. "There was something I wanted to tell you."

"What's that?" he said.

"I know you were lying."

He looked at her sharply, then smiled. "When?"

"On that poster."

"What poster?" he asked.

"On your wall. The one about 'The Hole is Greater than the Sum of Its Parts.'"

He laughed. "Oh, that one. How was I lying?"

"That was you, you were talking about. Somebody got a piece of your ass, good."

"Oh Leslie, you just know it all, don't you?"

"There are some things I tend to get the last word on. And I know about that shit. People always show their ass when they talk like that."

"All right, baby, since you know it all, why don't you come on up and meet the guys," he said. "They might need some of your wisdom, too."

Upstairs, he introduced her as 'My girl, Leslie," his arm across her shoulder, and she wondered what the hell that meant.

The guys comprised a band that had come up to perform for the weekend. Four of the guys were Latino, with Reggie's best friend from high school, Andre, playing the congas.

"We're up here to look after my man, here," Andre said. "Out here wandering in the wilderness."

That's certainly what it is, she thought, liking him right away for saying that. "Good!" she said. "He needs it."

She hung out with them for the rest of the afternoon, helped them set up the instruments in The Grille, where they were going to play.

But then Reggie vanished. 'Figures,' she thought. 'I need to just stop looking for him. Forget about him.'

She started wandering around the crowd that was waiting for the band to start. They did, and the Santana music filled the room, too much for the space. People starting dancing and cruising with the music. She saw Danny Cohen, who'd been her best friend/brother figure the semester before and went over to him. He was the guy who Reggie had given the black power salute to in The Grille that night he did the Nixon routine.

He'd had a girlfriend himself for a while and they hadn't been seeing much of each other. He looked drunk. She was glad to see him, remembering what a safe haven he had always been. He looked up at her, a big, superior grin on his face, "Just look at that fat nigger," he laughed, pointing at Andre. Danny was a bit portly himself.

She was outraged, disgusted. He'd deceived her all along. She'd thought he was parodying hypocritical white liberals, but all the while he'd just been ridiculing black people. He was just a common, ordinary racist. How could she be such a fool?

"Shut the hell up!" she said. There was a look in his eye of regret, like he realized he'd gone too far, but it was too late. She never spoke to him again.

* * *

The Feeding Frenzy

It was a Sunday afternoon and Leslie got hungry. She walked over to The Grille which was on the ground floor of Reggie's dorm, and she felt a pang of grief. Of course, she wouldn't run into Reggie. He wasn't in his room. God only knows whose room he was in. That moment when she'd confided to him how alone she was in the world and she'd felt, for an instant, that he'd encircled her into his world was another one of those brief moments when life felt normal. But, as usual, that had vanished. It always vanished.

Peter Van Archdale was in The Grille. She sat down with him for a while. He'd once described himself as a fat freak. She thought it unnecessary for him to be so self-deprecating. He was a little heavy, but still a nice-looking guy -- long, curly, dark-blonde locks down to his shoulders and carefully chiseled Anglo-Saxon features that coincided with his upper-class origins. Erudite. That was a good word for him. He expressed himself in an interesting, chatty way that made her think of Masterpiece Theater. Very pleasant. Engaging.

She'd gone with him for a while the semester before. She would have liked him more, but he was so condescendingly sour in his view on everything and everybody. He talked about his rich parents with condescension. He was condescendingly struck with how close (!?) she was to her family. Then he referred to her as one of the lost-soul girls who just wandered around looking to hook up with somebody, who didn't know who they were   . She distanced herself after that, though they still chatted occasionally in a more brother/sister kind of mode about their romantic exploits with others.

"Whatcha been up to, Peter? Or should I say, who ya' been up to?"

"I've already been through all the interesting girls," he said.

"And nothing more to do with any of them?"

He shrugged. "And what about you?"

"Missing Reggie," she sighed.

"You've really got it, don't you?" he said. He pointed his finger to the bridge of his glasses and tapped them further up his nose, cocking his head backward as he did so. There it was again. Condescension.

91

"What?" she asked.

"A kink for spades. I mean, one is okay, out of curiosity," he went on, "but two and it's a kink." He was referring to a black guy who'd visited the campus the first semester whom she'd hung out with for a few days. She hadn't slept with him. He was gay, actually, but apparently that was the buzz.

She looked at him speechless for several moments. She saw the room expanding, then contracting around him, as if with some cinematic effect intended to bring him intensely into focus. She felt herself in a free fall.

"Serial miscegenation," she muttered.

"What?" he said.

"The great American crime," she replied. She rose from her seat and continued muttering, not expecting to be heard, "Can't be a good reason to like *them*. That's impossible. Everybody knows that. Everybody. There can only be one explanation. . .

". . . I'm nasty." She walked away. Trudging back to her room she felt despair. She'd just been dehumanized with something grossly racist. It had been leveled at her, her dignity, and it was something nobody would ever care about happening to her. As Reggie had said himself, it was something she'd never have to deal with. No one would ever believe it was happening to her. She was on her own.

* * *

Kinks

Srđa and Jovanka were waiting anxiously for Leslie to get back to her room. They'd heard the exchange with Peter. They flew on ahead, trying to collect their thoughts. Srđa felt particularly guilty. This was the hard part of connecting her with her identity.

"What is it?" asked Jovanka.

"Persecution," he said. "It follows us wherever we go."

Jovanka started crying, then pacing angrily.

Leslie got to the room and didn't bother turning on the lights in the semi-darkened room. She sat staring at the walls, her breathing protracted as if each breath were a sigh.

Jovanka was still pacing, then she plopped onto the bed next to Leslie. She threw her arms around her. *"Lane moje,* it's beautiful what you love. You're loving *us.* Your heart is so right."

Leslie started crying.

"Even without knowing who you are," Jovanka went on, "you still know all on your own that the world hates people like us as much as it *needs* people like us."

Donna, her roommate, her real roommate who'd had the room to herself a good part of the semester, burst into the room and flicked on the light. When she saw Leslie sitting on the bed she flinched, startled.

"You scared me!" she said. "What are you doing, sitting in the dark? What's wrong?"

"That asshole," Leslie said.

"Who?"

"Peter van-head-up-his-ass."

Donna laughed. "What's he said this time?"

"He told me I have a kink for spades."

Donna was gathering some books in her arms, about to leave. She paused for a moment as if looking for a way to say something helpful, "Well, you know, Leslie, why do you think it is, out of all the people here, you picked him?"

That cinematic effect lurched the room around again, but Leslie kicked back at it angrily. "Obviously, I have a kink for spades!"

Donna hurriedly left the room. Leslie hurled her book onto Donna's bolster and then broke into helpless tears. She sobbed for a while.

"Come on now, my girl," Srđa said, kneeling in front of her and tapping under her chin. "Let's hear some of that argumentation you're so good at. Come on, I know you can do it. Give the world a piece of your mind."

Leslie snorted, 'Have I thought why I chose him?' she thought defiantly. 'Okay, let's just look at this rationally. If I'd met a boy I thought was really smart and cute who talked about all the unusual, unpopular things I always talk about, who's expressive and passionate and unabashedly attracted to me, who admires the same people I admire, who was raised by the same kind of hypercritical asshole I was, if I chose such a boy *and he was white,* would anybody be asking me why I chose him? Would they?? Or is the question absurd, in the absurd way white Americans think about anything to do with black people? And as far as liking 'them' is concerned, why shouldn't I? They make more sense to me than any of *you* do," she said, talking to the white people in her head, the ones who'd begun playing the part of a derisive, incessant chorus.

"Indeed," smiled Srđa, placing his hand on her head. "There's that old fire."

"Yes," said Jovanka, who was still holding her hand. "We are with you in this all the way."

It happened next, the weird things white people do, at New Men's Dormitory, Leslie's Brave New World the semester before. There was a lot of drinking going on. Hard liquor tasted nasty to Leslie, so she'd literally only had a taste, but the boys were drinking a lot. She looked around the room and, even though it was the same crew she'd hung out with the semester before, Danny Cohen wasn't there, she wasn't with him anymore, and something had changed. It dawned on her that her position was insecure, a lone, unattached female in a room full of drunken males. She left.

Bobby Miller came after her. "Hey Leslie," he said. "Where are you going?"

"Back to my room," she said. "I'm tired."

"Come on," he said, backing her against the wall and circling his arms around her. "Don't go."

She'd never felt threatened by anyone's arms before. Her stomach lurched and her body tensed into an enormous impulse to flee.

"No, really, I gotta go crash," she said, trying to disentangle herself and hide her panic.

He wouldn't let go. Her adrenal spiked so high she overpowered him. She managed to shove him off. She wrenched her shoulder doing so.

He laughed at her as she sprinted away.

"Don't be such a bitch," he said. "You gave it to that 'coon, you can give it to me," and he laughed even louder, sliding down the wall onto the floor.

She raced back to her dorm, at first as fast as she could, till she slid on some ice and almost fell. She stopped, winded, her side aching. She leaned against the wall of glass in front of The Grille, which was now dark and empty. She looked out across the rolling field of decayed snow, bright in the moonlight. Her shoulder still ached from fighting off Bobby. She smacked the glass with the heel of her palm in anger.

That was flat-out racism, directed at her, right below-the-belt. And the one person who should be supporting her had abandoned her to them .

Then she trudged on. It made no difference if she ran or crawled. She had no defense. And no one to defend her, except herself, and how was she supposed to do that all by herself?

* * *

94

Jovanka Sees What's Next

Jovanka chased through three layers of reality to find Srđa as quickly as possible. He was in a rainforest catching colorful frogs.

"No!" she cried. "This is wrong. She won't be able to handle it."

"Handle what?" he asked.

"She's going to see too much all at once. She's going to end up in the Woods at Brežje. In the pit."

"No!" he said. "That *is* way too much."

"Come on, baby," she pulled at him. "We have to be there."

* * *

Sacred Ground

The weather had shifted swiftly into spring the day after the incident at New Men's. Leslie was hanging out in somebody's dorm room. The harsh afternoon light was impeded by smoke from the hash pipe. It hung like a thick cloud. Reggie happened to be there too. He'd come in after she had and sat across from her. They exchanged glances, nothing more. The guy from New Men's who sang like James Taylor came in. He had some windowpane. She'd never done acid and wasn't particularly interested in doing so.

He was talking to Reggie. Apparently, he thought Reggie and Leslie were still together.

"Yeah man, it's really mellow. It would be a perfect day for you two to take a long trip, in more ways than one, hiking the Wakarusha." It was the thought of her and Reggie out in the warm sun hiking the river, and not the acid, that prompted her to put it on her tongue, impulsively, after he'd put it on his.

Then Reggie vanished. Of course, she thought.

She went back to her room and spent the day alone, forlorn, dejected, on a "bad trip." What was wrong with her? Why was she still mooning over this jerk who kept betraying her, all the while causing her so much trouble?

A line started repeating itself nonsensically in her head. 'That thing that's missing that will never be mine.' What the hell does that mean?

Jovanka whispered in her ear again. She was actually saying, "That thing that's missing that you must find," but Leslie heard otherwise.

Leslie tore through her drawers looking for a red sweater. She had to wear something red, no idea why. Then she made the mistake of looking

95

in the mirror and could see all the gruesome layers of her face, past the skin to the bare muscle, and the eyeball, all the way down to her skull, which she recognized as her own. She was astonished that she'd never been able to see all that before.

She wanted the day to be over, so she tried to go to sleep. She lay there a long time, seeing snakes dance across the ceiling. She did not dislike snakes, so she adjusted to what she knew was a hallucination and tried to just enjoy the dance. The mantra kept repeating itself, 'That thing that's missing that will never be mine.' It made her cry. 'Stupid. Why am I blubbering over something I don't even understand?'

Then she was sitting on a cold floor. There was a little girl, about four, sleeping in her arms. It was a dank, crowded basement floor – about fifty people, mostly women and children and old people, who looked very familiar, like family, Grandma's side. Only the children were sleeping. Everyone else sat with tensed anxiety.

The cold stone floor sucked the warmth from Leslie's body. Her hip joints ached. No one spoke. She could hear hoarse, exhausted screams from the next room. The old woman across from her crossed herself and said, "Beauty can be such a curse. Poor Smilja."

The woman next to her spoke. She was holding one hand with the other, trying to keep it from shaking. "I remember when all this was just a joke," she whispered, her face flushed with fear and rage. "Everyone was telling it, remember? 'What do Croats do differently than us? Nothing, they just blame everything they do on us.' I heard it myself, more than once. The waiter made a mistake with someone's check, and he said. 'I don't know how that happened. That's not how we do things here – not like those Serbs.'"

"And then just this morning, when the soldiers came to herd us all together, remember when the motorcycle slid on some ice into a ditch? How the *Ustaša* got off the motorcycle, kicked at the road and said, "You Serbs will pay for this!"

"But how could such a joke come to this? Is this just a dream?"

Leslie awoke from the dream, no longer in the basement. Where was she? The back of her head was like pulp, her arm twisted behind her head. Nearly in the dark, she tried to move but was pressed on from all sides by others. They were cold. A ray of light penetrated from above and in that light, she saw Smilja's blue, lifeless face, a few inches above hers, a beatific smile frozen on it.

Shock seized Leslie as she realized where she was. It was a grave. She was buried alive in a mass grave. Her skin froze, she started to retch and convulse and lose consciousness again, but then she heard a voice. It was the little four-year-old girl, happy and excited, calling her from that shaft of light. Then Leslie's dying brain understood what Smilja was smiling about. She didn't need to stay there in that pit in the woods at all – unlike those raptors who had put them there.

They will never leave it.

Leslie woke up to get out of the pit. She squinted in the brightly lit hallway to the bathroom. She was no longer hallucinating but feeling anxious. Back in her room, she tried to read something dull to quiet her fears that she'd find herself back in that pit under a pile of dead bodies. That line was echoing in her head again like a song that wouldn't shut up, 'That thing that's missing that will never be mine.' She started blubbering like a baby. She thought she was ridiculous. Near dawn, she fell asleep again, but at that moment when she dropped into sleep her mind flashed on exactly what the line meant, but just as quickly the comprehension vanished.

Then Leslie dreamt that she was in the Quonset hut that was used for art classes. She was at the far end of it, away from the door, when the floor began to liquefy into quicksand. The tables and chair were sinking into it, as was she. She struggled to reach the wall in time. First, she scrambled in panic across desktops not yet submerged. As soon as her weight was on one, it began to sink much more rapidly. She was moving as fast as she could, but she became more and more immersed in the quicksand. Luckily, she reached the wall just in time and was grappling her way, hand over hand, along windowsills towards the door. As the floor continued to liquify, her struggling roiled it and decomposing bodies churned up into view – blackened bodies of a woman with a toddler rigor mortised into her arms.

She realized the monumental enormity of the place – it was sacred ground and she had to tell somebody, she had to tell *everybody*. She kept scrambling along the walls. She woke up before she could escape. She wanted to return to the dream so that she could escape but was too afraid she'd dream that she couldn't get out. It wasn't until dawn that she fell asleep.

She awoke late the next morning, overwhelmed by the dreams. She started to write them down, to make sense of them. What she'd seen was mesmerizing, with a sense that there was way more to it, something that was the most important thing in the world.

Jovanka and Srđa tried to counsel her.

97

"My love," said Jovanka. "You feel the truth. You would have been terrified and disgusted otherwise."

"Yes," said Srđa. "All you want is to speak for us. Your priorities are straight as an arrow."

She looked for refuge in the mundane. She went down to the dorm basement to do some laundry. Marilyn was there, the beautiful girl with the yards and yards of naturally curly hair and the weird vibe with Reggie. Seth's girlfriend. They spoke, and she asked Leslie what she was up to. She told Marilyn that she was writing about a dream she'd had. Marilyn seemed interested and drew her out.

"It was a mass grave of massacred black people," Leslie said, telling Marilyn her mistaken interpretation of the dream.

At that, Marilyn changed abruptly. She had been showing a respectful, intellectual interest typical of the students of the tiny college that graduated more students who went on to obtain terminal degrees than Harvard. Her mood shifted abruptly. She smiled a crooked smile and looked directly into Leslie's eyes, too directly. "You're really into that, aren't you?"

"What do you mean?" Leslie asked. Her recently acid-soaked brain was still free-associating. Leslie's own voice sounded to herself like sheep braying.

Marilyn continued with a sexualized smile, projecting an intimate familiarity aggressively, without consent, "I know what it is you want," she said sassily, almost flirtatiously. "I know what you're looking for . . ."

Leslie could see that Marilyn was savoring the predatory moment, about to pounce, but she was unable to react defensively. All her brain could come up with was that addled line, 'That thing that's missing that will never be mine.' She said nothing.

Then Marilyn attacked, her eyes glittering lustily, drilling intensely into Leslie's. "You just want a big, black cock," she hissed.

Leslie went catatonic, catapulted from the previous night's vision of sacred ground, free-falling helplessly. She slammed into the village stocks, naked, her ankles shackled spread-eagle while the villagers pointed at her vulva and laughed. What kind of creature was she? A woman being raped by another woman?

Then all she'd seen between Marilyn and Reggie flashed in her mind. The weird, intense vibe between them. Reggie so disturbed. Marilyn so ashamed. Leslie figured it out. Marilyn had raped him too.

Still smiling her crooked smile, Marilyn sauntered away, picking her teeth as if she'd just eaten, then slipping that hand into her back pocket, along with Leslie's humanity.

Another unwelcomed, acid-soaked vision flashed in Leslie's mind. Marilyn, much younger, her eyes full of betrayed terror, as a man who resembled her in a familial way was covering her mouth and sliding his hand down the elastic of her waistband, into the front of her pants. Leslie's gut wrenched at the image that would call for a sympathy towards Marilyn. She in no way wanted to give her that.

Still reeling from the violation, Leslie trudged her way up the stairs with her basket. There was a landing in the stairwell going up to the dorm rooms, encased dramatically with glass. Leslie stopped there, not wanting to proceed.

She fled into the left side of her brain. She counted up all the attacks she'd suffered in the past few weeks since it had become public knowledge that she was no longer under Reggie's protection. There was no longer a male in the mix one might anticipate a punch in the nose from. Everyone she had encountered in this brilliant hippie dippy haven had something to say on the subject, and it was all gross.

She'd thought, naively, it was just the ignorant people, in the working-class Bigot Belt she'd grown up in, who were steeped in self-deceiving racism. Now she knew. She leaned against the wall, looking through the plate glass at the many dorm windows ahead of her. A paroxysm of anxiety overcame her.

She would never be safe around any of them. And Reggie didn't want her because he thought she was like them. He was more like them than she was – a thought she knew she could never explain to anyone, yet she knew it to be true.

She had nowhere to go.

Once more, that senseless line skated across her brain, 'That thing that's missing that will never be mine.'

* * *

Because She Can't

She awoke the next morning integrating all the craziness – all the violations and visions – into one bead of pure anger. She knew exactly what she had to do.

For once Reggie was in his room when Leslie knocked.

"What's up?" he said as she entered and plopped on the bed on the other side of the room, her feet on the mattress, her legs crossed in front of her, her arms hugging her knees, defensively.

She paused for a while, arching her eyebrows in bitter defiance. "All these white people keep raping me," she said.

He laughed. "What are you talking about?"

"They think they know me," she said. "They think they know what I want."

"What *do* you want?" he asked.

She tried reaching for her own reality, obviously irrelevant to the world, and thought about Archie's little prodigy. She pouted, "I'm supposed to be good for something."

"What do you mean?" Perfunctory question. He didn't want to know. She glared at him. He relented, "What have they been doing to you?"

"They think I'm kinky for loving you."

"What did you expect them to think?"

She showed him, she let tears well up in her eyes. "I didn't expect it to screw me up so much."

Finally, he was feeling her. He crossed over and sat next to her, his hand on her knee.

"Maybe you should chill out for a while," he said.

No, he wasn't feeling her! "What do you mean?" she demanded.

"Just leave it alone for a while," he said.

"That's all you can say to me?" she asked, shoving his hand off her knee and raising her voice. "Get lost? That's all you can say?" She squared off to him defiantly, "Why should I?"

"Because you can," he said.

"Because I can!" she said. "How do you know what I can and can't do?"

He got up and sat back on the opposite bed.

"I can't," he said. "But *you* can."

So, all that mattered was what the world did to *him*.

"You could stop getting in their beds," she said.

There was a long silence. "You can stop getting into mine," he said.

"I've been into a whole lot more than just your bed," she said.

"Have you?" he asked. "Why are you here? Why have you been with me?"

"Because I love you." There, finally, she'd said it.

"How can you even know me?" he said.

"How can I not? If I can't know you, I can't know anything."

"I'm just something novel for you to play with," he said.

100

He thought the same thing they did!

There was an old soda in a Styrofoam cup on the desk next to her. She threw it at him. It splattered all over him and the bed. "What the hell!" he said. She jumped up before he could and threw a tee shirt at him.

"All right, then," she said, standing over him as he sat back down and wiped himself with the shirt. "I'll get lost. But know this," she fell to her knees in front of him and grabbed him by the front of his shirt. "I'd go through all that and a hundred times more for you, any day of the week."

She kissed him till she started crying again. She patted his chest, touched his cheek, it felt unbearable that she would never touch him again. She stood up. "That thing that's missing that will never be mine," she said since something nonsensical seemed entirely appropriate. She left.

She didn't care who saw her crying. Halfway back she changed her mind. Her tears got angry. What was she thinking? Why should she love him? He was a total asshole. There wasn't anything again she would ever do for his sorry ass!

* * *

Amelia Adopts Leslie

A month later Reggie and Leslie got an apartment in Lincoln Park and applied to the University of Illinois, Circle Campus.

She was about to leave Shimer College with a Jewish guy she'd started seeing after she and Reggie had broken up. She was eating lunch by herself when Reggie sat down across from her. She was surprised. They hadn't spoken in a month. "You're doing what?" he said when she told him her plans.

"We're gonna hitchhike to California."

"That's the craziest shit I ever heard," he said.

"What would be crazy would be for me to try and go home and live under my racist father's roof after living under yours all winter. I know the limits of my sanity and that would be exceeding it."

He looked at her for a moment, as if taking in what she'd finally confided.

"Then come stay with me," he said.

"What?" she felt her jaw dropping, then caught it and jutted it out instead with her head back, indignant. "What are you talking about? You don't know me. You don't *want* to know me."

He leaned towards her, his head down, looking up into her eyes. "I wouldn't be asking you that if I didn't want to know you."

"Why?" she confronted. *"Why* do you want to know me?"

He paused for a moment. "Because you're special."

She cocked her head sideways. "In what way?" she demanded.

He relaxed, sat back in his chair and smiled. "You're not like anybody. I can't make any assumptions about you. I can never underestimate what you understand. You cared about me. You understood me. You took heat for me and I ignored it. I've been an ass."

"I wouldn't call you that."

"You wouldn't?"

"No. I'd call you an ass *hole.*"

He cracked up and clapped his hands together. "I guess we'll have to agree to disagree on that one."

"I guess we will," she replied, fighting the impulse to laugh with him, then regained her distance. "Why should I trust *you?* What have you ever done to deserve it?"

"Not a damn thing. I in no way deserve it." He leaned towards her and spoke in a near whisper. "If you ever see me getting high again, leave me behind on the spot and never look back. I haven't even been here. This is crazy shit being the first and only, with all these student radical revolutionary racist jerks. At least with bigots, you know where you stand. These fools don't even *know* what they're dishing out."

She thought about all the below-the-belt slams she'd taken. "Exactly," she said. "And don't *want* to know."

"I'm getting out and never coming back," he went on. "Come with me. I don't deserve it, but I want it. If you can't go home again because of the line you crossed to be with me, you might as well have something to show for it. Let me make it worth the trouble, if I can. I want to try. You deserve that much."

She felt her eyes starting to tear up, but blinked it away.

He looked around the room disdainfully. "You don't belong with these fools. Come with me."

The next day she was in his mother's kitchen. Her neighborhood was a semi-*bougie* island in the South Side ghetto. Amelia was a pretty, dark-skinned woman, tall, slender and graceful like her son, with an easy grace.

"Listen, baby," Amelia said, taking Leslie's hand. "Reggie told me what you're going through with your family, and I want you to know I appreciate that you care about my son and that you'd go the distance for him.

He told me all about it. Of all the girls at that school, you were the only one who wasn't afraid to be seen with him. That takes a special kind of person, and I appreciate it. You are always welcome here."

Leslie's eyes started to well up and Amelia hugged her.

"I'm gonna miss my mom," Leslie found herself saying. "I still haven't told her."

"I know you'll miss her, honey," Amelia said. "And I know it doesn't begin to take her place, but you can call me momma any time you want."

"Thank you," Leslie said. "Thank you. So, momma," she said, laughing a little, self-consciously, "what do you want me to do?"

"Baby, you just chop me up some onions, and that will be all I need."

After she had finished with the onions, Leslie wandered into the dining room. There was a family portrait on the wall from when Reggie was little. A surprisingly light-skinned man stood behind him in the photo.

Leslie felt Amelia's eyes on her. The lady was smiling at her warmly.

"That's Reggie's daddy," she said.

"Reggie favors you," Leslie said. She turned to Reg and teased, "That's a compliment."

"I know that," he said.

From what Leslie had already heard about the man, she knew he was anal compulsive and domineering. She thought she saw that in the way he had his head held back, looking down into the camera, with his hand possessively on his son's shoulder. She thought he looked arrogant.

"Yep," began Reggie. "Pops was from out in the sticks in Virginia, the product of a venerable old southern tradition. And this went on all over the place. A white man of any kind of means at all would have him two wives, one white and legal and another, black and on the side. That's what Pops was, a side-son.

"Gross," Leslie said.

"He used to tease me being as how I was from Mississipi," Amelia said. "Black on black parents, but I'll tell you, I do not envy him. Not one little bit."

"What was their relationship like? The father and son?" Leslie asked Amelia.

"His father didn't do much of anything with him, other than to fuss him out."

Leslie laughed. "Sounds like home." She looked up from her plate to see Amelia looking at her warmly, curiously.

Encouraged, she went on. "It's always intrigued me when people could so readily explain why their family was a mess, when it can be cast in some grand scheme of rank injustice. I wish I could do that. Instead, all I can say is that my father is an abusive fool and I can't stand to be around him."

"There's reasons for everything," Amelia said, again making eye contact that made Leslie feel understood. "I don't suppose he's any more of a fool than any other fool."

"What's this?" asked Reggie. "Fool equality?"

"Yeah, a new holiday – Fool Equality Day," said Leslie.

He leaned over towards her and made a goofy face, "well, I'm a fool for you, baby."

She'd noticed he was different when he was with his mom. Softer.

A few weeks later they'd both found part-time jobs and an apartment in Lincoln Park. The very next weekend she got to do a real boyfriend/girlfriend thing. The kind of thing she'd always missed being able to do, back in that high school her parents had moved her to, so she wouldn't have to go to school with the coloreds – that high school where nobody had ever asked her out. But those days were over, and she had a real live, live-in boyfriend. Someone to share her days with. They went down to the museum – the Museum of Science and Industry in downtown Chicago.

They'd wandered past a number of exhibits. They entered a high-ceilinged hall several stories high, filled with a long progression of identical glass cases, close together, over five-foot square and a half inch thick. Inside each was a half inch slice of a human being. Leslie imagined they must have had a 12-foot diameter round saw blade to do it. Perhaps they'd frozen the person first to make the slices cleaner. There was a body cut horizontally. A downward tour, first into the brain, then sliding down to the chest, no breasts, had to be male, just his lungs, his heart, his stomach, his guts, his genitals, the two round steaks of his meaty thighs.

The next human being was cut into vertical slices. When the slice was of the center of the body the vivid profile of a very short, moderately overweight, middle-aged woman leaped shockingly into view, an incredibly intimate profile. She was naked not only externally, but every bit of her inner self, her brain, her viscera. Leslie was quite sure the woman or her family had not donated her body to science. No, what Leslie saw was an abandoned, anonymous woman, alone in the world, that science had claimed for its own purposes. A homely, short, black woman nobody cared about.

The man's body was much more anonymous. In a few slices, it was possible, from his complexion and the texture of the hair on his head and his pubic hair, to make out that he was black. A nondescript black man.

They reached the end of the display and left the hall. They passed by a group of black teenage girls. One of them pointed at the two of them and called out loudly to her friends, "Look, salt and pepper."

Looking for some fresh air, they found their way to Grant Park near the ornate, Victorian-era water fountain. They stretched out in the grass while the fresh scent of water flung twenty feet into the air intermittently wafted over them. Leslie watched fluffy white clouds careening across the sky while Reggie chewed on the sweet end of a blade of grass. He touched the end of her nose. The woman's profile was still on her mind.

"If she'd been anybody else they would have taken out the middle slices," she said.

"Who?"

"The sliced-up woman."

"Oh, her. You think so, huh? You mean, if she'd been white."

"Obviously."

"You're going to start worrying about all that, huh?"

"What do you mean, start? I was raised to worry about that. All my childhood. Topic Number One."

"By who?"

"My father."

"I thought you said he's a bigot."

"He *is* that."

"I don't understand."

"It's simple. He raised me to be the opposite. That's not hard. Even a child can do that.

"But why?"

"It's a mystery." She turned on her side towards him and tapped the end of *his* nose. "My quest in life. Figuring out why, the hell, he raised me to care about all this so much." She blinked away a wateriness she felt welling up in her eyes. "*Why* is it such a big deal?" She re-composed herself, smiled and made her tone light-hearted, "You gonna help me on my quest?"

"Don't know that I can."

"Nah," she sassed and turned onto her back to look up into the sky again. "You just want me to shut up and be white."

He propped himself up and looked at her, pleasantly askance, also playing. "What kind of shit is that?"

"Mine," she said, still looking at the clouds.

He laughed and lay back on the grass. "I like your shit."

She felt him slide his hand under hers and grasp it.

"Good," she said.

Srđa and Jovanka had tagged along on the museum excursion and were there at the park. Jovanka had positioned herself at the base of the main jet of the fountain. With each burst of water, she was propelled high into the sky. She was laughing gleefully with each joy ride. Srđa was happily reminded of what a child bride he'd married. He was listening in on Leslie and Reggie's conversation. He motioned for Jovanka to quick join them. She heard the whole bit about the sliced-up woman.

"See momma," Srđa said. "I told you he would come along. He's 'getting' it, as they say."

Jovanka raised her dark eyebrows skeptically and spooned herself around Reggie. She put her hand on his forehead and closed her eyes. When she was satisfied she'd picked up on an adequate read she popped back up and faced Srđa.

"Nope, baby." she said.

"Nope?" he asked.

"He has no clue what she's talking about and he's a bit annoyed that she's changing the conversation to be about her. What's the word?"

"Upstaging?" asked Srđa.

"Yes, that's the word."

"Are you sure that isn't just what you're expecting, instead of what he's feeling?"

"No, she's right." Srđa turned to see none other than the sliced-up-woman. She was perfectly whole, however, and dressed elegantly in a peachy white satin dress, with large pearls sewn into her tightly textured hair to complement the pearls sewn into the front of the dress.

"There was nothing 'white' in the way that child reacted to the indecent butchery of my body they are exhibiting in there. There was not a shred of pity. It was different. It was outrage. May I ask what has happened to her family?"

"Butchery!" clamored Jovanka. "Aryan Supremacist butchery hidden from her. Hidden from the world!"

The lady shook her head sympathetically. "And still she feels it. I am so sorry for your suffering."

"As we are for yours," replied Srđa. "What brought you to such an end, if I may ask?"

"You may. I was traveling by train – I had a fear of flying – from my sister's home in St. Louis. I had decided at the last moment to take a detour and spend a few days as a tourist in Chicago, neglecting to tell anyone. I had acquired a habit of excessive independence harking back to my youth when I ran away from my parents' home in the south to attend a teacher's college. They were pressuring me to marry, but I had other ideas. My, how I loved teaching. While wandering the city I was abducted into a van. The intent was robbery, but I suffered a massive head injury. They stripped my body, dressed it in rags and left it in a rail yard. It's quite scandalous how little effort was made to investigate the possibility of a crime. I agree completely with your girl's deduction."

"But why are you so sure her boyfriend has no interest in her quest?" asked Srđa.

"His first reaction when she mentioned me."

"Yes!" said Jovanka. "You felt it too?"

"Yes – impatience. He was disappointed to hear her bring up the subject. He doesn't want her to talk about such things. He's a conflicted mess. He trusts her because she's different from most whites, at the same time he's looking for the white Nirvana of his imaginings, where he can ditch all these cares. He's hoping she'll take him there. How can she do such a thing? She doesn't live there."

"No, she's a displaced person trying to find her way home," said Jovanka. "They are headed in opposite directions." Then she added, to Srđa, "He's not the one, baby. We have to find someone else."

The next day was a leisurely Sunday. Amanda stopped by. "Boy, you better come out to the car with me and help me haul this junk up here."

"What junk?"

"Some old stuff I had laying around you can likely use."

A coffee pot, dishes, pots and pans, lamps. Lots of stuff to flesh out their near-empty apartment after many trips up and down the stairs.

"This stuff has been collecting dust for ages up in that attic, just waiting for this day when one of my chicks has flown the coop. And that day has finally arrived."

She smiled brightly and then her face crashed. She put her hand to her forehead and crumpled to the floor.

"Momma!" Reggie screamed. Amanda's eyes were open, but nothing was in them. Leslie ran to the phone and called 911.

They did nothing down at the hospital but pronounce on Amelia, victim of a likely aneurism. Her two sisters arrived and took over dealing with the hospital, whisking Reggie's little sister, Celeste, away with them.

It wasn't till he got home that evening that Reggie started to react. She heard him crying and got into the shower with him. She held him. "Why?" he cried. "Why? I need her. I still need her. I'm not ready to be on my own."

"You're not alone," Leslie said, though she felt lost too, unable to think of anyone else supporting her the way Amelia had done, immediately, without qualification. Life would be *much* harder without her. She cried with him, then was hit with dread at the loss she was about to experience herself when she came out of the closet to her family.

For several weeks Leslie would find Reggie in the bedroom in tears. He'd talk about Amelia – talk about things she'd done for him, things she'd said. The things she went through with his dad, how shortchanged she was when it came to being loved the way she deserved to be loved. "I hope I loved her enough," he said. "I wanted her to be able to see me do well and get some pay-back for everything she did for me."

"She still sees," Leslie said, crying with him. Seeing him show his feelings to her fulfilled her. She felt that a bond had been forged between them and that he would always show her his feelings.

For his part, he resolved it was the last time he would ever show his tears to anyone. He didn't expect her to stay much longer, she'd chicken out before getting her ass disowned over him, and then there'd be no one again who'd seen him cry like that.

His father's sister, Henrietta, took on the task of raising Celeste and assumed the role of the family's matriarch.

* * *

Leslie's Christmas Treasure

Leslie dreaded the onset of the Christmas season. She still had not told her family what was going on. All she'd said was that she was living with some roommates in Lincoln Park. She'd told herself she'd tell them the truth by Christmas. It was Reggie's first Christmas without his mother. There was no way she was going to desert him. Her place was with him. It had to be done.

She sat staring at the phone for a good while. She couldn't remember dialing but then she heard the phone ringing on the other end. Her mom picked it up.

"Leslie!" her mom said. She always said it that way when she heard her daughter's voice. There was always that exclamation point.

"Hey mom," she replied. "How are you? I got something to tell you."

"Good. I was just going to call you. You won't believe who was here yesterday."

"Why, what happened?"

"Three of the big wigs from SOS."

"I thought you quit, what did they want?"

"They came to beg me to come back!"

"Really? They couldn't live without you?"

"Nope. You wouldn't believe what's been going on. Well, okay, so you know they just hired some women to do inspections thinking they'd be pushovers. This was years ago."

"Yeah, I know, you've been telling me." She'd been telling Leslie for years.

"And I never let them by me, that's for sure. I don't care if I had to reject the whole night's shipment. What those jerks put me through."

"Yeah, I know." She'd been telling Leslie for years.

"So anyway, here I've been quit for almost six months now and the place has gone to the dogs." Deloris laughed.

Leslie did too. She'd jumped on Deloris' wavelength gladly, forgetting why she'd called. "No kidding?"

"No kidding! And they think it's 'cause I quit!"

"They figured it out, huh?"

"Yeah! Everybody's buying Brillo now! All these women are so disgusted. They're opening up their box of SOS and it's just a bunch of rust. That's 'cause they shipped it wet. They didn't do their job running it through the dryers right. They think I don't know, but I've done every job in that place and I know how it's supposed to be done and that's how I expect *them* to do it."

Deloris was on a roll.

"Or they'd be scrubbing away and get a sliver from the steel wool. You gotta cut that stuff right or it can cut somebody. It's terrible. And guess what?"

"What?"

"Stock prices fell."

"And it's all your fault?"

109

"It's all my fault 'cause I quit and there's nobody standing up to them anymore."

"Good for you, mom. I'm proud of you."

"So, they came, and they were sweet-talking me. The three of them sitting right there in my front room while I made them coffee. They want me to come back. I get more money, I get a big bonus and I get my pension reinstated like I never quit. They never did that for nobody before."

"You're one of a kind." Leslie felt a tear in her eye. Her throat constricted.

"And the best part, from now on, they listen to me. No more bullshit. They do what I say. If I say it ain't right, they fix it."

"Wow, Deloris saves SOS."

"So, what did you have to tell me, sweetheart?"

Leslie's mind went blank, trying to think of something else to say other than what she'd intended, raining like that on her mom's parade.

"What is it, honey? Is everything okay?"

Leslie stammered, and it came out, anyway. "It's about my roommate. My boyfriend. His name is Reggie. He's going to U of I with me. He's black."

There was a long silence.

Deloris' quick mind switched gears instantly. She flashed on a very hard life looming before her daughter, that she'd feared for her, a world full of scorn from whites, and black people who'd just use her. Her daughter would have no standing anywhere. Finally, the woman responded, her voice teary and resigned, rather than surprised. "So, I'll have to tell your dad?"

"I don't have anything to say to him," said Leslie.

"Okay," her mom said, sobbing. "I have to go now. Call me, call me every week."

Leslie was crying too. "Okay," she said. "I love you," and she hung up the phone.

She didn't tell Reggie what she'd done when he first got home. He wanted to go out for deep dish pizza, so they headed out. They stood waiting in the cold for the 'el,' the elevated trains that traversed the city, which was delayed. She had a thought that somehow inertia would overtake the world and they would just stand there forever, out in the weather. She felt something radiating from over her shoulder and she peered to see what it was.

There was a middle-aged white man standing fifteen feet from her. He was leering at her. 'There it is,' she thought, flashing on Marilyn's lascivious comment on what it was Leslie wanted in life, 'the Big Black It Leer – the second time this week, and it's only Thursday.' She cuddled closer to Reggie, the man's leer having sucked warmth from her body. She was cold. She wished she had more layers on. It felt like she had on nothing at all.

She still hadn't told him when they got home. They went to bed and he reached for her. She went through the motions of responding to him, but when she started to let herself go, tears started to flow. She turned her back to him, so he would not see her cry. She gave into the tears. The lovemaking took on a frantic quality.

"Baby, you're incredible," he said afterward. He thirstily drank a glass of water on the nightstand and quickly fell asleep. After a while, she gently extricated herself from his arms and went to the bathroom. She came back in the dark. A full moon was outside the window, illuminating the window shade. She watched him sleep and realized that the more she paid to be with him, the more precious he became to her. 'My treasure,' she thought, 'my treasure that costs a fortune.'

She spooned around him and wished she could hold him closer. That was as close as she could get, but it wasn't enough. It wasn't as much as she felt.

* * *

A Farewell to Mothers

She asked him to take out the trash. He forgot. So, she asked him the next day. He got in a rush to leave and forgot. As far as he was concerned, if it wasn't for her late ass, they wouldn't have been in a rush in the first place.

They got home that evening and the ugly old steel kitchen, which predated the concept of counter space, stank.

When she pulled the trash up out from the can, the paper grocery bag it was in disintegrated onto the floor. She laughed.

"What's so funny?" he asked.

"What so funny is you gotta clean that up. That's *your* trash," she said.

"My trash? Hell no, that ain't my trash. I would've never picked that bag up out of that can. My trash would have stayed in the can while I took it out to the big can. That's *your* trash."

Leslie looked at the wet disgusting mess on the floor and was slammed with a feeling of abandonment. Just as quickly as she'd laughed she began to cry. Reggie thought she'd gone *insane*.

"That's not me," she cried. "That's not who I am." She turned to him, sobbing.

"What in the hell are you talking about?" he said, dumbfounded.

"I told them," she said.

"You told who what?"

"I called, and I told my mom about us," she replied.

He sat down. "When was this?" he said.

"A week ago, Thursday."

"What did she say?" he asked.

"Not much, what's there to say? It's all been said, for years."

He got up, fetched the dustpan and started scooping the mess back into the can. She got some paper towel, dropped it to the floor and used her foot to clean up the wet mess. He put the smelly can outside the door. He sat down.

He watched her finish spraying the floor and wiping it with another wad of paper towels. She put them outside the door as well and washed her hands. He wondered if he was just a way for her to make some kind of statement. "Are you rebelling?" he asked.

She shook her head. "I'm being who I was raised to be. There's no way I wouldn't have loved you."

He'd been waiting for her to back down. He hadn't expected this to last. He thought she'd chicken out. He figured he'd go for it till it got to that point and he'd move on. No big deal.

"I had to tell them now," she said. "I couldn't let you go through your first Christmas alone." She crossed over to him, straddled him and sat with her face a few inches from his, looking into his eyes. The pupils in her eyes were so wide open. She was talking about his loss, but it was *her* loss pouring out of those eyes. Then she put her head on his shoulder and sobbed again. Her crying for her mother evoked his own. It was as if an apparition of his mother had just passed by him. The two motherless children cried together.

Amelia hugged them both, tears in her own eyes.

* * *

Sleeping on the Porch

It was the day before Christmas. Reggie and Leslie showed up at his family's home to help with preparations. It was on him to put up the lights on the porch no one had gotten to. Leslie was in the kitchen, helping Henrietta. Or trying to help Henrietta.

Leslie swept the floor and put the broom back in the closet.

She washed her hands and washed the green beans and started cutting them.

"Oh," said the woman, "just snap off the ends, leave them whole otherwise."

While Leslie did that Henrietta took out the broom and swept the floor AGAIN. Leslie watched her out of the corner of her eye, trying to catch a glimpse of something she had missed when she had just swept it. She didn't see anything. The floor looked perfectly clean. She was embarrassed.

Leslie offered the woman the washed and snapped beans. The woman took the beans with a distressed look on her face. Leslie sharply missed Amelia, her welcoming smile, and her forthright affection. Henrietta took the beans over to the sink and started washing them.

"Oh, I did that already," said Leslie. The woman continued washing them, turning her face away from Leslie. "They've been washed," Leslie repeated. Then she thought to herself, 'But they haven't been washed since I touched them.'

She left the kitchen and joined Reggie in the living room, where he was watching a football game. She had no attention span for sports and her mind wandered. She hated how easily people could make her feel inferior. She started feeling depressed. She leaned her head on Reggie's shoulder and pretended to be napping.

After a while, Reggie turned towards her. "You sure Aunt Henrietta doesn't need more help?"

"I don't think she likes me in her kitchen," Leslie said.

"She's a little phobic that's all," he said. "She's all right."

A little later Celeste came home, and Aunt Henrietta greeted her effusively. Leslie could hear the woman and the girl in the kitchen talking excitedly while Henrietta asked about her accomplishments at school that week and lavished her with praise. Leslie went into the kitchen for a glass of water. "Oh yes," said Henrietta to Celeste as Leslie passed by, "please cut that ham for me. It's so nice to have someone here who'll help an old woman."

At dinner, the conversation turned to Reggie's grandfather, who had also recently passed. That was Auntie Henrietta's father.

"What that poor man went through," Auntie said. Reggie had already told Leslie the story. His grandfather had been born to two unmarried teenagers in a small Virginia town. The girl was black, from a family who had, in antebellum days, been the clandestine bi-racial family of the man who owned them. The boy was white, from a family of merchants recently emigrated from Scotland. They both went on to marry others, but her husband never accepted her son. The situation escalated when the boy got to his teen years. His step-father turned him out. He was sent to live with his white father. He was not acknowledged as such, though, and was referred to as the "yard boy." He slept on the porch.

"He was such an industrious man," she said. "He made so much money selling liquor during Prohibition he built him a house, a nice house with two stories, my sister still lives in. They don't make them like that anymore."

"The man or the house?" asked Reggie.

"The man!" she said, annoyed. "What do you think I'm talking about?"

"You know I'm teasing you," he said.

Leslie helped herself to a second slice of the pumpkin pie she'd made. Nobody else had touched it. She was famous for her pie. She even told them that. She made her crust from scratch with half shortening, half butter – very flaky, and for the filling used only brown sugar and twice the sweet spices, a very dark brown, rich pie that surprised everyone with the intense flavors infusing the delicate custard. But no one there would even taste it. Actually, Aunt Henrietta had never touched anything Leslie brought, and Celeste followed her lead.

After dinner, Reggie clued Leslie in on the sleeping arrangements. The plan was for them to spend the night and be there all-day Christmas. "Aunt Henrietta's prim and proper," Reggie said. "She's not going to like it if you sleep with me."

"I didn't expect she would," said Leslie. Then she wondered to herself if the woman would prefer it if she slept on the porch.

She lay on the couch, unable to sleep. Reggie hadn't unplugged the Christmas lights on the front porch, and the light filled the room with a confusion of colors. The door was dead-bolted with no key present, no way for her to unlock the door and unplug the lights. She thought about Amelia and that made her cry, then her own mom would come to mind and she'd cry for her. Then she realized that she'd been resolved to comfort Reggie through this Christmas, but she was the one who needed comforting.

She left the garishly lit front room and crept into the bed with Reggie. She needed him to be the outside spoon. Once he was behind her, his arm encircling her, her mind settled, and she fell asleep for a few hours before dawn.

* * *

The U.P. Ghetto

The following summer they went on vacation to the Upper Peninsula in Michigan, commonly referred to as the U.P. Reggie had his first car, his aunt's castaway. They borrowed and bought some camping gear and headed out.

"I love hitting the tree line," she said, "when the pine forest takes over. Can you smell it?"

"Yeah," he smiled, opening his window more and taking in a deep breath. "I haven't smelled that since I was in Virginia at my Grandma's. Hooeee!" he shouted out the window.

He hadn't realized how hard the preceding semester had been on him till he let that whoop out the window. A sense of freedom and delicious carelessness swept over him. He cranked up the radio and began singing along with James Brown, pounding the dashboard to the beat. He grabbed her thigh and leaned over to kiss her, "We's living now, baby!"

She realized how long it had been since she'd heard him cut loose in the vernacular. She'd missed it. She loved that. Natural and full of life.

* * *

Putting Reggie in His Place

They got to the campground an hour later. A craggy old man looked at them with incredulity as they pulled in. After they paid and signed in he told them to follow him and he'd show them to their campsite. He led them past many a lovely, vacant spot all the way to the back of the campground to the scrubby part, and who was lodged next to their site but a black family. Everyone else in the campground was white.

Reggie was highly annoyed. He grabbed the borrowed old tent. He held the tent bag as high as he could and let all the aluminum poles crash to the ground as loudly as possible, muttering something about the U.P. ghetto. When the poles were all settled, he picked several of them back up and tossed them noisily back onto the pile.

"Encore," said Leslie. He picked up a bunch of the poles and let them crash several more times.

"Ooowee," said Leslie, "look at this jigsaw puzzle." She started unfolding the tent. "Help me, please," she said to him, motioning to him to pull the side opposite to her. She figured once she saw that layout, she could start figuring how the poles should be configured.

"All right," he said. "Now that we can see the rod carriers on the tent, the configuration of the poles will become apparent. You know what to do with a rod carrier, baby?"

"It might could come natural," she said. She started sorting the straight poles by size.

"Okay, all the poles with curves are identical," he said. "So, it's simply a matter of height on the other poles."

She took one of the shortest poles and tested to see if it reached the first, obviously shortest-serving rod pocket at the base of the tent. It was too short.

"Obviously," he said, "that joins with another pole." He was sounding a bit superior in his tone and it was getting on her nerves.

"Yes, I only got 99 percentile in mechanical reasoning," she said. "But that was only on the girls' scale. On the boys' I was only a 98 percentile. Obviously, I should defer."

"Sarcasm becomes you," he said.

"Oh, you think that's sexy, I'll give you a whole lot more," she said. "Just keep it up."

"I'll keep it up for ya'," he countered, grabbing his crotch in a macho gesture.

"You keep up that know-it-all shit, boy," she said, wobbling her head sassily, "and I might just have to put you . . ." She defiantly repeated the gesture with her own crotch, "in your place!"

She had been wondering when she'd get the opportunity to deliver that one-liner that she'd recently thought up. Apparently, she'd hit the right timing.

He let out a loud whoop of laughter and swung his arms out, then crossed his hands over his chest, still laughing. He staggered towards her, as if weak in the knees, and grabbed her wrist. "Yes, indeed," he said. "That certainly *can* humble a man."

She laughed with him.

"That was a good one, Lez," he said. "I gotta admit, I really liked that one."

"I know you do," she said. "All the time. Now are you going to help me erect this tent, so I can put you in your place, or are you going to leave the erection to me?"

He snapped his neck to the left to see the couple next door as they walked by and said, "Hi, how are y'all doing?"

He stepped closer to Leslie and the tent and muttered, "Fools think I'm going to talk to them just because we're in the ghetto together, they can go *on* thinking."

They finished setting up the tent. Reggie's mood had brightened, though he was still restless.

"Let's get the hell out of this ghetto," he said.

"And go where?" she asked.

"To paradise," he said. "Let's follow that river up a bit, and find a nice place, just for us."

"You sure?" she asked.

"Yeah, grab a sleeping bag. Let's go."

They hiked a ways upstream and found a beautiful spot in a bend of the river. They built a fire and zipped the two sleeping bags together.

"Now, this is what I'm talking about," he said as they gazed up at the stars, pulling from a bag of trail mix. They gazed at the incredible depth of stars above their heads. "Now this is *my* place in the universe," he said. "A jug of wine, a bag of trail mix, a universe of stars overhead, and a white woman about to put me in my place."

Leslie laughed merrily. "You think so, huh?"

"Oh, I know so."

She giggled. "My favorite political statement," she confided.

"Really? Putting me in my place?"

"Hits the spot for me," she said and laughed so hard she had trouble catching her breath.

They drifted off into some relaxed lovemaking, punctuated with laughter when the days' one-liners echoed in their minds.

They were falling asleep to the sound of the river gurgling next to them, as an amazing mist rose up through the moonlight around them. Leslie was entranced with the incredible beauty around her. Reg was already asleep.

She marveled at the fascinating proportions of his face with its Phoenix-like beauty. It always made her happy to see it in anyone, coaxing her to imagine what it must be like to be blind to yourself and then see

117

again. She never grew tired of it, always felt incredibly lucky she had him to look at every day. His eyes opened.

"I love you," she said, and to herself, 'my treasure.'

"I love *you*," he replied.

Around three in the morning, they woke up, freezing. Their sleeping bag was not water resistant and the mist that had arisen from the stream had penetrated through it, bringing their body temperatures dangerously low.

"Shit," he said, "I can't find the lighter." The fire had gone out. "We gotta keep moving," he said. "We gotta get up out of here before hypothermia gets us. Get back to the car and turn on the heat."

Leslie started coiling the conjoined sleeping bag.

"Leave the mess," he said. "We'll get it in the morning." They put on their wet clothes and shoes and started moving downstream in the dark. The moon had set and it was very dark.

"Ow," Leslie cried out as she was scratched by an unseen branch.

"You all right?" he asked.

"Just a scratch," she said.

He hurried along.

"Can you please slow down a little?" she asked.

"We need to get warm," he said.

"We also need to avoid twisting ankles," she replied. Hers was already hurting from when she'd rebounded from the branch that scratched her.

He continued hurrying forward while she fell behind. "Keep up!" he shouted when she lagged behind.

"I can't!" she shouted back. "Help me." He doubled back to her. "Which ankle hurts?"

She pointed and he took position alongside her so that she could lean on him.

They'd reached a spot where a fenced pasture intersected the path along the river.

"Good," he said. "We can cut through here."

"Cut through where? she asked.

"This field," he said.

"That cow pasture?"

"Yes," he replied. "It's a shortcut to the campground."

"Full of cows," she said.

"Yeah, come on."

"Where there are cows, there are bulls," she said.

"Yeah?"

"Bulls with horns," she said.

"Okay."

"I'm in no condition to be running from bulls with horns. I don't intend to be running from two-ton pissed-off cows, either."

He sighed in irritation.

"If you want to go that way, go," she said. "I'll be all right, as long as I can move at my own pace." She picked up a long stick and continued along the river bed, using it like a blind man uses a cane.

"Stop playing the martyr," he said.

"I am not being a martyr. I am perfectly capable of going on my own adventures. Making my way along a riverbed in the pitch-black dark while fending off hypothermia in the Upper Peninsula is my adventure of choice at the moment."

"Wait up," he said.

She stopped.

He took his place next to her again.

"That's a good idea," he said, referring to the stick.

They reached a stretch where there was a sandy shoreline to walk along the riverbed and made some unimpeded progress. There was even a bit more visibility.

"You warming up? he asked.

"Yeah," she said. "I'm okay."

"I'm sorry," he said.

"For what?"

"For dragging you out here."

"You didn't drag me," she said. "It was a good idea. I'm glad I came."

$$* * *$$

The Scam Years
School of Engineering

Reggie was admitted into the School of Engineering at IIT. He wasn't sure when it had started, but he'd go whole stretches of time now, when he was simply a person living his life and threw himself into a world with clearly defined answers and a comfortingly predictable reliability.

By then he was a double orphan, his father having died the previous year and he qualified for a full scholarship. Mathematically gifted, he'd also lucked into a programming gig, one of the first. It was pretty boring, working with punch cards and an enormous mainframe with a tiny "brain." Still, he was making twice the hourly wage Leslie was getting.

Leslie's strategy was to do three years at the University of Illinois, Circle campus – which was the low-cost equivalent to a junior college of the time – nice, slow and easy. Then, when she'd been self-supporting long enough, she'd get herself a scholarship for two years of film school.

She wanted to go into filmmaking because she frequently dreamed long, involved plotlines in full Technicolor in her sleep. She figured if she could do it in her sleep, it would be an easy job for her. But more than that, she felt like her experience of life usually tended to be 180 degrees removed from what anyone thought she was experiencing as if she were invisible. She craved the opportunity to be herself in the world. Not a whole lot else mattered to her. In the end, she'd have been in school as long as Reggie, but without a graduate degree. She didn't care if she had degrees that showed off how much she knew. All she cared about is that she had gained the knowledge she wanted to have.

She applied for scholarships at one point but didn't get any so she just took the minimum number of hours she needed to qualify as a full-time student, worked part-time in a relaxed pace, enjoying the journey.

* * *

Leslie's Scam

Leslie was putting herself through school by way of her scam. Growing up, she had taken six and a half years of piano lessons, which made her quite dexterous. She taught herself to type in a few weeks and within a year was typing 90 wpm. On top of that, she'd taken two years of Latin, so she could spell any medical or legal terminology.

She was putting herself through college as a typist. She could get a new job, with benefits, within three days any time she wanted. Since she'd get the highest scores they'd ever seen on those lame tests they gave her, she'd be paid top dollar -- top typist dollar anyway, for whatever that was worth. The problem was that the work was so boring that after a few months she generally was NOT the most productive typist, so her rate of pay became a source of irritation.

She never got canned simply over the productivity issue. It would start with the jokes. In Chicago, in the Seventies, bigots ruled. They certainly ruled the water cooler culture. It was the unspoken law in Chicago that, at any point in time whenever a room became occupied solely by white people, the reigning bigot would whip out the latest nigger jokes.

They could be quite rank, like the dead black baby you hang by his hair from the ceiling with Velcro joke, sick shit like that, but woe to the trespasser who failed to laugh. That person became suspect. Everybody in the room knew that and shunned the trespasser from there on out. And considering she was in a position, so to speak, where conceivably, so to speak, she could be mothering a gorgeous nappy-headed bundle of joy herself, she was particularly stony in her silence.

This went on commonly in the Seventies even after the hiring quotas came into effect and some poor soul of color would be hired and placed in a nice, large office that was the very FIRST office anyone entering the office suite would see. Leslie had no idea how these sacrificial lambs survived in those jobs – she certainly wasn't.

Those dear lambs, of course, never hung out at the water cooler, though certainly were in earshot, but, so long as they were not actually in the room, the jokes went on. No one yet had realized that a lucrative new field in the practice of law was being born as those poor token souls got the last laugh all the way to the bank, prosecuting the hapless jokesters.

The longest Leslie had remained on the job after being identified first as a suspect, and then actually seen with Reggie by any other individual working in the office, was two weeks. If aware she'd been found out, she'd start looking forward to how much more she'd be getting paid in two and a half weeks after she'd started her next job at a higher rate of pay than the one she was about to be canned from. This was happening so often that single-handedly she was raising the rate of pay for typists throughout the city.

It had started innocently enough. Leslie was quite adamant that she would never, ever make Reggie feel like she was hiding him, or treating him like a back-door man. When the first incident had hit, it had occurred entirely by accident. After a few occurrences, however, with the consequences of greater variety in her work life at a higher rate of pay, since it was customary to always pay a bit more than the previous employer, she could look forward to liberating herself from obnoxiously racist white people. Added to that was the safety net that, since she was being let go, she could always claim unemployment compensation if she needed to. The two of them just naturally went for some 'accidental on purpose' incidents.

The same pattern was repeating that she had been raised on by Archie, where her contrary behavior in this regard had been so amply rewarded. She was perfectly adapted to her role in life at the vanguard of that first wave of white girls crossing the color line.

* * *

The Vanguard

Being in the vanguard is a bitch, she thought, as the elevated train, referred to as the 'el,' squealed its way around a curve. She'd just lost another job. She and Reggie were heading uptown to a house party. Of all the people in this el car, she thought, how many of them were seeing a couple like them for the first time? She was a first. The first white female any number of people were seeing with a black male and reacting to.

She supposed that was why the fat lady across from her was glaring at her. The *Big Black It Glare.* That malevolent, dehumanizing stare that oozed such contempt. The old bat definitely knew what *it* was that Leslie wanted. That this *it* that Leslie wanted should be so reprehensible was rather baffling, considering the fact that she was, after all, a female in a heterosexual relationship. If she hadn't wanted *it,* the two of them would logically need relationship counseling. But no matter, this *it* was different. That was abundantly apparent on the old woman's face.

Compounding all that, Leslie had fleshed out, so to speak, her limited experience on the matter and referred to some physiology articles. Reggie was, in all respects, perfectly normal. That was the compounded irony. She was being persecuted – slut-shamed – for being perfectly normal, involved with someone who was *also* perfectly normal.

Leslie flashed on the old woman's life and knew why the woman thought that *it* was disgusting. The old woman had felt that way ever since her uncle had molested her when she was eleven. That scenario continued to unfold in Leslie's imagination as she and Reggie got off the el at their stop.

The insight that Archie had given her, that when white people talked their racist trash they were, in fact, talking about themselves, their own deep-down, dirty secrets, was only deepening. She knew what an intimate thing racism really is and every time they looked at her contemptuously now they were whispering their secrets in her ear, contaminating her with way more information than she wanted. She just knew them too damn well.

Only now the racism was being slammed *at her,* in a completely below-the-belt way, making the unwanted intimacy a direct violation. She wasn't listening to them talk about others. They were talking about *her.* *She* was the nasty, despised thing.

Leslie was still feeling contaminated the next morning by those two violations, the one that happened to the old lady as a girl, and the one she'd inflicted on Leslie with her virulent glare. Leslie sat down to write a story about an eleven-year-old girl who got molested by her 29-year old uncle in the basement of her grandparent's house, just to get it onto paper and out of her head.

But as soon as she'd moved on from that issue, the latest firing was sitting there to be contemplated. The job that had preceded this loss was a lot easier to lose. At least the loss of it had been easy. It had been a simple typing job for a real estate management company inhabited by straight-up racists. They managed buildings that had been white forever and were going through the rocky road of desegregation. Their resentments and insecurities at having their livelihood threatened and regulated were voiced daily and explicitly. That's where she heard the "porch monkey" crack she was going to write about, with Srđa's help, when she started writing articles under Reggie's name.

When she could bear no more of it, Leslie and Reggie made a date for lunch at the cafe on the ground floor of the building where she worked. By then their ambitions had escalated into a plot to garner as many of these firings as they could, in a kind of sting, and then publicize it, file a lawsuit and go somewhere with it. The office controller was the one to spot them. That Monday she was called into the Human Resource guy's office and told to clear out because of her soft productivity.

She walked out of there glad to be rid of them, eager for whatever opportunity lay ahead, and expanding her folder further on these firings.

* * *

Office of Economic Opportunity

She and Reggie had already decided that after the next firing she would go down to the new Office of Economic Opportunity and file a discrimination complaint. She'd been tied up in knots for days, rehearsing in her head how she should tell her story. She was confused because the scam aspect of it was not going to go down well.

"What should I say about the scam?" she asked Reggie.

"You shouldn't say anything about it," he said as if it were that simple.

"I don't know how to tell stories and omit shit," she said. "I'm a very poor liar."

"That's not lying," he said.

"Yes, it is. It's a lie of omission. I need to find a way to explain it up front."

"Okay, so that's how you were coping with all the firings."

The next morning, they got down to the office. Before they entered the building, Leslie turned to Reggie, "What am I doing here?" she said. "They're just going to laugh at me."

"Come on, baby," he said, pulling her by the hand. "You'll be fine."

Srđa and Jovanka, of course, had shown up and had her back, literally. They were lined up behind her chair. Jovanka's arms were crossed in front of her.

It was an incredibly long half-hour before they finally called her into the office.

A black man in his early sixties was her interviewer. In her imagination, she'd pictured herself having to talk to someone white and her first response to him was a sense of relief, that this would be someone sympathetic. She'd also imagined Reggie would be with her, but he was not allowed in.

Of course, the interviewer was unable to exclude Jovanka and Srđa so at least she had them in there with her.

"Okay Miss," he began. "I've read your complaint and I have some questions."

"Okay."

"Now you're saying that you've met with hostile workplaces because you were being exposed to extreme racist comments throughout the day, to which you could not respond compliantly, and as a result, you would be ostracized."

"Yes. Everywhere I go."

"And then when it became known to them that your boyfriend is black, you would systematically find yourself fired."

"Yes, within a few weeks."

"I've looked at the reports from the employers you list and they are fairly unanimous in claiming poor work performance."

"That's what they say, but they'd been content enough with my performance until this would come up. I mean, okay, I'm intelligent with great manual dexterity. I score really well on their screening tests, but I'm also a bit too intelligent to be doing such boring work, but I've got to put up with that while I'm in school. After a while, I get bored and I become just average in my work. But nobody's ever fired me over that. That's just the excuse they use."

"Well, if we take this before a judge, there's going to be all that documentation of slow work product," he said. "And then there's the other, obvious issue, that this is, frankly, Miss, a big city. Unless you were blatantly flaunting your relationship, there's no reason all these employers would have even known about it."

Jovanka was highly annoyed. "We've lived on these shores for 61 years, how much longer are you expecting us to live in hiding?" she asked.

"I'm supposed to hide him?" Leslie asked. "I'm supposed to hide who I am? Like that's what's right? Every other woman in the office can have a picture up of her husband or boyfriend, except me? That's what's supposed to be accommodated? I thought these laws were supposed to be making things normal. It's normal for me to have to hide who I love and who I am?"

He seemed to be getting annoyed. "And then there's the issue that each time you change jobs, you're experiencing an increase in pay, without any period of unemployment. You can't demonstrate any financial loss as a result of your firings. You seem to have boxed yourself into a corner with this, you're now making more money than your work performance justifies."

"She's boxed herself in?" asked Srđa. "They've boxed her in!"

"Frankly, Miss," he said, laughing. "This is looking like a game you're playing for attention. The courts are swamped with people with real problems, who are losing jobs they need to survive because they are trapped in a condition which they cannot escape, in a world that remains hostile to their survival. Not what appears to be some middle-class white girl on a lark. I'm sorry the world doesn't like your relationship, but it's what you've chosen, and you can escape any time you want."

"I'm alone in a very racist world that finds me contemptible," she said, "making close to minimum wage, putting myself through school for three years without any financial backing now that I've been disowned by my working-class parents," Leslie said. "Why are you seeing me as affluent? What's your bias?"

"I'm sorry, Miss. I appreciate that you're in love and I hope you two will be very happy together. I understand, the way the world is, that your relationship has a lot going against it, but at this time I don't think you have any kind of case this agency can assist you with."

She left the office as quickly as she could with a straight face. Reggie looked at her expectantly and she shook her head. The minute the door closed on the elevator and they were alone, she burst into tears.

"I'll just keep on hiding," she said as bitterly as she'd ever expressed herself. "I'll just keep on hiding like they're right. I should be ashamed. Shamed. Nasty."

As they made their way to the car she said to him, "Don't ever expect me to do anything like that again, okay?"

"Okay," he said and opened the car door for her.

* * *

Chapter 4
Still Losing

The Cute Girl Cousins

All that Office of Economic Opportunity mess was over a job she was happy to lose, but the next job loss had been harder to take. It wasn't just typing. She took care of clerical work, but she was also a film editing assistant. It was a cutting house for several ad agencies, high up in the John Hancock building with an impressive view of the lake and Michigan Avenue.

It was a strange crew. They were slam out of Cicero, at the very heart of the Bigot Belt. Cicero had become a white island amid the sprawling southside ghetto. It had persisted as white by way of a reputation of vigilantism. The word out in the street was that, if a black man were to drive through Cicero after dark, he might not ever be heard from again. Neo-Nazism had taken hold there with a vengeance. Leslie's parents had grown up in the neighboring community of Marquette Park.

Needless to say, the Cicero-based cutting house was very odd company in the largely Jewish advertising world of Chicago. Her boss, Rick, was a very nice-looking man, with a kind of Elvis look to him. This was a job that could go somewhere, so as skeptical as she was of how far she could trust them, she minded her manners and gave it a shot.

Leslie had been there about three months, things were okay, though she was having trouble getting any real editing work to do. The guy who was supposed to be training her seemed to be keeping those roles to himself, keeping himself indispensable and her rather useless.

Then one lazy Sunday morning at home, Reggie's cousin, Natalie, showed up. Natalie, though shorter, had Reggie's good looks and was more outgoing. She breezed into the kitchen, found some bacon in the fridge and fried it up. Leslie sat and ate bacon with scrambled eggs and drank too much strong, rich coffee with Natalie.

"How many jobs have you lost?" she asked Leslie.

"Oh shit, I don't know. How many is it now? she asked Reggie.

"Eight, I think," he said. He'd just woke up, was still in the sweats he slept in. He was scratching at a wild bed head, pouring himself coffee.

"In how long?"

"Three years," she said.

"Eight jobs in three years, over him?" she asked. "Damn, boy, you sure are one hell of a burden."

He grabbed his crotch, "I'll give her a burden."

"Ain't no big thing," Leslie said.

"That's not what you said last night," he countered, sitting down at the table with his coffee cup.

She laughed merrily. "I was talking about getting fired."

"I'll fire you up, now," he said.

"How do you put up with this boy?" said Natalie.

"I love the 'naughty boy' routine," Leslie said. "It's perfectly appropriate. Sex is funny. Seriously, there ya' are trying your best to be your sexiest, and then you knock over the lamp."

Natalie laughed heartily. Leslie leaned in closer.

"Did you know that the most popular Voodoo God of Haiti is Gede, who's the god of death, sex and," she said, starting to laugh, "and practical jokes! Seriously, you gotta love a mind that could come up with a combination like that." She cracked up.

Even Reggie was laughing at that point. Leslie went on. "Everyone loves going to the services when Gede shows up 'cause they know it's going to be a really good comedy act. Gede 'possesses' someone who becomes a stand-up comedian and tells everybody's business in the most embarrassing way possible, but everybody's going to be laughing *with* you, so it's cathartic.

"Which would be like living in the lap of mental health luxury," she went on, "but this is labeled an 'inferior' religion."

"Are you smoking weed?" Natalie asked.

"No, I just got up."

"That's Leslie," Reggie said. "She wakes up like that, you ain't even got your eyes open yet and she'll be hitting you with this intense shit, but it's kind of cool because all of a sudden you're tripping out into Haiti where people are very healthy mentally because they've got this really sophisticated religion that laughs at sex. I mean seriously, you would have to go to Vegas to beat that show. I'm telling you, Natalie," Reggie said. "I think I'm going to check into this religion next."

Both the girls broke up laughing. Leslie touched his arm and swung in her chair to be facing him. "That would be really good for you," she said. "I really hope you do that. I mean, seriously, Gede would have a field day with you and next thing you know you'll be on a whole new level."

He laughed with her.

"Seriously, Reg," Leslie said. "That is the perfect religion for you. Forget about the whole Judeo/Islamic/Christian thing and just go to what suits your nature. Hell, I'd even go there with ya.'"

"You would, huh?"

"Hell yeah," she said. "What do you think I keep you around for? So, you can take me where I wanna' go!"

Natalie poured some more coffee. "You need to start filing some lawsuits about all those firings, girl."

"I tried that."

"What happened?"

"Shit happened. I just got my feelings hurt. There is no point pursuing this. Nobody is going to care. Believe me, nobody is going to care."

"I care," said Natalie.

"Well, that's just cuz you love me, cuz," said Leslie.

"Oh, that is so true," replied Natalie. "Why don't you come with me?"

"Where?"

"Marquette Park," Natalie said. "The Neo-Nazi March that was supposed to be in Skokie is in Marquette Park this afternoon. There's a counter-demonstration. Come on with me. It'll be fun. You coming, Reg?"

"Hell no," he said. "I wouldn't go anywhere near those crazy fools. Besides I gotta study. If you go to that crazy shit," he said as he shuffled down the hall with his coffee, "don't be calling me to come rescue you from some damn Nazis. I told you to stay away from those fools."

As they were leaving he called out to Leslie from the bedroom, "You better not be making any political statements while you're out there."

Leslie pitched a fit of laughter. Then, finally, when she'd straightened herself up from leaning against the wall and could talk again, "You got it, baby," she called out as she pulled the door shut. "You and only you."

The girls drove off. "All this flak I'm taking is not really over him, you know," Leslie said. "It's about who I am. I mean, being with him just makes that manifest. What's the point of living if you can't exist in the light of day?"

They were stopped at a stop light. Natalie looked over at her long and hard. "What do you mean? she asked, "about who you are?"

That's what Leslie liked about Natalie. When she asked a question like that, she really was looking to understand, not just looking for an excuse to unload her own presumptions like everybody else in the world was doing.

"Remember what I told you about King Martin?"

Natalie smiled. "Your imaginary friend?"

"Yeah. The guy practically raised me. If it wasn't for him I wouldn't have gotten any approval at all from my dad. I don't know why, but my dad's racism was hooked into this enormous hot button I had to keep pushing if I was going to have any kind of life at all. And along the way, I just came up not thinking they way white people think."

"You aren't," Natalie said.

"What do you mean?"

"I knew you before," Natalie said.

"No shit? Like in another life?" She took in a big gulp of air, that rushed to her head as if it were an intoxicant.

"No shit. Remember when I met you, at Celeste's graduation party and everybody was teasing me that I looked like I saw a ghost."

"Yeah?"

"It wasn't a ghost I saw. It was you. I knew you before."

"When? Where?"

"I don't know, I'm trying to remember. We knew each other before. You're not really white."

Leslie felt goosebumps at the suggestion of another dimension opening up. "I saw something once. About a mass grave I was sinking into."

"I saw fire," Natalie said.

Srđa and Jovanka always showed up for goosebumps. They were in the back seat. "What is she talking about?" asked Jovanka, wrapping her arms around Natalie from behind and touching Natalie's head with her own, as if listening.

"I don't know," said Srđa. We'll have to find out more about this girl."

"You think she's one of ours?" asked Jovanka.

"Could be."

"I don't think I could have been black," said Leslie to Natalie.

"Why not?"

"I like black people too much. Black people never like black people as much as I do."

Natalie cracked up.

"Especially Aunt Henrietta," Leslie added.

Natalie nodded her head enthusiastically and laughed. "Yeah, she can get pretty rough."

"Did you hear what she said, that black women on welfare should be sterilized? That shocked me and I'm from the Bigot Belt. And she doesn't like me at all. But she's gotten so comfortable with me being around she'll talk about the dirty white people right in front of me, and then she'll never touch my cooking, and if I pass through her kitchen she'll disinfect it.

"And she thinks I'm too loud. Everywhere we go she's always behind me going, "Shhhhh, shhhhh. Some trophy you are."

Natalie laughed. "I'm sorry," she said.

"Oh, it's all right. At least I know she won't be stuffing my head and putting it on the wall."

"What?"

"You know, a trophy."

Natalie groaned. Then she shuddered. "Don't even say that," she said.

"What?"

"Something terrible, there's something terrible that happened to you."

"It's not terrible," Leslie said, sobered. "And it didn't happen to me. I've had it easy. I just get fired and get to take a few days off work. And people looking at me like I'm a slut. In the scale of the universe, it's small potatoes."

"Not to me," said Natalie.

"Thank you."

Natalie reached for Leslie's hand. Leslie started to cry. "I hate it," she said. "They're making me crazy."

"I know, baby," Natalie said.

"So, tell me what you see, what you feel?" Leslie asked, changing the subject back to a previous lifetime she was more in the mood to deal with.

"We were like family, and there was danger. Violence, and you were protecting me. And there are always these spirits around you."

"Really, what kind?"

"They're very sweet. They really love you."

"What do they look like?"

"One of them looks like you, the other looks very kind and wise. They're in the backseat right now."

Leslie turned around to look at the back of the car and let out a loud whoop of laughter. "Stop it, girl," she said, slapping Natalie's hand, "you're making me crazy!"

Natalie laughed as she turned into a parking space. "Girl, you ain't seen nothing yet."

* * *

The Love Feast

Leslie and Natalie got to the rally and had an absolute blast. The counter-demonstrators never really confronted the Neo-Nazis because the cops kept everyone separated. It just turned into a big love feast among all the counter-demonstrators. All day long Natalie was introducing Leslie to everyone as her cousin – and she knew everyone. All the freaks and the militants thought it was really groovy what a cute pair the two cousins were. They were the belles of the ball, who'd set the table of the love feast. Leslie had one of those rare experiences in her life when she felt like she'd just stepped into a normal world. Everything just felt normal. Even her family was normal.

But that evening was purely paranormal. The two girls went over to Natalie's apartment. It was totally North African. Moroccan motif. Hookas and oriental rugs. A hoot. She'd suspended an old parachute from the ceiling over her bed like a harem-style canopy. The girls lounged on the waterbed's maroon satin sheets, eating fresh, sweet cherries. In place of a headboard was an ornate Oriental rug.

"So, are they here?" asked Leslie after squirting some canned whipped cream into her mouth to go with the cherries, her body slipping into a state of extraordinary relaxation.

"Who?"

"My spooks," Leslie said, not knowing the proper term was 'Guardians.'

"No, not now. It's just us," Natalie said, lying on her back projecting a kaleidoscope of colors from an odd little flashlight onto the canopy overhead. She sat up and reached for the hooka. "This is some really good hash. Have some, you're gonna need it." She passed it to Leslie who took a few hits. Natalie laughed. "Your mouth is all stained from the cherries."

Leslie blew her a kiss. "Why am I gonna' need it?"

"You're not ready for me."

"That's what you think."

"That's what I know."

"Yeah, yeah, yeah," teased Leslie. "Go ahead, lay it on me. I'm as ready as I'll ever be."

Leslie propped herself on a pillow so she could observe Natalie staring at the ceiling, who then reached for some cherries. Natalie took a hit of the whipped cream. She overdid it with that squirt and messed up her face. She laughed at herself and licked after it.

Leslie laughed at the faces Natalie was making in doing so. 'You got quite a tongue there, girl," she laughed.

Natalie grew quiet. "We're hiding in a closet. Our home has been invaded. They keep shouting, 'Where are those cockroaches?' We can hear everything getting smashed."

Natalie gasped suddenly and bolted upright, her eyes wide open in terror. "They're opening the closet door!"

Then she calmed down. "She's here now," said Natalie.

"Who?"

"Your spook. She's holding my hand." Natalie's eyes were tearing up. "Oh Lez! I can't explain it."

"What?" Leslie's heart leaped in her chest.

"The energy in her touch!" Natalie began panting and crying. Leslie reached out to her.

"It's okay," said Natalie. "Just beautiful. *So* beautiful. That gold aura shimmering around her face, like light made out of electric gold." She looked at Leslie, tears glistening in her luminous eyes. "You are *so* blessed!"

Leslie began whispering rapidly, "That's why I pay all these dues I don't owe." Then she pleaded to Natalie. "A fortune." She felt an urgency. "Ask her something, anything, just ask her something. Talk to her."

Natalie focused her eyes, then shut them. "I'm sorry," she said. "She's talking, but I can't understand her. I'm sorry, I can't understand what she's saying."

* * *

When Leslie got home she walked a few steps up the stairs to the second floor, then stopped herself and laughed. She wondered if she was going brain-damaged. She lived on the first floor. This was the third time she'd done that.

Jovanka was sitting at the top of the stairs, amused at Leslie's prescient anticipation of the future tenant. "Not yet, my girl," she said.

Once inside her apartment, she found Reggie was on the bed, working equations, books sprawled all over it with abandon. She loved the energy that emanated off of his powers of concentration. He may have played the wastrel when she'd first met him, but what emerged out of that fling, his last as a boy, was an enormously disciplined young man. Pride, she thought. She'd wanted to feel that way about him and as it turned out, he was making it so easy.

She nuzzled him and whispered in his ear, "You's the man."

"Huh? he said, scratching his ear. "Hey baby," he mumbled absently.

She went into the kitchen looking for a snack. There were some soft, soggy vanilla wafers in the pantry. She turned the oven to 'warm' and put the wafers in to crisp them back up. She made them both some chamomile tea with honey and took it all into the bedroom.

He sipped his. "Not sweet," he said.

"Oh, wrong cup," she said and switched them.

Finally, he was done working. He gathered up all the books and set them on the floor. "There she is," he said, smiling and pulled her to him. "My baby knows I like it sweet."

She kissed him back. "Oh, I know what you like now."

"Something happened," he said.

"What?"

"DeFillipi called."

"Really, what's he talking about?"

"The assistantship. It's mine."

She bolted upright and flailed her arms. "Woohoo!"

"Paid. Minimum wage, but paid."

She nestled next to him and kissed his cheek.

"So, how'd things go with the Nazis?"

"Amazing. I had an absolutely spectacular day."

"Make any political statements?"

She laughed merrily. "Not yet."

"Oh really?" he said with interest.

"Seriously," she said. "Natalie tripped me out, totally. She can see my guardian angels."

"That girl's crazy."

"I like her crazy."

"It's just her wild imagination."

"Well, if it's just imagination, it's world-class imagination. As far as I'm concerned, there's no such thing as 'just' imagination." She was about to say, 'She gives me some superb attention,' but held back.

"She says something terrible happened to me in another life, and I'm not really white."

"Oh, you're white all right," he said playfully, pulling her leg across his.

"You think so?"

"I know so." He closed his eyes, savoring the day's good news. "We're on our way, baby," he said. "It's all coming together."

* * *

For all the fun Leslie had going to the Neo-Nazi counter-demonstration, there were repercussions. About a week after the march Cicero's neighborhood newspaper published an article covering the event, and what should there be but a picture of Leslie and Natalie, the cute little girl cousin hostesses of the counter-culture love feast, arm-in-arm.

Leslie's boss, Rick, propped the page up against the backsplash in the coffee room. Leslie came in, while he was there, with Daniel, the other editing assistant, and was taken aback by the photo. "Oh shit," she said, picking up the paper and turning towards the two of them, hoping everybody was just going to laugh it off.

"You know," Rick said, his eyes cold, raising his head up and breathing out sharply. "It's people like you who give those idiots credibility. If everybody would just ignore them, they'd disappear."

"Okay," she said, her shoulders knotting up.

135

A little later she went out to the bathroom. When she opened the door coming back into the office a deafening sound assaulted her. An enormous crowd was shouting at her. Rick's Nazi tape.

"Zeig Heil! Zeig Heil!"

Then the sound abruptly vanished. She could hear Rick and the senior assistant tittering in Rick's office.

She went about her work, pissed as hell. They thought that was funny, huh? She took her lunch break. She came back and opened the door. Immediately the huge crowd of Nazis assaulted her again, this time even louder.

It was so loud even Jovanka and Srđa heard and showed up. Jovanka was crawling the walls, literally.

Leslie was livid. What the hell was wrong with these jerks that they thought that was funny? And what were they going to do to her next? Was she supposed to trust them? Yeah right, Mr. Liberal-Can't-Stand-the-Neo-Nazis.

Out of curiosity, she left the office for another bathroom break. She stood outside the office for a second, just to make sure the tape wasn't playing again. The sound of her opening the door, which triggered the door chime, also triggered Mr.-Can't-Stand-Nazis to turn his sound pollution tape back on.

She'd had enough. She called Reggie.

"Come here and get me," she whispered. "I'm about to be abducted by Neo-Nazis."

"What?"

"Please, come get me. Please. I'm quitting this time. Come here and defend me. Please. I need you to defend me. Wear the panther suit and come get me."

She waited until Reggie would have been due to arrive and headed out for another bathroom break. Then she waited in the hall for him.

At the door, she stopped and motioned to Reggie. "Watch what happens when I open the door."

Immediately the tape of the *Adoration of Hitler Magnum Opus* hit them like a huge wall of sound falling on them like bricks. But before Rick could reach the switch to cut it off, Leslie had marched into his office with Reggie in tow.

Reggie was dressed in black, wearing his black beret and a pair of sunglasses, the outfit he often wore for Leslie's job discrimination stings. He stood facing Rick down with his arms crossed and his head cocked doing his impression of a Black Panther. He was absolutely stunning in that role, Leslie thought. It always made her so proud.

136

Even Jovanka, who ordinarily thought Reggie fell short of her expectations, put her hand on his shoulder.

"Rick," Leslie said. "This is my fiancé, Reggie. That girl you saw in the picture is his cousin, my soon-to-be cousin-in-law. Reggie, this is my boss, Rick."

Rick stood up with a broad grin and offered his hand. "Nice to meet you, sir," he said.

"What's with the Nazi tape, man?" Reggie asked, keeping his arms folded.

If Rick was intimidated, he covered it with a laugh. "Just horsing around," he said.

"Oh," he said. "You think that's funny?"

"I'm sorry, Leslie," Rick said, almost hiding a sheepish expression. "I didn't realize you had family ties in this regard. I, personally, hate those Neo-Nazi fools, and they really are incompetent losers. I know that for a fact, and if everybody just ignored them, they'd still just be in their basement talking trash. I'm sorry I took that frustration out on you, Leslie," he said, and then to Reggie, "your girl here is very talented," he said. "I never met anybody before who typed 90 wpm."

"So, what do you want to do, Lez, you want to dump this tip or give this dude another chance?"

"We can talk about it over the weekend," she said.

"Fair enough," said Rick and shook her hand. "I'm serious, I wasn't thinking about how that might make you feel."

Jovanka blanched and lunged at Rick. "How do you think we felt when they hauled us off to a death camp!" Srđa pulled her off. Rick swatted at his neck as if bitten by a horsefly.

Leslie looked at him hard, as Reggie pulled her by the hand out of the room. Once she was out of the room, she rushed with pleasure that Reggie had come to 'rescue' her. She smiled and babbled to him girlishly, "Who me? I was waiting for the fascists to come haul me off to a death camp. I'm sure they would've taken me right off the bat, in the first batch, and nobody would've even noticed."

She decided to go back in on Monday. She knew she was kidding herself and everyone else saying that she waited to be fired just to cover her ass in case she needed to claim unemployment. The real reason she stayed till she was fired was that she wanted them to prove to her face what they really were. If no one else noticed, at least she would know.

That titillated disgust she could feel radiating off them as they imagined her getting it on with a black man was real. She wasn't imagining it, and she wasn't going to own it. She wasn't going to leave it slamming *her* below-the-belt. They were going to show their ass. They were going to own it, and she was going to leave it on them, not on her.

Two weeks later Vi, the office manager, showed up and went into a long song and dance about how much Rick liked her, but business had slowed down so bad that they were just going to have to cut back. But he'd give her references and help her get settled someplace else.

He never did.

* * *

Driving with Natalie

Natalie had her own car – she had her own apartment, all by herself, and her very own car. Of all Leslie's friends, Natalie was the most accomplished even if she was only a few years older. For all her paranormal talents, her livelihood was purely pedestrian – an accountant.

"I'm surprised you can stand it," Leslie commented. They were on Lake Shore Drive, heading north, the lake glistening to the right. "I mean, isn't it horribly boring?"

"No, not once I get into it. I'm totally schizoid. When I'm crazy, I'm crazy. When I'm rational, I'm rational. I split the two up totally. I mean, I realized early on that I was a totally nonconformist kind of person and I had to be able to take care of myself completely independent. I was not going to be accepted, so I had to depend on no one. I had to have my own."

"So where are we going?"

"I have no idea," Natalie said as she shifted her little Mazda into fifth. "Just look for something."

"Like what?"

"Something that makes you curious."

"I have no idea." Leslie looked out the window and sang, "God bless the child that's got her own."

"That's got her own," Natalie added, finishing the refrain.

"No fair," Leslie said. "You sing better."

"I like to hear you sing," Natalie said. "Singing's not for sounding good, it's for the expression. And yours is always authentic."

"I like that. Thank you." Being with Natalie was always the best.

They drove on for a while, looking for something that would make them curious.

"Oh my god!" said Natalie. "There it is!" They'd turned a corner, and there it was. The Baha'i Temple, most of its height not yet visible to them.

"No shit, you didn't know you were coming here?"

"No idea."

138

They parked on the street and approached it. Then they took several short, flower-bedecked flights of stairs upwards, trying not to stumble with their heads craned to take in the vaulted dome that glistened like white lace cuddling up into the baby blue blanket of sky.

Natalie gasped. "Oh my god, the spirit of this place!"

They climbed more stairs. Natalie opened the door. Leslie wasn't sure if they were supposed to enter but Natalie pulled her by the hand inside.

Natalie stood reading a phrase chiseled into the ceiling, "So powerful is unity's light that it can illumine the whole earth." They sat down in a row of chairs in the center of the sanctuary. The girls craned their heads to peer into the dome over their heads. Then Natalie got on her knees, burying her head in her hands in a posture of prayer.

Kneeling was new to Leslie. Deloris had insisted her kids be raised Protestant. Archie, who had no use for the Catholic church he was raised in, was the ever-willing chauffeur. That upbringing had never included kneeling, but Leslie felt emboldened being with Natalie, so for the first time in her life, she got down on her knees to pray.

She closed her eyes and tried to think of a prayer but could not think of anything except her mom. That led to confusion since she couldn't ask for forgiveness without admitting fault, an unjust notion she refused to capitulate to. Then she remembered something about a goal in Buddhism or was it Hinduism – the pursuit of emptiness – so she just went with that sentiment.

"It's okay to pray for your mom," Natalie said. "Send her your love."

Leslie started to cry. Natalie put her arm around her shoulder. Leslie turned onto Natalie's shoulder and sobbed. She was startled that her tears flowed so readily. She knew it was Natalie enabling her. Reading her mind. That was becoming commonplace. 'What would I do without these people the world wants me to do without?" she thought, and she cried some more.

When they got back to the car Leslie felt buoyant, like a happy child.

"I'm starving," she said.

"And I shall feed you, my dear, *Lettuce Entertain You* is just up the street."

"Cool gruel," Leslie chirped.

"Oh, it will be more than just gruel."

"You're so good to me, cuz. What would I do without you?"

* * *

Leslie had to do without Natalie the next week when Natalie got swamped with work. Leslie had had a rotten day and needed to talk to her but couldn't, so she went out for a bike ride by herself on the royal blue racer she'd been maintaining since she was twelve. She never liked riding on the surface streets, but it was only a mile to Lincoln Park and the reverie could begin. She loved Chicago. The glorious path along the lake's edge broadened her spirits as soon as she hit it.

She parked her bike next to a vacant swing set and lounged on a swing, swaying back and forth the way she'd always loved doing as a child. She remembered the day she met King Martin. She still remembered that, the day she found out how to please her dad. That crazy man – who now refused to see her – who would not allow her under his roof because she'd followed the path he'd set her on. If this world thought she was crazy for liking black people and being on their wavelenth, it was a sentiment her dad had very clearly cultivated in her. It never failed that if she wanted his approval – however left-handed approval from him might be – all she had to do was rip his racism to shreds.

She remembered that time in her senior year of high school, he came home from work in a furious funk. Deloris had left her sewing on the kitchen table. It was in Archie's way, so he flung it across the room.

"What in the world!" she admonished indignantly, picking up the fabric and several straight pins that had come loose.

"You got a whole house to leave your stupid junk, you don't have to leave it in my way!" he countered, his voice oozing disgusted contempt. "Stupid bullshit!"

Leslie was waiting for her turn. It didn't matter what, he'd find something to jump on her for. Deloris was still clucking her tongue as she put Archie's plate and the dish she'd made for dinner on the table. She set everything down noisily, in protest.

Oh good. Archie's hot-weather favorite. Shultz. Leslie called it Shitz. It was disgusting. Cold, gelled soup. Homemade, meat-flavored Jello with lots of nasty chicken bits in it, the consistency of thick phlegm. Skin, bones, fat, gross tidbits Archie would soon be literally sucking up like a glutton.

Deloris knew Leslie wouldn't touch it, so she gave her daughter a plate with a peanut butter and jelly sandwich.

Archie had his ammunition. "What's the matter, you still some stupid little kid who can't eat what's on the stupid table?"

"I was never a stupid little kid," Leslie replied, her brow lowered, hunkered down for the ensuing warfare as he spewed his toxic contempt at her.

"Huh? Your mother slaves over a hot stove to make some real food and you gotta snub your stupid nose at it? Wait till the day when you're really hungry and you'll wish you had some decent food. Stupid."

He went on like that while Leslie launched into her peanut butter and jelly. The peanut butter was sticking to the roof of her mouth, so she refrained from arguing for a spell.

Then the shift came, and she knew her reprieve was on the way.

"Goddamn niggers!" he cursed, shoveling a large spoonful of the congealed cold soup into his mouth. "Can't even keep their stupid jalopies running, stopped in the middle of the expressway. Traffic backed up for miles. Sat there all goddamn afternoon."

He paused in his tirade while he noisily sucked the spinal cord out of a chicken neck bone. "Stupid niggers can't do nothing right!" he proclaimed, his mouth glistening with grease and his eyes sparkling with rage.

Since the 'stupid niggers' at their house never seemed to be able to do anything right either, in his eyes, it was obviously a topic of relevance. He was, as usual, bringing the controversy to his daughter so that she could bring peace and order back to his domain.

"Oh yeah," she said blithely, with the snotty tone he preferred to all others, "like that stupid guy, Solomon Northup, who wrote all about the time he got kidnapped into slavery."

Leslie heard Deloris exhale and settle in for the evening's entertainment. "He spends the evening playing the violin for everybody and feeding them a delicious fish dinner out of the fish trap he's invented. He *had* to do that because, after working an eighteen-hour day in the hot sun, all they were being fed was worm-infested bacon." Her mom involuntarily scowled in disgust.

"Then he gets up the next morning and repairs stuff nobody else knows how to fix. That pisses off the crazy white guy overseer who hates him for being such a know-it-all and goes after him with a hatchet, so Solomon beats the crap out of him and runs off. The guy gets some buddies to go after Solomon with dogs. But he outruns the dogs and disappears into the swamp since nobody knows he can swim, and the dogs lose his scent once he's in the water. He spends the rest of the day swimming through the swamp *alongside a bunch of alligators.*"

Then she started laughing merrily. She could see she had Archie in the palm of her hand, who was trying to hide his interest. "What kind of Triathlon is that? The 'Louisiana Down-the-River Triathlon?'" Then she looked at Archie in dead earnest, as if she pitied Solomon. "How much more could a man like that have accomplished if only he'd been white?"

She let out another whoop of laughter. "Not much!" She had both parents in abeyance at that point. She could see the tiny, involuntary upturns in the corners of their mouths. "How could he?" She laughed some more. "I mean, how many talents can one person have? A musician, an engineer, an athlete, an author who instigates a war of liberation . . ."

She looked at the placated Archie whose mood had now shifted, soothed by the comfort food and the comfort tale that had vindicated all the 'poor negroes,' including the ones at *their* house. He had encircled the bottom of his bowl with a necklace of petite neck bones, clean and white as pearls.

He was quiet as a lamb the rest of the evening, snoring through the evening news in his recliner – a lamb that snored, anyway. Nothing soothed his soul better than one of Leslie's book reports. He couldn't possibly have encouraged her more to do them.

Chuckling at the memory, she backed herself up for a nice long glide on the swing. Her life felt pretty together, considering she was estranged from her family and getting sniped at constantly by racists anytime she appeared in public committing that outrageous act — walking with her boyfriend. All the racist persecutions from the white people just to be stereotyped by black militants who were in fact, ideologically, the people she was the most like — seeing as how Archie had raised her to be a 'black militant' herself — though they willfully insisted on seeing her as the opposite. What a crazy-ass life.

But she had found a good niche for herself. Her best buddy was Natalie which meant she had a lioness in her corner who seemed always to be mistaking Leslie for her cub. Leslie wished she could return the favor but the best she had come up with was to crochet Natalie a tam in her favorite color yarn.

Reggie got weird about it. Like he was jealous. So, she crocheted him one in black, to go with his panther suit. Who could know when another black beret might come in handy in such a wardrobe?

But life had settled into a fairly satisfying routine. School half the day, work half the day, evenings at home with Reg, seeing Natalie at some point on the weekend and talking most days on the phone.

She knew she loved Reg more than he loved her, was resigned to it. She kicked at the pebbles in the groove under the swing and remembered Groucho Marx's line about not wanting to be in a club that would have him as a member. Is that what her love life would always be like? She could only love someone who didn't really love her? How screwed up. Why? Why was she stuck with that bullshit? She wasn't doing any better than grandma, who was such a chump for grandpa – still waiting on him hand and foot while he treated her like a dog.

Earlier that day, at school, she'd been waiting in the hallway for a class to start, next to a room with an opened door. She peeked inside. A small group of radical sisters were rehearsing for a program about the effects of generational oppression on their present-day life.

All these patterns of dysfunction were so familiar. Like not expecting to be loved due to lack of self-esteem. Leslie chuckled as she eavesdropped. The first thing she did when she could choose her own life, her own friends, was to surround herself with people who could pin the source of their all too familiar dysfunctions on something tangible like racism. Those same people who filled the libraries with stories Archie loved to hear, to placate his own ravaged, and ravaging self-esteem.

She shifted to better see them. One of the sisters glanced up at her. Then she glared at her. She walked over to the door and shut it in Leslie's face. Her face reddened as if she'd been slapped.

Leslie went into the bathroom, locked herself in one of the stalls and cried. Then she was late for class and the teacher embarrassed her over it.

When she got home, Reggie fussed her out for forgetting to pay the light bill. The lights were off. He went into his favorite rant about being trapped in a crab bucket full of shiftless negroes. He and Archie should do a duet, she thought. She tried to call Natalie, but it kept ringing. She remembered it was tax season.

With no one to talk to, Leslie grabbed her bike and went for a ride.

She didn't like these new swing seats made from canvas. It was pinching her ass. She sighed.

It made no difference that she'd spent her childhood soaking up all these stories, taking in all these theories on what to do to escape this dilemma of being the designated stupid people who couldn't do anything right and were worthless. And the first thing she does when she comes of age is surround herself with them and attend to them, listen, listen, listen to everything they tell her so they know that, for her, they hang the moon.

But when it came time to acknowledge her and let her into the conversation as someone who also mattered and needed attention back, that's what she got. The door slammed in her face.

She was on her own. That's okay, she thought, she'd steal the answers for the 'designated stupid people' anyway, for herself. When nobody was looking. That's what she was doing there. Regardless of what the

Marilyns of the world might say on the subject, that's what Leslie wanted 'those people' for.

She gave the stones a bigger kick, got back on her bike and rode home.

* * *

The weekend finally came, and Leslie spent the morning with Natalie. Afterwards, Leslie got home and was shocked – the last thing in the world she expected to see.

Reggie was VACUUMING!!!!! She thought she was hallucinating.

"What the hell are you doing?" she laughed.

"I can't stop sneezing," Reg said, angrily. "Damn dust. This dump is covered in dust."

"So, you're interested in taking charge of the vacuuming? Good idea."

No reply to that one. He went back to vacuuming like a maniac for over an hour. He even vacuumed the molding over the doors. Then he showered, got dressed and went out. His Saturday night out. Alone. He didn't take her, didn't say a thing, just left and didn't come home till after two.

"Where the hell have you been?" she said when he came in, following him into the bedroom.

He said nothing.

"You know I'm laying here in the bed wondering if you're dead somewhere. You're some statistic. Maybe Chicago's finest gotcha. You're laying in a morgue somewhere." Her eyes misted up. "Or you've found a new roommate."

He towered over her, grabbed her hair and pulled her head back then gave her a long, deep, aggressive kiss.

Then it was *his* eyes that were watery and impassioned. "Maybe *you've* found a new roommate," he said.

"Me?" she said, incredulously.

"You don't know?"

"Know what?"

"Natalie's a dyke."

Lez was stunned. She sat down. "No," she said. "No," she repeated, rocking herself and crying. "No."

He sat across from her, his arms crossed, watching her cry. "She's just been trying to pull you," he said. "All this bullshit about past lives and ghosts is just that."

"No!" she jumped up angrily. "No! Not everything people say when they want someone is jive. Not always. Is what you said jive? Oh no, that's

144

right. You never said anything, never pursued me. You never made any effort at all, sincere or jive. I just threw myself at you and you figured, 'Why not?'"

"Lez, don't start."

"Nobody wants to know why I'm here or what I need. Just Natalie. She's the only one who cares who I am, and now you're telling me that's just bullshit."

"I care what you want."

"No, you tell *me* what I want."

"What are you talking about?"

"Last week, when I told you about the *seance* Natalie did for me."

"The what?"

"The *seance*, when she told me that long story about my family from a long time ago, the homeless people on a long journey, running away from slavery, remember? And I told you and you smirked and said to me 'Why are you dwelling on this bullshit? You can do anything you want in the world, and you go looking for this bullshit?'

"I've thought about it all week and I've figured it out – what you're talking about. I can do anything I want. In other words, I'm white and the world is my oyster. Why don't I just forget about this shit and move on? Except that doesn't make any sense, because that means, why don't I just leave your ass behind? Why am I bothering with you? You're just dragging me down. Is that what you think? I'm stupid for being with you?"

He looked at her in that dumbfounded way Archie used to look at her. Then he laughed. "*Nollo contendere,*" he said holding up his hands, then grasping both of hers with them. Why was it so easy for him to take charge like that, she wondered? His eyes were near, laughing into hers. "Very stupid," he said, "and I hope you never wise up. Listen, Leslie, you have to be patient with me. Okay? I'm just not deep. I'm not. I'm really just a simple guy. I'm good at math, mechanics. That's it.

"And I don't know what to make of all this talk. It's overwhelming. Okay? We talk about it, and we talk about it, and where the hell does it go? What does it change? Nothing. It doesn't change a damn thing.

"The only thing that's making any sense to me is that if I just keep getting up and going out that door and making an effort maybe all I'll do is make a little money and live a mundane, middle-class life. And if I can make you happy giving you that, it's yours. That's all I have to offer."

She was silent, awed that he had just spoken about the future in that way.

"It isn't just talk to me," she said. "What's there is very beautiful, the most precious thing in the world. I see you in that glow and it's not bullshit. It's the most real thing there is. And if we can see it, then we can see ourselves clearly for the first time. And that *would* change things. That's the *only* thing that will change things."

He smiled and brushed a wisp of her hair away from her eye. "I like listening to you," he said. "I may not have much to offer in kind, but I like listening to you."

She doubted it. He used to like it, but that was changing. She held her peace. She thought of Natalie. Always something, always something was wrong. "Don't take away my friend," she said, her voice breaking with a sob. "There's so little in this world for me, don't take her away."

He circled his arms around her, "You sure she can't pull you?"

"If she was taller than me and had a dick you'd be in big trouble."

He laughed.

"This isn't the first time me and Nat competed over somebody. And last time she won."

"Who was that?"

"Some bitch in high school. Me and Nat have the same tastes. Feminine girls, high-minded, idealistic."

"You're stereotyping me," she teased. "I'm really a tomboy. But it probably had nothing to do with you. That girl just liked girls. I don't. Not that way. There's nothing I can do for Nat," Leslie said. "I just don't have it in me. You're the one I'm addicted to."

"I see the same things in you she does," he said. "I just can't show it."

"That's my fantasy," she said. "I spend the day with her and I feel loved, like somebody appreciates my love. I've got a whole world thinking what I love is nasty shit. I need to think somebody appreciates it. And she makes me feel that way like she sees me, and it means something. All this means something. We're connected. And I want to believe that's what you feel . . ."

"Please believe me," he said. "I see you, I do. The world's hard on you because you're ahead of it. I just hope I can do as much for you as you do for me. It's the women in the family who are good at showing that. Not me. But I see it. Please believe me."

She did for a minute.

Later that evening she lay awake listening to Reggie's breathing, deep asleep. She remembered what he said about her being ahead of the world. He couldn't possibly know who she was to say that. She wasn't ahead at all. She was way, way behind him and would never catch up. Nobody even thought she should. He was getting up every day and engaging something she could only dream about. If he were still impeded by his father's abuse it was not holding him back in terms of achievement. If anything, it just made him more driven.

She, on the other hand, was holding herself back in more ways than she could comprehend. At this rate, she would be nothing except another 'could have been.'

* * *

It was a cold, sleazy day, icy rain was driven pell-mell by strong cold gusts of wind. Reggie was driving. They were coming back from the airport. It was quiet, except for the radio, which kept wandering into static. Leslie shut it off. She was desolate.

They'd just dropped Natalie off. She was on her way to San Francisco. Moving there.

Leslie hadn't let on that she knew about Natalie's orientation. She continued to hang out at Natalie's every chance she got.

It touched her – now that she could see that Natalie's impulse towards her, at least in part, was to woo her – the way she went about it. Reggie was totally wrong. There was nothing jive about Natalie's efforts at all. To see her devoting so much energy and effort into mind-melding with Leslie, trying with all her might to reach into Leslie's existential dilemma and meet that need, touched her beyond measure. How profoundly this woman deserved to be loved, but Leslie could never give her what she needed. She was just in her way. Natalie needed to move on, to find someplace to stand where she'd have a chance to find a true mate.

So, when Natalie took her out to eat and made the announcement about her move to San Francisco Leslie was happy for her.

"There's something I've never told you about that lifetime when we knew each other," Natalie said. "In that lifetime we were gay. But in this lifetime, only one of us is."

"I know," said Leslie. "I know." She was glad they were in public and there was pressure not to break down into tears. "I know I have to let you go," Leslie said. "You deserve to be really, really loved, more than anyone I've ever known. I can only love you as a friend, as a cousin. As such I would take a bullet for you, please know that, but you deserve so much more."

'And what do I deserve?' thought Leslie as they continued driving through the rain back to her life that had grown so much colder.

* * *

More Spooks

The apartment had an exposed brick wall, in vogue at the time, but cold in the winter. Jovanka entered the room, astonished to find a window wide open to the winter squall outside, that cold rain Reggie and Leslie had driven through from O'Hare airport, now blowing into the room. There, sitting in the shadows by the window in a rocking chair that had never been in the room before, sat a decrepit old white man in a 19th-century white seersucker suit.

"Who are you, old man," she challenged, "and what do you want here?"

"Who are you, and what are you doing in my home?" he countered.

"This is not your home, old man. My Goddaughter lives here," she replied.

"It's not *her* home," he said. "That little wench has no rights here at all."

Srđa appeared and placed himself between his wife and the old apparition. "She has as many rights as she wishes," he said.

"What is your claim here?" Jovanka asked. "Why are you here?"

The old man pointed his cane towards the bedroom where the two young people slept. "That boy belongs to me," he said. "And I care about what belongs to me, as much as any man! He is mine and he will strive as any man must, to prevail in this world and keep in line those who belong to him."

"You don't frighten me, old ghost," said Srđa. He moved past the old man and shut the window. "Blow your cold wind somewhere else."

When he turned the old man was standing next to the fireplace and beside him was Kata's Croatian husband, Leslie's grandfather. The two men were smiling smugly.

"Da," said Leslie's grandfather, "that girl will learn her place, and the proper order of things."

* * *

More Logic, Less Feeling

Lez was getting on Reggie's nerves. He had committed himself to becoming a grown-up person in a grown-up world who shouldered the responsibilities and pressures of grown-ups.

The pressure to be a Type A person obsessed with upholding standards was part of the job description of an engineer. It was justifiable. People's lives could be lost if those standards were relaxed. But there was that subtle racism always slipping out from people's unconscious presumptions that he, as a black man, couldn't cut that kind of discipline. What a hoot. They didn't even know what anal compulsive was.

How about the time his father had everyone stand at attention half the night because somebody left the cap off the toothpaste? There was no doubt in that house that there was to be some attention paid to detail.

Not that Leslie left the cap off the toothpaste. There was just an impetuousness to everything she did – a thoughtlessness, a carelessness, she was beyond a space cadet, never really in the present, always lost in some dream world, like a child, talking loudly, blurting out whatever crossed her mind, all emotional. Impulsive.

When was she going to grow up? It was getting on his nerves. And the more he upbraided himself for feeling that way, the more he felt it.

It annoyed Reggie that she was starting to annoy him, annoyed with himself that he would feel that way towards her. He knew she loved him to a fault and was obviously going through hell to be with him. Maybe that was part of what was annoying. It was putting a lot of pressure on him to be 'worth it.' And somehow in that sense that she was seeing something in him worth all that trouble made him question if she was really loving him for who he was, or just some fantasy of what he was. Was he, at the end of the day, *real* to her?

And the scariest part was he was starting to feel what his father must have felt when he was being an ass. If that's all he was going to be, why should he even bother being in a relationship? Is that what reality was like? Did he have to compromise himself in such a gross way in order to achieve success?

It was all too depressing. He found himself preoccupied more and more with logic and equations and trying not to feel anything at all.

That night while Reggie slept his great-great-grandfather stood guard over him, pleased with the state of mind the boy was easing into. He despised those who accused him of not thinking his mulatto children were human. Those boys grew into men just like the rest, and with his help, they'd grow into the kind of men who took charge of those around them and did as a man ought.

And if they had to turn off their soft side, toughen up, so be it. The important thing was to put themselves on the side of what's right – what's strong and superior. All the more difficult for these boys, considering the riff-raff surrounding them. But Reginald would do fine. Just fine.

As long as he ignored that silly wench at his side who insisted on glorifying riff-raff.

* * *

The Goal Post

They sat at the table silently, both studying. Leslie remembered the first time she'd seen him, in The Grille, that brave boy outnumbered a hundred to one, holding court, winning the last word. She was so proud of him. That was the first thing she'd felt in his regard. Her hero. And he was still at it, running circles around them in everything he did at the University. The Illinois Institute of Technology, no less. If he had to be twice as good, he had it made in the shade.

She stretched her stockinged foot out to his bare foot and stroked it. He looked up at her. She smiled. He went back to his book. The toaster popped up and she went to it.

"Want some tuna?" she asked.

"Yeah, sure." She made them both sandwiches and sat back down at the table. He scarfed his down quickly and got back to working his math. Leslie however, was eating at a leisurely pace, reading. He'd never noticed before how noisy she was eating. It was all that breathing through her nose.

"You okay?" he said. "You got a cold or something?"

"Just a little congested, the dry winter air. No big thing."

"Let's see if we can get you a humidifier."

"Thank you for worrying about me," she smiled flirtatiously and touched his foot again.

Not worrying about you, bitch, he thought to himself. Just trying to get rid of that damn irritating whistle while you breathe through your narrow-ass nose.

She kept up with stroking his foot. "What's with all the footsie business?" he said, withdrawing his foot.

"Thought you liked it when I stroked you," she said, still flirting.

"Yeah, baby, I love it, but not when I'm studying," he said. He gathered his books up and went into the bedroom.

She felt it in the air. The Archie Effect. The 'I can't do anything right, excuse me for breathing' ambiance. She took her book into the front room and lay down on the couch, trying to read. She put a Billie Holiday album on the turntable and gave up the futile effort to read. She sat there while a blue funk rolled in on her.

"Leslie!" Reggie shouted.

"What?" she said.

"Will you come here, please?"

She entered the bedroom. He was standing next to the dresser.

"Every goddamn day I get up and there's your panties laying in the corner. Can you please pick up your shit?"

"That's where you keep throwing them!" she said acidly. "All the time, like clockwork. The same exact spot." She put her hands on her hips and cocked her head. "What's there, a goalpost over there? I'll tell you what. I won't let you take them off anymore, and that way, they won't end up in that damn corner."

She had to go a far piece to get the last word on that one, wasn't quite sure if she wanted to go that far, but there it was, out there.

He felt foolish, sat down on the bed and started to laugh.

"What?" she said.

"Come here," he said and pulled her to him. He wrapped his arms around her waist while she stood over him. He ducked his head penitently. "I's sorry," he said. "Please, please, let me keep taking off the panties and throwing them in the corner. I promise, I'll pick them up myself every day and never bother you about it again. Just please, please, don't stop giving up the panties."

She laughed and flopped across the bed. "I think we need a break."

"You're brilliant," he said. "Absolutely brilliant."

* * *

Banging in the Store Room

The department secretary was a known 'ho. Reggie had heard all about it. He'd noticed she dressed oddly. The other secretaries dressed like secretaries, just casual office stuff, slacks with a conservative blouse, that kind of thing. But Doreen was always dressed in a cross between professional career woman and slut. Classy clothes, just a tad provocative. And then she started wearing chocolate-colored lipstick, about the same time she started smiling at him real sweet when they'd pass in the hallway. The shade was popular with the sisters, but on her, a white girl, it was odd, provocative. Of what?

He was hanging with Abe, another of the assistants, smoking some weed at the guy's place when he got the low-down on Doreen.

Abe was a case in contradictions himself. He dressed conservatively, button-down shirts and corduroy slacks, but he had long, curly-ass, Jewish-style curls that somebody had twirled up into dreads. Reggie wondered how long that would last once ol' Abe got offered a fat paycheck. How long would those counter-culture ideals hold out?

"She's kind of a nymph," Abe said, taking another hit and passing it to Reggie. He then strained himself to talk while simultaneously trying to hold in the smoke. "It's like she's a nerd groupie."

Reggie laughed then took a hit. Abe went on, "She'd applied to IIT herself at one point and had gotten in, but she had to drop out when her old man died. She's got a diabetic mother on dialysis, so she's got to do the family thing and work. That old sob story."

"But she's apparently thinking some dude is going to do all the work getting the degree then bestow all the benefits on her. And all she has to do is screw her way around the department and she'll be *In Like Flint*. Crazy crap like that. But I'll tell you, man, if the walls in that storeroom could talk. That is one wild piece of ass."

"Oh yeah?" said Reggie. "When'd *you* hit it?"

Abe smiled a tad guiltily. "Last Christmas break. I put in a *lot* of overtime," he said laughing. "A whole lot more than I'd intended. Damn, if I could only get that kind of overtime every day . . ."

"I hear ya'."

Abe picked up a book on his end table and tossed it to Reggie. *Portnoy's Complaint*. "Funny shit," Abe said, sucking in another toke of weed. "Guy was so horny he'd jack off with a piece of raw liver."

"What?"

"Yeah, he'd steal it out of his mom's fridge, slip off to the john with it, then slip it back in time for dinner."

"Funky," said Reg, "I ain't eating at his house."

"Indeed," Abe leaned back and sighed. "Damn, that bitch was something else. If the walls in that storeroom could only talk. . ."

* * *

Yup. Reg could see that the bitch was definitely coming on to him. He'd needed her help collating a syllabus for the professor he was assisting. Every time she passed something to him, she'd touch his hand. Swap some skin. And the way she smiled, penetrating eye contact. Then she asked him to help her get some paper down in the storeroom. *The* storeroom. He went in, chuckling to himself, and there she was. Her arms outstretched, balancing a large box on the top shelf, her top showing a gap between her skirt, revealing the bare skin of that tight waist contrasting intriguingly with that big ass of hers.

He grabbed the box and she extricated herself, giggling. He brought the box down and set it on the floor. When he rose back up, there she was, turned square on to him, with that look on her face. Hungry, flushed. The door was within his reach. With just a flick of his wrist, he slung it shut and thrust his tongue deep into her mouth. She dropped her jaw deep with a moan and took it, then panted in his ear as he groped her. He reached up under her skirt. No panties, just her. The bitch wasn't even wearing underwear. He sat her on the table and spread her legs.

He was doing her hot and heavy when the door opened. DeFillipi.

He glared at Reggie. "My office," was all he said. Furiously he pulled the door shut. Still frozen, Reggie felt nothing but the cold, air-conditioned air on his bare ass.

Like chastened children, the two awkwardly dressed, not even looking at each other. Reggie made his way to the office of the Department Head, Dr. Michael DeFillipi. His legs felt awkward under him, the way they did at 14 when he shot up a foot in height and they seemed like someone else's, like he had limited control of them.

"You need to know," the middle-aged white man said, feigning composure. His cheeks were red, and his bushy eyebrows drawn together in contempt, "that it was not my idea to admit you to this department or to give you an assistantship. You did not get in here on merit, okay?" He paused for a moment to let that drama sink in.

"That pisses me off," he continued, still struggling to contain his revulsion. A drop of his spit hit Reggie's hand. "And you just need to know that if you pull any more of that disgusting, low-life, trashy ghetto shit on *my* floor, I will have your ass out of here so fast you won't know what happened."

Reggie felt too assaulted by the words to respond. He turned on his heel and tried to march away indignantly, but his bandy legs could not pull it off. He knew he just looked like a fool.

He stopped at the drinking fountain and doused his hand with the cold water, but it still felt filthy with DeFillipi's spit. He got back to the conference room. Doreen had disappeared. Flushed, he finished the stapling. It wasn't until he thought of Abe that a whisper of dignity wafted by him and he seized onto it. Abe! What if Abe had been the one DeFillipi had caught in that storeroom with Doreen? What would they be doing now?

He imagined the two of them in the parking lot, saying goodnight and laughing about *Portnoy's Complaint*.

* * *

Hard Old Rubber

Later that afternoon Leslie picked Reggie up. He got into the passenger side. He grimaced as he looked over at her.

"What's wrong, sweetie?" she asked.

"Nothing, tired," he said, leaned back and shut his eyes. "Headache."

Several cars ahead of them, in the close traffic, someone opened a door nearly into the path of a car. A domino chain of cars slammed on their brakes.

"Shit, Lez!" he shouted. Angry. He was *angry* with *her!*

"It's not *my* fault!' she countered indignantly and pointed at the traffic. She continued driving then glanced over at him sideways. His eyes were open. As she braked at a stop light, she could see him mimicking the action, unconsciously, with his own foot. She could feel him tensing up as she made a turn and had to swerve a bit as a pedestrian stepped off the curb, trying to jaywalk. She sighed. Back seat driving. It made her nervous. She hated how easy it was for people to make her feel unsure of herself.

He'd had two accidents since she'd known him, the usual over-confident, risk-taking young male kind of accidents. She had not yet had *any* accidents, and scarcely any tickets. Statistically speaking, she should be doing ALL the driving. Yet on the rare occasions when she did drive, she had to put up with this bullshit. She sighed.

They got home. He lay down on the couch while she fixed dinner. Once it was simmering, she joined him in the living room. He did look stressed. She put his feet in her lap and massaged them the way he liked. His breathing slowed like he was napping. She left him to sleep.

He woke up and fixed himself a plate.

"What *is* this shit?" he said.

"Oh, it's that new Hamburger Helper shit. I thought I'd try it."

"It's nasty."

"Yeah, pretty much."

"What else ya' got?

"I don't know. Scrounge around. I gotta write that paper."

She heard him leaving the apartment. So, there he was again leaving without even telling her where he was going. Common courtesy? The minute the door shut the room felt unnaturally empty and silent.

She flopped onto the recliner and sat there for a long while, her mind unable to think of anything but the emptiness of the room. It seemed a foreign place she had no claim to. There was nothing she had claim to.

* * *

Reggie went down to the lake, by the chess pavilion. It was dark, a mild autumn night. At the shore, he jettisoned rocks out into the water that skipped furiously along the surface, like the report of a machine gun. He did not want to think. There was nothing *to* think. Just *do*. Blue lights sparkled from across the lake. He shot another stone towards it, skipping many times, obliterating that damn sparkle. Like that titillated sparkle in DeFillipi's eye, as he rebuked Reggie.

The same titillation in that bitch's eyes. Marilyn. That bitch at Shimer. Sitting on his bed, naked, long blonde curls snaking around those big perky titties, while her eyes glistened with contempt.

"You think you're so hot," she jeered prettily. "Knocking everybody over like you're just such a stud." She reached her hand behind his neck and pulled his face closer, licking his lip like a kitten, then whispered in his ear, "but all you are to everybody," she sat back and looked him straight in the eye, her eyes still glittering like blue-green gems, "is a naked ape."

He didn't hit her. In his imagination he did, but he restrained himself. He could do that. He could push anything in the world down and restrain himself. He had that degree of control.

He was walking back to the car when a blinding burst of light suddenly smacked him in the face. He froze in place. Cops. He was all right. He could push anything down. He waited, motionless.

"The park is closed," came a voice from behind the spotlight. "What's your business here?"

"Just had to get away from all that female yapping."

Both cops laughed. "I know how that goes. Is that your car?"

"Yes, it is."

"You have a good night, sir." The spotlight disappeared, and Reggie waited a moment to overcome the blindness it left him with.

He hit the ignition and wondered how many times that night they had flipped that spotlight onto a white man.

* * * *

It was late, and Reggie still hadn't returned. Leslie tried to go to bed but laid there awake, remembering the old days at Shimer when he was racing through other girls like a speed demon. Something was up.

It was after midnight when he finally got in. She got out of bed. He was in the bathroom.

"Damn, you scared me," she said.

"Sorry," he said. "Just went for a long walk."

155

"Did you get something to eat?" she asked.

"Yeah, I had me one of those greasy burgers at that joint up the street."

"Okay," she said. "You coming to bed?"

"Yeah, in a minute."

"My shoulders and neck are all spazzed out. Could you massage them?" she asked.

"Sure, baby, I'll be right there."

But he wasn't. She lay in the bed, her neck aching for his touch. He finally got into bed.

"Will you rub my neck?"

He looked sleepy, drained.

"You all right?" she asked.

"Sure, I'm fine. Turn over," he said.

She turned on her side, her back to him and he started to rub her neck. After a few minutes, she felt the movement of his hand slow, then start back, then slowed, stopped. He was asleep.

She lay awake nearly the whole night. She hated that. The worst torment she could imagine was to be a vampire lying in a crypt for ages, awake, aware, with nothing to do but think, waiting for sleep that never came.

In the morning, the muscles in her shoulders were like hard old rubber. She felt like she had the flu coming on, everything ached, and her head was in a fog. She stayed home from work while Reggie, still cold and distant, went on to the University. Then the idea that had been trying to get into her brain all night hit her. She had cut herself aloose from her family for nothing. She didn't have him. She had nothing.

She lay around all day trying to rest, but she still couldn't sleep. She was watching the clock, waiting for Reg to get home, look after her and dispel that fear that she was nothing to him.

He entered the apartment and dumped his books on the old recliner.

"Hey," she said.

"Hey," he returned.

He went into the kitchen and she heard him banging around. She followed him.

"I'm starving," he said. "Whatcha got?"

"The flu," she said.

He looked up at her and squinted. "You better see a doctor. This is the third time this winter you've had the flu."

"He can't find anything wrong."

"No," he said. "You look fine."

What's that supposed to mean? she thought. "Could you go down to the Jewel and get me some chunky chicken soup? I haven't eaten anything but *Cream of Wheat* all day."

He went out and came back three hours later. By then Leslie had eaten some scrambled eggs and a peanut butter and jelly sandwich. She tried to sleep but, again, her mind couldn't rest, listening for the sound of Reggie's key in the lock. When he came in he had one small bag with a can of soup in it.

She laughed. "Whatcha do, take a slow boat to China?"

"Sarcasm becomes you," he said.

"I know what you like," she replied. As he brushed past her, she grabbed him by the collar. He stopped, and she kissed him. "Thank you," she said, still holding his collar.

"No problem," he said, still looking like he wanted to brush past her.

"You gonna keep me waiting again tonight?" she flirted.

"I might," he said, shifting his interest towards her. He gave her a lingering kiss. "And I might not." She kissed him back. If she did have competition, that competitor was going to have to go some.

"Well," she said, stepping back, still flirtatious. "Let me know when you make up your mind."

She stepped back into the bedroom and got back in bed. When she looked up, he was standing in the doorway. "Whatchu' looking at?" she challenged, playfully.

"Nothing much," he replied.

"Is that right?" she said.

"You still want a massage?" he asked.

"Sure," she said.

"Turn over."

He straddled her and started working her shoulders. "You *are* tight," he said. He grasped the muscle with both hands and squeezed with a rolling motion.

"Oh shit, that is *so* good," she said. "You have no idea. That muscle has been screaming out for you to do that for two days, screaming in my ear, constantly."

He worked the other side similarly, then her neck. Then he worked his thumbs along down her spine. He sat back and worked her thighs. Then he worked her lower back. When he got to her panty line he pulled them back.

"You gonna knead my ass?" she asked.

"Oh, I'm gonna need it," he said.

The panties hit the goal post Leslie had drawn on the wall.

157

The massage and the sex did a lot to help her unwind from the vise of tension that had bound her, but her mind started up again just before she finally fell asleep. She got him to take care of her, but he only did it because there was something in it for him. He hadn't done it just for her, just because he cared about her and she needed his help.

The thread of tension was still hissing at her. That doubt was gnawing at her again. She doubted he really loved her. She figured she was out in the weather. Alone.

She'd cut herself adrift, like flotsam and jetsam. That's all she was. She had jumped ship thinking she was claiming some brave new world where she could finally be with people she understood, who made sense to her, whose narrative was profound, meaningful in a way that resonated with her beyond anything else.

But she'd forgotten about one thing. There was nothing important about her story. She was just another insignificant girl sinking away into a morass of depression that no one would ever care about. She did not matter at all. She couldn't even go home to her parents for a while to recuperate without it being a devastating defeat. Unthinkable. Suicide.

* * *

Jovanka was livid, pacing in the living room while Srđa listened. "Our story isn't important? Do you see what this world is doing to her? To us? We can just be rubbed out like ants in the pantry? Before they can get into the sugar? Vermin to be disposed of? Depressed? Who wouldn't be depressed? How much more depressing can you get?"

"Shhh, my love," said Srđa. He pulled her down onto the couch beside him.

"She's not finding herself," Jovanka continued. "She's losing herself. When is she going to find out that what she's seeing in them is us?"

"As soon as you figure out how to show her," he said. "And I know you will."

It was the very next day that Jovanka pulled out all the stops and spread herself far and wide in Serbian Heaven, putting out the word that a black American Balkan scholar was needed – someone who knew at least a fraction as much about Serbia as Leslie knew about black America and could treat her like an equal, not like someone who had it easy, whose struggles made no sense and had no importance.

* * *

158

People With No Push

Reggie finished the semester. He had the immense satisfaction of having the second highest GPA. He couldn't think of those scores hanging on the wall without thinking of DeFillipi's face, having to read them.

Damn DeFillipi. Fool. Reggie was his father's son. He could stand rigid as a fence pole for a week if he had to, working calculations all the while. You want anal compulsive, tight-ass shit? You don't even know what it is.

He thought about Leslie. He didn't know *what* was going on with her. True, she had to kill time before she was off her family's taxes long enough to qualify for financial aid, so she'd wandered through three years of liberal arts at Circle. She was finally in film school at Columbia, but she'd taken the last semester off. And did nothing.

Halfway through the summer before, she'd given out. She'd lost another stupid job and this time she did claim unemployment and she laid around the house doing nothing. It was driving him straight up the wall. He had no time for people who had no push. She only had two more semesters to go. What was she waiting for?

And why was she taking film anyway? The competition was so stiff. He just didn't see her having that kind of aggressiveness. She was just way too sensitive. She played a very good defense, but playing offense? Forget about it. She didn't even know what it was.

* * *

Down for the First Count

Leslie lay on the couch, listening to the bathroom sink dripping. She couldn't sit in the living room without hearing it unless the bathroom door was shut, but laying on the couch she just listened to it.

The fatigue had never left her, and the spasmed muscles. Her MD could find nothing diagnosable, so had referred her to a shrink. She reluctantly went, terrified he was going to confirm what she feared. She was turning into another Uncle Joe. She was losing it. She'd even dreamed about vines growing up the steps to the vestibule so thick she was trapped inside.

She wanted to stop that damned annoying drip but she couldn't muster the resolve to get up off the couch and shut the door.

Reggie was passing by. "Will you shut the bathroom door?" she asked. "That drip is driving me up the wall."

He stopped, looked at her and sighed. "Did you call the landlord yet and tell him about it?"

"Yes," she lied. A new pattern was surfacing that made it hard for her to pick up the phone and call people, particularly people in authority. She recognized something in it that reminded her of Archie. For all his machismo at home, when he'd confront authority, a cop, a bureaucrat, he'd be all obsequious, hat in hand, humble. What was really funny was that's the same manner he had the few times she'd seen him having to talk to black people. What was that about?

Reggie closed the door. Then he stopped and faced her again, interrupting her reverie.

"You know, Lez," he said. "I'm out all day at school, taking classes and assisting, and I realize you got your little unemployment checks coming in and all that, but I'm paying more on this tip than you are at this point, and I would just appreciate it if I could come home and there's something to eat and it's not a dump in here."

Although it was the umpteenth time he'd given her that speech, she did appreciate that he was speaking calmly this time, so she tried reiterating her position calmly as well. "I have no energy," she said. "I can't get out of bed."

"You could if you had to," he said.

"Glad you're such an expert on the subject. Of course, that expert shrink I'm seeing thinks it might have something to do with being around somebody who's fussing me out every time I turn around. I was starting to feel a lot better last week. Remember? I told you about it. And what happened? What was your response?"

* * *

Reggie's Response

Leslie woke up feeling happy for the first time in weeks. The windows had been open throughout the night, allowing birdsong and a gentle breeze into the room. The ambiance of birdies, Mighty Mouse and her imaginary friend, King Martin – the first time she'd won her father's respect – washed over her. Reg lay on his side, facing her, silhouetted in the soft light. Reclaimed beauty. Phoenix beauty.

A sense of pleasure buttered over her. She often thought of Marilyn, that crazy girl from Shimer, the first to persecute her for doing the forbidden thing in America, for seeing what was really 'huge.' That 'those people' were really beautiful, clever alchemists who could turn mud into gold. If only she could sass off to the Marilyns in the world the way she could to Archie as a kid. If she could just keep the vibe she felt at that moment, maybe she could.

"What?" Reggie said, smiling, his eyes still closed.

She nestled in closer to him, "You should keep your eyes closed all day. You hear me better that way." She whispered in his ear, "My sweet thing." Then singing, "Don't you know you're my everything?"

Feeling strength and energy percolate throughout her body again after so many days without them was pure joy. She got busy putting her house back in order, really got into it and the pretty house she loved to keep reappeared by mid-day. Then she got busy cooking a nice meal. She wanted to surprise Reggie.

That would certainly do it, she chuckled. She had never really acknowledged that it was her job to cook and clean for him. If there was a division of labor between them, there really wasn't anything she could think of that he was doing on a daily basis that would be the *quid pro quo* to her doing all the cooking and cleaning. But, on the other hand, she knew he enjoyed being pampered, he *was* putting in long days, and she wanted him to feel as good as she was feeling.

She made angel hair pasta with pesto, fresh tomatoes, and basil, lemon and strips of marinated, sauteed chicken breast, with a baguette she picked up at the Italian restaurant on the corner. They wouldn't tell her their recipe for the delectable olive oil dip they served with the baguette rather than butter, but she'd experimented and had it very well replicated.

Excited at the prospects of him getting home, she heard his key in the lock. She smiled at him broadly when he entered the kitchen, shuffling through a pile of mail.

"Hey sweetie," she said. She crossed over to him and gave him a kiss.

"Hey," he said absently.

"I felt good today!" she said.

"Good, looks nice in here," he replied.

"How was your day," she asked.

"Screwed up."

"What happened?"

"Had to spend the day in the same room with that asshole, DeFillipi, waiting on the damn massa's table. Racist, anal jerk," he muttered and headed down the hall.

She was draining the pasta when she heard a huge clatter of noise coming from the living room. She ran in there. Reggie was standing at the coat closet with an empty laundry basket in his hand, which he then tossed angrily into the middle of the room. While cleaning, she had gathered some of the stray clutter into several laundry baskets, wanting to see the end result of the clean room right away, to keep her motivated to get through the whole apartment, and left the sorting out of all those odd items for later. The baskets were in the closet. Reggie had thrown all of it across the living room, returning it instantly to the disheveled condition it had been in before all her hard work.

"I'm sick of baskets," he said, "I'm sick of the half-assed bullshit. If you're going to do a job, do it right!" he yelled.

She plopped down onto the floor and broke down into a fit of tears.

He grabbed his keys and left the apartment.

By the time she got up from the floor the food she had on the stove had burned. She threw the shiny new pan into the sink, turned on the water, and realized too late she'd warped it when it gave off a loud cracking noise.

She flung herself onto the bed and cried for the rest of the evening.

The next day she was more depressed than she could ever remember feeling. The flu-like symptoms had returned, and she could hardly move. She stayed in bed for the next week. Reggie expressed no concern, just irritation, impatience.

Nothing in her life made any sense. His annoyance with her and his disrespect were two things she was intimately familiar with. Her father had raised her on them. With him, she had a defense that had gotten her through her childhood. But with Reggie she had none. This had gone too far. She didn't even want him to touch her anymore. She was too angry, too disappointed.

Everyone thought she was crazy for venturing so far from where she belonged. She knew what was really crazy was that she hadn't gone *anywhere*. She was stuck in the same old shit, no matter what she did to get away from it. She was utterly defeated. She was just going to end up like Uncle Joe. *The Ultimate* victory she had won with Archie, when she confronted him with the truth about what he'd done to her and asserted her independence from it, was bullshit. Pure illusion. Nothing had changed. Nothing had been won. It was all pointless.

We still can't love each other, she thought. We're stuck in the trap and we still can't love each other. Then she felt grief knowing that the instant Reggie had thrown those baskets full of trifling things across the room he had lost claim to the innocent, wronged child at the mercy of an abusive father, that he'd told her all about, and that she'd loved him for, the person like herself she could relate to and care about. There was now nothing there but emptiness, empty as those baskets. He had co-opted. He had become what he hated.

All there was in the world were vampires who sucked the blood out of other people, like bigots, to make up for what they lacked in themselves. Nobody, anywhere had gotten anywhere better.

She had tried telling Natalie, but things had changed. Natalie had met someone and was in love. Somewhere along in the conversation Leslie realized that Natalie had detached herself. She was letting Leslie go. The sympathy in her voice sounded perfunctory. It was a kind of loyalty to her new love. Of course. Leslie had to back off. Give Natalie a chance for happiness. Leslie cut the conversation short.

She crawled back into the bed that had been imprisoning her for weeks – the bedroom that had become her Dungeon, and wondered how long before the man-eating vines strangled the life out of her.

* * *

Great Uncle Henry

Srđa and Jovanka heard an odd creaking sound coming from the stairwell in Leslie's apartment building. They investigated and there someone was, hanging from the ceiling. It was Reggie's great-uncle, Henry, who had died as a young man in the 1930's. Jovanka flew to the top of the rope and untied it while Srđa lifted the young man down from below.

Following his lynching, Henry had two siblings that disappeared to New York, passed for white and were never heard from again. Having those two as siblings had left Henry fatally maladapted to his rural Virginia environment. He was perfectly comfortable looking people with fair skin in the eye.

A number of white people had noticed it and were annoyed as hell with his uppity behavior. Then when the rumor started that he was messing around with the Puryear girl, that was it. He was apprehended slipping away from there one afternoon. The ardor with which the girl denied there was anything between them sealed his fate. They lynched him the next day for rape.

The young man opened his eyes and spit at the two of them. "I curse you," he said. "This town can rot in hell for what it's done to me," and he vanished.

Jovanka was desolate. She sat on the steps and put her head in her hands.

"What, my love?" asked Srđa.

163

"This is what Reggie is punishing her for," she said. He sat down next to her.

"Yes," he replied.

"It won't ever stop, will it?" she asked, then sobbed, "Haven't we been through enough?"

"It will stop," he said, his voice catching on the lump in his throat.

* * *

Magua

Leslie was on the near empty 'el in the middle of the afternoon, on her way to see her shrink. He'd told her to think of stories from her childhood that stuck out in her mind. She remembered a story her mother, Deloris, had told her when she was about fifteen.

They had some Serbian neighbors – the only Serbs she ever knew. It was the husband who was a Serb. Mike Strojanović. Archie would go over and have a few beers with the guy and had him make some kitchen cabinets for them. Archie was really impressed. Groove and tenon joints, the whole nine yards, not just carpentry, but real cabinetmaking. They were done European style, free-standing. Built to last a lifetime.

"This you will give to your grandchildren," Mike had told Archie. "Put in will."

Leslie thought Mike was scary. He was a slender, sinewy kind of guy whose body language was strange to her, with an over-abundance of coarse, dark, body hair contrasting sharply against his olive skin. He had an intense kind of energy that felt intimidating to Leslie. He was one of those DP's who'd come to America with 45 cents in his pocket and in ten years had built up a carpentry business and bought his own house outright, without hardly even learning English.

Leslie had grown up hearing the term DP used as the acronym for the words "dumb pollack." It wasn't until she reached the sophistication of a well-read teenager that she understood it was really supposed to mean "displaced person." But the 'dumb pollack' term was extremely popular in her Slavic neighborhood. Few escaped being labelled as such from time to time.

There was a 17-year-old girl in the family, Maria, who was the only teenager Leslie had ever seen who would pile very energetically and cheerfully into washing a sink full of dishes, without being asked. She was Anne's child from an earlier marriage. Anne and Maria were supposed to be German, but they didn't look like it to Leslie. They looked like dark, southern Slavs to her, but nonetheless, they were German.

When Leslie was twelve she babysat the two youngest kids, Mikey and Millie. Millie was four, and Leslie was helping her in the bathroom when Mikey, who was about eight, came to the door, pointed at his little sister sitting on the pot and laughed at her derisively. "She doesn't even have a dick!" he gloated. Leslie thought he was an embarrassing and disgusting example of Old World sexism, though no one had yet coined that word.

Deloris was chummy with Anne but then became aware that Mike was beating Anne up. She felt sorry for Anne, but she distanced herself after that and told Leslie what was going on.

At one of the Croatian picnics, she had talked to a man who had come from Serbia with Mike, along with eight other fellows who'd served in the military. They had all been imprisoned and abused by the Germans in a prisoner-of-war camp. He told her that at the end of the war they all made a pact that they would each marry German women and then abuse them to get even for the abominations the Germans had done to them. And he said that they had all done that. They'd all married German girls and all of them, except him, were mistreating them.

He couldn't do it. He loved his wife and didn't want to ever hurt her.

Leslie wondered if anyone would ever love her like that, or if she'd just always be one of the nine.

* * *

Abnormal Psychology

Leslie had started seeing her shrink the past summer when her bout with depression had knocked her off her feet. She was in the middle of summer break when it hit her. She thought she was in a chill mode, decompressing from the school year when she found herself unable to get out of bed. She'd just lost another stupid, meaningless job two weeks after a rumor went around the office that she slept with black men, though that wasn't the terminology used. That wasn't what was bothering her, though her shrink kept coming back to it. She was getting tired of him harping on it. She knew it went deeper. It wasn't the persecution. It was the pointlessness of it that went way back.

She remembered her grandma. The time they'd gone on vacation to Idyllwild Resort in the Ozarks. The rest of the family had a cabin to themselves, but Leslie and Grandma stayed in the lodge and shared a room.

Grandma washed out all her clothes every night in the bathtub and hung them on the shower rod to dry. Leslie never saw such a cleaning person in all her life. Her mom had told her the story. She'd tried to show Grandma how to use a laundromat, but Grandma wouldn't go. That's when her mom figured out that grandma couldn't read or write. When asked, Auntie Babe admitted grandma couldn't read or write in any language. All the instructions on the machines were too intimidating. She continued washing all her clothes in the bathtub.

The two would lay in bed each night, there on vacation, and talk. Grandma talked about the Old Country, but only to say that it was a bad place. And Grandma told Leslie not to eat too many potatoes the way she had, and gain weight. She told Leslie about her marriage, that grandpa had stopped loving her a long time ago, while she had kept on loving him. He'd been dead for four years already. "And I still love him," she said, her voice breaking in a sob. Leslie was embarrassed for her grandmother that she would be such a chump to love someone who had always been so disrespectful and domineering towards her.

"It's not the jobs," Leslie said to the shrink. "It's Reggie. I'm worried that I'm going through all this bullshit for someone who doesn't even love me, I'm just there for him to vent on.

"But then again, I'm not just doing it because of him, if it wasn't him, I'd still be the same person, and all this would still be happening. It's not like it's his fault."

She started to blink away tears, "I just don't want him to make my life absurd. I can't be strong if it's all absurd."

"What do you mean it would still be happening?" asked the shrink.

She hesitated. She knew he was her doctor and all and he had an obligation to be respectful, but she didn't know how far she really could trust him.

"I'm not really white," she said. She instantly regretted opening that subject.

"How so?" he asked and started writing.

"I don't think like white people," she said. "black people are way more familiar to me, and make more sense, and are more admirable." Her voice caught. "I've always felt that way." As soon as she said it she felt enormously resentful that in his notes he was certainly classifying all that as something aberrant. He looked up at her.

She leaned forward and told him with as strong an expression of conviction as she was capable of, resenting the fact that she even had to say it, her eyes blasting him with the outrage welling up in them, hissing at him, "*This is not something that's wrong with me!*"

On her way home, she realized it was gone. The depression was gone. She got home feeling excited. She started cleaning. She had to get her life together, immediately.

She never did housework anymore without some loud R&B playing. The upstairs neighbor had always been a pain in the ass about it being played too loud and would pound his floor with a broomstick to signal his demand for their silence. But now he was gone.

He had moved out, complaining that the apartment was haunted by a pirate by the name of Dust Pan who kept offering to help every time he used his broom. He told that to the landlord, and the landlord immediately figured he'd cut his losses and let the guy out of the lease before he became even more of a liability. He knew from experience that it could take months to get a delinquent, mentally ill tenant evicted. Leslie had run into the landlord coming down from the apartment. He laughingly asked Leslie if she'd seen the ghost too. That's when he told her the story. They both laughed about it.

She had a multi-album set of Motown's Greatest Hits that was her favorite. She had it cranked up and was doing her dance-cleaning routine. She was dancing like no one was looking when Reggie arrived home and startled her.

There was a glint in his eye she hadn't seen in a long time.

"Niggerish looks good on you," he said.

She laughed and continued dancing and singing, playing to him. He crossed to her, his face directly above hers. She looked up to him, still sultry.

"What looks good on me?"

A little while later, they lay on their bed together, nestled contentedly. He combed his hands up through the hair at the back of her scalp and pulled her head over to his. He kissed her.

"I'm sorry," he said.

"For what?"

"I've been an ass. You're right. I'm taking all this pressure out on you. I don't know why you put up with me."

"Tradition," she said.

She hadn't seen him cry since his mom died, but his face contorted into tears. He covered his face with his hands. "Tradition is a bitch," he said, then he looked at her more intently, directly than he had in a long time. "I love you. I wish I could say I deserved you, but I don't."

They lay nestled together for a while, him stroking her hair.

She put her hand on top of his and looked into his eyes, pleading. "If this happens again, if I get depressed again, can't work, don't kick me out. If I have to go home to live in my dad's basement," her voice broke, "I'll never get out."

"No," he said, his own voice uneven. "I would never do that to you. I promise. But you're going to be fine. Just fine."

Early the next morning she called an office temp agency and was working a typing job an hour later.

* * *

Chapter 5
The Magic Words

The Vision

The guy the temp agency sent her to work for, the day after she'd muttered the Magic Words to her shrink, was aspiring film producer, Michael J. Davidson. He was an escapee from the advertising industry who'd talked his best friend, a wealthy fellow from the North side, into bankrolling a film production company. She was a film student. What a coincidence.

There were still painters at work when she got to the penthouse suite in a Michigan Avenue high rise. It was an old, mediocre building and the penthouse was small and odd-shaped, but she could see someone had just sunk a chunk of change into sprucing it up and making it look trendy. The best part was a balcony that overlooked Lake Michigan.

She was banging away at a letter he needed typed up when he complimented her on how fast she was. They got to talking and he found out she was in film school.

"Really!" he said. "Perfect. Come on, let's talk."

He ushered her into the screening room. That was a proactive term since he had absolutely nothing to screen, never having produced anything, but it set the proper ambiance. He was prototypically wholesome. From his sparkling blue eyes to his dimpled cheeks, a Donny Osmond knockoff, he was the 'boy next door' who exuded goodness, light and charity with every breath.

"I want you to understand what the dream here is," he said. "Things are changing in a phenomenal way. The Networks are like dinosaurs, dying out, while cable is going to sweep the landscape, and we need to be there, giving a voice to under-served families, ordinary middle-class people who want to see their vision of reality on TV, who want their children to have decent things to watch that speak to who they are, and not the degenerate junk that the television moguls are foisting on them."

Leslie wasn't quite sure who the degenerates were or who these poor disenfranchised people were, but she had the feeling he must be talking about the folks in his neighborhood, up there on the North Shore where the poverty line cut-off was at six figures. But it fascinated her to see how he viewed himself and his own.

At the time, Leslie was working on a script that was very similar to the movie that came out several years later, *"Three Men and a Baby."* Michael asked her what she was writing, and she showed him. Most of the things she wrote, that she was really interested in, were about her experiences in the No-Man's-Land she inhabited between black and white, but she knew nobody was interested in that coming from someone like her. If they were interested, it was in how they could read it to bolster their own twisted perception of her and when commenting on it, had ample opportunity to let her have it in a big way, the way Marilyn had, so she was always working on the acceptable stuff she would allow people to read.

He read it and had his wife read it and she told Michael he needed to stop bothering with writing himself and let her do it. He talked a lot about how he was going to utilize her talents once they got the ball rolling.

"You in?" he asked.

Was she! It was a long shot for her in the sense that she lived in a radically different world than the one he was likely to appreciate, possibly even respect, but she would keep her private life detached and go for it.

* * *

Not the Meathead

Another exciting opportunity dropped into Leslie's lap in the month after she'd uttered the Magic Words to her shrink, by way of Reggie's cousin, Antoine. He had a friend named Melvin who had gone off to Hollywood and was writing TV sitcoms. He also did ad agency work and was frequently in town. He'd come out to hang at Antoine's house. Antoine was like Natalie, friendly, open-minded and welcoming. He'd seen a little of Leslie's writing, so he talked to Melvin about this interesting white girl his cousin was going with who was writing about bigots, it was funny stuff, and did he want to read some of it? Melvin said he saw no reason not to.

So, Leslie and Reg went over to Antoine's with a copy of a story Leslie had written about her and Archie called *The Gold Mine.* It was about the day Archie had clued everyone in on what was really going on with the pool they liked to go to. There was news in the paper that it was now a private country club and could only be used by its members. Archie was very proud of himself that he understood what was really going on. "They're just saying that to keep out the coloreds!" he informed all the boobs around him who lacked his savvy. He then packed everybody up and took them on down to the pool. When they got there the lady at the gate asked for their membership card. So, Archie told her he thought they were just saying that to keep out the coloreds.

She looked at Archie like he was a lizard. She didn't let them in.

Leslie couldn't tell the story without doubling up with laughter.

Melvin was a slender guy of average height, dark complexion and an intense way of observing and listening to everyone around him.

They were all sitting in Antoine's kitchen, a typical Chicago kitchen of the era, pre-counter space, filled with large white objects, including the steel sink unit, and the steel kitchen table and chairs. The window offered an unobstructed view of the fire escape. Melvin took the story out of the manila envelope and started reading it.

Leslie was surprised and a little taken aback that he was going to read it right in front of her and everyone else. What if he thought it was lame? She'd be able to feel it even if he tried to be polite. It might be excruciating.

It wasn't.

Everybody else in the room had started chatting and Leslie had gotten her attention away from the 'pins and needles' mode it was in when Melvin let out a good laugh.

"You think he had a gold mine in there," he said, laughing out loud. The line was referring to Deloris's comment on how deeply Archie was picking his nose. That fond memory from childhood never failed to crack Leslie up – Archie asserting his dominance in the family by freely picking his nose in front of everybody – so she joined in the laughter.

"What a little smart ass," he said, looking up at her. She felt an incredible rush that her writing was eliciting a direct response she could feel, as in a performance.

"So, you're trying to write *All in the Family* stuff?" he asked.

"Nah," she said. "This is from my childhood. We were doing this stuff ten years before *All in the Family*. If anything, they're ripping us."

Melvin laughed.

"And I was not," she repeated. "I was NOT the Meathead."

He laughed again, with his laser beam of attention focused on her.

"I was the *prodigy*," she said. "We were like the Mozarts. Daddy was grooming me."

"For what?" he asked.

She laughed and blushed a little, then motioned to take in them all. "He raised me to contradict him."

"Why would he do that?"

172

"Because he was contradicting himself. All he was ever doing when he was talking about y'all was talking about himself," she said. "And it always touched that old Negro's heart when I stood up for him the way I did."

He laughed like she'd just said something uproarious, like he had followed exactly what she was saying.

"Well," he said, "let me see what I can do. I know the people writing for *All in the Family*. You might be useful to them."

"Thank you for noticing," she said.

He laughed again. Damn, she thought. He makes me feel like I'm so damn clever. What a high. And what an incredible chance. The whole world could change. She could have her say in the world and people would like her for it.

* * *

Sunshine

"Good morning, sunshine," Michael said cheerfully as she got into the office. "Let me get you some coffee."

"Oh thanks," she said, always enjoying his little attempts to be egalitarian.

"There you go, my dear."

"Thank you," she replied, taking a sip.

"Look at this beautiful morning!!" he shouted out to her. He was out on the balcony. The lake was twinkling gloriously in the summer morning sunlight. She picked up her coffee and joined him out there.

"Hello world!" he shouted to the universe.

She laughed with him. She'd been working there almost half a year already. She wasn't sure when she'd started to trust him a little, but with the way he talked about his wife with her, confiding about their relationship, she'd decided she could trust that he was not going to make any moves on her, and that she could take him as a kind of brother figure. He was from a part of the world – the upper middle class – that was very strange to her, that she really only knew about from the media, but he was so welcoming and so damned wholesome, she'd become quite fond of him.

And then, of course, there was all he was offering her. When she'd finally graduated that spring, she was the envy of her peers, already having a job in the film industry, assisting a producer. Of course, they still hadn't produced anything, but nobody needed to know that.

The subject of Reggie had never come up. She never even mentioned that she had a boyfriend. She was starting to feel like she could be more forthcoming with him, but the silence had become a habit with her and she let it stand. He did actually run into her once when she was with Reggie at a street festival, but Natalie was also there, so it was likely he thought those two were a couple.

"Well, do you have your passport?" Michael asked.

"No," she said. "Why would I have a passport?"

"So that you can come with us to the Cannes Film Festival."

"Really?" she asked. "When's this?"

"Next May," he said.

"Wow, that will be very cool," she replied.

"I know I'm asking you to put up with a lot while we're in formation, but I don't want you to give up hope. Keep up with that writing. I'm serious, I know we're going to need you for that."

She was beyond excited and very, very grateful.

Her routine during the day included more than just manning the huge word processor they had. A Vydek, the latest technology, it was the size of a desk and used floppy disks that were six inches wide and held about 25 pages of text. She'd taken to it like a duck to water and was unable to write on anything other than a word processor afterwords. She knew that everything that was going on was going to put her out of business as a typist, but she thought it was a ridiculous job for a human being, so good riddance. People needed to learn how to do their own damn typing.

She was also responsible for reading the *Hollywood Reporter* and reporting on the latest to Michael. She helped him write his proposal, quoting information from articles on the changes to the industry looming on the horizon. And everything she did for him he always gushed over, as if he was representing the reigning white, Republican, world order. Ever since *Leave it to Beaver* they were portrayed as the kindly, humane, civilized people who could be trusted to handle authority well, and at bottom, that's the real reason they were in charge of the world.

She thought it ridiculous that she was contemplating such a possibility, but he was making a compelling example of it, and if it was going to bring her good things, who was she to refuse them?

And then she heard back from Melvin, the Hollywood writer Reggie's cousin had introduced her to. He called and asked if she could meet with him at the Chicago Club. He bought her lunch and they chatted. She basked in the laser beam of his attention once more.

"So, tell me," he said. "More about this girl in the story."

"Oh, you mean me, huh?" she said.

He laughed. "You're so forthcoming."

"What else is new?"

He laughed again. It was like having a laugh track running all the time, only it wasn't phony.

"So, you're saying your bigot of a daddy encouraged you to your present lifestyle?" he asked.

"Oh, you mean the way he set me up with y'all?"

He laughed again. She thought it was fun the way he seemed to be encouraging her to speak on the outrageous side.

"Yeah," he said. "I'm having trouble taking that in, though I have to admit, there's something there that strikes a chord."

"It's like I was saying. The guy really is a closet Negro," Leslie said. Again, Melvin laughed. "I don't really understand why it is, but, whatever the reason, he talks about y'all exactly the same way he talks about us, his immediate family. Can't none of us do anything right." More laughter from Melvyn, looking her in the eye like he was just *so* enjoying her. "He made it *very* clear who *we* were. The only difference between us is that he talks about us all negatively, but he likes it when I talk positively about y'all.

"The positivity never applies to us, though. And he never believes anything I say, he just wants to hear it all the time. But it was very clear that he thought saying something positive and defensive was extremely intelligent, admirable and impossible to refute, since he never could. Of course, it didn't make any damn difference, but it was sure fascinating to him.

"This is what I think it was," she went on. "I read Alex Haley's account of the Middle Passage in *Roots* and I was disappointed. It was too factual, I mean, it's no big deal, the guy's a journalist, not a poet, but there was no feeling there, so I'm looking for some kind of fiction that's going to let me feel this unimaginable experience.

"Then in *Ms.* magazine," she went on, "there was a chapter from Andre Schwartz-Bart's *A Woman Named Solitude* and his passage on the Middle Passage is the most intense piece of prose you can imagine. But then, he would be the perfect person in the 20th century to be able to describe that, since he was a Holocaust survivor. He survived Auschwitz, and he went on *that* cattle car ride. He wrote about it in his first book, *Last of the Just,* and the passage in there about the cattle car trip, is just like Alex's." She leaned down towards him and spoke very earnestly, "Dry, factual, no emotion."

"It's *distance*," she said. "They say that all the time about a writer, 'he needs some distance.'

"But when Andre wrote *Solitude*, it was pure emotion. He was in love with a brilliant Guadalupe woman he collaborated with, his wife, Simone. They wrote *In Praise of Black Women* together. The *Solitude* story is based on a Guadalupe folk heroine.

"And when he writes about the first girl in the story, who becomes the main character's mother after taking that dreaded ride, it all totally comes alive. It's nothing but sheer, intense feeling. Nary a fact, just dreams about being a maggot in an old tree trunk, and practicing how to swallow your tongue, because it's the only way you can kill yourself when you're chained up, but hard for a female, and worrying if you'll be able to find your way home so you can sleep under the rice patty until it's time to be re-born again, and putting together a death song. It's just the most poignant stuff you can imagine." She saw an intensity in the way he was looking at her that gave her the feeling that, if they were alone, and she hadn't had a boyfriend, he would have just touched her. She sat up.

"But it's something like that going on with my dad. We get to this variation of the inferiority theme – the one that applies to us – where there's enough distance and the lights go on and he can function rationally. I don't know what's behind it, but it's extremely important."

"Wow," Melvin said. "That is very heavy."

"Yes," she said. "It's a way for us to talk about ourselves. We see ourselves clearly in y'all. And guess what?" she said, learning forward playfully.

"What?" he asked.

"We're fabulous!" she said.

He laughed.

"You gonna argue with that?" she teased.

He laughed again. "So how does he take your relationship now?" he asked.

"We don't talk anymore," she said.

"Oh, so he set you up to do it and now he won't talk to you anymore because you went ahead and did it?"

176

"Yep," she said, suddenly quieted. "We may be fabulous, but we're also a mess."

"Sounds familiar," he said.

"You have no idea," she replied.

* * *

Staggering

Leslie did a lot of thinking about Melvin after that lunch, still talking to him in her imagination. She would have felt very attracted to any handsome man she could talk to on that level. But the world he could open up to her! It was rather staggering. It wasn't exactly her ambition that made it attractive, but her isolation, and her hope that she wasn't understood because she needed to be around people who thought on a broader scale.

She felt qualms though. She was still with Reggie, which troubled her, not with guilt but with irritation that she still felt attached and loyal to someone who was not treating her well enough to deserve it.

Within a few months of their big makeup following her discovery of the Magic Words in therapy, he reverted to his trifling critiques over every move she made. Archie, Jr. For all her trouble crossing the Great Divide and dealing with a world of funky-ass racists over it, all she got was Archie Jr. All those dues for nothing – all the firings, the nasty stares, the insults to her dignity – her life as a shunned person.

She could have stayed home and been paralyzed with depression with much less effort. The world might be a ghetto for some, but for her it was a Dungeon – following her wherever she went.

All he was getting off on, anymore, she thought bitterly, was swiping at her with petty criticisms, pissing her off, then calling her a bitch for fighting back. Behind that, she wasn't giving up nothin.' Let him wander. Please wander. Leave me the hell alone. She was thinking that more and more often, wondering when the critical mass would be reached and she'd just go ahead and do it.

There was, of course, the significant hurdle that she was too broke after her illness to strike out on her own. Or was she just finding an excuse because she was stupid enough to still have some fantasy that things would work out?

She and Melvin left off their conversation with plans to meet again some time during the next month when he would be back in town. When he did call her a month later she gladly set off to see him again.

Melvin explained he would be making some calls from his room till she got there. He gave her his room number. Reggie had gotten into a persistent habit of failing to return home without explanation. She left him no notice either. She approached the hotel with the room number written on a piece of paper like a wild card she had obviously decided to play, or she wouldn't have been walking up those steps. She gulped.

He was on the phone when she arrived, seated at the little round table by the window. He motioned for her to take the chair across from him. He finished the call.

"Hello!" he said, smiling broadly. He got up and kissed her on the cheek. "I've thought about you so much. It is *so* good to see you."

"Yeah, it sure is," she replied. For a moment they regarded each other.

"I hope you don't mind if we have room service. I'm waiting for another call."

"I don't mind," she said, admitting to herself that she was glad he'd thought of an artifice excusing the privacy. They ordered up some food and chatted a bit.

"How's your boyfriend?" he asked, with a look of assumed concern. "How are you two doing?"

"Hanging on," she said, "by a thread."

"Really?" he said. "Sorry to hear that."

"Really?" she said.

"No, not really," he replied with a laugh. "Regardless of all that, I want you to know I think there's something special about what you have to say. There's a voice there that will get you into a lot of heat, but it should be out there nonetheless."

"I'm already in a lot of heat," she laughed. "Your opinion is very important to me," she said. "Thank you."

"I talked to my buddy in New York who works with Lear and he's not against talking with you at some point. Could you get yourself there?"

"I suppose I could manage."

"Let me know if you need help."

"Thanks," she replied.

The meal arrived.

"So, what are you working on these days?" she asked him.

"I'm trying to get myself going as a producer. There's gonna be a lot of programming needed with cable coming in. I got buddies who can front me money and access to facilities to get a production done so I don't need but diddly up front. Everybody gets paid on the back-end when it hits the channel."

That's what my boss is doing," she said.

"What's his name?"

"Michael J. Davidson."

"He worked at Marsteller?" he asked.

"Yeah, yeah he did."

"I know the boy scout," he said.

She laughed. "Boy scout. You got that right. Did you two work together?"

"He took over my position when I left," he said.

"Wow," she said. "Did you know each other well?"

"Nah, not really. We were in different departments. So," he said, "I got a buddy who needs some half hour stuff to fill in a slot and what I'm thinking about is dramatizing your little story."

"Really?"

"Yes, really. What you think, I'm jiving you?" he said with a charming conviction.

"Oh, I'm sure you'd never do such a thing," she laughed.

WBMX was on the radio in the background. A slow jam came on. He turned it up. "I love this one," he said.

He popped up exuberantly and pulled Leslie up as well. He brought her into his arms and they started dancing. She was startled to suddenly be so close to him, at the same time relieved to be expressing the energy that had been percolating for the past month. She was astonished at how much that energy was amplified by what she felt radiating from him.

As the song finished he kissed her.

"You okay?" he asked.

"Yes," she replied. "I'm fine."

"Yes, you are," he said. "Very fine. Thoroughly exceptional."

* * *

Melvin was going to drop her home with his rental car. They got into the elevator. Once alone, he hugged her again. She put her arms around his neck and kissed him.

She was still wrapped around him, giggling when the elevator door opened and who was standing there but Michael J. Davidson. There was

179

a frozen silence that seemed to last minutes till Melvin recovered the moment with a loud greeting and proffered hand.

"Hey man!" he exclaimed. The moment was played out in a perfunctory fashion as the two chatted briefly about the ad agency they'd both worked at. Leslie said nothing, her mind still reeling with apprehension about her boss's new knowledge of her. Michael got off at the ground floor with a warm farewell.

As the elevator doors closed, Melvin jiggled her hand mischievously and looked her slyly in the eye, "Fool looked like he saw a goddamn *spook.*" Leslie laughed with him.

"So to speak!" she said wryly as they exited on the parking level. She wondered how what Michael witnessed was going to come back to haunt her. Her gut lurched.

* * *

Boy Scout Shit

On the elevator ride up to the office the next business day she girded herself. 'Let's see how the Boy Scouts do with this shit,' she thought.

Michael came in a bit late. Everything was cool. Just a normal morning, phones ringing, typing to be done. Around eleven, Paula, the accountant, had to go out to a doctor's appointment, leaving Leslie and Michael alone in the suite together. Leslie was in the screening room, collating copies. Michael was in there with her, doing his egalitarian routine of helping her with her menial chores. The document she was preparing was a synopsis of a project about a basketball team.

Michael started reminiscing about his days in college, playing on the team. He was talking about the positions he played and how he mostly just sat on the bench during games.

In the two years she'd known him she'd never heard him once refer to black people, let alone say anything disparaging. He looked at her for a moment, as if he were trying to tell her something significant.

"Yeah," he said. "I remember those black dudes on the basketball team with me, how they'd walk down the hall, arms around each other like it was no big thing. All that uninhibited physical energy."

Leslie was immediately taken aback. He considered that little bit uninhibited? Really? Oh shit, let me guess why he's talking about that.

He asked her to dictate a letter. They went into the other room and she sat down at the Vydek. She could feel his presence behind her and

180

she relaxed with the routine of the moment, hoping the apprehension she'd felt a moment before would pass. He stepped closer to read what she'd typed, then closer to puzzle out something displayed on the screen. Then he got closer still, till she could feel him leaning against the back of her chair. Then his arms appeared over her head as he reached down to the keyboard in front of her. He fumbled with the keys, trying to make an edit himself.

Stunned, she froze as he rested his arms on top of hers.

No, no, no!

Then he rested his head on top of hers. She had stopped breathing, still frozen in place.

She could feel his aroused breathing in her ear.

She still couldn't move.

When he'd finished with his correction and began to stand back, his hand brushed across her breast, lingering for a split second that lasted an eternity.

She jerked herself up, the chair tipped and fell onto him. He caught it. "Get off me!" she hollered.

"I'm sorry, I'm sorry," he said. "I didn't mean it that way."

"Uh huh," she said. "Just get the fuck back, motherfucker, get the fuck back!"

He did, retreating back a step. She hurriedly grabbed her belongings, some Vydek discs with her writing on them, whatever, and left.

She never returned.

* * *

The Second Funk

She couldn't tell Reggie everything that had happened, so she just edited the story a little, making the encounter between Michael and Melvin seem innocent.

She saw a glimpse in Reggie's eye of fleeting jealousy as he got the picture, but it passed instantly. It was obvious to her that he didn't care enough about her to *be* jealous.

"It's incessant," she said with bitter tears. "There's nowhere I can go, no one I can trust to respect this about me. He was the last. I'm not crazy, I'm not paranoid, this is how they ALL think."

He shrugged, and she knew what he was thinking. He wasn't listening to her, feeling for her. He was dismissing it, thinking about how he went through that all the time, why should it be any different for her? She wasn't just someone going through the same trauma, needing the same support. She was white. When it happened to her, it didn't matter, it got filed away in some denial zone he kept handy for those occasions.

She wasn't really his woman, never had been, she thought bitterly, why would he support her? All she was to him at that point was a lease he didn't want to break. He needed a good credit rating for the life he had plans for.

She started a hardening process. If everybody was so *cock* sure they knew exactly what *it* was she wanted, she'd show them all.

She wouldn't want anything.

Their love life, which had been dwindling for months, became nonexistent. She knew that would drastically hasten Reggie's incentive to find a new 'roommate' and she braced herself for that fall. She didn't know where she would go if she weren't able to work. She was not counting on his promise not to kick her out if her parents would be the only place she could go.

She filed for unemployment, claiming sexual harassment from her employer, a legal concept only a year or two old at that point. Michael didn't challenge it. Her benefits began promptly.

She was frantic to talk to Melvin, but realized he'd never given her his number. Desperate, she looked him up in the Hollywood Reporter's movie business directory she'd taken home from work and never returned. There she saw his bio.

About him and his famous actress wife.

Nonetheless, she tried writing a cryptic note to his agent, asking questions about the 'project' based on her short story that he'd talked about doing, hoping it would elicit a response.

She never heard back.

She cocooned herself into another long, deep depression.

Reggie was obviously on his last nerve. She did give him credit that he made no mention of kicking her out.

Several weeks in she found something extremely cathartic. She began writing about racism. She pretended she was a black male by the name of Reggie Wilson, spoke with absolute abandon and let the world have it.

It was titled "Maintaining a Healthy Distance."

"We may be preparing ourselves for a professional career of some sort, investing a great deal of our effort, our time, our heart and soul into it, perhaps accumulating student debt. We're risking a lot in the hopes that we will find a bright future for ourselves, but there's an undertow here that will never quit. Not in our lifetimes."

It went on from there, describing the unconscious racism to be found deep in the minds of nearly all white people, that can be counted on to sabotage and derail any meaningful partnerships with them in the business world. The piece ended with a hope for an independent livelihood, off the grid, that did not depend on mainstream support to survive. She submitted it to half a dozen publications under Reggie's byline. It was accepted right away.

He thought it was a hoot. It thawed out some of the ice that had solidified between them. She watched him reading it in newsprint, looking impressed. As he looked up at her he smiled warmly and covered her hand with his.

"So, you've figured it out," he said.

She realized he interpreted the article to mean that she understood what life was like for *him* - not that he understood what *she* was going through. That still meant nothing to him.

She withdrew her hand. He was the only person in the world who knew it was her writing that, but still, nothing at all was communicated to anyone. It didn't matter how many people read what she'd written. No one heard her. She was completely alone.

Chapter 6
Leslie Meets Daniel

A Random Coincidence

Leslie was sitting on the steps of the brownstone she lived in with Reggie, snapping a bowl full of green beans. She finished, got up and walked back inside. The door closed behind her as a U-haul truck pulled up to the curb. Dušan's very great grandson, Daniel, got out of the driver's side. Nikola and his girlfriend, Bojana, a slender, misty-eyed girl, emerged from the passenger side. They all soon began carrying furniture and boxes up the steps.

Srđa was on the steps, watching in disbelief. He turned to Jovanka, speechless. When he saw the joy on her face he realized that her dream was coming true. Their dream. She'd made it come true! Leslie was going to be rescued!

Jovanka raised her finger in front of his face and smiled mischievously. "Don't ask," she said. "Don't *even* ask," as she skipped happily up the steps to check on the three young people.

It really was just a coincidence — a Serbian Orthodox guardian angel 'coincidence.' Jovanka had overheard Daniel talking about moving, so she'd taken to repeating the words "Lincoln Park" whenever she saw his eyes entering a rapid eye movement phase of sleep. That was at the same time the second guy in a row upstairs started to see ghosts and decided to move. Of course, by then Dušan was fully in cahoots with his ghost pirate routine. He made sure everyone else who came to look at the apartment got a cold chill. At least till Daniel looked at it.

Jovanka caught a lamp cord Bojana was about to trip on just in time.

"This is so nice," said Bojana, as she entered the apartment. "I get a really nice feeling from this place."

* * *

She's *Been* Ready

Several days later Leslie saw her little friend Kiasha from the basement apartment, a dark chocolate wisp of a girl in cornrows, on the steps, talking to the new tenant.

Leslie knew someone had moved in upstairs from the quick footsteps that were traversing the space for hours on end. Somebody was obviously busily getting their act together in a new space.

She wasn't sure if that's who Kiasha was talking to. Whoever it was looked interesting, so she joined them and sat down on a step.

Jovanka and Srđa appeared at the landing at the top of the stairs, standing above them, flushed with excitement.

Kiasha ran over to Leslie and wrapped her arms around Leslie's neck.

"Hey sweetie," said Leslie as she returned the hug.

"Have you met our new neighbor?" asked Kiasha. "This is Daniel. He's gonna be a doctor!"

"This is it! This is it!" exclaimed Jovanka, squeezing Srđa's hand so hard he winced, then laughed.

Dušan was leaning against the wrought iron fence at the bottom of the steps. He clipped a fingernail, polished it against the fabric on the front of his shirt, then blew on it. He looked very happy with himself.

"Calm down, my pet," Srđa said. "Before you mangle me." He wrung his hand out teasingly, quite excited himself.

Leslie noticed the same details that Jovanka had when she'd first seen him in the lecture hall some months earlier. An average-height fellow solidly built, a medium complexion with a raw umber cast to it, who exuded an intense curiosity and discernment. Leslie thought him a nice enough looking fellow.

"Hey," said Daniel, offering his hand, then explained for Kiasha, "Actually, no, I'm not going to be a doctor like at a doctor's office. I guess I'll go into teaching and people will call me a doctor, but that just means you've taken all the schooling anybody can get on that subject."

Leslie turned to Kiasha, "That's what you're going to do someday. I can just tell." The little girl took her hand. "'Dr. Kiasha,' that's what everybody's going to call you." Leslie saluted her.

The little girl giggled then ran down the steps, as if to tell her mom.

Leslie laughed. "Adorable." Then she asked Daniel, "What's your field?"

"I'm researching the Ottoman occupation of the Balkans, modern-day Yugoslavia."

"Look, look!" Jovanka squealed, "they're not wasting a moment's time."

"The *denouement* is at hand," concurred Srđa.

"Really? I'm Croatian on my dad's side."

"Oh, then y'all pretty much just missed it."

"Missed what?"

"The Turkish occupation. It was mainly of the Serbs."

"I don't really know much about the difference."

"There was little difference originally," he said. "They were like the Dakota and the Lakota. But the Croats were occupied by the Austrians, while the Serbs were occupied by the Turks. And because of that, the Croats were westernized and became Catholics, while the Orthodox Serbs were forced to assimilate into the Middle East and obstinately refused to convert from Orthodoxy to Islam."

"My grandma was Orthodox before she got married," she said. "She converted to marry my grandfather."

"Oh, well then," said Daniel. "She couldn't have been a Croat. She had to be a Serb."

"Eureka," cried Jovanka, tears in her eyes. "No longer are we in hiding!"

Leslie asked, "Why do you say that?"

"Because that's their black and white. That's what defined your ethnicity, the religion. It's weird shit, I know, but it's the way it works over there. It's kind of like people using religion the way a gang uses its colors."

"I wonder why she didn't tell us we were Serb." Then she smiled sardonically and feigned whispering, "Oh, I know . . . 'cause grandpa thought he was *better* than Serbs." She reached over confidingly and touched Daniel's knee with a wink. "He thought he was better than us, too. . . So what was going on over there?"

"People were being very hard on minority Serbs. You don't know anything about any family over there?"

"Just about an Aunt Sara who lost six children and a husband in WWII." Daniel blinked.

"Did you see that blink?" asked Jovanka. "Did you? Did you? He *feels* us, he really *feels* us!" The two men nodded, enjoying her excitement, though being men, they of course, had little to add outright to a discussion of feelings. At least out in public.

"How'd you get into all this?" Leslie asked Daniel.

"I did a master's thesis on the Ottoman Empire. I thought I was going to be defending how advanced they were in their political strategies. They'd use proxies - people from a conquered country to police their own - rather than brutalizing their subjects with their own forces. But the more I looked at it, the more it looked like just a slicker way to mess with people.

"Then I started noticing how the Serbs were dealing with it and I got hooked. Incredible support structures. But then y'all have been dealing with this shit for so damn long, and it built up so slowly there was time to adjust the cultural infrastructure, not like the abrupt shock we were thrown into. Fascinating."

She laughed mischievously. "So, if that was our black and white, what does that make me?"

"Actually, you'd be lucky to just have to be black," he said cryptically.

She was startled to hear him say that, and recognized immediately how unusual he was to be conceding such a possibility. "Meaning?" she asked.

"I'm sorry," he said. "I'm putting too much on you."

"No, tell me," she said.

"The truth? I'm just going to upset you."

"What?" she pressed.

"Tell her, tell her," said Srđa. "She's ready."

Jovanka, who had come to sit directly behind Daniel, her arms wrapped around his shoulders, whispered in his ear, her eyes misty, "Son, she's *been* ready."

"Were they mean to us?"

"They were more than mean," he said. "In World War II, Croatian fascists were exterminating their minority Serbs by the hundreds of thousands, as racial undesirables."

Leslie was trying to take that in, as if the portal to an alternate reality had just opened for her.

"My baby," whispered Jovanka hoarsely. "You're a child of the Holocaust."

Daniel was very moved, "Baby, you's a child of the Holocaust."

Daniel saw her eyes begin to shine with a thin film of water, shining over the large orbs of her eyes with a fascinating luminosity, as her pupils dilated with strong emotion, her irises sparkling gold. He'd never seen anything more beautiful.

"*I knew that!*" she whispered hoarsely, choked with emotion, and ran up the steps.

* * *

Reggie was seated at his desk. She ran to him. "Reggie!"

"Wait up," he said, holding up a finger while he finished his calculation. She stood over him, her hand on his shoulder, while she caught her breath.

She felt a shift, as everything fell into place. Too much to think about at once. Whoever the hell that guy Daniel was, what he'd just told her explained everything. Every choice she'd ever made, how she felt about *everything* in the whole world.

She gazed at Reggie, and the word she'd been looking for, for years was suddenly obvious. The racist world, meaning the outside world, used nasty words, 'lascivious, perverse,' for what she felt towards the people in her life, the black people, the people of color. No, no, the word was 'loyalty!' That's exactly what she'd been feeling! Loyalty towards her *own* – a feeling impossible to deny that dictated who had to be loved and supported, at any cost.

"Wassup?" he said, looking up to her.

"We were being exterminated!" she said, still panting, not from being out of breath, but from strong emotion.

"Huh?" he looked up at her, his eyebrows furrowing at the onslaught of her passion.

"Grandma was passing for Croatian! We were Serbs, not Croatians. Croatians were exterminating us!"

"Wow, that's heavy," he said, attempting to make the transition from calculus to high drama. She could see he was distracted and unable to take all that in.

"I love you," she said. He smiled slightly, then turned back to his math.

She went to the bedroom and lay down. So many thoughts were racing through her mind. She lay for a while as one connection after another realigned with the new paradigm. Her mind gave out in exhaustion and she fell asleep. Her second depressive episode ended when she awoke with a feeling of excited elation.

She was no longer invisible. Someone, that guy on the steps just now, who lived upstairs could see her.

To hell with Dungeons.

* * *

Daniel Observes a Tenacious Identity

It was morning and Daniel heard some indistinct fussing coming from the street below. He idly looked out the window to see Leslie getting into the car while Reggie upbraided her. Daniel had not realized she was with a brother. "No shit!" he thought.

"Can you ever get anywhere on time?" Reggie cried, loud enough for Daniel to hear, as he slammed her door shut.

Daniel laughed. "You can tell who's the *nee*-gro in that relationship," he said out loud and laughed some more.

He thought about her throughout the morning. He thought about his buddy Nikola, the Serbian guy he'd run into in the hall who was translating for him. Nikola's reason for attending Howard was one thing – that black people were more familiar to him than white because of what he understood of the history – but her instinctive responses over such a span of time were another. If people of color were, in fact, more familiar to her, with no conscious knowledge of the reasons why, it would be staggering. And judging from the look in her eyes when she'd found out who she was, that's exactly what was going on.

Authenticity fascinated him. People going through the motions, pretending loyalties they would abandon in a heartbeat if the opportunity arose was something he'd seen all his life and despised. Jive. But this tenacious sense of identity was inexplicable. Epic.

What a fascinating girl. He hoped he'd have a chance to see her again, soon.

* * *

The Hapless Eavesdropper

Leslie was sprawled on the couch, studying. Jovanka was lurking nearby. Leslie may have unconsciously heard the noise of someone in the vestibule opening a mailbox, but Jovanka was taking no chances. She slipped up to Leslie's ear and whispered, "Go get the mail."

Leslie got up absent-mindedly, picked up the keys and went out to the vestibule.

"Oh hi, Daniel, there you are."

"Hello sister," he said, "it's good to see you. How have you been?"

She noted the appellation and was touched. Except for Natalie, and before her, Amelia, nobody ever used that kind of familial term with her, no matter how well they knew her, even when they said it constantly to everyone else, even total strangers. "Pretty blown away," she said.

"Yeah, I can imagine. I hope I didn't speak too soon with all that information. I'm sure it would be pretty mind blowing."

"Too soon!" she exclaimed. "What's it been, 35 years since all that nasty business in WWII happened? What can be too soon?" She grasped his arm and jiggled it excitedly. "No, it's like I've been waiting all my life for somebody to tell me that. There's been so much going on that was such a mystery that makes sense now!" She laughed and flailed her arms over her head, "Go ahead, blow me away!" Her voice loudly echoed up the stairwell.

There was an awkward silence behind his visceral reaction to the un-intended sexual innuendo. 'No,' he thought. 'This is serious, calling for complete respect.'

"Listen," he said. "I'd like to see what I can find out about your family, if you don't mind. I've got access to all kinds of resources."

"Oh, I'd love that!" Her cheeks were flushed like a little girl's.

"Just get me whatever information you have, and I'll see what I can come up with."

"Oh," she said, bubbling over, "you're so good to me!" She hugged him.

"My pleasure," he said as she bounced back into her apartment. She just as quickly bounced back out. "Oops," she said. "I forgot I was getting the mail."

They both laughed as Daniel made his way up the stairs.

Everything about her was so free and expressive. He had become recently aware that he enjoyed seeing that in European Americans and had given it some thought. He had decided it had to do with the veneer of self-restraint that had been so stringently applied for at least three generations in his own upwardly mobile family.

All that strident energy, all that self-consciousness, all that self-deprecation, all that anxiety-ridden inhibition! More importantly, all that intolerance towards most of the people in their world – other black people. It was beyond tiresome to him. He supposed that white people displaying a passionate exuberance represented the possibility of living in a state of parity without all that compromise. Easy as a Sunday morning. Life could just go on – normal, human life.

A short while later, he was upstairs slogging through Nikola's translation when he heard Leslie's excited voice again. And then there was Reggie's voice and the obvious sounds of lovemaking. He shut the window.

When the commotion had finally subsided, he succeeded in refocusing his attention onto his studies. Then the aroma of chicken, garlic, onions, olive oil and peppers drifted up from the floor below. His stomach growled but would have to wait. He had nothing in the house to eat. He

192

was about to go out when there was a knock at his door. It was Leslie, flushed and happy, her hair wet from a shower. The sight of it made him melt.

"Hey," she said. "I just talked to my mom and she got this information for me." She handed him a piece of paper. "That's everything we know. Grandma's name was Roknić, she was born in 1894 and she came from a tiny village by that name in an area called Vrginmost."

"No," he said, flabbergasted. "You're kidding!"

"What?" she asked.

"Now *my* mind is being blown. We got a book two months ago about Vrginmost in the Forties. Nikola's already translating it. This is too weird. Too many damn coincidences. Why did we get that book? Out of all the many districts in Croatia? Why did I move in here? I'm not into this kind of paranormal shit at all. Why did I bump into Nikola? It's not at all anything I expect, but here it is."

She thought of Natalie's "séance's" with Leslie's ghosts and smiled at him knowingly, "Just go with it. These are some really nice spooks. They're not going to take you anywhere you don't want to go, even if you don't know it yet."

"Spooks?" he questioned.

She paused for a moment. It would be too much to try and explain Natalie. "Just those kinds of coincidences. Like I wonder something and some book flies off the shelf at me."

"Oh really," he said, smiling. He looked down the stairs towards her apartment. "You've got books flying around down there?"

Her head was down as she smiled up into his eyes, freely. He didn't want to presume but he could swear she was flirting with him.

"Tch," she responded and nudged his arm. "No more than you," she seemed to notice his jacket for the first time. "Oh, you going out? I'm sorry. I didn't mean to hold you up."

"Yes, somebody's driving me wild with a taste for something Mediterranean – some Mediterranean food," he stammered.

"Oh, I'm sorry," she said. "Am I overdoing it with the garlic?"

"Is that humanly possible?" he said.

"Then you should try some Thai food. There's a dish I made once that calls for *twelve* cloves of garlic. "

"Well if you make it again, make sure you invite me over for dinner."

"You got it," she said and disappeared into her apartment.

He wished he did.

Not a week had passed when Leslie dug up that recipe and made some Thai food. Daniel was coming over. He'd found something for her about her family.

She was in the kitchen. A pile of vegetable peelings still sat on the kitchen table where she'd chopped them. Daniel had already arrived from upstairs and was opening a bottle of wine. Reggie abruptly breezed through the kitchen, so she offered him a forkful of the heavily garlicked Thai dish. He evaded her with an emphatic, 'Hell no.'

"I'm serious, Reg, everybody has to eat some of this, in self-defense," Leslie said, laughing mischievously. "Come on, now." She followed after him with the fork.

"No thanks," he said, leaving the room. "I'll just leave the two of you to your own devices." He headed back to his books.

"Oh honey, I didn't mean for you to go hungry," she called after him.

He popped his head back into the kitchen. "No, seriously," he smiled. "I knew you were making this mess, so I had me a burger on the way home."

"Traitor," she teased. Then to Daniel, laughing, "I bet he makes me sleep on the couch tonight. Come on, dig in."

Daniel helped himself to a generous forkful. She sat down across from him and watched him with amusement. When his eyes lit up at the strong flavors, she burst into laughter.

He struggled to suppress his own laughter given how full his mouth was. He savored it and finally swallowed. She laughed again. He thought her laughter was as infectious as a child's. Natural and full of life.

"Good God!" he finally said. "That is up*standing*!" He took another bite.

"The first time I made this a lady came to the door, canvassing the neighborhood. The minute I started to speak to her and that garlic breath hit her, the look on her face, oh god, I'll never forget. She was doing such a good job being polite, but she couldn't hide it. She was like 'what kind of heathen is this?' Just standing there, wilting."

"Twelve cloves, huh?" he was laughing with her.

"Yes, I had to mince twelve cloves of garlic. My fingers are going to smell for a week."

He grabbed her hand, sniffed it, and burst out laughing.

"You better get going with that anti-garlic self-defense yourself," he said and motioned for her to eat.

After a few forkfuls he pulled some papers together.

"All right, you were waiting for a report on your family," he said. "You are in luck. I found something right away. There was a major incident,

194

famous throughout the Austrian Empire, that was making headlines for months. It happened in your grandmother's little village, when she was three years old. That was in 1897. A precursor to the unrest that caused World War One, namely the Imperialism of Austro-Hungarians."

"Wow," said Leslie.

"I got Nikola to translate some of Gojko Nikoliš memoirs. He's Sjeničak's only famous son in the twentieth century, ambassador to India. He talked about how the people in Sjeničak were so remote to the rest of the world, they might as well have been in the jungles of the Amazon, and their experience with the world was so harsh that any kind of crazy plot would seem believable. According to him, your grandma would have seen old men – refugees from Serbia no doubt – with their backs a mass of scars from whippings. Oh, did I tell you yet? Serbs were enslaved by the Ottomans for 500 years."

"Enslaved?" she asked.

"Peonage slavery," he explained. "Like Jim Crow. Amazingly like Jim Crow."

She remembered that picture she'd seen of Peter Gordon – an American slave turned Civil War soldier -- with his back a mass of such scars and realized what Daniel was alluding to.

"Krajina means 'frontier' or "No-Man's-Land,'" Daniel went on.

Leslie chuckled wryly. How many times had she used that phrase to think of the space she'd been living in now for five years, that forsaken place between black and white?"

"What?" he asked.

"How could that be *my* homeland?"

"Y'all lived in the frontier between Europe and the Middle East. You basically were in a war zone for 350 years. But when the Ottoman empire faded, so did your livelihood as border guards and you became *very* poor. People were living in shacks that provided less shelter than a barn.

"You'se poor *nee*-groes were *so* poor by then that things were getting very tense. Over 20 people – two of them Roknić – were indicted in the Sjeničak Revolt – your grandma's Roknić hamlet was within the town of Sjeničak. Well, the revolt was basically a race riot, and guess who their defense attorney was? Guess who the court-appointed lawyer defending these illiterate Serbs was?"

"Who?"

"One of the founding fathers of genocidal hatred of Serbs," he said. "The Grand Wizard, himself, so to speak, defending the *nee*-groes."

"You're kidding," she replied.

"And that, I am told," he said, "was business as usual. That, and the fact that the whole incident had been incited by an outsider, likely the politician who won the next election, none of which was ever investigated for one single second."

"Damn," said Leslie. "This would have been the big event of Grandma's childhood. God only knows what her memories of it were."

* * *

Kata's Michigan Avenue Career, 1939

Kata, Leslie's grandmother, opened the office window. The cool night air refreshed her face, and she looked down at the Michigan Avenue traffic twenty-odd floors beneath her. The traffic lights looked festive.

She pulled a handkerchief from her belt, took off her glasses and wiped the sweat from her face. She sighed deeply. She returned the handkerchief to her belt, so that it could dry before she needed it again. She put her heavy, horn-rimmed glasses back on. They obscured her large, expressive eyes. When she stepped back she knocked into her bucket. It sloshed some wash water onto the floor. Her knees ached as she knelt back down with her wash rag and sopped up the spilled water.

Then she saw that the water had spread further. It was soaking a newspaper at the bottom of a stack of papers, a mistake she was not permitted. Her stomach knotted as the pinched face of the man who oversaw her came to mind. She wrung out her wash cloth to absorb the water there. She picked up the paper. She could not read in any language.

There were drawings of an assortment of American flags at the top, and a caricature of an ape-like black man being booted. She opened the page and placed it on the windowsill to dry out. She remembered Balatin.

Kata was thirteen when Balatin got out of prison, after serving a ten-year sentence for his part in the Sjeničak Revolt. That was the same year thirteen-year-old Kata's parents died. She was sent to live with impoverished distant relatives who would teach her, by example, the meaning of the saying, "You show your worst face to an orphan."

She was just stepping out of the hen house, eggs in her doubled-up apron, when she almost walked into Balatin. He was the most frightening person she'd ever seen.

She looked up at his enormous height, a hulking man heavy with muscle, his head covered in coarse black hair, a thick black beard covering nearly all of his face, eyebrows like bird's wings, nose hair, ear hair, coarse black hair at his neck, his hands, it seemed, everywhere save the soles of his feet and the palms of his hands. She gasped. He saw her and laughed.

She ran to the house in even greater embarrassment. As she ran, one of the eggs slipped from her apron. Ðuro, a small, slight man, head of the household she now was part of, barked at her. "What are you doing, you stupid thing? Why are you running? Do you think we have food to waste? Huh? We have your stupid face to feed, don't we? That's enough of a loss."

"Leave the girl alone," said Balatin. He smiled at her. "It's not her fault I frighten children." He took a coin out of his pocket, crossed the distance to her in a few broad paces and handed it to her. "Take this to Karlovac and buy yourself a sweet," he said. "But don't tell them Balatin gave it to you, or that you're from Sjeničak, or they'll spit on you."

The two men laughed, Ðuro looking up at him admiringly. "Nobody in Karlovac will bother you," he said. "You know, they put in the road because of you."

"They put in the road so they'll have an easier time keeping track of us," replied the huge man. "And deciding the Serb question."

After Balatin had left, Ðuro talked about him repeatedly, as if he were a hero. Ðuro presided over the Sunday dinner table like a professor. "Twelve years ago, the Hungarians tried to take us over and tax us into slavery and take away our language. They tried to trick us by running their flag over our church, but our elder brother by way of my mother's sister, Balatin, got everyone in the village to stop them."

After washing the dinner dishes, Kata slipped away from the cottage. On the hillside overlooking the field were the ruins of an ancient walled fort sacked in the 14th century when the Serbs were enslaved by The Turk.

She remembered the summer picnics they would have there. Her grandfather would chant the old history stories, sardonic tales cast to instruct everyone on who they were, and how they could survive peonage to their colonizers. With nearly universal illiteracy, they knew more of their own history than the average English farmer, who was literate, of the same era.

Her grandfather would accompany himself with his *guŝlar*, a single-stringed, home-made instrument. She heard the tales about the beautiful maidens who'd lived in the fort. As a little girl she'd pretend she was one of them.

Franjo was there, the Croat boy on a neighboring farm. She told him about Balatin.

"Balatin? THE Balatin? Balatin, the Gorilla?" The boy laughed. "Did he scare you?"

"Oh, my Lord, yes," the girl exclaimed. "He's so ugly! Cousin Đuro says he's a hero. He stopped the Hungarians from taking us over."

The boy started laughing. "I don't want to offend you, but that was some crazy nonsense. Ignorant, ignorant nonsense. There was no Magyar plot, and the people in Sjeničak are so ignorant, they didn't even know that the Austro-Hungarian flag was *already* their flag, being part of the Empire. They slowly beat three poor men to death, all afternoon. Two of the men were Serbs, even. They just got killed for wearing suits. Shameful, shameful riot. And Balatin was the ringleader."

Kata was at once vindicated in her fear of the man and embarrassed to be related to him.

"Sjeničak was in headlines all over the Empire for months. And the worst part was about that poor man, the last one left alive, hiding in the priest's house, waiting, while that giant, hairy creature, Balatin, climbed to the roof and then burst through the window. He scooped the poor man up, dragged him down the stairs and threw him to the crowd.

"Half of Europe was talking about him, for weeks on end. We have no idea why Balatin wasn't hung with the other three. He was the one who spread the rumor in the first place." He looked at her. "I'm sorry," he said. "I didn't mean to embarrass you."

"I'm not embarrassed," she said, though she was. She knew that everything he said was true. Everyone she knew was brutal and ignorant, except her parents. She hated them. She had felt a shock of homesickness, shock that all the adults of her early childhood had vanished. She started to cry. "I miss my parents, they never talked about things like this. They talked about things we could do something about. I can't do anything anymore. I'm just two arms that do whatever they're told," she said, sobbing. The boy touched her hand.

She was still in a morose state when she got back to the *zadruga,* a multi-generational compound with encircled structures forming a fort of sorts.

It wasn't much of a *zadruga* at that. Đuro's brothers had all gone to the Americas. The largest of the cottages in the compound had caught fire the year before and stood in ruins, reminding them daily of their defenselessness in a hostile world. As she entered the cottage where Đuro's small children chatted about, he lunged at her with a belt. She cried out as he struck her with it.

He pushed her against the wall. "If I ever catch you holding hands with that *Hrvat* whelp again, I will throw you out. You can sleep in a ditch. Do you hear me?"

"Good," she said. "I'd rather sleep in a ditch than have to spend another moment with you."

He slapped her face. "You Roknić think so much of yourselves. We'll see how much you think of yourself when you've lived in a barn for a while."

With that he pushed her out the door. She marched off to the barn defiantly.

She slept in that barn for the next three years, alongside field mice that made her flesh crawl. They were burrowed alongside her under the haystack she slept in through the winter. On one frigid night she'd slunk back into the cottage, but the beating Đuro tried to inflict on her sent her running back to the barn in relief.

Then at seventeen, her father's brother, who had made it to America years earlier, scraped together the money for her passage and sent for her. She miraculously boarded an ocean liner transporting her to America, just before the First World War was commencing. He had work for her already lined up, scrubbing floors. Indoor work. She was going to work indoors!

She was in transit, in Hamburg, when she saw a drawing in the newspaper. An ape-like man in Serbian dress was being beaten with a huge German fist. She recognized the word 'Serbien" and guessed at the rest. She flushed with embarrassment, her heart pounding wildly, wondering if everyone there could see it in her. Did it show? Could people see? Could they tell that she was from the family everyone knew were the apes of Europe? *Did they know that was why she was so ugly?*

"Serbians Must Die"
Brother Balatin, the poster child

Kata snapped herself to attention. How long had she been sitting there? Dreaming about the past, when she had so much floor to scrub? The night was not endless, however endless the dimly lit hallway seemed that she knelt on, and had to scrub by morning. Permitted illumination only in the area she was working on, she sat in a dim pool of light as the hallway lurked behind her into a black infinity.

When she finished the hallway, her arms aching almost as much as her back, she returned to the office where she'd left the newspaper page to dry. *The paper was gone from the windowsill!* Panicked, she looked around for it, then realized in terror that it must have flown out the window. She had no idea what kind of trouble that would make for her. She closed the window with a sense of dread.

She got home in the early morning light and put her pay envelope on top of the icebox.

That first week, when she'd come home proudly with her first pay envelope as a married American woman, her husband, Stevan, had slipped in behind her, his arms around her waist, then he snatched the envelope

200

from her. She thought he was playing and reached for it, while he held it above her head. Then just as easily, above her grasp, a cigarette dangling from his mouth, he took the money from the envelope. He turned his back to her while she continued to giggle.

He turned towards her and handed her a portion of the money. "Here's for the grocer," he said. "In the future, leave the envelope on top of the icebox." He pocketed the rest. It soon vanished onto a sidewalk, his bet on the throw of a pair of dice.

That became the first condition of their marriage.

* * *

The Second Condition

Kata stood in a long line waiting for the lamb at the Croatian picnic. She was expecting her first child, generously swelling her belly. It was the Roaring Twenties.

The old man ahead of her turned to her with a mischievous smile, "You know," he said, "some of us have to stand here and wait for the lamb, but the truth is, the best cuts go out the back door as soon as it comes off the spit."

"I'm sure," she said. The old man was still smiling, like his intent was to flirt with her. He'd already had enough to drink to forget himself.

She looked over to the young men playing in the band and waved. "My husband," she said to the man, as an admonishment. "He's playing the *tambritza*," referring to the small mandolin that lent the rapid percussive harmony to the Balkan music, similar to Greek, they were playing. The man tipped his hat in deference.

The lamb was worth waiting for. Several days earlier it had been rubbed with many cloves of garlic, then salted. Early that morning, before dawn, all the lambs had been set on spits between beds of coal and slowly roasted till the savory rich skin was crusty and salty with an intense flavor, impossible to forget and longed for on many a cold, winter night dreaming of summer picnics.

She looked out at the festive crowd, the many Croatian families -- complete families with mothers and fathers and old people, and healthy, happy children.

Here she was now, half a world away in America, where there was always enough food, and always work for willing hands. Soon she would have her first child and her home life would be whole again.

201

It was a perfect day in late spring. People sat at tables under the trees, listening to the music. She admired how peaceable the assembly was. No loud, drunken Serbs breaking into fights. No rude young Serbs pulling girls to dance with them under protest. She liked these people better than the bitter, hardened people she'd left behind.

Kata listened again to her husband playing his *tambritza*. He nodded his head at her smile. She was so proud of him. Such a handsome man, and so ambitious. He could even read and write. He carried a little address book with him always that he was using as his own personal dictionary, writing new English words in it as he learned them.

Her husband joined her at the picnic table. He was disappointed in the lamb she purchased. He had asked for some from the hind leg, but the best of that had, of course, long gone out the back door.

"You have to watch them," he said. "You know a hind leg from a rib, don't you?"

"Leave her alone, Stevan," said Marta, the wife of his friend, with whom they were sharing a picnic table. "There was not much left. She did her best."

Kata smiled gratefully at the young woman. She admired how confidently the woman carried herself, and was excited that she was being so welcoming.

Marta surveyed Kata in an overly kind way that made Kata apprehensive. "What town is that you are from, dear?" she asked.

Kata was flustered, not sure what to say, so she told the truth. "Sjeničak." She waited for Marta's reaction. It was there – disdain. "But I was just baptized," she said, referring to her recent conversion from the Serbian Orthodox Church to the Roman Catholic.

She was hoping to see the same pleasure she'd seen in the priest's face during the ceremony. What Kata saw, however, was scorn, as if the woman had just confirmed her suspicions about Kata.

* * *

Stevan was furious later, as they left the picnic. There were still puddles of water from the night's rain in the path. He stomped into each one, splashing muddy water onto Kata's legs. Kata dropped back and followed him from a distance, dejected by his mood.

"Zašto si tako glupa?" he turned back and demanded. "Why are you so stupid?" The confusion on her face irritated him even more. "Now we have to move. We have to find another church."

Kata despaired.

"Why did you have to tell them you were just baptized?" he demanded. "Now they know, stupid!"

He stepped back away from her and looked down at her with disgust.

"Now they know you're a *Serb.*"

He said it like it was a dirty word, as it was commonly said by Croatians about the Serbs who lived in their midst. Kata had never heard him say it that way before. She had no rebuttal. Nothing in her life in the *Krajina* No-Man's-Land had prepared her, in any way, for a rebuttal.

"I didn't know what to say, she already knew when I told her what town I was from."

"So stop telling them, stupid," he said. "Do you think I'm going to be shamed like this for the rest of my life? If you want to remain my wife, don't you ever mention it again, not to anyone. Not your friends, not your neighbors," he poked Kata's swollen belly, "not your children. No one.

"Do you understand? No one had better ever find out you're a Serb."

With his decreal of that second condition she understood that she had not escaped her identity as third-class citizen. She had only confirmed it.

* * *

Leslie's Kitchen, 1:30AM

Leslie had long since cleared the table of the pungent leftovers. Jovanka, the ghost, was observing them with a great deal of satisfaction. She noted, as the two chatted, their body language. Daniel was relaxed in his chair, his legs crossed at the ankles, stretching out far under the table. Across from him Leslie stretched out her own legs, wide spread. Jovanka giggled mischievously. Who said she was no matchmaker?

She put her arm across her goddaughter's shoulder and whispered in her ear, "Sit up like a lady." Leslie sat up and crossed her legs.

Leslie smiled at Daniel. "I guess that could account for it. Grandma's horrible self-esteem. It's not so much like she was passing, as surrendering."

"Passing is always surrendering," Daniel observed. "Horrible psychological scars."

Reggie, who'd been gone for several hours, came into his kitchen, filled up a glass with water and gulped it. "You two still at it, eh? The history buffs."

"It's more than just history," Leslie said.

"I'll say," muttered Jovanka with a wink.

Daniel laughed.

Reggie had a hunch what Leslie's mood would be that evening. "Don't stay up too late," he said. He swept the hair up at the nape of her neck and kissed it. He made eye contact with Daniel as he stood back up and smiled. "Nice of you to come by, brother," he said, offering his hand. The two shook.

As Reggie left the room Jovanka stuck out her foot to trip him. His foot skidded into the floor a bit and he stumbled slightly. Once gone, Leslie turned back to Daniel.

"But how could all this influence me so much, without me knowing?"

"How would it not?" Daniel replied. "How could so much energy just evaporate into nothing? That makes no sense. I don't know what your family has been through, but I'm sure it was horrible. It's just unthinkable to me, it depresses me, to think that all that could happen to so many people, all at once, and it just disappears into thin air, like they don't matter. I'm glad it influenced you. I like that about you. You make sense to me."

Jovanka could see how much Leslie was savoring that thought. She was looking up at Daniel with a shy smile that glowed.

Then Leslie's expression saddened. "How much could they have suffered? she asked.

"It was bad," he said, wondering if he should tell her about Jasenovac.

"Yes," whispered Jovanka. "Tell her everything. Tell her what happened to me."

* * *

Jasenovac, Croatia, 1942

Twice a year, Kata was able to persuade her husband to write a letter to her family in the Old Country, but their letters to her stopped coming as the years of the Second World War started to unfold. She was now a middle-aged woman. Her children had come of age. Her two sons were serving in the U.S. military. She had no idea what might be happening to her family in the Old Country.

The last she had heard, one of her nephews had just joined the Domo-brani, the Croatian home guard. Her older sister had sent that letter, along with a photo of him in uniform, and a sarcastic remark that her son had defected to the Catholic church as Kata had, as if that made them partners in crime.

 So, she heard nothing except what others would read to her in the newspapers, or what she heard on the radio. She knew Germany was in-vading all of Europe and that fighting had broken out between the Croa-tians, who'd sided with Hitler, and the Serbs who had brazenly defied him. Serbia was, in Hitler's opinion, the smallest, crummiest excuse for a country in Europe. It took many times more might to subdue it, how-ever, than he'd anticipated. But Kata had no idea what was happening with her own family. She certainly knew nothing about the kiln at Jasenovac.

The brick kiln had been re-purposed. It stood in a remote backwater, too swampy for settlements, and near the Sava River that flowed to Ser-bia. Let the carcasses float back where they belonged, the guards joked. Jasenovac shared a rail line with Auschwitz death camp. Both were trans-porting their respective victims with the same cattle cars. The comman-dants at Auschwitz were appalled at the levels of sadism at Jasenovac and called for an investigation by German High Command.

Let them kid themselves, the Jasenovac personnel rued. If those hyp-ocritical German prigs at Auschwitz weren't enjoying themselves too, why did they insist all the Jews be sent to them, so they could have *that* sport?

The guard, Franjo, saw Kata's niece, Jovanka, whom Kata had never met, shivering in the cold, spreading her thin coat as best she could around the infant she held at her chest. She was shivering just as she had the day before, when he'd touched her. "You won't be cold for long, my dear," he quipped.

Jovanka and her infant *were* shivering, the baby from the cold, Jo-vanka from fear. Srđa had told her about the kiln, when they were on the mountaintop, where there was clarity. The scent of what smelled like barbecued pork wafted past her. She stood paralyzed, choosing to believe this was just another iteration of her nightmare. Her stomach lurched with nausea.

But then she remembered her baby and what was important. She brought the baby close to her mouth and whispered repeatedly with many kisses, "Don't worry, my little lamb, *lane moje,* everything will be fine. Just stay by momma. We are going to be with grandma now and everything will be wonderful. Just you wait and see. This will be the best thing ever."

Franjo wrenched the baby from Jovanka's arms. Both mother and child shrieked hysterically.

Jovanka continued screaming till they got near the door into the kiln, a door large enough for a man to walk through. Everybody always shut up once they got there, their mouths agape. He did not break stride as he held the mother at arm's length, while, with his other arm, he slung the screaming baby by her leg and tossed her. Lightly, he only need toss the baby lightly, since the updraft was fierce from that inferno and would grab her more passionately than her own mother.

He didn't even need to lay his hand on the mother – that *Krajina* trash ran into the inferno after her nit.

Franjo would win the pig this month. They could win suckling pigs for discovering new, more efficient disposal methods. Last month, somebody won it for demonstrating how inexpensive it was to tether Serbs together, drive them up to a cliff side, bludgeon the first few, throw them off and the rest would just be dragged along effortlessly. This month's helpful hint would be, 'Why struggle with the mother when she will follow you effortlessly if you take her infant?'

The prigs at Auschwitz were appalled to hear they cremated their vermin alive. Liars, as if they wouldn't also enjoy watching a stupid *Vlach* bitch dance that dance.

* * *

Jovanka and the Baby Escape

Jovanka's only thought as she hit that wall of flame was to reach her child before death overtook them both. Her overriding fear was that her baby might lose her way. She did manage to scoop up the baby before she collapsed, shrieking, or so it appeared. In reality, she was still running, with all her might, her child in her arms, when she hit the other side of the chamber.

She passed right through it into a lush green field filled with wildflowers and a large crowd of picnickers. It was a sunny morning in spring. The delightful scent of rotisseried lamb, heavily garlicked, wafted in the air.

Her family was nearest. Everyone was standing, cheering. It was deafening. She thought it must be a sports match, but everyone was looking at her. They were cheering her! Her Uncle Pavao, who'd always been so hard to please, pounded her on the back. There was a big smile on his face. He had all his teeth. "That was fantastic, my girl!" he said. Then he turned to an old buddy, "Our teenage girls have more guts than grown men elsewhere!"

Almost all her relatives were now hugging her, crying with joy. So was she. Half the people in her village were right there.

"So here you all are," she said. "And I thought you were all dead!"

That huge crowd -- everybody in it -- laughed merrily. She'd never felt so clever in her whole life.

Mama looked so fit and trim. She took Jovanka's baby and held her high above her head. The baby giggled.

"What a day!" Jovanka leaned against the fence behind her. A sensation flashed in her mind of hitting into a wall of flame. Her legs were suddenly wobbly. "Momma," she cried and reached for her. As her momma embraced her she could feel a huge wave of sympathy wash over her from everyone surrounding her. She cried for a while, attended to intently by all. Everybody loved her and felt for her. She could feel it washing over her like a balm.

"Mama," she said, smiling again. "This sure is some health resort. You look twenty years younger."

Mama laughed and touched Jovanka's cheek tenderly. "Yes, *lane moje*, this sure is *some* health resort." Then she hugged her daughter, the baby in the middle. "I knew you'd come through just fine, no matter what. My little sharp shooter. . . I have a surprise for you."

She looked over to her left and then motioned with her index finger for someone to stop hiding and come to them. It was Srđa. Jovanka let out a gasp and raced into his arms. She began sobbing.

"*Ne, ne*, now what's all this?" he said.

"I wanted you to live a long life. You had so much to do! It's not right. I wanted you to live for a long time and do lots of great things. All that education wasted!"

"Energy is never lost, *srče moje*, my heart," he said. "I've got lots to do, and lots for you to help me with. Seriously. You get some rest and I'll tell you all about it. Prince Lazar wants to see you."

"Prince Lazar wants to see me? *The* Prince Lazar?" she said in disbelief.

"Yes, you, exactly."

* * *

Jovanka Gets the Royal Treatment

Serbs tend to expect overmuch from their heads of state since two of them were saints. Lazar was the second.

He was king when the Serbs were conquered by The Turk in 1389. He died on the field of battle, at Kosovo, on the day Serbia was enslaved for the next 530 years. He is revered as a hero.

In Serbian Heaven he became something of an eccentric, preferring to dress like a monk and/or beggar. He became heavily involved in micro-managing the emotional well-being of every Serb who ever mentioned him in prayer. As a result, his psyche morphed into an immense consciousness that bore little resemblance to that of a normal human. He quite enjoyed it. He was known to carry on multiple conversations in multiple places simultaneously. No one could keep up with him.

"Oh, my girl, there you are!" he effused when Jovanka entered the dilapidated shack he insisted on inhabiting. She was nonetheless in great awe and terribly wide-eyed as he hugged her warmly.

"Oh please, please, sit down," he continued. "You've been through such an ordeal. You must be exhausted. Did you make sure she rested?" Lazar asked Srđa.

"Oh yes, I did. She slept for a good long while." He put his arm across her. "It's such a joy to be reunited. It's hard to even think about what's still going on down there. It seems so distant."

"Yes, yes, you're exactly right, my son. But we must think about it. I have it straight from the horse's mouth, God does not intend to do without Serbs in the world. The world needs more Serbs – the people who can be relied on to choose the heavenly kingdom instead of the earthly kingdom.

"It's of course forgone the Axis will be defeated. It's been forgone ever since that wet spring God sent in '41 that turned the roads into Russia to mud. That and Hitler's irrational fury at a country full of defiant Serbs. Once it's over it will be a high priority to get our numbers back up.

"And personally, I'm particularly fond of the Roknić family."

Jovanka blushed and laughed like a shy girl.

"Have you seen Vaša yet?" Prince Lazar asked.

"Oh yes!" said Srđa. "I saw him the other day. I told him everyone knows now how right he was about what was coming, and how many lives were saved by his warning everyone."

"Yes, well Jovanka, I know it's a joy to have nearly everyone in the family here together at last, but the problem is that it means there are hardly any Roknić left on earth. One in four Serbs in your district have been dispatched here, but the casualties for your family in particular, with so many in the vanguard of the resistance, are much higher. I don't have to tell you about the reprisal that took your family. There were many more."

There was a knock at the door.

"Oh Sava, you read my mind," Lazar said to the scholarly-looking gentleman in an 18th century suit who'd come to the door.

"Yes, I did in fact. My pleasure."

"You're just in time. I'm filling Jovanka in on our plans for your Roknić cousins' resurrection," Lazar said, then addressed Jovanka. "You have an aunt in America who was caught up in the first phase of the Aryan atrocities. Sava, why don't you fill Jovanka in on that?"

"Certainly," Sava positioned his spectacles, which he no longer needed since his vision was now perfect, but he didn't feel like himself without them, so he kept a blank pair with him at all times.

"Let me first comment on the state of the world, when, after all I went through pushing the new, improved alphabet through, my own little cousin never even learned to read or write. That says it all. The Hapsburg regime deliberately denied them education.

"Then she fell victim to the Croatian Aryan Wannabe's first effort – to 'Kill the Serb in the Head' – to force conversions onto the vulnerable. Some who were starving were coerced with the offer of a barrel of flour for anyone who converted. Others were feeling so badly about themselves they could be deceived into betraying themselves and becoming enslaved to their enemies in the worst possible way – willingly.

"Then came the next generation whose souls were at terrible risk of being taken by the Devil himself. That man, Franjo, who threw your baby into that kiln? Three of his grandparents were Serbs!

"So many of our children are lost over there. Their heads filled with lies about us, trying to live lives with no love for themselves at all. Your auntie is in great distress. Every day when she wakes up she prays the Orthodox prayer and is so ashamed that she betrayed her own. And every day she's treated like a dog. And every day she fears she has lost her soul forever into the *Tuđina*.

"Her younger son is very protective of her and is likely to be receptive, though he's very confused about who he is and angry with the world. He has two souls. His Serbian soul is the one he's loyal to, but his Croatian soul is the one he obeys. He betrays himself with every breath."

Lazar jumped back in. "The thing is, you two were to have another child, another daughter, but that's been interrupted, so the thinking is to give that little soul to your cousin Archie, and with your intervention as her Guardians, her Heavenly Godparents, her *Kuma*, to help that poor family find themselves again. There are so few Roknić left, every last one is important. If you two will consent to sign up for Guardian training, we can get things rolling."

Srđa could see that Jovanka was excited. "Of course, we will," he said. "It's the least we can do."

So, it all ended up, after all the intensive Guard training, with Jovanka and Srđa haunting a working-class Chicago suburb in the Fifties. It hadn't been ten years for them, seeing as how they had been in a different time zone, so to speak. It seemed like just a few months when Jovanka found herself cooing to this new baby, who'd just been born to her American cousin, Archie. There her little goddaughter was, Leslie, just as beautiful as her firstborn daughter. The baby whimpered a bit, hungry.

"Shhh, now, little one," she said, enveloping the baby with her arms, euphorically. "You are always safe with me."

The baby's New World mother came to her, grasping right through Jovanka's arms. It was Jovanka's first experience as an invisible one with no physical substance at all, in other words, a ghost. The sensation was an intrusive kind of tickling. The new father, Archie, stood in the door-way – her Aunt Kata's son, whom she had also never met. She recognized him from the photograph that had hung on the wall next to the icon of their family Slava, Saint George, in the home that was now nothing but ashes blown to the winds.

"*Dobro*," she thought. "Good. Everything is good. Srđa, as always, was right. What's good never dies."

* * *

Leslie's Kitchen, 2:30 AM

Daniel paused for a bit, then said, "I've counted 226 Roknić so far who perished at Jasenovac. Out of one little district – how many could have been left?"

210

The body count hit Jovanka hard. Instead of the image of a crowd of happy picnickers, the ones who'd greeted her on her first day in Heaven, the image she liked to hold onto, she flashed involuntarily on the terror, and unimaginable loss -- everyone had endured. She wrapped her arm around Leslie's shoulders, her eyes tearing up and she buried her head on Leslie's shoulder.

"I always knew about them," Leslie shuddered, placing her hand on her shoulder and rubbing it.

Jovanka remembered it was these two who were now her mission and pushed her melancholy aside. She crossed over to Daniel. She wanted to see Leslie's expression.

Leslie was looking intently at Daniel, speaking emphatically, as if pleading for his understanding, her mud-into-gold eyes glazed over again with tears that made them sparkle luminously. Jovanka was already aware of the effect that sight had on Daniel. She smiled.

"I keep seeing them in other people!" Leslie exclaimed.

He smiled. "That's what you see in us?"

"Of course, isn't that obvious?"

Jovanka stood between the two of them, feeling the electricity of emotion being amplified as it shot back and forth between them. She could hear Leslie's astonishment.

'He feels me!'

To which Jovanka could hear him reply,

'Yes, I do, with such pleasure I can't hardly stand it.' He smiled tenderly, reached across the table towards Leslie's hand.

"It *is* obvious, and I can't tell you how much it moves me."

As he placed his hand over hers, Leslie felt an energy that had been bouncing frenetically inside her all her life become instantly grounded.

* * *

The Revolt or the Race Riot or
Whatever the Hell It Was

Reggie had not gone into the bedroom while Daniel told Leslie about the revolt or the race riot or whatever the hell it was. He had sat in the living room and he had listened. And he proceeded further in his process of letting her go. Whatever anyone else said, he'd just spent all those years with Leslie because he cared about her and he liked her, and he enjoyed her, and who the hell knew if he really loved her or not. What the hell is love, anyway?

But he was sure that he could not, nor did he want, to love her the way she now wanted to be loved, and that made him sad, for he saw in himself a flatness that depressed him. He could never do for her what Daniel was doing. He was too cynical. He didn't believe in that shit. It made no difference. It had made no difference for him, why would he muster it for her?

All the horror stories in the world about what had happened in his family to make everybody so screwed up didn't make a damn bit of difference. Everybody stayed just as screwed up anyway. If that's what she thought she needed for herself, she could have it. But he couldn't give it to her. He just didn't have it in him and didn't *want* to have it in him anymore. What would be the point?

All that foolishness he'd indulged in during his militant phase was purely adolescent. As if bitching about the inequities of the world was going to make any damn difference. Nothing touched it. Nothing touched what ailed him. If anything, the relief of being with someone white was letting go of all those pointless illusions that commiserating about that shit was going to do any damn good. And now she wanted to take him back into that pointlessness?

No, Simone understood him better. She was the girl he was slipping off to see when he left home with no explanations. He gave no explanation because he knew Leslie would not demand one. He knew she was letting him go. It was becoming clear where he really belonged. It was about somehow slogging away at that deep-seated shit. Just understanding where it came from wasn't cutting it.

He would miss Leslie, but he could not take her where she wanted to go. He didn't resent Daniel. Actually, he was quite relieved that the guy was hopefully taking this enormously needy girl, alone in the world, off his hands. And, to be honest, the situation was a hoot. He laughed.

He saw it right away. Anytime she talked to Daniel she'd come back all happy and bubbly and *ready*. He supposed some of it might have been for him, or she was trying to still feel it for him, but she was just kidding herself.

And to be a really nice guy, he'd leave it up to her to figure that out for herself. And if that involved a little something for him along the way, for old time's sake, why the hell not? He *was* going to miss her. Maybe he could use a little time in letting her go, himself.

* * *

It was 3AM before Leslie finally got ready for bed. She was enormously gratified by the exchange with her new friend, Daniel. Her new, true friend. And more. Just being in the same room with him woke up a side of her that had been getting beaten around everywhere she turned. The negative attention it had brought her was relentless and withering. And that's exactly what she'd become – withered.

But there it was, as right as rain. And hers. She'd paid for it and it was hers. It was hers every minute of every day she'd ever breathed on this earth, she owed no one a thing for it. But still she'd had to pay, again and again for her own damn birthright.

And it was superb. What she was seeing and what she wanted was superb. Her birthright was every damn thing she ever thought was beautiful and deep and, and . . .

She stepped out of the bathroom and was startled to realize that it was Reggie in the bed. After all that with Daniel and she had to get in the bed with Reggie. He turned onto his back, stirring towards her and she was struck again, how it is sometimes with a bad habit you're trying to break, that's so damn tempting. Why did he have to be so good looking? He was better looking than she was. Why did he have to bother with her? Keep tempting her with something she couldn't help but be attracted to. He was perfect. Phoenix perfect.

"Hey baby," he said, smiling groggily, as if he'd been waiting up for her.

'Oh, so it's 'hey baby?'' she thought. 'You think I want your sorry ass when I could have someone who appreciated me? There's a lot here *to* appreciate, if you'd ever cared to notice.'

"You gonna just stand there or are you gonna come to bed sometime tonight?" he said, teasing her sweetly.

"I might," she said. As she climbed in, he rose up to put his hand behind her neck, guiding her face to his.

When their lips met it sparked an explosion of beautiful anger she disguised as pure passion.

'You think I'm giving this to you?' she thought. 'No, baby, I'm showing you what you *could* have had if you'd had any sense, what you've been missing all along. What you will soon *be* missing forever.'

And as he reached up under her nightshirt, "Yeah, go ahead, see what that's really like, that will *never* be yours."

* * *

Daniel in the room directly above theirs thought Reggie was laying it on a little thick with all the noise. Like Reggie was trying to be as loud and talkative as he could so there'd be no doubt how good *it* was.

And all that banging. Everybody knows all it takes is a balled-up pair of socks between the headboard and the wall to tone that shit down, but this guy was going for the drum-line with a big bass drum, in an up-tempo. It all ended with a flourish.

Daniel lay, thinking of her, how deeply she moved him and how much more he wanted to know. He knew it should concern him that his dissertation research was becoming sexualized, but he didn't care. It would either make the work superb or ruin it. It didn't matter which, as long as he could find out more about this girl.

Was this little white girl really from a parallel universe? And if she were, what would that do to his conception of the cosmos?

Jovanka sat on the bed next to Daniel, watching him fall asleep, her arm encircling his head as if he were a child. "So, you want to understand our universe?" she said, seeing he was deep asleep.

She leaned down and kissed his cheek. "You already do, my son, *moje sine,* you already do. You just have to let yourself *feel* it. The devil's set many a snare to keep you from it -- you know who I'm talking about -- but I know you can do it. If anyone can, it's you."

* * *

The Reprisal in Perna

Daniel wondered if he should see if Leslie was home. Nikola had just translated a section of that Vrginmost document Daniel had told Leslie about. The one that *just happened* to be about her family's district that had arrived a month *before* he'd met her – that odd little 'coincidence' that had so shocked him.

He wasn't aware of another coincidence. Nikola had inexplicably and randomly chosen to first translate the chapter about *Jovanka's* village.

"Yes, of course!" Jovanka said, tapping her foot impatiently. "Go see if she's home. She is, I can tell you that right now, so go see her. Go on! Do you have any idea how *long* we've been waiting for this?"

Almost as fast as Jovanka, Daniel flew down the heavy 19th century staircase, blackened with age, with a rapid staccato of footsteps. He raised a flurry of dust that was highlighted by a sharp shaft of afternoon light in the foyer that smelled of old wood. He knocked on the door. Leslie answered it with a broad smile as if she already knew it was him.

"Hey!" she said. "Come on in. I heard you double-timing it down the stairs." She plopped onto the sofa, picking up some books strewn across it. She set them on the end table. She patted the cushion next to her, gesturing for him to join her. "What's up?"

He had paced quickly into the room and began circling it in the quick way he had when deep in thought, which was most of the time. "Okay, Nikola scanned through that Vrginmost document I told you about and decided to start with the chapter about a town called Perna. He'd noticed something."

"Yeah?" Leslie asked, intrigued, motioning again for him to sit. He was too far away.

"There was a resistance in the town, instigated by two men, that turned out to be considerable."

He was still pacing. It had been a week since they'd spent half the night together, in her kitchen. It amused her to see how hard he was working to get it, which she knew he was, when he had to know he already had it. Her eyes started to water when she realized he was making all this effort to make sure she understood how much *it* was worth to him.

"Really?"

"Yes, that little town pulled together in an amazing way. There was a passage mentioning that this scantily-armed group of illiterate peasants stood up to a modern army for months. The first airstrikes of the Croatian Fascist State were visited on it." He had been dying all week to see how she was going to respond to this story.

"Wow!" she said.

"What the three of us did was write down the names of all the casualties, each on its own index card, and then put them in date order. This book lists alphabetically each person who died in the war, their name, birthdate, town, date of death and manner of death. It was quite a monumental effort someone went to, putting it together.

"You sweethearts!" Jovanka exclaimed, throwing her arms around Daniel and planting a kiss on his cheek. Her eyes were moist.

"So, anyway, once we did this, the story popped. Nikola had a hunch that recorded in those dates was an event, a reprisal on the families of those two men."

Srđa appeared. He sensed Jovanka's tension and rushed to her. She had popped up to plant that kiss on Daniel and was pacing nervously in the same space where he was pacing. Daniel gave up trying to occupy that space and sat down next to Leslie.

Srđa tried to reach for Jovanka but she was moving too fast. "He's talking about the reprisal?" he asked.

Her chin quivered, and she nodded, her eyes watery, finally stopping to face him. He wrapped his arms around her. "You sure you're ready for this?" he asked. She nodded again, and they squeezed in together on the recliner. It creaked.

Daniel and Leslie looked in that direction absently.

Dušan was leaning against the wall, in the corner of the room and laughed. Those unconscious perceptions of the living always amused him.

Daniel picked up the pages of Nikola's typewritten translation and interpretation of the events in the summer and fall of 1941 in the town of Perna, Croatia.

"It all started when the fascists attacked the village in the valley, Poljans. The people in Perna could hear the screaming, and all the men . . ."

"And one girl," interjected Jovanka.

". . . slipped to an agreed upon point of ambush and attacked the fascists as they were returning from Poljans. As I said they put up such a resistance that it wasn't until September that they began to weaken. Here, read it."

He handed Leslie the document.

Jovanka crossed over to the couch and sat closely next to Leslie, on the other side from Daniel, her hand on Leslie's thigh.

* * *

Perna, September 14, 1941

"Lane moje," Jovanka whispered into Leslie's ear, "your grandmother lived in Sjeničak, but I grew up in a neighboring town, Perna. And we were ready. When the gunfire, the screaming and the wailing in Poljans

drifted up from the valley in July 1941 to us in Perna, we poured out to our rendezvous." She pantomimed holding a rifle. "We lay in ambush and attacked the *Ustaša*.

"My uncle was among those first members of the Partisans. The Partisans are the only reason there are any of us are still alive. But our family paid the price when *Ustaša* committed their reprisal on us.

"All our men were in the field, among the first volunteers to the Partisans. Even my broken down, alcoholic daddy volunteered, gave up his drinking, just like that, and before you know it, he was his old self again. A super marksman.

"But then, in the very early morning hours of September 14, 1941 the *Ustaša* pulled into our compound. As luck, or God would have it, I was in the outhouse when they burst into our courtyard. So, I climbed the tree next to the outhouse and hid.

"From the height I had climbed I saw the first stabbing. I saw my father's first cousin, or his sister by way of his aunt, as we would call her, Milka Tanasije Roknić, bayoneted by a *Ustaša*. He pulled the blade out of her body, ran his finger along it and licked his finger. I threw up.

"I recognized the young Croat boy who had done deliveries for the feed merchant and had often eaten at our home. Often, we had shown him our hospitality. He could never make a delivery without being fed and entertained like a member of the family.

"He's the one who led them to the Poštic *zadruga* nearby, our cousins. He took them straight to the cottage of the Poštic man at the head of the Partisans. My best friend, Milka, was nursing her baby, Evića, and making bread.

"Let me tell you how we make our bread. She would have had to wake up throughout the night to keep a good fire burning, so there would be lots of coals. She'd set out several liters of dough the night before, then in the morning she would have cleared a circle in the center of the fireplace, then placed some large squash leaves on the fireplace floor. As she was about to empty the dough onto the leaves, the *Ustaša* burst into the house, awakening everyone.

"There were six little kids in the tiny house that housed two families, all sleeping in one marriage bed, what you call a double bed. While they lay in their bed, three at the top, three at the bottom, all cuddled together, still asleep, a *Ustaša* quickly began piercing each child in its gut with his bayonet. The last two, out of his reach, woke to see what was happening and tried to run, shrieking from the room. One *Ustaša* caught the youngest, a girl with long, reddish brown hair, shining in his hand as he jerked her up underneath him and slit her throat. The other, a little boy was snatched by another *Ustaša* in the main room who, smiling as if this were sport, tossed the beautiful child onto the end of his comrade's bayonet. The child's shriek ended abruptly as it pierced his lung.

"What should have happened that morning, Milka should have poured that dough into the fireplace and covered it with the baking lid." Jovanka clasped her hands and made a triangle shape with her arms. "The potter makes it. Like a Chinese hat. It would already be piping hot, then it covers the dough, and coals go over it. Everybody was supposed to wake up to the scent of some wonderful, fresh-baked bread that morning, but no.

"Instead they grabbed little Evica and put *her* under the lid.

Leslie gasped. 'My God!"

"That little baby," Daniel confirmed.

Leslie shuddered.

Jovanka continued, "Someday you can go see that lid at the Military Museum in Belgrade. And bring some flowers for little Evića."

After a pause Leslie said, "When I go to that museum someday, I will bring her some flowers."

Jovanka could not speak, either, for several moments as she wept for Evića. Then she remembered the joyful little girl she saw every day brightening Heaven and she swept away her tears. She continued.

"Then the commanding officer said to Milka, 'Serve that dish to your uncle, Marko, in Hell,' I know, because she told me, but she did not tell me this in Hell. She told me this in Heaven.

"Then they took Milka, shrieking, half-mad, out into the yard. Several of them raped her and her aunt Kata while the others were setting the house on fire. While being raped, her mind left her body and regained its clarity, and she saw, in the doorway of her burning house, a beautiful angel holding Evića.

"Then the *Ustaša* stabbed her, and while she was still alive, threw her into the burning house. Within fifteen minutes, everyone in the house had been killed and was being burnt up in the fire. Once dead, they departed from their front doors and began their ascent, looking back in disbelief at the unfortunate soldiers who were now as damned as they were blessed.

"But back at the Roknić *zadruga*, I saw with my own eyes as my cousin, Boja Radicanin, ran into the woods with several *Ustaša* chasing her. In minutes, they brought her back to the burning houses, pulling her by her hair. One then bayoneted her, and while she still lived, threw her into the inferno inside the house. She screamed her agony and then was heard no more on earth.

"The last cottage they came to was that of my hero, Anka Roknić. She told me about it later, in Heaven. She had moments to think of an escape. She had a thought to send her children out the window in back, but there was a soldier lurking there. She hid her two youngest under the bed. She ran into the kitchen and found a kitchen knife when the fascist thugs entered. She rushed at them with the knife. Immediately they bayoneted her.

"She fell to the floor while they moved on to the others. Her head was clearing when she heard her invalid mother-in-law screaming from across the house. One of the soldiers had lingered in her kitchen, tearing off a piece of bread from the large loaf she'd baked the day before. She leapt out at him with her kitchen knife. She went for his throat, but he blocked it and she only cut a deep gash along his shoulder. They fell to the floor, with him screaming, as she continued slashing at him. "You scream like a girl," she hissed in his ear.

"Two Ustaša ran into the room and finally managed to bayonet Anka once more. As she lay dying, the soldiers hurriedly left, dragging their bleeding comrade with them, anxious to get him to the medic. They set the house on fire.

"In their haste they had missed Anka's two youngest children she'd hidden under the bed. The children could hear the trucks departing and slipped out of the burning house in time. Somehow, in all the smoke and confusion, we missed each other and fled in different directions. I did not know of their survival till much later.

"I also learned of another person who survived, another young mother, Evića Roknić. She'd been bayoneted in the courtyard and left for dead, with her three-year-old son, who'd been killed while in her arms. She was found and taken to the hospital, where her wounds were healing. Ustaša, nonetheless, found her in the hospital and finished her off while she lay convalescing in her bed.

"By the time the sun was fully risen, 105 people lay dead, 57 of them little kids. There was even a newborn who was thrown, uninjured, into one of the burning houses."

Daniel looked intently at Leslie. She did it again. She turned to him with those intense eyes that opened onto her soul and pleaded with him to enter into it. "It's too much," she said. "No wonder we weren't told." Then she clutched the pages up to her chest.

219

"It got left to me to sort this out. That's how long it took to just be able to speak about it.' She sobbed quietly.

"You okay?" he asked.

She brushed aside her tears and sat up straight, her eyes resolved with a beautiful anger. "Of course! It's the least I can do. We still on for tonight?" she asked.

"Sure. Nikola and Bojana are excited about meeting you."

"Bring it on," she said.

* * *

The Pub

They met at The Pub for deep dish pizza and some Bock beer -- Nikola and Bojana, Daniel and Leslie, an international crew. Reggie had been invited as well but begged off. It was a trendy place with a greenhouse of Italian herbs growing in the front window, and deeply cushioned booths of high old oak woodwork forming cozy partitions under an eleven-foot stamped tin ceiling. Acoustic rock played softly in the background. An easy place to talk.

"It's the damnedest bit of history I've ever encountered," said Daniel. "It's like somebody took a cookie cutter and made the same cookies there as here."

"What do you mean?" Leslie asked.

"Well, let's start with 1389, when you all got kidnapped to another continent and held captive for hundreds of years," he said.

"Kidnapped where?" she asked.

"All right," he admitted, "So you all didn't go anywhere, the borders just shifted. You woke up one morning and were no longer in Europe, you were now a part of the Middle East. But the analogy is relevant because it meant that you were foreign enough to the people who enslaved you to make them that much more callous. You were less human for it, like we were. You were held captive for hundreds of years by people who did pretty much whatever they wanted to you."

Nikola cut in. "It was not quite so uniform. There were always the mountains," he said. "Where, as they say in West Virginia, 'Mountaineers are always free.' For us, there were always mountains where rebels hid and made The Turk miserable. We made much trouble for him, always."

"Good," Leslie said.

Nikola nodded at her with a smile. "In the plains, where most people had to stay, since the mountainside produces little food, people were treated badly and suffered many abuses, but there were always the mountain rebels who gave everyone hope. But Bojana and I are from the *Krajina*, like your family. And that is another story. "

"The uppitiest negroes of all time," said Daniel.

"Really? Is that why I like them so much?" she said."

"They say it's in the blood," said Bojana.

"That's what Starčević said," said Daniel.

"Oh," said Nikola, "so you *have* been reading."

"Starchy bitch who?" said Leslie.

"Starchy bitch, Starčević, was the founding father of the Croatian nationalism, by way of being the founding father of genocidal hatred of Serbs." Daniel said.

"His mother was a Serb, and he had some Serb blood on his father's side too. In the 19th century, he was calling for Croatian independence, and claiming that the Serbs living in Croatia must be eradicated. They could never be trusted, would always side with each other, it was just in the blood. And that was the rationale that led to the extermination of a fourth of the Serbian population."

"It looks like it was half of my family," Leslie said.

Everyone fell silent, then Daniel took another big gulp of beer.

"Okay, I will tell you *Krajina* history in a nutshell," he said, facing Leslie. "It's 1560 really, but for the sake of analogy we'll say it's 1860 and the South has just seceded from the Union and fired on Fort Sumter. But the North decides not to vex itself fighting the South itself so what it does is just spread the word through the grapevine for the slaves to make their way to the Mason-Dixon line. If they do, not only will they get 40 acres and a mule anywhere along that line they want, but horses, guns, uniforms and military training. And they get to keep whatever they can steal from The Turk. So, what do you think, Lez, you think our boys are gonna hold that line? 'Cause that's all they have to do, is hold that line, and all that is theirs. And the best part is, they get to kick the ass of those motherfuckers they've been slaves to. Think they can do it?"

"Yeah, they can do it," she replied.

"Yep, for 350 years, y'all held the border of Europe." he said.

The pizza came, and everyone dug in enthusiastically to indulge themselves in the orgy of melted cheeses and chewy crust. Daniel started rapping the table, his eyes lit up with a new thought.

"That's it! That's one of the main differences in the two populations. We *were* literally dragged to another place where we had nowhere to run, where we stuck out like sore thumbs. We *couldn't* fight. We were profoundly de-militarized, while y'all were profoundly militarized. Exactly the opposite extreme. Interesting. Interesting to see what effects that will have."

"You will see," said Bojana. "In the end, it turns out much better for you."

"Yes," Daniel said. "A militarized, armed minority. That could be deadly . . . for that minority." The two nodded. "Like the Indians here," he added. "Interesting."

"Exactly," said Nikola. "Just like the Indians here."

"Okay," Daniel went on. "So, let me back up to when it all started. It was 1389 when the Turks colonized the Serbs. That means Serbs, who before that were sailing to China and doing art that surpassed what was going on in Venice, were suddenly serfs."

"Slaves," said Nikola.

"Yes," said Daniel. "A serf lives in the same conditions as a Jim Crow-sharecropper. Slavery didn't end with Civil War. It just shifted into peonage." Daniel rapped on the table. "And that is a form of slavery."

"Yes," said Nikola. "We have always called it that."

"So, say you're struggling to feed a family, somebody comes along, steals most of your crop, and if you try to hold back on that, he impales you. If you leave the patch of dirt you're sentenced to work, any Turk can do anything he wants to you. You have no rights he is bound to respect. He's also stealing your sons whenever he pleases, and oftentimes your daughters for harems."

"Eee-ooo," said Leslie.

"And if he wants to, he can spend your wedding night with your bride, and get first dibs at her."

"The Right of the First Night," said Bojana, patting down her black hair, which had frizzed up in the night air.

"So that's what's going on in Serbia, while the Turks were trying to invade further westward, but they can't get past the damn *Krajina* Serbs living in what's now Croatia.

"During the same time period, the neighboring Croatian population was being held in abject serfdom to the Austro-Hungarians. There were stories of Hungarian lords chasing naked Croatians with dogs for sport."

"Damn," said Leslie.

222

"Hot damn," he seconded. "That is not a good situation to be in. So, what you had with the Croats was a 'po white trash' mentality brewing that was going to turn its ugly head on the Serb border guards with a vengeance."

Bojana interrupted. "What is 'po white trash?' I never heard of such thing."

"Oh sorry," said Daniel. "I forget myself. Poor white trash, meaning the poor whites living in the South. They tend to descend from the Scottish, Irish and poor English who were the first slaves in America. Once it became obvious how much more profitable and manageable it would be to enslave Africans, those white slaves were bought off to become the new slave drivers."

"Ah yes," said Nikola. "Balkanized. We wrote book on that one."

"Definitive, eh? Divide and conquer," smiled Daniel.

"You betcha," said Nikola. He turned to Leslie. "With a vengeance. Imagine what happen if black people can become white people."

"What do you mean?" asked Leslie.

"All you need is a little water sprinkled on head," he gestured the act. "And presto - chango you are now a new white person. Imagine what happens. Will the new white person be better to those still black than other white persons, or worse?"

"Worse," said Daniel. "Much worse." He turned to Leslie with an excited thought. "This is what has been blowing my mind. All you have to do is look at those 'new whites' in Croatia – the Serbs who had converted to Catholicism, thereby becoming Croats – how gory their violence was towards their former "own." They were the *worst* of the Ustaša."

"Yes, I can believe that," said Leslie. "It's the bigot mind. They're always talking about themselves. It makes sense. The more literal they're like the people they hate, the more they *would* hate them."

"And what that means," said Daniel, "is that alleged 'curse of Ham,'" he brushed his cheek to indicate the color of his skin, "has a huge silver lining. It has imposed a unity you can't really see until you look at a similar situation where it was absent. Croatia in the forties.

"So," he went on, "the 'new' whites joined forces with the newly freed Croatians. The minute the Austro-Hungarian empire collapsed the Croats went from hating them to wanting to *be* them. They'd spent centuries despising their Germanic occupiers, but the minute the occupiers left, there was a sudden obsession to be Germanic themselves. And a sudden despising of their Slavic cousins.

"So, by the end of the 19th century you could see the beginnings of the Aryan Supremacy dogma starting in Europe, and there were Croatians stirring that pot from the git go, headed by your friend, Starchy Bitch, the 'new white,' or I should say, new Croat.

"By the Depression the situation had gone totally rancid and you had average Croats succumbing to classic scapegoating, looking for any excuse to be hating on you'se poor nigras.

"If you go and look at some of the documentation on Croatian attitudes and stereotypes of their Krajina Serb countrymen, it basically comes down to them seeing y'all as a bunch of rough, tough ghetto thugs living on thievery."

Leslie smiled incredulously. "What ghetto?

"It's not uncommon," said Nikola, "to find the Kordun, another word for Krajina, referred to as ghetto."

"Yes," Daniel said. "Ghetto is a European word. We're the ones who borrowed it. And remember, you all were never paid for holding the border of Europe. Just allowed to keep what you could steal. So how are you going to be seen? A bunch of lazy thugs, living on their thievery. Then when there were no more Turks to steal from, you were just laying around, bitching about it instead of hustling at some honest work. Of course, by then it was easy to forget that the Serbs had no other options. The land they had was usually poor, high ground. If they failed as farmers, that was why, but you know how good bigots are at sidestepping facts like that, and that's what they'd become – bigots.

"Some claim that the first genocide of World War II was committed by the Croatian Ustaša on *Krajina* Serbs." There was a silence. "In some villages it would be as much as 60% of the population exterminated. And the level of sadism was so off-the-wall there's tons of documentation of Nazis condemning the barbarity. Hitler even complained about it."

"Too heavy," said Bojana, wincing nervously and retreating behind Nikola's arm.

"I'm sorry," said Daniel.

Daniel reached across the table and touched Bojana's hand. Leslie's hand was on the bench between them. He covered her hand as well.

* * *

Leslie Wonders If She's Real

Reggie was already in bed when she got home. As she slipped into bed he stirred.

"Have a good time?" he asked.

"Incredible," she said.

"Good," he said. He turned towards her. "Anything left for me?" he teased.

"Oh, a little bit," she teased back. He ran his hand across the contour of her hip and pulled her leg across his.

A question that had come up before that she'd never asked, jumped into her mind, and the asking of it seemed suddenly to be an easy thing to do. She sat up and leaned to face him. "Am I real to you?"

"What do you mean?" he said.

"Am I real to you?"

"What kind of question is that?"

"It's just a question," she answered.

"Why would I be living with you if you weren't real to me?" he replied, and then went on tersely, "as real to me as I am to you."

She stopped short at his honesty.

"You don't think you're real to me?"

He sighed. "I don't think I have the energy for this conversation."

She wondered why she was still in his bed. "Why do *you* think I'm here? I mean, America is quite adamant. It's been telling me loud and clear for a while now. 'You nasty 'ho.' Why do you think it's so important to me that I'm finding out the real reasons I'm in this space? Or are you trying to tell yourself that I'm just here because you're such an exceptional guy."

"What 's wrong with that?" he said.

"It's racist," she said.

He sighed. "Leslie defines racism."

"It's racist because it's saying the only reason I could possibly want to be around someone black is because he's exceptional. Black people, as a whole, no way. There's nothing about them, as a whole, that anyone could like or want to be around. There's only one thing a white woman could want if she keeps laying up with black men."

Marilyn flashed in his mind. "Shut up," he said.

"Shut up? What are you talking about? I'm supposed to take all this filth these good white folks are throwing at me all the time in silence?" she asked, also thinking of Marilyn. "There's never time for me? It's

225

never my turn to get some attention? Some support? It's just about you? Always just about you?"

He stopped himself short. There was nothing to fight about. He'd already made up his mind.

"Well, what do you want to do about it?" he said.

Now she was silent, thinking about letting him go. Then she started crying. She covered her face with her hands. He put his arm across her.

"You *are* exceptional," she said. My treasure, she thought, my Phoenix. Then she became pensive, trying to think how to explain what she wanted to say. There were no words in American English.

"We *are* the same," she said, choking up again. "We are both from the same kind of people. Vicious racism deprived me of my own, who I still need, and that's what I saw in all of you. Us, alive and well."

She reached for a tissue and blew her nose. "Does that make any sense? Do you understand what I'm saying?"

His eyes were heavy as was his arm around her, "Yes, baby. I understand." His voice sounded tedious.

She lay awake for a while after it seemed he'd fallen asleep. She was wondering how it would work out. When they broke up. The lease was up in another month. Is that what he was waiting for?

* * *

The Biograph

The next day Leslie answered the excited knocking at her door. It was Daniel.

"Lez," he said in a rush, "grab your coat, there's still time to make it."

"Time for what?"

"There's a movie at the Biograph tonight, it's about a Serbian girl in New York in the Forties. A classic."

"A classic about us?" she said. "Really?"

"Where's Reggie?" he asked. "He needs to come."

"I don't know," Leslie said.

"It's Saturday night and he's out and you don't know where he is?"

"That's about the way of things around here," she said.

Daniel stood stock still and looked at her hard. "He's a fool," he said. "And you know what? I'm glad. Come on, girl," he said, taking her hand. "Let's go."

As the sugar and the caffeine from the Coke hit her bloodstream along with the popcorn, Leslie rushed on the original *Cat People* plot line. It was soon obvious what the moviemakers' perspective was on Serbia – a primitive, backward country full of superstition and evil black arts.

She had already started laughing when it got to the part about the black panther. The Serbian girl in the story lived next to the zoo and loved sitting in the dark, listening to the panther scream. And every day she went to visit him.

"Too bad she couldn't just move in with him like I did," she quipped. Daniel's laughter in response was too uproarious for the setting.

The theater was fairly full of people trying to watch the camp, horror classic. The two were the only people laughing, trying to suppress it, without success.

"Okay," Daniel whispered, 'that's the gist of it, she thinks there's a curse on her and if she has sex with her new husband she's going to turn into a black panther and eat him for lunch."

Leslie slouched down in her chair, trying not to laugh loudly and failing. People turned their heads at her, annoyed. She was trying to whisper but was too convulsed in laughter to manage it when she said, "Then he be sayin.' 'Hit me with that again!'"

Daniel was laughing just as loud.

The usher flashed his flashlight on them. They quieted down.

Once the movie was over, it was a delight to be out in the crisp night air and able to laugh and talk freely. Daniel loved seeing Leslie so excited and intense. She was skipping, actually skipping. "No," she said. "It's so genius! How did they know?" she said, grabbing his arm with both hands, still laughing.

"Sociologically the film really is significant," Daniel said. Leslie thought that was a really funny statement and continued with delighted laughter.

"White Americans *would* be terrified of Serbs. Serbs are their worst nightmare," he continued.

"Serbs started out perfectly high functioning Caucasian people," Daniel went on, "who went through all the exploitation, all the abuse, the subjugation, the oppression, the lynching, the raping, the impoverishment – the whole nine yards people of color have been subjected to here, and they turned out exactly the same! They are a white racist's worst nightmare."

"How are we the same?"

He took a step towards her and looked her closely in the eyes. He shook his head. "I'm trying to define it. It's very subtle. Then maybe it's not, maybe it's hitting me in the face. What is it about us?"

"That makes us so special?" she asked, first as something she was giving him with her whole heart, and then as something about herself that made her coy and sure of herself.

It was that point in the conversation, where, had it been a date, they would have kissed, but it was not a date. They continued walking quietly home. 'Home,' she thought with immense satisfaction. 'Our home is the same place.' She grasped his arm, just above his elbow, as a lady being escorted home is allowed to do, date or no date.

When they got to the vestibule there was music playing in Leslie's apartment. "He's home," she said. "Home early for a Saturday night. Thank you," she said. "That's the most fun I've had on a Saturday night in a long time."

"My pleasure, lady," he said. "My absolute pleasure." He gave her a little peck on the cheek and headed up the stairs, two steps at a time. Leslie remembered those times when she'd started walking up those stairs as if they were taking her home.

She got into the apartment and felt rather smug, wondering if the tables had turned and Reggie was staring at four walls, wondering who the hell *she* was with on a Saturday night.

"Hey baby," he said. "Have fun?"

"I had a blast," she said. She headed into the bedroom and shut the door.

* * *

Daniel lay awake, in a rush over Leslie. He had a running fantasy that was in his mind more and more. It had started with a theoretical question he had asked himself. 'Let's say I came from a culture where people had just lived through centuries as slaves, and then headed into a century of getting exterminated. How would these people look to us, who'd been through the same time-period as slaves, but now, it looks like, anyway, are achieving a relative emancipation?

'How would I process everything I saw about them? What would they make me feel? What would I see through those filters?'

She had a glow on. He could feel it any time he was near her. He knew there wasn't much she couldn't cite. It wasn't just the knowledge, or the rapt attention to acquire it. It was the tenderness. The awe. The joy. It was in her passion. Seeing something no one else could see.

He wanted to see what she saw.

* * *

Cousin Sava

Leslie left the apartment door open the next afternoon when she went upstairs, but she didn't say a word about where she was going. She knocked on Daniel's door and he answered it with a big smile. As she entered the apartment she stopped him as he began to shut the door and whispered, "Leave it open. Give him more courtesy than he shows me. It will gratify me."

"Oh, you're so right," he replied, loudly. Leslie laughed conspiratorially.

"Okay," he said, walking down a long hallway towards the kitchen. Leslie followed, watching him. Reggie's lanky build had always been interesting, but Daniel did an equally interesting average -- broadly muscled with very quick reflexes. As if Reggie was doing masculinity in the latitudinal mode, while Daniel was doing it in the longitudinal. When she entered the neat kitchen two places were set with some popcorn in the middle and sodas. Two large posters from old classic movies were on the walls. 'Oh my God,' she thought. 'He has taste and isn't afraid to show it."

Propped against an old wine bottle was a book in Cyrillic script. On the cover was a distinguished looking gentleman with very sensitive eyes, sensual even, wearing a fez. There were medals on his chest.

"Who's this?" she asked.

"That's your cousin's protege, Vuk Karadžić."

"My cousin?" she asked.

Daniel produced another book. On the inside plate was a photograph of a statue of another distinguished looking gentleman in an 18th century suit, the man with the spectacles and perfect vision in Serbian Heaven who'd dropped in on Prince Lazar. She was amazed.

"That *is* my cousin," she said. "That's my cousin George."

"You're kidding," he laughed.

"No, what's he doing in that get up? she asked. "That's a *total* likeness."

"He and his buddy here wrote the alphabet, the Serbian Cyrillic alphabet. He's Sava Mrkalja, from Sjeničak, which your grandma's hamlet was

229

a part of, and where there is documentation of Mrkalja and Roknić marriages, a small, isolated village, isolated for centuries."

"They did the same thing Sequoia, the Cherokee, did, in the same time frame, here. They devised a system of writing that was so good an old man could be taught to read in a few weeks. Nikola caught the connection with the names."

"Oh my god!" said Leslie, "Sequoia's one of my favorite people."

"And your poor cousin went through hell over it."

"What happened?" she asked.

"Okay, he started out a poor but brilliant kid who was sent to school, sponsored by the Serbian Orthodox church. Then he was a teacher, still being paid by the church. Then he wrote a book calling for the simplification of the alphabet. The church didn't like it. He tried to prove his loyalty by becoming a monk, but that didn't work out either.

"In a couple of years he was homeless. He became depressed."

"Depressed?" she said, trying not to sound self-conscious. She knew it ran in Daniel's family, too, but she still was reluctant to tell him about her experiences with it.

"A deep depression," Daniel went on, "then it sounds like schizophrenia. He was tutoring some guy in Latin and up and attacked him with a knife. Totally crazy act. Soon after that he drowned himself in the Kupa river.

"Shit," said Leslie.

"A few decades later Vuk was able to push the alphabet through."

"What's Vuk's book about?" she asked, picking up the book written by the man in the fez.

"Compiling the songs of the Serbian people," Daniel said. "The literature of an illiterate people. He gathered folk songs and compiled them into a set of books."

Leslie gasped. "Wait here," she said. "I'll be right back." She ran down the stairs to her desk, almost running into Reggie as he exited the bathroom. She grabbed a manuscript. "I gotta show him!" she said and ran upstairs. She brandished it breathlessly at Daniel.

What's this?" he asked, leafing through it.

"A screen adaptation of a Charles Chestnutt story I wrote. I applied for a fine arts grant to produce it." She looked at him, teasing him with a pretended impatience, her eyes glittering. "The literature of an illiterate people!" she said.

"No shit," he said.

"You don't know Charles Chestnutt?" she asked.

"Not really, just heard of him," he said.

They're variants of B'rer Rabbit and Conjure Woman tales he compiled from freedmen and adapted," she said.

"That's right," he said. "That's what these are," referring to the protege's book, the guy with the fez. "A guidebook on how little guys can outsmart and outfight the big guys."

She brandished a big smile. "And I didn't get the grant because they thought I should do something 'more germane to my own personal narrative.'" She laughed, savoring the irony.

She thought about that nagging harpy that she often argued with in her head, the one that was always needling her with America's racist delusions that there was something degenerate or perverse about what she liked and loved. She started laughing.

"Everything I've always loved about y'all. Everything I thought was so *interesting*, and so *important* . . ." the joy she felt made her feel giggly. "Are all the ways we're the same!"

Then her eyes began to water over. "It's the first time in three generations any of us have felt good about ourselves, even if we didn't know that's what we were seeing."

Daniel reached across the table for her hand.

It was when she realized she did not want his touch to end that she withdrew her hand. She picked up the books and held them close to her chest.

"They're for you," Daniel said.

She smiled at him. She got up from her seat and crossed to him. He stood up and circled her with his arms. "Thank you," she said. "For this incredible gift." She rested her head on his shoulder, then stood back. "I have to go. I have to get my life straight."

"I understand," he said.

* * *

Rosemary's Chicken

Reggie came up with the idea that the three of them, him, Daniel and Leslie, go down to Lincoln Park and play some handball that Sunday. Reggie ran into him in the vestibule and chatted with him at length. Then he came up with the idea about the handball.

All the while they were in that vestibule Leslie had been thinking about how she'd broach the subject of their failed relationship, but when he came back into the apartment, talking about the handball, she just decided to go with the flow and see where Reggie was taking this.

She got up early that Saturday morning and roasted some chicken drumsticks with rosemary for a picnic lunch. 'Evergreen chicken' she thought as the fragrance filled the apartment. She cut up a bunch of *crudities* and threw some croissants into the basket, too. It was getting time to go.

"Are you going to get up, or what?" she asked in the bedroom doorway.

"Can't, baby."

"What's wrong?

"Feel like shit."

She got onto the bed next to him and felt his forehead. It was cool and his color was good. He seemed fine. "What's wrong?

"My gut's in a rumble."

She laughed.

"What's so funny?" he asked.

"That's one of those things you say, and nobody ever wants any more details."

He laughed with her a little.

"It's like if you want to stay home from work, just call up and tell them you have diarrhea."

They both laughed.

"What am I going to do with the picnic I made?"

"You two go on. Have fun."

She felt a pang when he said that. Was this it, finally? She nestled close to him and played with his hair. She still liked twirling it around her fingers, making little spikes. "You gonna be all right without me?" she asked.

Was that an expression of guilt in his eyes, or loss? she wondered. "I'll be fine, baby," he said.

She patted down the spikes she'd made, or tried to anyway, and kissed him. There was a knock at the door. She hugged him wistfully, not wanting to let him go. "Love you," she said, suppressing a lump in her throat.

"Love you," he replied. Wistful himself, he watched her leave. Yes, he *was* going to miss her, but it was for the best that he let her go. He went into the kitchen. Good girl, she left him a plate, with four drumsticks of that damn chicken. He scarfed it. Yes, she was a sweet girl. Sweet, sad girl.

* * *

232

"You sure you're okay?" Daniel asked as he shifted gears.

"I'm fine," Leslie replied as they made their way down to the park in his jeep.

"You look worried. Worrying if Reggie's okay?"

"No, he'll be all right." She smiled for Daniel. "I'm fine." Then she thought about who she was riding down the road with, who her 'boy-friend' had just set her up with. Crazy. She'd spare him the details. "Everything's fine."

"Yes, yes, it is," he said. "There's something I intend to do with you that's much more fun than handball."

She laughed, not quite sure where he was going with that. "And what's that?"

"Oh," he said with an apologetic smile, as if realizing how that statement might be interpreted. "I'm going to interview you. This will be part of my field research."

"And what is it you're researching?"

"The persistence of identity in an endangered population."

"Whoa. That's deep."

"*You're* deep."

She was speechless. She'd gotten so much negative feedback from the world, so many nasty words, and now this one, profoundly respectful word swept them all away. Just like that.

* * *

She spread her blue, round tablecloth under a huge, old oak. The bike trail in front of them was full of joggers and cyclists taking in the fresh, balmy air rolling in off the vast, glittering lake – a brilliant noontime in early June. Daniel set aside the plastic laundry basket with one corner missing, damage left from that terrible day when Reggie had flung it across the room.

"Hungry yet? Wanna eat?" she asked.

"Oh, I can't wait. I woke up dreaming of chicken this morning, salivating at that aroma you were enticing me with."

"I was enticing you?" she said, handing him a paper plate. Their eyes met.

"Can't fault a man for dreaming."

Her mind grabbed a snapshot of that moment that she was sure she would never forget, however long she lived – that afternoon, under that tree in Lincoln Park, eating rosemary chicken with Daniel.

"I don't believe there's much I'll ever fault you for," she said, imagining that to involve a very long spell of time. She piled his plate with four drumsticks, a croissant, some carrot sticks and celery. Then she handed him a bottle of wine and a corkscrew.

He gobbled a large mouthful of chicken before setting himself to the task of opening the wine. "This bottle is going to be greasy," he said.

"We'll just have to kill it, so we won't drop it later," she said.

"Good idea."

"So, you were going to interview me, huh?"

"Yeah," he said. He looked at her intently from head to toe. "Yes, you'd make a good subject for an interview, even with poor lighting and no makeup."

Yep. He was flirting. Responding in kind, she looked at him with her head cocked, smiling, squinting her eyes a little. "Yeah, but are you sure there will be enough intellectual engagement to maintain my attention span?"

"You doubt my capacity?" he flirted back.

"No, now back up there," she said. "I said nothing about your capacity. I questioned your intent."

"Fair enough."

"Anyway, before you start interviewing me, there's something I want to tell you."

"What?" he asked.

"What you said the other day, that you weren't religious anymore. You're pretty much agnostic now."

"Yeah?"

"You're wrong. What you think about is all about your spirituality. I haven't gotten it figured yet, but your intellectual life *is* your spiritual life. You haven't forsaken the "Faith of Your Fathers" as they say. You're just taking it further."

He touched his forehead as if struck by a thought.

"What?" she asked.

"Nothing," he laughed. "Just a little déjà vu I guess, memory of a dream, perhaps. My great-grandfather and a philosophical dude with a Russian accent. Tolstoy maybe." He shook his head and smiled at her. "Never mind. I have recurring dreams about Tolstoy. So where am I taking things?"

She smiled, "Hell if I know, but I'm kind of hoping I'm there when you find out."

"I don't know how comfortable I am in such a lofty position."

"It's not lofty. It's just you."

"Thank you. Enough about me."

"No, one more question. I'm curious when this similarity between Serbs and Black Americans first hit you. When did it first occur to you?" she asked.

"I'll tell you when it first blew me away. I was reading some Bosniak, do you know who they are?"

"No. Yes. Tell me again."

"Bosniaks are people who were originally Serbs who converted to Islam during the Turkish occupation. They're in what's now the Bosnian Republic of Yugoslavia. Though, most of the countryside in Bosnia is occupied by Serbs. The Bosniaks are the more affluent people living in the cities. It's hard to keep things straight because everything's in reverse. The Moslem people were the privileged class, the Christians were the po' folks being taken advantage of, and everybody looks identical. Very confusing. A lot of the Bosniaks were descended from those boys I told you about, who'd been stolen from their families."

"The janissaries," Leslie recalled, trying to keep up with the complicated history.

"Yes, so this Bosniak is recalling how harmonious the relations were between them and the Serbs in the good old days of Turkish colonization, that it was idyllic practically. Then I happened upon a description of the legal code of the time. In those good old colonial days, in any lawsuit between a Serb and a Turk or his Bosniak quisling, the testimony of the Serb was inadmissible in court. He could not testify against a white man, oops," he said, feigning an unintended slip, "I mean a Moslem. The *déjà vu* blew me away. You have to remember that religion in that system was the delineator *for the racism.* And, like I just said, the inferior ethnicity was clearly the Serbs, who had no civil rights."

Daniel was talking at a fast, excited clip. Leslie loved watching those mental wheels spinning away, making his eyes glitter.

"Think about it," he went on. "All you have to do to get your civil rights is convert to the occupier's religion, and not only do you get full privileges, now you can do whatever you want to people who a minute earlier had been your own kind. Maybe you have no intention of doing anything bad, but anytime some twisted kind of personality comes along, he can go hog wild crazy with it. I mean, how much more can you do to bitterly alienate people? So slick. I mean, it's like what I was saying at the pizza place. The silver lining to the immutability of American color-coded racism. There's only so far we here of color can go in betraying one another. It can get so much worse. And you only have to look at this story to see it."

"Yes, yes, yes!" Leslie said loudly, sitting up excitedly and pounding Daniel's arm. Her own wheels had been spinning while she was trying to listen to him. "We had no rights those in power were bound to respect. It's too much. To think that for the past 18 years, ever since I was six years old, I *just happened* to be fascinated with the people here who had just been through *that very thing*." She was feeling really stoked with the synchronicity, combined with a wine-induced bout of free association. "Not that that would ever matter to white America."

Leslie began miming a representative of that white American bias, an old man with a deep male voice. "Oh, but that's just coincidental, that has nothing to do with anything. . ." She winked repeatedly with a snide expression. "Everybody knows she just wants a . . ." She left the sentence dangling provocatively.

"A what?" Daniel asked.

There was no way she was going to say it out loud, that *non sequitur* Marilyn had laid on her while she did her laundry that half of America seemed to be taunting her with every time she turned a corner. That Big Black It. If she ran inside to escape those taunters she'd find herself in a room full of them leering and sneering and groping and ridiculing her with it. Then it would turn into that nightmare when you go up to the head of the class and realize you forgot to put any clothes on that morning and everyone's laughing derisively at you, chanting 'We know what IT is *you* want.'

It IT **IT!** She was in a country obsessed with IT. That monument they had set up in every town square in America – a monolith twenty feet tall – not a glorification, but a dehumanization. That animalistic IT only a debased whore into bestiality could want. That's what they were flashing at her every day. That's how white America perceived her, whether they knew it consciously or not.

Her expectations on the subject might mimic a paranoid delusion, but it was quite real. It was really happening to her, all the time, and no one seemed aware or in the least bit concerned that they were doing it, making those outlandish, obscene presumptions. It was just ordinary, everyday, common-as-dirt. . .

. . . racism.

Nah, if she said it out loud it would ruin the joke. He would have to guess it. Besides, she wasn't going to say something like that. She was a lady goddamn it! Why had everyone forgotten that? She motioned for him to try harder, reaching her hand out towards him, palm-side up, beckoning him as if they were playing charades. He laughed and shrugged his shoulders.

"Is it bigger than a bread box?" he asked.

Leslie fell backwards onto the grass in a fit of laughter. "Never!!" she said. She sat back up and continued giving clues.

"Oh, it's not something you say in polite company, not that there are very many polite people in *this* country. And it's definitely *not* a stereotype you'll ever find *any* brothers protesting. You'll never see any one of them *ever* get up on a soapbox and proclaim . . ." she raised her fist, hamming a deep, passionately indignant male voice, "Not me!"

Daniel cracked up for a good while. He got the joke. He laughed and then he looked at her with that look, that eye contact that telegraphed he *felt* her, he *heard* her. He understood what she'd been going through. He was conveying that ordinary, common-as-dirt thing. It wasn't pity, not remotely. It was just a simple, respectful acknowledgement. All she'd ever wanted.

"And here you are," he said. "In one piece."

Leslie soared. He got the joke on that subject she could never even raise with Reggie. Reggie would just shut down with his own bruised feelings and leave her on her own, as if she, too, were insulting him. Him, him, just always about him. *She* never mattered at all.

But here with Daniel, she was 'on.' He was liking her being up on her own stage. She had secret monologues she knew she would rarely, if ever, get to whip out on anybody, but it seemed her moment had finally arrived.

"But I can tell you a carefully guarded secret."

"What's that?" he asked.

"What a *real* woman thinks about all that."

Still the perfect audience, he said, "And what does a *real* woman think?"

"A *real* woman? A *real* woman in love?" She began hamming up a bit of female melodrama. She clasped her hands together in state of rising ecstasy, "Whatever *it* is, is . . ." throwing her arms out wide and letting the last word explode "*PERFECT!!* We're never fickler. And it's a good thing, too."

"Why is that?" he asked.

"Can you imagine what the world would be like if women were choosing men over something that stupid? I mean, what do we call a man who's a fool?"

"A dick," he hooted, turning some heads of passers-by.

She looked around and whispered, "How come all those people are staring at me? She continued hamming it up. "Oh no, not that. You don't think they think I want a . . ." She covered her mouth, feigning shock.

Daniel laughed.

"Or maybe they just think I'm too loud. Yeah, that's probably it. That was the first thing someone told me when I went to that Serbian party. The monumental first thing I learned about my people's culture, knowledge of which had been withheld from us, like a Holy Grail, for generations. Longed for unconsciously, hauntingly, something we just couldn't live without. . .

She leaned towards him and uttered grandly and loudly ". . . loudness!"

Daniel laughed.

"So Milja," Leslie continued, "is telling me about how her sister got in trouble at work because people thought she was mad. But she wasn't mad, she was just LOUD."

"But I've always known that, I've always known that people have thought I was mad or crazy or crude or whatever because I was animated and I was LOUD. I was hoping to be so in an interesting way, real and honest and natural. Sharing what I feel."

"That was one of the things that was such a relief about hanging with y'all. I didn't feel like such a loudspeaker. Y'all are almost as loud as we are!"

"Almost as loud, huh?"

Daniel made eye contact again, and they stayed there for a moment. He was lying on his side, his head propped in his hand. "And you just couldn't live without that loudness?"

She grasped his wrist urgently feeling like she could almost cry, this was that important.

"No, how can you live without loudness? I mean, this is something that's quantifiable scientifically. Do people who live in highly-stressed environments survive better if they can express what they feel? And get a warm touch in response?

"You can't express what you feel if you can't get LOUD. It's not uncouth. It's not common. It's common sense. Never mind what it does to your nervous system to live without loudness. But why are you even bothering to live if you're not really feeling any of it? And if you're really feeling it, baby, you're gonna get loud. It's guaranteed."

He grasped her hand. "This is quite a body of thought here. How long have you been thinking about all of this?"

There was so much electricity in his touch she had to work at focusing her mind back to the idea at hand. Again, she did not want him to let go. "All my life," she said. "Since childhood. Since I was old enough to think conceptually."

"Maybe we should partner up on this," he said.

Leslie was caught short because the first feeling that popped up was that he was asking her to be his. But no, no, he was just asking her to partner on the project. Too late, he saw the first thought.

He smiled slyly and laughed. She wasn't sure of his reaction. Did he like her first thought? He had to. She was sure he was at times flirting, and if he was just trifling with that, he wouldn't be risking working with her, would he?

Then he went on, "I was asking you to seriously consider working together on this project. There's too much you instinctively know. There's too much I'm trying to find out. We complement each other," he looked at her and laughed again. "Our two populations complement each other in really, really fascinating ways. You have a bachelor's, right?"

He was still holding her hand.

"Uh huh. I have a BA in film making and you could call it a minor in Philosophy. I have two years of Latin."

"Excellent," he said. "We could probably pull it off. I'm so golden at the moment, don't know how long it will last, but I'm a big paycheck to them. I could insist that you be admitted and find a grant that would enable you to attend. You could do a thesis that would append to the dissertation, which could be prolonged while you catch up."

Leslie's first thought was of Melvin, the guy who was going to 'produce' her story. Then several thoughts argued against that first thought.

"Just think about it," he said. "I don't mean to rush you. I know you already have a life, and probably plenty of priorities."

"This is my priority," she said.

"I know that," he said. "But a lady gets to take her time making up her mind . . . This will be funny. We get to find out how far these white men will go to get revenge on a black man, old Ralph X, the professor I worked under, who bested them. They gonna pay for their 'lackey' to have him a white woman on his team? Think I'm pushing it?"

"You're insane," she said. "You sure you ain't a Serb?"

Later, as he was driving them home, she looked out the window. She thought about his proposal. She smiled. Then a little harpy voice nagged at her. What was she doing? Did she really think she was ready to be risking it all yet again, when in the end she might just end up 'useful' to yet another dude?

She woke up the next morning, not at all sure where things stood. Reggie had already gone on to class. Had they agreed to break up? Was it over?

She went to eat a bowl of cereal and there was Reggie's lunch, in a bag on the table. He forgot it. She laughed at herself as she re-organized her day around an extra errand, bringing Reggie his lunch. Such a little woman, she thought. What am I thinking? What exactly is it I'm thinking?

* * *

Leslie's Big Black Separatist Party

Leslie's life was changing, radically. The more she thought about it, the more obvious it became. Like she'd just told Daniel, what she'd been seeing in black people was herself and hers. Every other thing she was learning about Serbs was something she was very familiar with. It was always something that was on that big, long list of things she loved about black people – and that liking was the Magic Button that had brought her back from the genocided hell Archie had raised her in.

She was detailing her front room, thinking about all these things. Company was coming. As usual, she put some Motown on the turntable. The music totally energized her. She was singing and dancing along. The white world was so intent on persecuting her, telling her what she loved was nasty, whereas, to her, it was incredibly beautiful. She was happy. Beyond happy, she was in a state of near bliss.

She'd written another article under Reggie's byline. It began with, "We are so beautiful, we are all we need." It had already been published when she had to run down to Reggie's school, the Illinois Institute of Technology, to give him the lunch he'd left on the table. She was in the hallway walking with him to his lab class when several people had stopped him to compliment him on it.

One was Camilla. She was a tall, beautiful girl, attractive in much the same way Reggie was, with large, finely sculpted features, and a flawless complexion of the same hue. They looked good together. She was prominent in the student political scene, and was doing a lot of similar writing herself. Leslie noticed how intently Camilla was regarding him. It was an odd sensation for Leslie. Camilla was, in reality, complimenting Leslie on the way *she,* Leslie, thought, and was regarding her boyfriend in some elevated spotlight because of it. She could see Camilla was more than just intellectually turned on.

She'd figured out a while ago that her own jealousy around Reggie had worn itself out. There was nothing much to be jealous of, now that she understood what his sexuality was about. On a really deep level, it was entirely superficial. He really didn't care much at all who he was with, as long as she was reasonably good-looking, and he was doing it. Nothing personal. That's just the way he was. And the fact that he had no interest in this deep thing she was about was just another aspect of his superficial nature.

Yep, her attachment was pretty much gone. She found herself regarding Camilla's possible crush on her man from a distance, like a spectator with little stake in the outcome. What did interest her was that Camilla wanted to bring Reggie, and by extension, Leslie, into focus. She was dying to find out how the world was going to accept this revelation of her true identity. How would that change things?

"We're trying to schedule another meeting," Camilla said to Reggie. "As soon as we get a location lined up, I'll call you."

"How much space do you need?" asked Leslie. "How many people?"

"About twenty," said Camilla who was still facing Reggie, as if he were the one speaking.

"You all can come over to our place, if you want. I don't mind," Leslie replied.

"Sure," said Reggie. "That would be cool."

Camilla looked at Leslie, as if noticing her presence for the first time. She seemed apprehensive, but then smiled broadly at Reggie. "Want to say this Sunday evening, at seven?"

"Cool," he said.

Leslie was detailing her front room, getting ready for the company. She got some refreshments together and then got dressed. She had invited Daniel, but he had a conflict. She would have felt a lot more supported if he could make it, but it couldn't be helped.

If Leslie was supposed to feel odd being the only white person in the room, she didn't. For years now, she'd pretty much been the only white person in the room most of the time. No big thing. Whenever there were more than a couple of people in the room she was accustomed to being seen but not heard. But she was excited that, tonight, she was giving herself permission to be her own self. 'How many more lifetimes are we supposed to live in hiding?' she asked herself.

If this was the part of America she'd assimilated to, why should she accept being a second-class citizen in it? No, it was time for her to be bold and be herself. Time to be assertive and get what she needed to live in her own world. She'd already paid a fortune in dues she didn't even owe to be there. She absolutely deserved what she needed to survive there in one piece.

She was well-aware of the resistance she might meet, but sure her reasons for being included were irrefutable. Anyone reasonable would have to see that. As if on cue, Diana Ross started singing "I'm coming out." Leslie laughed as she sang along.

"De-colonizing the mind" was the name of the support group Camilla was leading. Now that Leslie was aware that her life had been totally ruled by the fact that her family had been colonized for centuries, she tripped out extravagantly on what perfect sense it made that the topic had always fascinated her – and that her defense of people in that position had always been synonymous with a defense of herself and hers. She was home, had made herself at home no matter how strong the current she had to swim against. No, there was no reason for her to hide who she was. It was a beautiful story.

She'd just finished dressing when the doorbell started to ring. Reggie took charge of answering the door, greeting their guests. She was taking coats and throwing them on the bed, then fetching drinks. About fifteen folks showed up and sat in chairs, some on the floor. Leslie curled up in a corner of the couch. They all chatted while the latecomers arrived.

Camilla, seated in the armchair Leslie had dragged to the head of the room and directed Camilla to, waited fifteen minutes, then dug in. "I want to welcome all those folks who are here for the first time," Camilla began. "This is a support group for folks interested in healing the wounds of a racist, colonizing world that has prevailed for centuries in defining us as less than human. It's a tall order – 400 years of brainwashing aren't going to be washed away in a day. But we're here to begin that process. I want to thank Brother Reggie for opening up his home to us, and to thank him for the inspiring words he's been sharing with us in *Brother Voice* newspaper.

"I want to start by reading a little bit of his article, to put us in the mood, so to speak."

242

"I love women in the mood," Reggie quipped. Everyone in the room laughed. He sat in a chair across from Leslie. She observed a little bemused eye contact between Camilla and Reggie. Camilla began reading.

We Are So Beautiful
by Reggie Wilson

We may have grown up every day of our childhood feeling like the world was a bleak place filled with nothing but our own impoverishment, whether it be physical, or mental, or emotional, surrounded at every turn by messages that told us we were nothing, we were ugly, we were stupid, we were worthless.

I certainly did. It compromised everything I touched. I could not see myself, except shrouded in the lies of centuries. Brutal lies, from brutal people which left us paying untold dues we never owed, still paying daily for the privileges of people long since moldering in their graves.

The lies had so overwhelmed us that we had no clue at all who we really were. And who were these people I'm from, who could be so maligned? What was the truth behind those lies?

Absolutely astonishing people thrust into an unimaginably difficult predicament who found their way out of an inescapable bondage pressed on us by an insurmountable foe. But we found a way, by way of our faith.

Leslie felt a rush of excitement and affirmation as Camilla read her, Leslie's, thoughts summarizing her heritage and identity. Every word of it described precisely how she'd always felt about the world, all the while she'd had no idea why. She felt like her life was on the verge of a kind of fulfillment that had always eluded her. A tingling surge went up her spine.

"It goes on from there," said Camilla. "But we can talk more about that later. Why don't we first introduce ourselves? If you will take a few moments to introduce yourself and tell us your interest in this topic, it would be great."

She nodded in succession to everyone there.

Except Leslie. Leslie shifted in her seat, crestfallen. She looked up at Reggie, who did not return her gaze. Then Camilla turned her attention on her. "I appreciate your willingness for us to meet in your home, but we might feel more comfortable if we had the space to ourselves."

Leslie's heart pounded, falling as precipitously as the flight on which she'd just soared. But instead of leaving she began speaking, "I'm not here as a spectator. I am deeply invested in this issue, myself," she said. "There isn't a word you just read that doesn't come from my heart. I am from people who have lived through six centuries of either colonized slavery or life as a persecuted minority. My own family was totally traumatized by it. The only sense I've been able to make of it has come from Black America." She was having trouble keeping her voice steady.

Camilla stared at her for a moment, still looking harsh. "How long ago?" she asked.

"It's still going on," Leslie replied. "My own family was culturally genocided fifty years ago, grandma was passing for the people who, 30 years ago, were exterminating us. That's why we survived when so much of the family didn't. She didn't tell us who we were. I think her husband, who was from the people exterminating us, wouldn't let her. We were just left floundering with all the symptoms of cultural genocide. But I figured out who we really were by who was *familiar.* Identifying with and loving black people was the key to my learning to love myself and recovering my identity." There it was, she'd laid her soul bare, her heart still beat in her throat. If her words were trashed – that would be unimaginable.

"Wow," said Sherry, a strikingly pretty young woman with a *cafe au lait* complexion and light brown curls tinged with gold. She was sitting next to Leslie. "That's beautiful."

Leslie smiled at her gratefully. "Thank you. It *is* very beautiful to me."

In her peripheral vision Leslie could see Camilla looking at her with a stony face. Leslie looked up at her, "It's like a parallel universe. For centuries, the same kinds of things happening to the same kinds of people. Until this century, when the unthinkable has been happening to us, while what you all have been making happen here is like a dream come true." Camilla's face was unmoved. "It's what has sheltered me and helped me recover my identity."

Then a male voice chimed in. "Who? Where? What? What mythical universe is this?" Leslie looked across the room at a dark-skinned fellow named Zack with corn rows and a dashiki brightly-colored in oranges and reds. He was smiling smugly, his eyes glittering as he surveyed Leslie like she was a hamburger and he was very hungry.

"It's not mythical. It's the Balkans. Look it up some time," she replied.

Then another guy in a back-turned baseball cap named Spike, jumped in, chewing gum, "Yes, but you're forgetting something."

"You think so?" she said. Her sinuses were burning, as if she'd just breathed in pepper dust.

"You trying to tell us you ain't white?"

Leslie looked around the room. Except for the three confronting her, no one was looking at her. Not even Reggie. So, it was coming to that. That quick. The Big Dismissal that no one was going to question. It didn't matter what her story was. She was perceived as white. That's all that mattered. The tingling she felt a moment before turned into a shiver of fear of the imminent attack she knew all too well. "How do you define white?"

"How do I define white?" he asked. He began ticking off his points with his fingers.

"White means you can drive down the street without the pigs pulling you over just because they noticed you're a brother."

"White means you can apply for a job and not worry if they've filled their quota or not, because if they have, you're shit out of luck.

"White means you can apply for an apartment and get it.

"White means you can browse through a store without somebody following you around trying to catch you stealing something.

"White means *you* get to decide whether you give a shit about what happened to your family on the other side of the world or not. If you want to just move on and forget all about it, you can."

"On what are you basing the assumption that I don't know all that?" she asked. She stared him down and brushed her cheek with the back of her hand.

Spike returned her glare, "If you knew, you would know why we don't want you in this room."

There was a long silence. She fell full force with a thud from that precipitous height she'd just been on. She tried to re-fill her lungs.

She closed her eyes and tried to speak from her core. "It's not a room," she said. "It's a dungeon that I will never escape, because no one will ever see that I need to." She opened her eyes and looked to Reggie. She locked onto his eyes and wouldn't let go. "They'll just be annoyed with me, disappointed in me that I haven't rescued *them*. They can't see me. All they can see is 'white.' And what they would excoriate me for doing to them, they do to me, every day. That will never matter. And that will keep them in the dungeon with me." She looked around the room, trying to make eye contact. "All of them."

Camilla met her gaze. "I really have no idea what you're referring to, nor do I see how you could presume to tell us where we are at."

"Because it's where *I* live," Leslie replied.

"You can't."

"How do you presume to dictate that?"

"I don't presume, it's *your* people who have presumed that."

"You don't even know who *my* people are. Don't even know that you are much closer to escaping that dungeon than we are."

Zack jumped back in. "Every time you hit that door, you can escape any dungeon you want."

"That's *your* fantasy," Leslie said. "That if you hit that door and suddenly you were white everything would change. The truth is that, when you are from colonized people, the damage goes very deep and persists for many generations, even if you're transplanted halfway around the world and nobody knows that's who you really are. Not even you."

"But this is perfect," said Camilla triumphantly. "A perfect example of extremely subtle white racism. You'll notice as soon as she's in the room, she must be the center of attention. She's leading the conversation. She's telling us about *our* oppression. Typical white racism."

Leslie was silenced by shock. The highly alienated life she had been living, rejected and/or attacked by nearly every white person in her world because of her commitment to the black people in her life was a meaningless joke. She could be persecuted by racism and accused of it as well? Her mind started to unravel. It was not possible for it to occupy both spaces. Gears were stripping into a space devoid of meaning, a seemingly bottomless dungeon into which she was falling at a terminal velocity.

Camilla went on, her voice full of contempt, "We came here to this brother's house, because of the beautiful words he used to describe our reality and because a white woman lives here she has to take center stage."

Leslie snapped. That was the way to halt her free fall. Anger. The Serb in her took over. She got ghetto. The Krajina ghetto. She leapt from her seat and towered over Camilla. "Get the hell out my house!" she shouted. "Those were *my* words you loved, *I* wrote that article. You loved every bit of it, you understood every word. But you're addicted to the American disease of polarity and must objectify anyone not passing your paper bag test, you hypocritical bigot. Get the hell out of my home!" Reggie had circled her waist from behind. She knew he was not backing her up. He was just restraining her to protect Camilla.

"Let me go, you son of a bitch!" she shouted.

"Lez, shhhh, shhh, just calm down, it's okay." He didn't look reassuring. He looked embarrassed.

"It's *not* okay," she cried. "This is a stupid lifetime. It makes no sense at all. I'm just going to spend my life loving people who will never love me back. I'll just be someone for them to use. That's all I've been to you. Useful."

The room was silent, everyone was staring at her.

"Since this is my room and I'm refusing to leave it, and you don't want to discuss colonization issues with me in it, and I refuse to stop talking about them, I guess you'll just *all* have to leave."

"Okay, everybody," said Camilla smugly, gathering her things. "I'll be in touch with you all about our next meeting. We'll talk about why it's not in our best interests to sleep with the enemy."

Reggie had to restrain Leslie as she lunged at Camilla. "The enemy? The enemy gets fired over you, and molested, and disowned and humiliated and shunned and risks their life? You bitch!"

As they were filtering out of the apartment she could hear someone in the stairway muttering about a typical white martyr complex. "What does she expect us to do, worship her?"

She stomped to the bedroom and furiously slammed the door. She flopped onto the bed and stared at the ceiling. This nightmare isn't going to end, she thought. I'll be lost forever in this foreign land. This *Tuđina,* she thought.

Where did that word come from?

Something had just changed. Strange things were popping in her head. Had she really gone insane?

Reggie entered the room. He looked angry. "Well," he said. "That went well."

"Shut up!"

"What did you *think* would happen?" he asked. "Why are you so god damn naïve?"

"It's not about naïvete!" she shouted. "It's about necessity. All these brothers out here having a high time, pulling in these white bitches. But there isn't a one of them that's given a second's thought about what those girls need. Think of all the attention and support I've given you all these years, while you've been making your way, the only one in all those white rooms, going all the way back to Shimer. I've got news for you, buster. A woman doesn't pull a man into her world. He pulls her into *his*. So, what have you ever done to support me, when I'm the only one in all these black rooms? Huh? The only rooms left to me after all those white people threw me out of their rooms for 'slumming' with your ass.

"You don't even *want* to know why I'm here. I tried to tell you last week, when I came home from that party, that Serb party where I overheard some people talking about 'The Turk.' So, I find out that the term means EXACTLY the same thing as 'The Man.' Identical usage for identical reasons. And what was your response?

"You yawned, you yawned! You didn't want to know. You want me to just shut up and be white, that little cherished stereotype of a white girl you have running around in your head. Well, guess what? That's not who I am and if it *were* there's no way on God's green earth I would have put up with all *your* shit.

"That's the whole problem between you and me, baby. I'm not white enough for you. And what I really am, you don't like at all. I've been crazy going through all this shit for you. You wouldn't cross the street for me."

He glared at her but made no reply. His book bag was in his hand which he was filling with some clothes. Finally, he muttered, "Who the hell do you think you are, telling everybody you wrote that?"

"Well, you know, if you'd done anything at all to defend me in there, I would have continued protecting your interests. The truth is, you don't deserve it."

He threw a balled-up pair of socks into his bag. "Well, you're absolutely right about one thing. I *don't* give a damn. You're on your own," he said. "Do what you gotta do. I'm done." He left.

She picked up a shoe and hurled it at the shut door. Then she broke down into some serious wailing. She was hurtling back down that dungeon hole. She hit the bottom again and bounced back up on a tide of pure anger.

She'd finally made people say what they were thinking, she thought bitterly. She'd been feeling it for years, even when it wasn't said. Especially when it wasn't said. Those silences. All the way back to Howard's silence at Emmett Till Junior High, that boy she had to sit behind for two years who never once spoke to her. His silence about Emmett. She heard a silence like that in high-fidelity stereo. That irresistible angst she knew like the back of her own hand that beckoned her the same way a bird's instinct would make it fly thousands of miles south in the fall.

Her life made no sense at all. She was trapped in a mind that could not stop feeling everything those people said, whether they said it out loud or not. Yes, those people. She remembered somebody calling her out, a black guy at a party, for using the word 'those' in referring to black people. It had to do with the racist way some white people have of referring to 'those' people with a little inflection to make it clear 'those' people were scorned. Leslie knew all about that. If she'd heard it once she'd heard it a thousand times. And then, once, she had made the mistake of using the words "those people" when gushing about their innovations in musical art forms and she had been severely and publicly reprimanded for racist behavior. It was as devastating as it was absurd.

Of course, there was no inflection in her voice to indicate scorn. Her usage was entirely innocent, but that was irrelevant. What *was* relevant was that she had a 'white' skin tone, was phenotypically European and she used the word "those," referring to 'black people." But she'd learned her lesson and was carefully censoring herself.

She was supposed to go her entire life without ever using such a basic phrase. "Try it," she said to the four walls, "Try going for a week without ever using the words 'those people.' Let's line up two groups of people. Tell us which group is wearing hats. If you point your finger at one group and say, 'those people.' BZZZZZZT. You are banished to Siberia forever as a godawful racist."

That's what it meant to be white in America living on black turf. She was expected to do the impossible, the unnatural in a constant state of deference to OTHER people's bad behavior, not hers. *Her* thoughts, *her* intentions, *her* behavior was of no significance whatsoever. Ever. It was not a state that could be sustained by any human being. It was precisely the state imposed on black people in America, and lo and behold, they were imposing it on her, then leaving her without the one thing that helped them survive it – each other. Is that all she was there for, to be their scapegoat? Is that all her life meant?

That guy at the party was presuming on *her*. He was being willfully obtuse. He had way more than enough information to know exactly what she was really saying, but he had an opportunity to vent on her and he was going for it. He, for once, had that privilege and he was going to exercise it.

Then she remembered the time she took something she'd written about one of her firings to an older, black dude who had an experimental theater. She went back the next week to get his response. But he didn't talk to her one-on-one like she expected. Instead he started talking about it while he spoke to a group of people, about twenty-five people, all black.

He ridiculed her.

In front of all those people. Grandstanding at her expense.

"Until somebody hears what's happened to us, don't expect us to be worrying about some little mess of yours."

Who was he, the Equal Opportunity Commission's guy's brother? The one who'd laughed her out of his office when she reported all the firings she'd experienced? She had tried really hard to forget those incidences, but she was losing it. She couldn't anymore.

She talked to the empty room again.

"Until somebody hears? What do you think *I've* been doing? Why doesn't that count? Why am I such a nothing in this world that you can take these pages that have it dripping all over them that that's what I'm hearing and then say no one is? How come I don't matter at all? Why am I just this nothing in the middle everybody's dumping on?"

Then she started talking, still agitated, to Reggie, who was no longer in the room. "And it wasn't any better when I got home and told you about it. And all you could say was, 'I go through that every day.' Of course, I know what you go through every day. *I'm* the one you tell. And I listen. Every time. Every time I listen. But it will never be *my* turn. What I've been busting a gut trying to do for other people will never even be noticed. Certainly, never acknowledged. And absolutely *never* reciprocated."

What had just been demonstrated in her living room affirmed that it made absolutely no sense trying to make the right response, since she offended people just by being white. There was no point trying to accommodate anything. It had no value whatsoever to anyone.

Her life was absurd beyond measure. She had gone through years of abuse now from white people for aligning herself with people who reviled her. People who were 100% sure that someone like her couldn't possibly exist and were seeing something completely different when they looked at her, and feeling 100% entitled to do so. And there was absolutely nothing she could do to change that. She was entirely irrelevant.

"But this isn't just about me!" she proclaimed to the universe. "These relationships between black men and white women can't work. A woman enters her husband's world. But there can be no white people assimilating to black people. The world can't become normal, with an equal flow in both directions, and black people are the ones enforcing that.

"You don't want things to get better, you just want to get *even*, and it doesn't matter which White Appearing Object you exact that revenge on." That's why those people in her living room were being so obtuse when she tried to explain the simplest facts about why she liked being around them – because they were the same, because they were familiar. They were being obtuse because they were offended with her temerity to suggest such a thing. She had no right to say that.

"I'm *not* the same. I'm less. I'm one of those nasty people who are inherently supremacist, uncivilized, exploitative, violent, sadistic, savage, inferior. That's all this is – petty, cheap, cowardly revenge on an inappropriate object. Just like those other bigots I grew up around. I can spot people like that a mile off."

She scornfully laughed at herself. What a fool she'd been, thinking she was getting somewhere, finding an answer to the generational issues her family's ordeal had infected them with – all of them, grandma thinking she was ugly and stupid and undeserving of love, her son, Uncle Joe, who never got out of the basement.

Leslie had thought this persecuted minority, the American version, had an answer and could help her, but she was falling for the same bullshit her grandmother had. 'All I've done is find another lifetime in which I am the inferior idiot who has no value, surrounded by people who think they're more important. They are *my* Croatians.

'And I'm that fool whimpering after them, wondering why they won't love me. If only just one would love me. . . '

She thought of Daniel. Promising so much. Seeming to appreciate who she was. Why would that be anything more than just another illusion? Just another one who thinks she might be useful.

She sighed with that lethargy that comes when nothing makes any sense, nothing has any meaning, instead is relentlessly absurd, seeing with such intensity people who deliberately had no intention of seeing her at all.

* * *

It got late and she lay in the dark, staring at the ceiling. She noticed someone sitting on the chair in the corner. She was not startled. It was someone in her family. A photo of him had been found in her grandmother's things, a very handsome young man with large, dark Mediterranean features and thick shock of wavy dark hair, dressed in a WWII uniform. Leslie knew, at that moment, that his name was Miloš, that he was a ghost, and as real to her as anything she'd ever seen.

"I know what you need," he said, "to recover from your grandmother's 'passing,' as you call it."

251

The recognition hit her like an enormous wave. She couldn't tell the difference between him and one of her living cousins. It was far more than just the way he looked. She decided this was entirely real and that she was not going to give her sanity another thought. She had nothing to lose.

She turned on the lamp next to the bed. The ghost, or whatever he was, remained visible to her, just better lit. Yes, this was real. Very real.

"There's a simple antidote to being baptized, as we call it. And I will tell you all about it."

"Why?" she asked.

"To help you, sister," he said. "I'm not going to leave you like this."

"None of us are, baby," said Jovanka, appearing from the shadows.

Leslie was looking at her mirror image, clothed in confidence and self-assurance, but she did not recognize herself. She could only see that the apparition was beautiful. Her sensation looking at Jovanka was that she was seeing someone much more clearly than she'd even seen a human – a super high-definition image much sharper than anything she'd ever seen before.

"*Srće moje*," Jovanka continued. "We know what you've been through, and we love you for it. You did all that to find us."

Leslie's eyes puddled. That's *exactly* what she needed to hear. She even knew what *srće moje* meant. My heart. Someone appreciated all this bull-shit she'd been through, that had taken her exactly to this spot, this very spot she'd been struggling to find! Then the puddle turned into an out-right liberation of sobbing. Jovanka rushed to hold her. Leslie'd never felt so embraced before in her life. It was as if Jovanka's warmth and glow was entering through her pores deep into wherever her own soul resided. And her soul, tangled into a hardened snarl of knots, gently unsnarled and relaxed into its natural state, like a warm bowl of udon noodles. She exhaled deeply and when she inhaled she could feel the oxygen molecules dancing excitedly into her lungs.

She thought of what Natalie had said about the electric gold the night she had the vision of Leslie's ghosts. She realized Natalie was right. "That's what haloes are," she said," they're benign electricity so pure and intense it's golden. It's an electricity that only energizes, never shocks. Like a kiss of energy. The kind that Tesla and the makers of the pyramids harnessed!"

"Yes, my girl!" said Srđa with great excitement suddenly appearing before her. He grasped her hands between his own.

She went on, already knowing who he was, "We're connected to them. Our philosophical base is closer to them than Western Europe!"

"Yes," he said. "The original church, our church, came directly from Ethiopia as much as anywhere else, and certainly *not* from the West."

"We are in the philosophical soup of the Mediterranean rim," she went on, her mind exploding with the concept, "half of which is African."

Srđa looked to Jovanka. "Look at this girl, I don't have to explain anything, she's already figured it out."

Leslie became sad-eyed again. "I've *had* to figure this out. These people in this crazy country say terrible things about me because I *like* people from Africa. I like the way they think." Then she looked cross and bitter. "I *have* to know this."

"I know, sweetheart," said Srđa. "I've seen what they've done to you."

"You're my Godfather," she said. "My *kum*."

He nodded, then became pixelated and morphed into a different, dear face from her childhood smiling tenderly at her.

"King Martin?" Leslie exclaimed. "Is that you?"

"Yes," Srđa said, morphing back into his own face, and taking her other hand. "It was just me."

Leslie started laughing. "It wasn't just me being crazy." Her eyes teared up. "You were there!"

"Yes, always," he said. "Listen, there are some things I've been dying to tell you. He took both her hands in his again, sat directly across from her and spoke to her earnestly. "You have to understand that it doesn't matter at all that the loyalty you've shown has not been returned. All that matters is that you gave it. That was a great gift you were giving, to us, and mostly, to yourself. And to the people you've loved, as well."

She cried again, releasing a world of hurt as the love in his words pushed it out.

"That was the path out of the hell you were in."

"The Dungeon," she smiled through her tears.

"Yes, your Dungeon. You always understood what was at stake. A great crime has been committed against your family, which left you buried alive, very deeply, and you took the only way out. You don't need to think of it any other way, or regret anything."

"I'm blessed," she said.

"Yes."

And behind that thought she saw no reason to be obsessing with her own situation. "With all you've been through, why would you worry about me?"

"That's *how* we got through it," said Srđa. "If our suffering has meaning in that way, and there is still hope for us, anything can be endured." He held her hand near his heart. "And you do give us hope. You didn't even know who you were, and you still *knew*. We are so proud of you."

Leslie choked up again in gratitude. She looked up at Miloš. "I'm sorry, she said. "I forgot all about you. You were going to tell me something I need to know that will solve my problem."

He shrugged with a smile. "When you're ready."

"Please."

Miloš smiled and moved over to the bed, facing Leslie. Jovanka was sitting on the bed next to Leslie, leaning on the headboard, holding Leslie's hand in her lap. Srđa sat in the chair. She was still astonished with the incredible sense of family, as well as how real Jovanka's hand felt in hers.

"It's a long story, I'm afraid, to make my point."

"But that's exactly what I need!" Leslie said excitedly. "I need to hear stories I can care about that somebody will *believe* I care about. Please tell me your stories. I want to know about your lives. When did you live?"

"We are all from your father's generation. Jovanka and I are your father's first cousins. Though we have no word for cousin. We have only the words brother and sister, by way of an aunt or uncle."

"Interesting," Leslie smiled. "So, you lived during World War II?"

They nodded.

"You don't mind talking about it?" Leslie asked.

"We want you to know," Jovanka said. "We want your family to know. No disrespect to your grandmother, she did her best, but it's best now for all to know." She nodded at Miloš.

"*Dobro*," Miloš said. "This is the story I wanted to tell you. It all started when I was just a boy, coming of age, and thought I knew everything, when I found my father lying in the street, surrounded by Croat children who were laughing at him." He looked up to Jovanka, speaking to her, "He'd passed out there drunk the night before and pissed himself."

Jovanka shook her head then gave her brother a sympathetic glance.

"And they were chanting that Croatian nursery rhyme every Croat child at that time was being taught.

"'*Srbe na vrbe*. . . Lynch the Serb.' But at the time I was just ashamed. I blamed him. He was the reason we were so hated. I had no understanding at all of what his life had been like. Living in a world with so little to go around, a world that made damn sure he would be the last to get anything. A world where any man's instinct to provide for his family was

254

constantly and deliberately denied. But I blamed him and left him lying there, tormented by those urchins. He never even knew I saw him there.

"I believed the lies that it was all our fault, and if we just stopped being the way we were and became like them, everything would be fine. That's when the Croat priest started courting me."

Leslie clapped her hands. "I've been listening to this story all my life!"

Miloš nodded to her and winked. "We know how carefully you've been listening, all duly noted. Anyway, back to *our* story. The priest told me there was no need to 'keep wallowing in a debased life. You can put all of that behind you.' His own father was a Serb, he told me and assured me that he knew what he was talking about. 'Put that nefarious Serbian Orthodox heresy behind you, be baptized in the true Catholic faith, and you can rise to whatever rank you prove yourself worthy of.' He handed me a pamphlet. 'Look this over carefully, my son.'

"And that's when I decided to convert to Catholicism, and in so doing I would become, in effect, a Croat."

Leslie laughed. "So, basically, you went from being the equivalent of black to the equivalent of white, just by getting a little water sprinkled on your head?"

"Exactly," Srđa cut in excitedly, "that's exactly how it works. Nothing has changed, except two things – who you have become loyal to, and who you have betrayed. But that's all it's *ever* about." His face was morphing back to the King Martin face in a short circuit-y kind of way. "Sweetheart, you have to stop doing that."

"What?" Leslie asked.

"You're the one who turns on the morphing switch."

"Oh, I'm sorry," she apologized, then she laughed. "But I *like* seeing you like that. You do such a good impression."

Miloš shook his head and smiled, "Yes, we've noticed."

Leslie smiled. "I'm sorry, go on."

"This story gets really serious, really fast." He paused for a moment and then began telling his story.

"I would often meet with a group of three other neophytes, young men, Serbs, undergoing catechism into the Catholic faith. Afterwards, we met at the inn in the Croatian part of town and drank wine together. The inn keeper knew us boys from church and was happy to have us come. He would make sure no one accosted us as 'not belonging.' Marko was the oldest. It had been four years since his conversion.

"'I'll tell you, Marko said. "The thing I really hate about Serbs is the way they lay around blaming everyone else for what's wrong. I watched my old man for years, nobody was to blame for our problems but that stupid, old fool.

"'You'd need more than two hands to count the number of stupid things that stupid man would do throughout the day that would spoil everything. All he could do was complain about how the world was abusing him, but he was abusing us!

"'Croats make sense,' he continued. 'You just keep putting one foot in front of the other and make the most of your life, being a part of the world, instead of lazing around half drunk, making more babies than you can feed, living in a hovel you won't even keep up, and complaining about losing border guard privileges fifty years ago we Croatians NEVER had. Yes, us,' he said, striking his chest with his fist, proudly '*Ja sam Hrvat, nisam Srbin!*'

"'I'm telling you, Miloš, if there was anything wrong with Croats, why would they welcome us in like this? They don't care who we've been. All they care about is who we are right now, and what we're willing to do, as men, to stand shoulder-to-shoulder with other men and make the world the best place we can make it.'

"I was so moved. My baptism was set for the next week. I was happy."

Miloš was interrupted in his storytelling by a knock on the bedroom door. Leslie got up and opened it. A very beautiful, but painfully bashful woman was at the door. Apparently, she was too shy to have just appeared in the room without knocking, even though she could have, being a ghost. She was dressed in a colorfully embroidered folk dress, red and green florals on black velvet, just like the one Jovanka danced in. Her hair was blue black and shiny, her cheekbones highly defined, with a full, sensual mouth. Her eyes were large and smokey against her flawless, olive skin.

"Marta!" said Jovanka. "I'm so glad you decided to come. Please, please, come in, *uđite*. Leslie, this is your cousin, Marta. Marta, *ova je tvoja sestra od padtetka*, Leslie."

Marta crossed to Leslie and kissed her three times on alternating cheeks. *"Kako ste, moja sestra?"*

Leslie thought for a moment, *"Dobro, hvala. A ti?"*

"Ljepa," Marta replied with a gracious smile, looking at Leslie admiringly, as if she were using the word, 'beautiful,' in reference to Leslie.

"Marta's story," said Srđa. "Yes, perfect. I love that story," then to Leslie, "She is one of the lost ones we found in America when events we'd been through repeated here. We thought your friend Natalie might be one, but she is not."

"Who is she then?" asked Leslie.

"She is one gifted with the ability to see other's lives as if they are her own. Much of what she sees are lives that are yet to be lived," he said. "But Marta, I'm sorry to interrupt. You came to tell us your story."

Everyone turned their attention to Marta, who just as quickly became shy. "It's still hard for me to tell," she said. "Jovanka, you tell her."

"Of course," she said. She took Marta's hand and stood alongside her.

"Marta had flitted across my path several times," said Jovanka. "Being allowed to come back as a Guardian takes a lot of testing and training. If you make it, there are some tough things expected of you. One of them is to find the lost ones, out there confused, who can't find their way home.

"Marta was one of them. She had also died by fire. It had happened in her church. She and everyone she knew were locked into their church and burned alive by evil men who thought us animals."

"No," said Miloš. "They would have killed animals humanely. Us they killed with deliberate cruelty."

Jovanka continued, "*Da*, so Marta had died in an insane panic and lost her way. She had not been fortunate enough to die with her baby in her arms, comforting her little one into the next world." Marta was flinching. "I'm sorry you have to re-live this. You are so brave."

"If it will help my sister, then I am fine."

Jovanka continued on with the story. "Poor Marta was trapped in a room filled with smoke and scorching heat, and in that mad crash of several hundred people her baby was knocked from her arms. She met death in a state of unspeakable fear for the safety of her baby, crawling on the floor, seeking her baby among flames."

Marta jerked her arm back reflexively, looked at it and began crying. Srđa wrapped his arm around her.

"So, she'd entered the next world in a state of confusion and panic that her little one was lost and alone. She would suddenly appear to me – frantic, crazed, and then disappear before I could catch onto her. I had committed myself to rescuing her.

"Then one day she came to me in a more focused state, screaming to me, "'My baby's in the church,' a vision of that church flashed in my mind. She grasped my hand and led me to it."

Jovanka continued. "We ran through some darkness, then through an angry crowd. I realized we were in Alabama in the neighborhood where King Martin lived, where Srđa and I had left him after a trip to India we'd been stowaways on, when your Godfather was researching good lines for you to use in your debates with your daddy.

"'At least we're invisible now,' Marta said, still pulling me along. 'They can't catch us anymore!' As we approached the church, a young man in denim pants and a cigarette behind his ear used it to light a molotov cocktail in his hand and throw it at the church.

"It bounced off the window frame. Someone inside started pulling the window shut with a pulley from below. We two Srpkinja flew through it just as it was closing, into the sanctuary filled with several thousand people, all *crn*, all black, dressed for church, sweltering together in the heat. I followed after Marta as she flew down to an 18-month old baby girl, crying fearfully. I had to admit that the little girl did look very much like Marta's girl. As Marta tried to take the girl's hand, and lead her away, I stopped her.

"'*Ne, ne,*' I said. 'The mob can see the baby. They'll hurt her. We have to stay here.'

"Marta did not argue, just wrapped her arms around the little girl. Again, Marta disintegrated into fear. 'They're going to burn up my baby,' she cried in horror. The baby's real momma was a light-skinned woman," Jovanka chuckled. "Actually, what we would have called a dark-skinned woman, who might have passed for Marta's sister. It was amazing the similarity. She also hugged the girl. I was on the other side, hugging Marta. That's when I saw King Martin coming to the pulpit.

"I said, 'Oh look, it's the King. Everybody listens to him. He'll get them to stop.'

"And that's just what King Martin had to say. 'I've just gotten off the phone with Attorney General Robert Kennedy and he has authorized several thousand federal agents and National Guardsmen to assist us.'

"The congregation broke into cheers and hallelujahs.

"Eventually, they did come and threw those things, what do you call them, that makes the air hard to breath?"

"Tear gas?" said Leslie.

"Yes, the gas that makes you cry. So, all the windows had to be closed even tighter and the people suffered even more in the heat. Then the mob outside returned and had to be tear-gassed again. It went on like that, it seemed like forever.

"Marta began rocking herself, starting to lose her grip, remembering her death. 'Why do they torment us like this? Why? I don't understand this. Why does God let this happen to us?'

"I tried to calm her. 'God has us in the palm of his hand,' I said.

"'God has us in the palm of his hand,' repeated the baby's mother. Someone at the back of the church repeated the phrase, and then another chanted it. The organist began playing a song with those words and a lady stood up and started singing with a strong, beautiful voice.

> "And He will bear you up on eagle's wings,
> bear you on the breath of dawn,
> make you to shine like the sun!
> And hold you, hold you in the palm of His hand."

"Someone called out the page number and soon the whole congregation was singing. Very early in the morning, a very snotty Alabama National Guardsman banged on the door and angrily told everyone they could leave. I'll never forget that. Where had I seen that before? Some things never change. Never.

"Some of the crowd stood in the cool lawn of the church. Marta sat down in the grass, still holding the baby's hand. 'They didn't burn us up,' she said, crying, 'somebody cared about us! They didn't let them burn us up in our church!' Her eyes shone with bliss.

"I said to her, with tears in my eyes, 'God was there in your church when they burned you up, and He loves you for it. He will always grieve over what we went through.' Then the mother pulled the girl with her towards a car that had pulled up to the curb.

"Marta followed the mother and child out to the street. She started to panic. 'That's not my baby,' she said. 'Where's my baby?' I clasped Marta's hand and pulled her away.

"'Come and I'll show you,'" I said.

"And I followed her," Marta said, finally forgetting her shyness. "Jovanka started climbing a tree. She was always such a tomboy. I was not so sure, but I keep forgetting I have no weight. I can't fall, so I follow her up into the tree to the very top." She had gotten very excited.

"And she says to me, look, look there to the sun coming up. But I hear first. I hear my little girl calling me from behind the sun. She has been there all along! And I spread my arms like they are wings and I fly to her."

Marta beamed at Leslie, "And we have been together ever since, and so happy." Tears were streaming down her face.

Leslie could feel some on her own cheeks.

"Those sorts of things went on all the time," said Srđa. "Do you have any idea how many of our lost souls were wandering the earth after what happened to us? And what it meant to them to see what started happening here just a decade later? How much it attracted them, to see it repeated but this time with some hope a mind can grasp, and how much that helped us to find them and bring them home?"

"Of course," Leslie said. "I know all about that," thinking about the odd journey Archie had set her on.

Marta had become fidgety. Jovanka turned towards her. "Do you need to get back?"

"Yes," said Marta. "It's time to nurse my baby.' She looked anxious, then apologetic, towards Leslie.

Leslie crossed to her and gave her a hug. "Thank you so much for coming. What you said. . . it makes my life make sense."

Marta returned the hug. Then with a nervous urgency, she left. Jovanka watched after her.

"She's doing so much better." Everyone looked sobered at the thought that ten years in Heaven had yet to completely heal poor Marta.

Miloš smiled at Leslie, who remembered he'd been interrupted in his story again.

"Well, insane woman who sees ghosts," Miloš said, "this ghost must warn you. There are some very foul-mouthed people in this next part of the story. We are talking about soldiers in a barracks, and some very sadistic soldiers at that. But it was the path that led me to the church in Glina."

* * *

Let a Man Jerk Off in Peace

"Every night it was the same thing," Miloš said. "Remember this is the Croatian Home Guard, like your National Guard, which was becoming more and more involved in Ustaša extermination of the Serbian citizens of Croatia, men, women, children – everyone.

"Lights would go out in the barracks and Ante would get going again, talking in his lewd, crude way about his Ustaša fantasies."

"'Yes,' Ante drawled. 'One day's delivery of Serb trash included a very ripe bitch. Tits like cantaloupes and that ass. How anybody can have such a small waist and still have such an ass, I don't know, but there she was. And us boys fucked her all-night long. And the more we fucked her the more swollen she got, and the tighter the fit. Perfect. And she never stopped fighting it.

"'You should have heard her scream. A night to remember. And we repaid her by saving her life for a whole two weeks until she finally stopped fighting us. What a hellcat.'

"'Shut the hell up,' I said. 'Let a man jerk off in peace.'

"'I'm just giving you something juicy to jerk off about, my brother.'

"'I'm not your brother,' I replied.

"Oh no?" Ante said. "Maybe we should throw you in that kiln along with that bitch. You can fuck her there. She'll be very hot."

Miloš was pacing angrily, his face contorted with disgust.

"The barracks got very quiet," he went on. "I knew they'd forgotten that I had been born and raised a Serb when they assigned me to the Karlovac district, and I had long since stopped telling anyone. Already the tide was turning for me. I was not telling who I really was – not because I was ashamed, but because I was afraid. And that changes everything."

Srđa nodded sympathetically. "Exactly," he said.

"For the past week," Miloš continued, "I had been helping with the roundup of civilian families of Partisans."

"Who are Partisans?" asked Leslie.

"Good question," said Srđa. "They're the people fighting the fascists, the Resistance. Some were Croat, many Serb, trying to defend themselves against the homicidal maniacs."

"Thanks," said Leslie. She turned her attention back to Miloš, who resumed his narrative.

"Our orders were to immediately execute anyone not in Croat uniform who possessed weapons, anybody outside their own village without a permit, and if there were any attacks on Croatian forces, that entire village would be transported to a camp -- men, women, children, old people.

"That day we had transported such a group from a village north of Karlovac. Since Vrginmost is to the south of Karlovac, there was no one there I knew. The families were transported in trucks to the railway line without incident except for an old farmer, probably senile, who was shot when he picked up a pitchfork and brandished it at a guard.

"We got to the rail line and loaded the people onto cattle cars. The stench from the cars was revolting. Urine, feces, vomit and blood festered in the warm, spring sun. The reflex of anyone entering the car was to recoil. Eventually it became necessary to shove people in, who often fell headlong into the filth. It was a disgusting day."

He looked over at Jovanka, who'd begun pacing. "You okay?" he asked.

She shook her head violently and proclaimed, "I am okay! When I'm not okay is when nobody talks. That's when I am not okay!"

Srđa leaned towards Leslie, "What she's talking about is that, in the years right after the war, it was made illegal to even talk about what was done to us."

"Really?" Leslie said, astonished. "I've heard people deny what a holocaust it was, but illegal to even say it happened?"

Jovanka was still pacing. "There are always extremes for us." Srđa grabbed her hand and made her sit in his lap.

Miloš had his hands cupping his face, keeping his focus. He continued. "I heard the commander phone in a request that the cars be hosed down between transports so that there would not be so much difficulty getting people into the cars. I doubted that hosing down the cars would help much. There seemed to be about a half inch of filth, layer upon decayed layer, lining the floor of the cars. I pitied the poor sap who'd have to hose that down and have it all spray up in his face. But they'd probably just get some prisoners to do it.

"We were to perform a similar mission that day. We piled into a transport truck and followed a long procession of them into the countryside. Ante regaled us with another story.

"'Let me tell you about Bukovica,' he said. My ears pricked up. I knew Bukovica, a dirt-poor town in a rocky hillside area with poor soil for farming. Many people had left over the years to try their luck as migrant workers in other countries. Many families had been split up that way. There were a couple of gypsy families there, but otherwise, all were Serb. I used to pass by there, on my way to visit a girl, and I scoffed at their backwardness. They were an embarrassment.

"Ante went on with his story. 'We did the work of missionaries, my brothers. We brought those poor, benighted heretics to the true faith, in a lovely baptismal ceremony at the church in Glina, and then we sent them all straight to heaven.' He laughed raucously.

"I kicked at him. 'Shut up, you foul-mouthed bastard,' I said. I caught a glance from Stevo, a tall, heavily-built fellow who also swapped dead Serb jokes with Ante. That glance told me that he was questioning my loyalty, I realized. I said no more.

"The next day I asked for permission to speak to my superior officer. I requested a weekend pass in order to visit my mother in Banski Kovačevac, a Croatian town in Vrginmost district. It was already in my charts that I was from there, a favor my enrolling officer had done for me, he liked me so much.

"I told the officer that I had received word that she was gravely ill and I wanted very much to visit her. I was careful to act like a Croat, which I was very good at. It's hard to describe the difference. Serbs are louder."

Jovanka laughed.

"They take up more space," he went on. "They touch you more when they talk to you and the accent is different. Croats try to act more 're-fined.' Serbs are rougher. Some like their honesty. Others think it is a brutal honesty. By avoiding those things and speaking with a Croatian accent I could blend in with them very well. The differences were really not that great, but at the time, many Croatians made a very big deal out of Serb characteristics and held them in great contempt.

"The officer looked over my chart. 'So,' he said, 'you are well-behaved and dutiful. Good. Yes, you may see your sick mother. I will give you four days. Do not wear your uniform while you are alone out there. There are some civilian clothes you can borrow and be very careful to keep your pass and your identity papers with you, at all times. Keep a sidearm with you also. And be careful. You are needed here, soldier.'"

* * *

Stepping into a Sugreb

"I thanked the officer profusely and headed out into the countryside. I traveled by rail as far as I could and then walked and hitched towards Perna. On the way I passed through Donji Sjeničak. Nothing was left. All the houses had been burned. I was not surprised. I had a third cousin, Vaša Roknić, who had stirred up a lot of trouble. His father was a contradiction in terms – a wealthy peasant."

Srđa jumped in. "The way we use the word 'peasant' is pretty much the way you would use the word 'farmer.' He's not the same as a serf, the way we were serfs to The Turk. 'Serf' means the same as 'peon,' as in 'peonage slavery.'"

"Thanks," said Leslie.

Miloš nodded his head at Srđa and continued. "The family land-holdings had increased over time, and by shrewd management, the family *zadruga* had blossomed into a thriving little micro-economy, with nearly all necessities provided within the *zadruga* itself, and with a cash cow, in this case, cash pigs, allowing the family to set aside the money to send a son to college. Vaša's poor father, Timo, had dreams of his son becoming a policeman. Vaša surpassed the father's ambition and distinguished himself as a law student and then a faculty member of the school of law.

"But then he went bad, in my opinion at the time. As the old people would say, he had stepped into a *sugreb*, the groove a wolf makes pawing at the ground. He became a Communist in 1934 and brought his family down."

Srđa interjected again. "I know you've probably heard mostly negatives about Communism, but the thing you have to understand is that, during the Second World War, the only big country that gave us any assistance at all in escaping the exterminations we were suffering from the fascists was Russia. Everyone else turned their backs on us. Even after we rescued 500 US airmen. An amazing feat for so small a country. So, at this point, we all realize that Vaša was right in what he saw coming. And of course, even *he* regrets the way the communists were to persecute us for our faith, especially in the Krajina. But that's another story for another day. So, anyway, Miloš, sorry to interrupt again."

"Thanks for explaining," said Leslie, then to Miloš, "Sorry."

"*Nija problema*," he smiled. "Where was I? Okay, I was back in 1938 when Vaša was sent to prison for his subversive activities, for a year. When he got out, he went right back to what he considered freedom fighting, trying to turn peasants into communists. And, on September 17, 1941, in German-occupied Serbia he was shot first and then hanged by

The Twelve Patriots, Vaša is sixth from right

the Wehrmacht, one of the so-called 'Twelve Patriots' – communist agitators – executed that day.

"Sjeničak was the largest village in Vrginmost, which means "Virg's Bridge." Another one of the rare college-educated people in the district was Gojko Nikoliš, the son of the village priest.

"You would think with the way Gojko's family had been treated during the Sjeničak Revolt, threatened by what I saw as an ignorant mob of Serbian thugs, crazy enough to threaten their own priest and his infant son. . . ."

"Yes," Leslie interjected. "Daniel told me that story. The mob went after the priest too?"

"Yes, Gojko's father tried to save those three poor men who were killed in the race riot. So, while I was a Home guard, a *domobrani*, I still felt that Gojko was a fool not to leave those ignorant peasants in the *Krajina* alone. He could have moved to a city and any sort of career he wanted, but instead he came back to Sjeničak as a country doctor, and fomented revolt in his spare time.

"From the man whose cart I was hitching a ride with, I learned that it was as I expected. The men of the town had been rounded up by forces of the Independent State of Croatia, in other words, the Croatian Fascists. The families of these captured men fled to refugee camps after their homes were burned. No one knew where the men had been taken.

"We learned much later that some had been taken to Jasenovac, where they were either incinerated alive in the kiln, slashed or bludgeoned to death. Others were sent to a German-run camp in Norway where a typhoid epidemic broke out.

"It was decided to eliminate the contagion coming from the Serb prisoners by eliminating the Serbs. They took the first batch out, marched them out to the woods, made them dig a big pit, and then machine gunning them all into it. The second half surmised this and refused to leave the barracks they occupied, so gasoline was poured on the building and they all perished in that fire.

"But I knew nothing about this at the time. What was clear to me was that the Serbs were, as Serbs always seemed to be, total fools, duped by the Russian Communists into their own destruction. My host on the cart ride told me that the women and children had fled to the Partisans. When I commented on the men's folly, getting themselves arrested, thus leaving their families unprotected, the old man looked at me with that crazy paranoia of old Serbs.

"'You really think,' the old man said, 'that there is anything we Serbs can do that will prevent the *Ustaša* from trying to destroy us? You really think that? We are surviving much better in the bush, sheltered by Partisans. And at least it's just the men of Sjeničak who are dead, and not the women and children as well, the way it was in villages who did not resist.

"'The Russians are our only friends. My brother was foolish enough to volunteer to be baptized in Glina. Now he's in a pit with hundreds of other baptizees.'

"I wondered again why I was hearing this crazy bullshit about Glina."

* * *

Ustaša Outdoing Themselves

Miloš continued with his tale while Leslie cuddled up with Jovanka. Srđa had seated himself in the chair, while Miloš paced as he spoke. "The old man let me sleep in the small hut he was living in overnight and in the morning, I walked to Perna. My family's *zadruga* was nothing but cinders. I cursed those damned Communists, Mirka Poštic, and his cousin, Mile Roknić, getting everybody to take arms against Croatian forces, rebelling against their own country's government. That's what had led to this. I sat on the swing next to the outhouse, the only structure still standing and cried angrily for my mother and my brothers and sisters. Perhaps they have escaped, I thought, and went looking for someone still in town who could tell me something. Those structures still standing were deserted.

"I found Bosiljka Bakić at her home. She was busy packing up a cart. A middle-aged woman, large as a man by way of height and a stocky frame, who stood in an uncommonly erect manner, spoke hurriedly to me. 'I am afraid to be here for even a few hours like this. They are not leaving no one alive, no one. The people in Petrova Gora saw what the Ustaša did to us in September but stayed in their homes. Then in May, the Ustaša came and killed twice as many of them. Now everyone lives in the refuge. I am only here to retrieve the grain I had hidden.

"'Do you know what happened to my cousin Pava Kljajic? They threw her alive into a mass grave and she dragged herself out. She could have saved herself, but thinking of her brothers, she followed the Ustaša and told them not to kill her brothers. She would give them money if they would leave her brothers alone. So, they told her, 'we won't kill you, we'll slaughter you.' And that's what they did.'

"She wiped at her eyes," Miloš continued, "then answered my questions about my next of kin. Jovanka was a Partisan soldier, fighting alongside our father and was newly married to another soldier. Two of my cousins on my Aunt Anka's side were at a refugee camp in Bosnia. To her knowledge, no one else was still alive.

"She answered, 'The damned Ustaša are outdoing their own policy. They set out to kill off a third of us, baptize another third, and exile the last third. But the truth is, if we agree to leave, they steal all our money and kill us on the road. Those they baptize they kill directly afterward, and the rest they just round up and kill at their leisure.

"'Son,' she said to me, 'why has it taken you months to come looking after your own?'

"I had no answer for her and was suddenly resentful of her meddling.

"I decided to take a side trip through Glina."

* * *

Washing Blood with Blood

Miloš continued with his story. "The Orthodox church stood in the center of Glina. The door was open, and I entered. An old woman was kneeling in front of the altar, scrubbing the floor. I entered the church and crouched in front of her.

"'*Dobro jutro,* grandmother," I said, 'how are you this morning?'

"'How am I? I will not be able to sleep until I have scrubbed out these stains!' she said. I realized from her accent and dress that she was an Hrvatitsa – Croatian. I saw no stains.

"'Why?'" I asked. "'What has happened here?'"

"'The first time they hired me to clean up the church they offered me five times more than I have ever received for such work. When I came down here I found out why. Everywhere was blood.

"'Then a *Ustaša* came forward wearing his special claw, a *Serboček*, or Serb Cutter, a curved blade attached to a leather strap he fastens onto his wrist to make slashing throats an easy job and he says to me, 'You will clean the church from top to bottom by this evening, or someone will be cleaning up *your* blood.

"'I worked bent at the waist or squatting for as long as I could, it was too revolting to kneel down onto all that blood. How quickly my wash water turned red, until it was like I was washing blood with blood. Many buckets I filled and poured out in front of the stone cross outside.

"'I tried to clean a spot for myself to kneel in, where it was clean, but the blood kept oozing out from between the stone floor tiles. I was frightened at the end of the day, because the church was as filled with blood as before. I, as well, stood in blood-soaked clothes, soaked in the blood of many, many innocents. If I was to die, I did not want it to happen until I had carried all the blood to the Savior, and that is why I cleaned it.'"

"I am sorry you have suffered this, grandmother," I said, realizing I could trust her. I had switched into my Serbian accent, knowing I would never again feel the same about having abandoned it.

"'But at dusk,' she went on, 'the clawed raptor said I had done a good job, paid me and told me to come back again in a week. And each week, for six weeks, I cleaned this church that will not come clean, and I must keep cleaning it now until all the blood has been poured out where it belongs. Now I overhear them say that they will burn it after one more batch, so I have so little time left. All day I wash it, but at night it returns again, and I must come back and do it all over again. If I don't hurry I will not be able to pour this sacred blood where it belongs.'

"Then, still on her knees, she moved to me and looked up into my face with a tender smile, 'You must take this money,' she said, 'sweet boy, for you look like the brave Serb who stole my girlish heart many years ago. Take it and give it to your brothers and sisters, if they still live, if not, find your cousins and give it to them. Feed them through the winter, for

I am not long for this world, and I am terrified of what will happen to my soul if I have not sent this money where it belongs.'

"With that, she gave me a purse. Inside it there were over two hundred *kuna*. There was too much joy on her face at being relieved of it for me to be able to refuse it.

Serbs in Glina Church about to be massacred

"I pitied her insanity. 'Dear *baka*, you can stop washing now. You have cleaned as much as you can, and what remains God himself will purify. Sleep in peace. We are indebted to you.'

"The old woman clasped me closely and began crying. "Oh Ljuban, why was I so afraid to love you? You are everything to me. But all I have of you is the blood of your children that I can't wash out. I don't want to wash it out, if it's all I have of you. Such precious blood to have spilled so freely.'

"'Sleep peacefully, my love,' I said, as if I had been possessed by Ljuban, possessed with his eyes, seeing the lovely young woman whose devotion had transformed that beauty into something sacred. The sight of it thrilled me. There were tears in my eyes. 'You have taken superb care of my children. I love you for it
with all my heart. And I always will. I know what you have been through for me. You are my hero.' The old woman cried in relief for a good while, clinging to my arm.

"I then walked her back to her home, holding my arm out for her to grasp. She held it closely, smiling blissfully, all the way. Once in her small one-room *kuća*, she fed me some bread and honey and continued to call me Ljuban.

"Sweet Mila," I said. "When it's safe for you to do so, I would like for you to find the Orthodox priest and ask him to baptize you. And it will be as if we were married, and you will forever be where you belong."

Jovanka was watching Leslie crying through the story and had circled behind her. She put her arms around Leslie.

"The old woman cried some more healing tears," Milos went on, "then settled down on a mattress next to the fireplace and fell deeply asleep. I left all my coins on her table, some clean money she could spend on herself.

"In the morning, I ate breakfast at an inn. The old cleaning woman, Mila, passed by the window, not seeing in. She was carrying a basket full of goods, smiling, talking to someone in her imagination.

"'Who is that crazy old woman?' I asked the innkeeper, speaking with a Croatian accent, knowing that from then on, I would only use that accent to deceive them, never again wanting to be one of them. "Why is she talking about people being killed in the heretics' church?'

"'Communist Serb terrorists,' she said. 'Good riddance to those heretics. It's the best thing that's happened to us in a long time. As for her, she was a whore to Serbs, a *Srpska kurva*. She has been shunned for many years.'"

* * *

Rednecks and Tire Irons

Leslie and her visitors were quiet for a few moments. Jovanka was holding Leslie's hand in her lap.

"Yes," Jovanka said. "That is how a Croatian woman who loves a Serbian man has been treated. She is shunned and tormented and possibly killed, and that is what she is called, a whore."

Leslie let out a sarcastic laugh. "Oh, you mean like those red necks with the tire irons?"

"Yes, we know all about the tire irons, and the firings, and the humiliations," Srđa said.

"Really? You know what happened with the tire irons?"

"Yes, a number of us from Serbian Heaven showed up. How do you think you escaped so readily?"

"Really? You saved us? Is that what happened to those good ol' boys?"

Reggie and Leslie had gone out for a bike ride and gotten back at dusk. As they pulled up to the house a pick-up truck pulled up alongside them.

Three burly young country boys, armed with two tire irons and a chain, poured out of the small, rusty, old truck, one jumping down from the truck bed full of junk. As he jumped down he stumbled and fell head-long right into the fellow in front of him, who then knocked into the guy in front of him.

"They went down like bowling pins," Leslie laughed. "We had more than enough time to escape to the foyer, though it was hard to tear our-selves from the sight they made."

"It *was* comical," said Miloš.

"Of course, it looked very funny to you," said Jovanka to Leslie, still holding Leslie's hand. "We were seeing something a little different. What you don't realize is your story has become quite popular. 'The poor *Krajina* girl lost in the *Tuđina* trying to find her way home by way of the 'Serbs in America' saga has caught on in Serbian Heaven. When the alert went out about those *Ustaša* you call Red Necks coming after you, six strapping young Serbs appeared – without appearing of course – and had quite a time with those goons.

"There's a trick to it," said Miloš. "It's something us boys practice up there, how to concentrate our energy towards a specific task like knock-ing into the back of someone's knee at just the right instant so that it buckles under his weight. With the right concentration focusing that en-ergy, a fighter can still fight without a physical body. It's quite an art."

Leslie continued, "When we got into the apartment I opened the front window. Reggie told them we'd called the cops, and I said, 'Get the hell out of here.'"

Leslie got quiet.

"What?" asked Jovanka, she was still holding Leslie's hand, which she shook gently.

"Then one of them said, 'Shut up, you whore. Fuckin' with niggers, god!'

Leslie was quiet for a moment, remembering the bite of that five-let-ter word.

"Then he threw his tire iron at one of the bikes we left on the sidewalk. It hit the sidewalk at a funny angle and ricocheted onto one of the other guy's shins." Leslie was laughing again. "That guy was cursing him out all the way back to the truck."

"Damn," she went on, "I could have died, instead I died laughing."

Miloš sat on the bed across from her and took her other hand, "That was quite a close call, young lady. But we were there for you, and always will be. Do you want me tell you the rest of what happened with the cleaning lady?"

"Yes," Leslie said. "What happened?"

Miloš continued, "I had a lot to think about as I returned to my barracks, which is what I decided to do. But before I left Glina, I slipped into the church once more. I knew there was no way to find a priest. They had all been killed or were in hiding. My business would have to be between me and God. I crossed myself, then prostrated myself before the altar. "Forgive me," I pleaded. "I have sinned against my family obscenely. I do not deserve forgiveness. Show me how I can help them. If it costs my life, I freely give it." On the way out, I spied one of Milka's wash buckets. There was still water in it. Very holy water. I cupped my hands into the water, and then emptied the water onto my head.

I got back the next day. My lieutenant asked after my mother. I told him she had passed away, and that I was very grateful that he had given me a chance to see her before she departed this world. The lieutenant told me to let him know if I needed anything, and he would put me on light duty for the next few days.

"Light duty left me working with Ante. We were set to the task of digging post holes for a fence. The ground was heavy with clay and difficult to work. If this was light duty, I'd like to know what would be hard? Being sent to murder Serb children?

"I didn't know how I would proceed. I'd come back to the *Domobrani* because there might be an opportunity to inflict the greatest casualties positioned there. The rest I had left to God in the pledge I made at the church.

"Then Ante started back in with his obscenities. 'Have you heard about the bricks they make at Jasenovac?' he asked.

"'No, I haven't,' I said. I looked up and stared him down bitterly. 'But I'd love for you to tell me.'"

"'Yes,' he went on meeting my glare with his own, 'there used to be a brick factory there, and a lovely, large kiln. The doorway is like a normal door, since men must be able to enter it to stack the brick about to be fired and remove it afterward. But now the camp is there, and they have found the most delightful use for it. First, they get the kiln going like a blast furnace, then they drug a batch of Serbs, till they can barely stand, they're so out of it,' he said, tittering.

Miloš paused in his storytelling and looked to Jovanka who had covered her face with her hands. "Are you all right?" he asked.

"Go on," she said. "Go on." Now it was Leslie holding her hand.

"'So, they line them up outside," Ante went on, 'then one-by-one they come and get them. Once inside one guard takes the feet, another takes

272

the arms and they toss the old Serb grandmother into the kiln. There's nothing so satisfying,' Ante joked, 'as hearing a Serb skull explode.'

"I reacted without intent. Before I even knew what I was doing I'd swung my shovel at Ante's skull. Ante was quick, though, and grabbed the shovel. It flung out across the yard. Then I went at him with my fists. I grabbed Ante's throat and began to strangle him. Ante pulled all his weight away from me, then rebounded forward into me. He kicked me hard in the groin. I lost my grip and retreated, waiting for the pain to subside. Ante leapt at me and we crashed to the ground. He tried to pin me down. By then, guards had descended on us.

"We were thrown into the brig, in adjoining cells. Late that night, Ante began to talk to me.

"'I know you are a Serb,' he whispered.

"'Shut your mouth,' I replied.

"'And do you know how I know?' Ante asked.

"I said nothing.

"'Because I am a Serb, too. Why do you think I have been telling everyone what's going on? So that I can tell who is with us, and who is against us. And I can tell you, brother, there are five of you ready to act when the time is right. There are five of you now, since you have joined us, which I know you have. The only question open is how we will do it.'"

* * *

The Six Patriots

"A plan was formulated. The goal was for us to disappear into the Partisan world fully-uniformed, fully-armed. Luckily, standing orders were to appear always in public uniformed and armed, even during short passes to town. A location was designated as to where we were to go. On the next day we were allowed a pass to town, so each of us would find that address and disappear.

"Fortunately, four came up in the next rotation and everything went smoothly as planned. Our captain was furious, however, at the group defection and canceled all passes indefinitely. I was thus stranded. An alternative plan was devised. On my next assignment of guard duty I would toss a grenade into the compound, another into the fence line, and in all the confusion I was to pretend I was seeking out the enemy, moving stealthily, firing at the imagined enemy, till I disappeared into the city.

273

"I bid my farewell to Ante, who would continue on with his job recruiting Partisans, while my life as a Partisan began. And that's when I found my father and my sister."

* * *

Borac Srpkinja

"Jovanka was quite the *borac Srpkinja*, a lady combat soldier," said Milos. "Now that she was with our father and me, the old days returned when we three would practice our marksmanship. My reunion with my father had been memorable.

"It was at a briefing for us snipers that I first saw my father again. I was astonished to see how much younger he had become. Sober, his health returned and his pride, he was, once again, the man I remembered from my early childhood. Jovanka and I were the oldest.

"Our father had been a migrant worker in France for three years while we were young, meaning there was a period of time when he returned when it was just us three, before the other children started to come. We accompanied him deer hunting when still eight and nine years old. Our family always did so well at shooting contests.

"After the briefing we stood before one another. I, shamed with the betrayal I had inflicted on my own family, him, I imagine ashamed of his addiction and the many failings it had created.

"'Can you ever forgive me?' asked my father.

"'If you can forgive me,' I replied, and we never referred to the past again.

"And there was Jovanka's new husband, Srđa." He turned to his sister and teased, "I hear it had been a short courtship."

"That was my doing," she said. "You see, it was Srđa who had found me after I survived the massacre of my family. I had spent about two weeks afterwards crying a good deal. I cried so easily because he gave me such intense attention, as if he enjoyed sharing in the depths of my soul."

"Which, in fact, I did," added Srđa.

"He was the first educated person I'd ever met. I began asking questions of him about his life and I could imagine nothing more fascinating than to go where he would go, and do what he would do. I had done well in school, and enjoyed exercising my mind, and the amount I could learn from him, and the kind of debates we'd get into left me highly stimulated.

"Did you know she'd been the Great Debater at school?" asked Srđa. "Every year there was a debate in the last two grades, the third and fourth grades, and each year she won it. In her last year, her teacher bragged about her to the class. 'You can just look at Jovanka to know why The Turk was constantly kidnapping our Balkan girls for his harems – beautiful girls, but a good deal smarter than they are good looking. The Turk knew he had little sense of his own, so he stole some of ours.'"

Jovanka continued. "I felt, with survival hanging in the balance every day the way it was, an urgency to cram in as much life as possible. I was not going to wait for anything."

"For my part," Srđa said, "I was mesmerized by her, but, being in my early thirties, I felt a huge burden of responsibility. I was sure I could trust myself not to take advantage of this young girl.

"That's when we started debating. It happened after a particularly harrowing day. Our little group, me, Aleksandr and Petra, had been part of a larger group on a mission that had been cut to pieces. Perhaps there were other survivors, but we were stranded in *Ustaša* territory, with our foundling, Jovanka, struggling to reach a Partisan cell.

"We were crossing the countryside at night, on a bridge, when a sniper started shooting. We all ran, scrambling for cover. I pulled Jovanka with me into a depression in the ground, the hole left when a huge dead tree falls, uprooting itself, surrounded now with brush.

"I had felt him snatch me so fiercely," Jovanka cut in, "that the momentum slammed me into his chest. I felt the warrior in him, that part of him that had been reacting steadily to threats of violence with an intense physical energy. I did not let him go but wrapped my arms around his neck, knowing that he would have no choice but to comfort the frightened little girl, but it was not my fear that motivated me. I had set my cap on him. I lifted my face to him and he kissed me. When I opened my eyes, looking upward, I saw the sniper!

"'Give me your rifle,' I whispered.

"'Why?'

"'I see him,' I said.

"'Where?'

"I pointed. 'Can you see him?' I whispered.

"'No, no, I can't.'

"He handed me the rifle. Carefully, I took aim and shot. The man fell from the nearby tree. We waited, wondering if he had been alone.

"I slipped out from under the brush, picked up a large rock and threw it a distance. It made a clatter. There was no gunfire in response. Srđa

275

hooted like an owl. It was answered by another. The two of us crawled out of our hiding spot and went towards the sound of the hoot. Both Petra and Aleksandr were unhurt. All four of us continued our journey.

"The next day the debate began. I proposed the topic. It was: 'Marrying the love of your life in a war zone is an imperative.' Srđa argued the counter-point.

"'The most important argument against that notion,' Srđa said, 'is the most obvious. The lady in question may become pregnant, seriously compromising her ability to survive the warfare.'

"'Nonsense,' I said. 'I watched my mother overcome many difficulties while nearly always pregnant. I've seen her plow a field while six months pregnant. And you also have to take into account that if the lady were someone like me, who would be in the field as a soldier, were she not pregnant, it may well be that being sidelined with a pregnancy could actually save her life.'"

"'Are you seriously suggesting that you will remain in combat, even after we've reached the refuge?'"

"'Absolutely,' I said. 'Could you see the sniper?'"

"'No,' he answered.

"'But I could.' I said. 'In times like these, I can't withhold an ability like that when it can help our people. That's what comes first.'"

"I don't want you in combat!" he said.

"'Then marry me and get me pregnant,' I replied.

"That was the last word in that debate."

* * *

Srđa Does His Best

"We reached the refuge in the village Rujiška in Grmec," Srđa said. "It was one of the Serb villages far away from any Ustaša strongholds, full of feisty Serbs and feared by the Ustaša.

"Frequent complaints of German SS officers and regular army were being made to Berlin, complaining that the sadistic brutality of the Ustaša was fueling a massive backlash that was very dangerous to the success of the Axis powers. But the Ustaša intent was deliberate. Those at the very top had made a conscious decision that, whether the war was won or not, the crimes against the Serbs were to be so terrible that the Croats and Serbs could never be friends again, and ultimately, however long it took, Serbs would be driven from Croatia, forever.

"The village priest married us."

Jovanka got up from the bed and gave Srđa a hug. He put his arm around her shoulders. He continued, "I quite willingly caught myself up in her life force to grab as much of life as we could, while we could. She did volunteer as a sniper. She was trained and she served on half a dozen missions before she reached her fourth month of pregnancy. I accompanied her to the refuge in Dvara and then reported for duty with my Partisan unit.

"In January of 1943 I was killed by gunfire during the Fourth Enemy Offensive." Jovanka held him closer. He paused for a moment and gulped. "On February 16, 1943 Jovanka and her baby were captured by Germans and killed at the Jasenovac camp. And that's when our next life began, much better than the first."

"Where is your baby?" asked Leslie.

"She's with my momma. They are very close. Babies grow very slowly in Heaven. We have much more of a chance to enjoy one another."

"How old is she now?"

"About the equivalent of four."

Leslie looked to Miloš. "And you? Were you also a casualty of the war?"

"No, my father and I both survived the war," Miloš said. "We returned to our family land and rebuilt. And this is the part I want you to know, Leslie. I went back to Glina, found Mila, the cleaning woman of the church in Glina, and brought her to live in my household. With great joy she was baptized into the Orthodox faith and became a *Pravoslava*. She lived out her days with us, content that I was her son.

"My wife, Anka, and I gave her many grandchildren. Before death finally came for her one night in her sleep, she had spent nearly a decade perfectly sane."

"Do you understand what I am telling you?" Miloš asked.

"You're telling me how I would like people to treat me," Leslie replied. "but I can't make a world where that happens. Nobody's going to invite me to convert to the black side."

Dušan, the shipwrecked sailor, Daniel's very great grandfather, his *Deda*, had been lurking in stealth mode all evening. He naturally wanted his entrance into Leslie's consciousness to be appropriately dramatic and now he could see that his moment had arrived.

"Why the hell not?" he shouted, bursting into the room. "What's wrong with those people?"

Leslie was thunderstruck. There, standing next to her dresser, shouting at her passionately, waving his fist at her, was no less than Sean Connery, in his prime! Without his toupee, thank god. "What are you doing here?" she asked, in a delighted shock.

"I am the very great grandfather of that young man we've gone through great difficulty delivering to your doorstep," he said, pointing to the ceiling. "Are you going to sit around here doubting your sanity or get on with the life you are supposed to lead?"

"But you can't call them 'those people!'" she said.

"Which people?" he said, squinting.

"Those people."

"What are you talking about? Oh, that bullshit. So, I can't say 'I like those people, I've just spent 400 years raising countless generations of them.'"

"No," Leslie said, and she had a good laugh. "It's not permitted."

"When have I ever worried about what was permitted? And for that matter, when have you?" He turned to Srđa and muttered. "Our teenage girls have more guts than grown men elsewhere." Then he turned back to Leslie. "How do you think you got into this mess?"

"Oh my God!" she exclaimed. "If your Daniel's ancestor, then Daniel's a Serb!"

"Of all my many living descendants he favors me the most," he said. "And that is because of what he believes. I will tell you the truth of what kind of people there are in the world. There are two kinds, just two kinds of people in the world. There are people who choose the Kingdom of Heaven and people who choose the Earthly Kingdom. This afternoon you had a room full of people who have chosen the Earthly Kingdom." He motioned to the other three. "This is ridiculous, you've been talking to her for hours, and nobody's told her about the meaning of the Battle of Kosovo?"

"What does Kosovo have to do with this?" she asked, still quite blown away and liking him immensely.

"It is very simple," he said. "There was a point in time, when we were sailing to China and rising in the world around us, when it looked like we would be the next Big Men in the world with our foot on everybody's neck. Do you know how much I hate people like that? I know it's not something you expect to hear from a ghost dropping in from Heaven. But it is my failing, what I have to work on still. I hate people like that. Don't you?"

"Yes."

"Yes, that's right." He was standing above her from quite a height, and poking his finger on her sternum, but she felt quite comfortable, even sheltered. "You weren't choosing black people. You were choosing the Heavenly Kingdom. You couldn't stand being in the room with people who think they're better than other people. It wasn't just because of who you liked, it was also because of who you didn't like. You don't much like white American bigots, do you?"

"No," she said.

"No, I don't either," said Dušan. "They get on my last nerve. It's The Turk all over again! Okay, let me finish with this. I keep getting ahead of myself, but I can't help it. I'm a Serb and we're impulsive as hell. Even when we're ghosts dropping in from Heaven. Anyway, that's the thing, we were about to become people like that, who think they're better than other people and God said, 'Oh no, not my Serbs! They're my favorites. I don't want them to become assholes like that.'"

Leslie cracked up. "That's what God said?"

"You're damn right."

"You swear like a sailor," she said.

"Naturally, I *am* a sailor."

"Oh, I didn't know that!" Leslie said. "Nobody's introduced us."

The other three all began talking at once, apologizing.

Dušan shouted them all down, "It's all right! I didn't give anybody a chance to introduce me. I am Dušan Kraljević. You may have heard of my brother, Marko. I was a mate aboard a vessel that sailed from Dubrovnik in 1530. We shipwrecked off the coast of what was then Chowan land, though now it is," he made a face, and minced, 'North Carolina.' Believe me, doing half-time between Serbian Heaven and the Chowan Spirit World I've heard my fill from people recovering from genocide. The stories you would not believe!

"Where was I? It was our grandchildren – some with blue eyes – that puzzled the English when they finally started exploring. Those sweet grandbabies. . . We left a lot of children, you know. Ours were the babies who survived. They had our immunities, you see, to help them survive all the plagues the colonizers brought with them. So, sisters were all sharing us. It sounds shocking I know, but it was really quite practical. And to tell you the truth," he said leaning in to her with mischief in his eye, "*we* didn't mind *a bit!*" He let out a raucous bout of laughter. "You see my point? A great many of the people in the Upper South enjoying some measure of Indian blood, black or white, are also SERBS!!!

Leslie's mirth knew no bounds. "You're crazy," she muttered.

"And the identity is hard-wired," he said. "Look at you.

"So, let me get back to that point I was trying to make about Kosovo before I interrupt myself again. The Angel of the Lord came to Prince Lazar the night before he was to face armies serving The Turk all the way from India to North Africa and everything in between. The Angel asked him 'Do you want the Kingdom of Heaven or do you want the Kingdom of Earth?'

"And being a very devout man, he answered right away, 'The Kingdom of Heaven. In the long run, that's what makes sense.'

"But the Angel says, 'Take your time now, if you choose the Kingdom of Heaven, *tomorrow you lose*. And if you choose the Earthly Kingdom, *tomorrow you win.*'

"Still he chooses the Kingdom of Heaven. So, we *chose* to be the ones with a boot on our necks, our daughters raped in harems, our sons stolen and a pole stuck up our ass if we bitched about it. We *chose* that shit. Crazy you think? No, think about it. You've seen what those evil bastards are, treating people like that. You don't *want* to be like them. They're *revolting*. Once you've been on the receiving end of all that evil, of *course* you would choose this.

"Once they start abusing you, you're not going to their damn church. Hell no. You've got your own damn church and you don't want to spend eternity with someone who does the kinds of things they do, with all that on their souls. You're not stupid. And keep in mind, if you choose not to be a slave, the alternative will be to be a slave *driver* to your own people. What kind of a person would choose such a thing? The most revolting person *of all*.

"That's the truth." He raised his arms and began preaching at the ceiling. "You want to keep railing at the Universe that you have no choice, but the truth is, if you did have a choice, this is what you would choose. And if you wouldn't, you're an asshole. I've got no use for you."

"Who are you talking to?" Leslie asked.

"Those assholes in your living room today."

"Oh, them."

"Am I right?"

"Sounds good to me," she said.

"That was your misfortune today, you just happened to run into a batch of people who have chosen the Earthly Kingdom. They think they can't choose the Earthly Kingdom, but that's bullshit. They have as much of a choice as anyone. And that's why they can't stand you, because you have clearly forsaken privilege and chosen the Heavenly Kingdom, when they lust after the Earthly Kingdom for themselves.

"Leslie, listen to me," Srđa cut in. "I know that what happened here today was very cruel, but it is not defining. Sherry will come by tomorrow, with her sweet potato pie, which she is already baking. When she does, you must tell her that her saints visit Serbian heaven all the time. They come with those pies, and we break out some *kolači* and boil some Serbian coffee and we talk till the wee hours about what we are to do with our errant children on earth, and we are always happy to have such wise people to commiserate with. Tell her that."

"*Da*," said Dušan, "exactly right. Those people in your living room today were lying to themselves, thinking they were looking for justice. They were just avenging themselves, like cowards, on someone defenseless in their care. Cowards are always the most plentiful.

"But that boy upstairs is taking a huge gamble. He is writing a paper that the people paying him expect will benefit them. In fact, it will indict them, so he is about to enter very treacherous waters. He already has a world of black people thinking he's a traitor, and he will soon have a number of powerful white people who will think the same thing. And there's only one reason he's risking all of it. You want to know why?

"Why?" Leslie asked.

"Because," said Dušan, "he has the biggest crush on you I've ever seen in four hundred years," said Dušan. "He's doing it for you. All that matters to him is that he can see you clearly."

Leslie was smiling, with tears forming in her eyes. "No willfully obtuse bullshit?" she asked.

"No," said Dušan. "Not a scrap. So, what are you doing down here? Why aren't you up there?"

"He's in Milwaukee."

"When does he get back?"

"Sometime today."

"Well then, you better get some sleep," he said. "You look terrible. You get that beauty sleep and then get your ass upstairs and getting on that life you're supposed to live."

Jovanka came near, "*Da, da, da*, sweetheart, you get yourself some rest," brushing Leslie's hair out of her eyes and kissing her goodnight. Then Srđa hugged her, while Miloš gave her a big smile.

He paused in front of her. "I don't want to make light of what your *Kuma* and Daniel's *Deda* have done for you, but the intent of my story was not to suggest that you convert to become something else. The point that

I was trying to make is that you be baptized *in your own*. We are waiting for you. It's time you take your place as a proper *Srpkinja*. It's time you came home. You are not a lost orphan ever again, hoping someone will take you in. You *are* home."

"Of course," said Srda.

Jovanka rushed to her with another embrace. "Yes, *srće moje*. You are home. You have always been home. We never left you, and you never left us. Now, to sleep."

Dušan turned out the light.

* * *

Sweet Potato Pie

It was after ten when Leslie woke up to the doorbell. She'd forgotten all about Sherry! The only one to defend Leslie at that Big Black Separatist Party Leslie threw. She put on a robe and buzzed her in. She'd meant to straighten up a bit and make sure there was enough coffee in the house.

"Come on in!" she said. "Oh my god, a sweet potato pie. You're so sweet."

"I'm sorry to drop in like this, but I didn't have your number and I was worried. That was terrible yesterday. I can't stand to see anybody treated like that."

Leslie picked a piece of lint off of Sherry's maroon sweater. "Neither can I. It's a religion with us. Come on, let's get some coffee going to go with that pie," she said as she pulled Sherry along with her. "Sweet potato pie for breakfast. I love it!"

She looked in the pantry and reached for a coffee can. "Oh good, just enough for a nice pot."

Sherry sat at the table while Leslie put the kettle to boiling and set up the Melitta filter.

"Are you sure you're okay?" Sherry asked.

"I'm fine, I got a lot of attention last night from just the right people," she said.

"Wow. Hook me up with them."

Leslie laughed. "That can be arranged." She laughed some more. "Actually, they got ceremonies for that."

"What?"

"Never mind, I'll tell you later."

"I was afraid what I was going to find," Sherry went on. "I pictured this lady I saw in a Bergman film last winter who was peeling the wallpaper off the wall with her fingernails, in a psychotic state."

"Well," Leslie said. "If I'm psychotic, I'm thoroughly enjoying it."

"Good, you seem really, I don't know, at peace. No, I take that back, you look excited."

"I am, somebody's coming home today."

"Reggie?"

"Hell no, Reggie's moved out. He's gone. Actually, he's been an apparition for a while now."

"I'm sorry."

"I'm not. It's about time."

"So, who's coming home?"

"It's kind of an Old World arranged kind of thing,"

"Really? That sounds dull. Are you sure you'll like him?"

"He's perfect. It's a match made in Heaven."

"Here's mine," Sherry said, and opened her wallet to show Leslie her family.

"Oh my God," Leslie said. "That's the biggest Jew-fro I've ever seen," she said of the man in the picture, sitting in the middle of Sherry and her little boy, whose hair was a bit more tightly curled than his daddy's.

Sherry had a good laugh. "I'll tell him you said that."

"Where did you meet him?" Lez asked as she poured the coffee.

"We were in the math department together."

"Oh, math. Now that's *really* sexy."

Sherry laughed as Leslie picked up a knife and cut the pie.

"It really means a lot that you made me this pie," she said, her voice breaking. Her eyes teared up. "Sometimes I just feel so invisible. And I'm just here for people to vent on."

"I know the feeling," Sherry said.

"I know you do," Leslie thought on that for a moment and decided to do something ridiculous. "And I'm going to tell you something, you're going to think I'm crazy. "

"What?"

"I dreamt about this pie."

"You did!"

"Yes, I dreamt that the sexiest angel you've ever seen . . ."

"Yeah?"

"He looks just like Sean Connery!" She was watching Sherry's face closely for the way she was taking in all this outlandish nonsense. She was liking it, amused in a very attentive way, like she had a few dreams like that herself.

"Wow!" Sherry said. "I *love* Sean Connery. He's beautiful, at least since he took his toupee off."

"He told me in the dream that you were coming over with a sweet potato pie and to tell you that your folks come visiting all the time up there, bringing these pies, and those wise old souls all sit around talking about us."

Sherry laughed. Leslie could tell Sherry was as aware as she was that they connected.

"I'm sure they do," Sherry said.

"You're all about how people feel," Leslie said. "You're like this satellite dish for other people's feelings. My aunt is like that. I'm not nearly as good at it. I'm getting too isolated. People shun me a lot."

"Me, too," Sherry said.

"Family?"

"Yeah, I've got a sister who's set herself up as a family counselor advising people in mixed relationships to abandon their marriages and stay away from the evil white people."

"Oh, nice. Does she preach this at family get-togethers with you and what's your guy's name?

"Ben. Oh yeah, we've been through that."

"And let me guess, he's wondering if the *gestapo* just showed up."

Sherry got quiet. "I went to Camilla's meetings because I want to keep moving forward. I want to stop letting this bullshit limit me or dictate my life and the first thing she wants to do is take away the only space I've made for myself where I *am* myself. I'm with someone who relates to me on the deepest level I've ever been on with anyone."

Leslie heard someone going upstairs. It sounded just like a suitcase banging around. Her heart started racing. "He's here," she whispered. "He lives upstairs."

Sherry laughed at Leslie. "Calm down, now. You'll be all right. How did he come to live upstairs?"

"Just a really, really unbelievable coincidence," Leslie said. "But we can take our time finishing our pie."

"Sit down here, and relax," said Sherry. "Never look too enthused."

"I can't begin to do that," said Leslie.'

"Neither can I," they laughed together.

"I was joking about the arranged marriage thing," Leslie said. "Remember yesterday I was talking about the colonized people I come from? Who lived in a remote part of the world nobody knows or cares about?"

"Yes."

"Well, this guy, this really attractive guy moved in right upstairs who's doing his dissertation about us."

"Oh my God," said Sherry.

"What are the mathematical probabilities of that happening?"

"Pretty much zero."

"I'm so lucky," Leslie said, her eyes were tearing up. "I'm living such a privileged life."

"Okay," Sherry said, rising. "You go to him then, but first put on some makeup and comb your hair. You look like you just rolled out of bed."

"I did just roll out of bed."

"Okay, then go do what you gotta do, and call me. Let me know how this all turns out. You know I'll be dying to hear, so don't keep me waiting."

They exchanged numbers and Sherry departed.

Leslie took a quick shower and got dressed. She was on tenterhooks. Once ready, she suddenly felt shy. She sat on her couch, all dressed up and acting like there was nowhere to go. What was that ridiculous feeling? Feeling chicken.

She had the nerve to cross the color line, a lone teenage girl, slam out of the Bigot Belt in Chicago, in 1970, only 12 years after a boy in the neighborhood had been viciously slaughtered for it, but she didn't have the nerve to knock on a neighbor's door, when she already knew he had the biggest crush on her in 400 years? She laughed.

* * *

Daniel smiled when he heard the knock on his door, knowing it had to be someone in the building since anyone else would need buzzing in from the foyer, meaning the chances were one in three it was Leslie. He'd just dreamt about her. That recurring Tolstoy character told him to go get Leslie, she was waiting for him. It was time. Woke him up early with it.

"Hello there!" he said when he saw her. In his head, Roberta Flack sang the line 'the trembling heart of a captive bird' while Leslie spoke.

"Hope I'm not interrupting," she said. "I know you must be tired from all that traveling."

"No, actually I'm feeling rather mellow," he said, leaning against the door jamb, closer to her.

She looked him up and down and smiled into his eyes, half shy, half flirtatious. "Yeah, if you were a cat, you'd be purring," she said, her pupils so dilated, so open to him, sharing eye contact, then he realized he had her still standing in his doorway.

He pulled her along with him towards the front room. "I woke up way early, raring to go. My first ambition, when I was a little kid, was to be a sailor. Get out and see the world. I love traveling." They reached the front room. "Come on and sit down. Want a Coke? Orange juice? Water?"

"Water would be good," she said.

He fetched her a glass, and felt a rush as he walked through the hallway towards her, her sitting there on his couch, waiting for him. Leslie. It's time. He sat down next to her, and turned to face her, his arm across the couch behind her. "So how did your big Separatist meeting go?"

Leslie smiled. "I threw my Big Black Separatist Party and they threw me out! Of course! What was I thinking?"

He laughed. Gutsy little iconoclast. "Why *did* you invite them?"

"You know those articles Reggie's been publishing?"

"Yeah?"

"The woman who runs that group quotes them. She loves them. Reggie didn't write them. *I* wrote them. I *needed* to write them."

He burst out laughing. "Good God, what a scandal! The big radical brother on campus' shit written by a white girl!" He kept on laughing. "Priceless! You are priceless!"

"*They* didn't think so," she said, still smiling, then serious, looking deep into what she felt. "It's like I'm not even here. Just this ghost nobody sees. I walk around thinking, feeling one consciousness, but everybody, white or black, attributes a completely different one to me. There was no way those people could rebuff me without being total asshole hypocrites."

"And they obliged you."

"You got that right."

"Hester Pryne," he said.

"What?" she asked.

"The Scarlet Letter."

"I know. Why do you mention her?" Searching his face intently.

286

"What everyone thought was her shame was her shield and emblem she was brandishing to the world."

"Something precious," Leslie said.

Her eyes almost crossed she was looking so inward. The longing on her face told him that she knew what he was thinking. She knew he knew who she was. True minds. "So, tell me what happened," he asked.

"The first thing that bitch did was ask me to leave."

"What bitch?"

"The bitch running it. The one who loves what I write, in other words, how I think. 'De-colonizing the Mind.' Of all the people in that room, my family was the most directly, most recently, the most violently impacted by all that shit. Nothing in over a hundred years has happened here like what we've just been through. Did you know Tito made it illegal to even talk about what happened to us?"

"Yeah. Nikola told me."

"This country is so bizarre. There cannot be any commonality on this issue. You could be kissing cousins experientially, but it won't matter, if you're white, that's all that matters and anything you say is assumed to be a dismissal and must be summarily dismissed in turn."

She'd become very animated, speaking quickly, intensely.

"So, she's going around the room letting people introduce themselves and she passes over me. In my own home, she passes over me. So, I told her I wasn't a spectator. My life is totally about trying to understand and undo the damage from being a persecuted, recently de-colonized minority. I've gone through hell trying to crack that nut, what with that scarlet letter they give any white female who crosses that line I had to cross to be with my own kind of people.

"And then half the room was attacking me that being white in America meant I couldn't possibly have any problems like that. Okay, so I don't really exist, I'm just this White Appearing Object they get to use for target practice. Oh that, and they hate my guts. And the other half were a bunch of cowards who let them get away with it. Including Reggie."

"Wow. Reggie did nothing?" Daniel smiled. Clearly, that impediment had disgraced itself.

"Nothing. Oh no, he did do something. He tried to keep me from clawing at that bitch. Can't even remember her name now I want to drive her from my memory so bad. She's got it as bad as any bigot I ever saw growing up in the Bigot Belt. People like her repulse me.

"Oh yeah, and he told me I was naïve, which just underscores his assumption that my identity MUST be white as defined by American racism.

I'm supposed to just set aside for my whole life what I need as a human being because there's this racial context that supersedes it. Always and forever. I'm not even to *think* about what *I* might need to exist in this time and place."

Daniel laughed. "So, Reggie had to protect her from you?"

"I threw them all out."

"Hallelujah and praise the Lord!" he clapped his hands together. "I wish I could have seen that. Of course, then they would have had to deal with me and I wouldn't get to see Hester standing trial solo, her head up, her eyes straight. I'll just have to imagine it. So, tell me how you feel about all this."

She looked stunned. Go for it, he thought. Give me what you feel. He reached for her hand. With his touch she cut loose. Her face crumbled into tears. She looked up into his eyes, pupils big enough to fall into. Keep them there, he thought. Keep them right there. And come here.

He pulled her towards him to hug her and she gave it up. To him. His girl. She sobbed loudly and fully for several minutes. The closer he held her, the more she wailed, in anger and despair. Then, finally she whispered, a lament, "That's the curse of my life. The people I recognize will *never* recognize me," she said. "They will *never* see me as an equal."

Something clicked in Daniel's head, like the wisp of a dream, a long-sought intent realized. He pulled her into his face excitedly. "That's *all* I want to see, and I *do* see it, and I can't tell you how *much* I see it, and how much joy that brings me."

Her wet face beamed. He didn't understand why people thought crying made people look bad. It made her beautiful, compelling, real. She sighed deeply and was done with the tears. Then she demurred playfully. "But there's something you need to know before you get too involved here. There's something I need to confess," she said.

"What do you need to confess?"

She smiled, "I really *am* insane. I see apparitions. I saw my ghostly Guardian Angel godparents, and my long-lost cousin AND I see your great- great- great- great- great- Serbian grandfather, too," she counted off five digits as she spoke.

"You can actually see them?" he said. "They just play *me* like a fiddle."

"I can now," she said. "When I was little I used to see my godfather, but I mistook him for Martin Luther King." She laughed. "But I saw them all last night, in total technicolor."

"Are they here now?"

She looked around the room and shook her head. "I think it's just us."

Daniel smacked his head with the palm of his hand. "So that's it! The Tolstoy dude in my dreams isn't Russian. He's Serb! Of course!" A host of forgotten dreams flashed in his head and left him high as a kite. Inebriated. "So that's who sent me on this quest!"

"What quest?" she asked.

"You already know what quest. This quest to find you. Ever since I was a boy."

"Ever since I was a girl," she said.

They were both quiet for a moment. Almost shy.

Then he jumped up and pulled her with him. "Come on, I've got to show you something." He pulled her into his bedroom.

She stopped in the doorway and teased, "You know momma always warned me about a man offering to show me something and taking me to his bedroom."

He was in the closet and laughed. He pulled out a box on a top shelf. He set it on the bed. She sat on it as he started digging through some papers in the box. He pulled out a child's drawing and showed it to her. She gasped.

"It's Dušan!" she said. "You used to see him?"

"I *imagined* him. We'd play pirates together. He taught me how to walk a gang plank."

She looked at the picture closely. "Oh my god, this looks just like him, those eyebrows and the hair. You've even got the copper bracelet he wears. This is incredible!"

"So, tell me what they told you. Was it like a dream?"

"I suppose I could have been dreaming, but it didn't feel like it. I remember it as real, and I completely believe everything they told me, completely believe that they're real and that they love me, and that they've been pulling for me all along."

He watched her talking, in his room, sitting there, like she'd always been there.

"And all I had to do to see them was to be driven stark raving mad by black bigots doing everything to me I've been watching white bigots do to them all my life, the same white bigots who've been persecuting *me* of late. It was an absolutely insane position to be in, and there was no way out except into an entirely different dimension.

"Oh, I've decided to convert to the Serbian Orthodox Church and make it official that I've chosen the Kingdom of Heaven. No ifs, ands, or buts about it. See, there are the two kinds of people in the world. Your *Deda*

Dušan told me about it. There's the people who choose the Earthly Kingdom who want to be racist to everybody else and steal the good life for
themselves, and the people who choose the Heavenly Kingdom who think
the Earthly Kingdom people are gross and wouldn't be caught dead acting like them."

"Excellent interpretation of Christianity," Daniel observed. He loved
listening to her ramble on, quite aware that when he did the same ram-
bling most people went glassy-eyed. What's wrong with them? he
thought. This shit is fascinating!

"Oh, and another thing," she said, grasping his arm excitedly and
shaking it. "I just figured this out when I was taking a shower. Okay, according to the legend us Serbs had the privilege of becoming slaves because we were God's favorites," she laughed heartily. "This is such crazy
shit. I love it!"

"Superbly crazy, brazen Serbian shit," he said. "Y'all *are* a hoot."

"So, I'm cooking up another legend. Okay, God could see that the way
the world was going somebody was going to be coming up with the he-
reditary slavery thing pretty soon since the world was getting so small,
and color coding was an obvious first choice for the building of a high-
end hierarchy. He needed the people with the highest emotional intelligence for the job. Nobody else could cut it and raise the level of civilization the way it needed to be raised – this absolutely miraculous feat."

"Everything that's been going on here," he said, picking up the beat,
"for the last few hundred years while y'all were being wiped from the
face of the earth."

She was struck silent, her eyes started to puddle up, and she nodded
her head. "We need help." She sobbed. He took her in his arms again. "We
need your expertise," she said. "Y'all are better at this shit than we are."

"I'm your man," he said. "No matter where it takes me." He cuddled
her again.

She leaned heavily into him, in a trusting way that gratified him. Give
her shelter. He rocked her. She seemed to become lost in thought, very
contented thought. Her eyelids suddenly looked very heavy. "I've had
like two hours of sleep in the last two days." She rested her head against
him and closed her eyes. After a moment she opened them again and
smiled at him. "See, I knew you were just trying to hustle me into your
bed," she teased. Her eyelids took over and shut themselves again. She
fell asleep. He gently shifted her head to the pillow.

He watched her sleeping for a few minutes. He picked up the drawing
of Dušan and thought to himself, 'So this is what this has all been about,

290

you old devil, you.' He looked around the room. "You hearing me?" He said out loud and laughed.

He got a blanket from the closet and covered her with it. He went into the kitchen and busied himself cleaning up the dishes he'd left unwashed since before his trip.

He remembered his drive down 94, starting at dawn, with a large coffee and the sun rising over the sparkling lake. His mind had been broadly synthesizing, percolating lots of little bits he'd picked up in the last month. Tripping out on the same shit Leslie was tripping out on, at the same time.

Nikola had given him literature on the Serb religion. Of course, everything was always in synchronicity. He was going to have such a field day with this mess, comparing the parallel cultures.

He could already see the overview. Serbs had survived and overcome their slavery by way of an interpretation of Christianity that emphasized heightened cultural values for loving and supporting one another in highly evolved ways that, according to their belief, God loves.

Black Americans had survived and overcome their slavery by way of an interpretation of Christianity that inspired them to love *their enemies* in highly evolved ways that, according to their belief, God loves. All of which convicted the whites of the slaves' humanity and led to their emancipation.

'Good God,' he thought, "can you imagine if the two could borrow from each other?"

Earth, Wind and Fire was on the radio. He beat the rhythm on the dashboard and sang along.

> "Shining star for you to see,
> what your life can truly be."

The song was still in his head as he dried the dishes, singing the song, realizing that highly complementary Serbian mind, now endangered, that was capable of persisting, of loving this beleaguered mutual identity, in ways he could not yet fathom, was in his care, needing his protection. And he had been nurtured since childhood to do just that. Life was good. No, it was amazing.

The song ended, and he heard someone downstairs. He went down to Leslie's apartment. The front door was open. He rapped on it. Reggie came out of the bedroom. "You know where Lez is?

"She's upstairs, man, asleep. She had quite a night."

"She all right?"

"Yeah. A little manic, free associating, probably just from lack of sleep."

"You a shrink?"

"No, and neither are you, but you damn well know what I'm saying, even if you do want to be obtuse about it."

Reggie held up his hand as if to concede the point. "Does she need to talk to me, you think?"

"Nah, I think she's let you go, man. I mean, she hasn't hardly mentioned you. Like there was no support in her world, so she made up another one."

"Sounds like Lez."

"Why'd you just leave her alone after those people did that to her?"

"I left her to you," Reggie said.

Daniel was struck silent for a moment.

"To me? I was in Milwaukee."

"Oh, I didn't know that. You got her?"

"Yeah, I got her," Daniel said.

"Well, I'm clearing out of here. I've left a number on the kitchen table she can call when she wants to talk logistics. The lease is up the end of the month and she can keep the deposit if she doesn't want to stay. Tell her that."

"Okay," Daniel replied. He went back upstairs. "Logistics," he muttered under his breath.

When he checked on Leslie she was sitting on the bed, looking disoriented and morose. "I heard you talking," she said.

"Yeah?"

"And this whole awful world popped back in my head. This world where I was giving all this support to the people around me and getting attacked by racist hellcats for doing it, but when I look for someone supporting me, the room is empty. They don't think I need it. I'm not really human. To anybody. That's how I think when I'm depressed."

He watched her talking beyond her fatigue, as if her brain was still thinking, streaming its consciousness while her body was already half asleep.

"It seems everyone in this country, with amazing uniformity, thinks I'm propelled by a disgusting and perverse energy – since that's pretty much how America sees a white female who consents to be in a black man's bed."

He touched her cheek.

"Listen," he said. "The energy propelling you is sacred."

She gasped. "That's the word! That's it!" Her eyes were sparkling with tears again in that way he loved. "The word I could never think of. It's just been the feeling of it, but the word I didn't dare. I would never dare."

She took his hand and pulled it to her chest, then locked eyes, her own filled with joy. "This is what I've been jealous of. Watching y'all do this ritual for each other – that takes at least one other person – that confers upon you the status of a human being – a status you've lived without for a very long time."

Then she beamed at him. "Now I can be a Phoenix, too!"

"A Phoenix?"

"Yes, rising."

"Oh, from your ashes."

"Yes, no more ashes," she said, another set of puddles glimmering in her eyes on top of a grand smile.

She regarded him very intently, still holding his hand to her heart. "It can't be that I've only known you a few months. I don't know when it was, or where, all I know is the feeling, and it feels like my rudder just caught a good current and I'm righting myself."

She pulled on the blanket separating them. "Come here," she said. "You're too far away."

"Too far away? I'm right here," he said, smiling but taking his weight off the blanket, nonetheless, then climbing in with her.

"Now this is some serious *deja vu*," she said. "I've been picturing *this* for months."

He laughed. "Really? Tell me about that."

"Why don't I just show you?" she said impish again, bringing her face in very close.

Lost passionately in each other, Leslie chanted, "Yes, touch me. I want you to touch me. I want everything about you. It's you I want."

Then, just a beat ahead, Daniel cut in with the deep, resonant voice Leslie loved. "You're the one."

* * *

Leslie and Daniel's kindred spirits were downstairs in Leslie's kitchen. Miloš was filling four shot glasses with šljivovic, plum brandy. Jovanka was cooking Serbian coffee, which is nothing like Turkish coffee, the main difference being that Serbian coffee is made by Serbs, while Turkish coffee is made by Turks.

"Do you think they'll ever figure it out?" she asked.

"Figure out what?" asked Dušan, who had helped himself to a piece of baklava and was making a mess of the honey dripping onto his hands, which he then meticulously licked with great relish.

Srđa was eating his baklava with a fork but was thoroughly enjoying Dušan's gusto. He caught Miloš' eye and they were both watching Dušan with amusement. "Here," he said, offering Dušan the plate, "Have another piece."

Dušan dug in with both hands, then looked up and noticed them watching him. He picked up the plate and challenged them, "Dig in, you sissies! Eat like a man!"

Srđa laughed, shrugged his shoulders and grabbed a piece. Miloš followed suit.

Jovanka brought the four cups to the table. "Figure out when they knew each other before."

"Before when?" asked Srđa.

"When did they know each other before?" Dušan said. "Nobody's said anything about this."

"You hadn't heard?" she asked. "I suppose it is something only us ladies will discuss. Vuk and Sava."

"Vuk and Sava who?" asked Dušan.

"Our famous boy. Oh, I'm sorry. I'm forgetting you wouldn't know about the only famous boy from our district."

"You're not saying . . ." said Srđa.

"Ne, ne, ne, ne," said Jovanka. "Nothing like that at all. They were like two brothers is all. Like brothers who are best friends who will take a bullet for each other at any moment. They were brothers to the death. It would have been better if . . . well it's better now with Sava coming back as Leslie.

"I'm sorry, Dušan," Miloš said. "We keep forgetting to explain. The famous boy in our district was Sava Mrkalja who began the effort to get the alphabet changed to save the people from the plight they were in from being illiterate. And Vuk Karadžić was his best friend and collaborator. All Sava and Vuk could talk about was saving the people."

"Just like those two," Jovanka said, pointing upstairs. "Anyway, these kinds of problems, like Leslie has been having, are best solved with the love of a man. A *real* man. It takes the energy of a real man.

"I will never forget what she said, 'I don't know when it was, or where, all I know is the feeling, and it feels like my rudder just caught a good current and is righting itself.' It's just so beautiful." She started dabbing at her eyes like a woman reading a romance novel. "To think it didn't matter how long it took Vuk to find his lost brother, whose lifeless body was drifting down the Kupa, only now the brother is reborn as a beautiful girl." She dabbed at her eyes again. "Who still feels Sava's defeat, but brother Vuk has returned and she has found her rudder."

"So to speak!" laughed Dušan raucously. Then he hit Srđa's arm. "I told you the boy was like me!"

He rose up and took her shoulders in hand and said. "Sister, I am thrilled beyond words to have you for my sister, and to celebrate, us three brothers are going out and getting plastered."

Jovanka protested, but it was no use as Srđa and Miloš were pulled out the door by their burly new brother.

* * *

Archie Rebuilds an Engine

Eventually, Leslie and Daniel came up for air and surveyed the world around them that needed to adjust to their partnership. Of course, it was imperative to share the big news with Archie about Leslie's big discovery. After all, he was the one who'd spent a decade programming her to go on that quest –whether he had any idea that's what he was doing, or not.

Leslie and Daniel were at Nikola and Bojana's for dinner explaining the issue. Nikola said the thing to do was just to show up. Just him, Bojana and Leslie. They'd get him straight.

"Come," said Bojana, "with us to see your father. Let him get the big family news first, then another time, he will be ready to meet Daniel. Then he will make perfect sense. Your *tata* will have time to think."

So, one Saturday afternoon the three of them drove out to the suburbs. Leslie was tied up in knots wondering how he'd react to her. Would he start screaming at her? Would he lock the door and not let them in? Would it be horrible? If it weren't for Nikola and Bojana taking her, there's no way she would ever get up the nerve to go see him.

Then she told herself that, in all those years of endless debates with him about racism, he had never been the least bit contemptuous with her. Those were actually his moments of clarity. As long as she was completely contradicting him on that subject, she was okay by him. So now, this would have to be okay, too. Right? That didn't stop her stomach from fluttering or stop her eyelid from twitching. Bojana said she couldn't see it. She was sitting in the front passenger seat. She reached her hand towards the back seat where Leslie sat and rested it on Leslie's knee.

Of course, Jovanka and Srđa were flanking Leslie. He had his arm across the seat behind her, and Jovanka had her hand on Leslie's other knee. Jovanka looked excited. Srđa did too. Today was the day for some major closure. Mission accomplished.

They pulled up to the house and parked. The garage door was open. "He's in there," said Leslie, hoping her voice wasn't expressing dread, "working on his car."

"Good," said Nikola and piled out of the car. The tall young man led the way with the two short girls behind him.

"Hey dad," Leslie said as they neared him. He looked up at her furtively. "This is Nikola and Bojana, they're from the same district as grandma. They've been helping me find out who we really are. This is huge." She'd already been filling her mom in during their weekly phone chats. Leslie was counting on her mom relaying the news to Archie. It looked like maybe it was working on him.

Archie nodded his head and mumbled, "How do you do?"

Nikola offered his hand. Archie took it. Leslie's jitterbugs abated. There was nothing phony about Archie. If he shook your hand it meant he wasn't going to bite you.

"They've got a lot of stuff to show you," Leslie said, motioning towards a box Bojana was carrying, "Can we go in?"

Archie nodded his head in the direction of the door. Leslie was amazed at how right Nikola was. Their presence awed him, mollified him.

Archie opened the door and walked in. While they entered he picked his newspaper up from off of the table. His head was still down, he wasn't looking at anyone directly. Then he looked up at Nikola.

"You can sit down," he said.

"Hvala," said Nikola.

"Nema na čemu," Archie mumbled faintly, as the two young women seated themselves around Nikola.

Leslie was floored. She'd never heard her father say anything in Serbian before. Grandma had never spoken anything but English to anyone, including her son. It had never occurred to Leslie that her dad knew any of it. It was as if this secret part of him had just opened up. The little immigrant kid the bullies beat up, taunting him about his 'liver lips.' The dark little immigrant family that would never think of travelling south, where they would have had to use the 'colored' facilities. All that mess his endless nigger jokes was covering, calling attention away from. But in that moment when Nikola said, 'thank you,' and Archie replied, 'you're welcome,' all that went away, and the world was just normal. One of those rare moments in Leslie's life when the world was normal. Respectable. No longer a Tuđina, full of genocidal, self-betraying collusions. And it was happening at her house! She batted away tears.

Nikola spoke. "Sir, first thing I must say, from story Leslie tells me, your instincts are super. You did not know our story, but still you raised your daughter to think the way *we* think. It makes perfect sense." Nikola then dug into the box starting with a large print on cardstock of the painting by Paja Jovanović, "Migration of the Serbs."

"Here is who we are. Thirty thousand of us who stood up to the Turk who occupied our country and made us their slaves. But we lose and run for our lives. Austrian crown lets us live in no-man's land between Europe and Middle East and all it costs is our blood. We keep The Turk from invading Europe for 350 years! We are best freedom fighters of all time! Many people benefit. But not us!"

Deloris walked into the room and did a double take. "*Leslie!!!*" she said, with multiple exclamation points at the end. Leslie got up and hugged her mom. She introduced her friends. Deloris went about joyfully making everyone coffee.

Nikola got back to his story. "Then when done with that job we produce Tesla and Mrs. Einstein. The first one, who help husband with his math. He did his best discoveries when married to her."

"And the world repays us with this," he brought out a picture of Jasenovac.

Leslie harrumphed sardonically. "Anyone sane would look at people like us and think, 'How remarkable, how did such a small population contribute so much? But look what we got. A death camp."

Nikola continued, pulling out a family portrait. "We found on list of those lost there, your cousin, Vasilije. He was your Aunt Sara's son. She is sitting in the middle. He is tallest boy standing. And that beautiful girl holding the two babies, she was sent to other death camp, Stari Gradiška, and disappears."

Jovanka and Srđa were standing behind Leslie. Jovanka looked behind her. The beautiful girl in the picture was there, looking on, holding the hand of her brother, Vasilije. They were both glowing.

"Oh Anka!" Jovanka exclaimed, there you are."

Leslie felt something behind her and turned. She saw her cousins! They were semi-transparent, but looked just like they did in the picture. Anka raised her finger to her smiling lips in a shushing gesture, reminding Leslie to keep a low profile on her new powers of perception.

"Later," Anka whispered.

Leslie turned her head back around, smiling. That was the kindest face she'd ever seen. She felt a thrill tingling up her spine. She thought to herself, 'sometimes it takes the paranormal to make everything normal.' She felt a certainty that life would be normal from then on. Every day normal.

Nikola went on. "If you want to know the story of your Aunt Sara and Uncle Rade, just read about parents of Malcolm X. Same story. Uncle Rade was farmer, miller *and* blacksmith. In that time, most Serbs in Croatia are super poor. Poor land for farming. No one hires them. Most Serb fathers struggle to put shoes on children's feet. But not Rade, no. Rade pays for all his many children to go to school. He is too proud to go into hiding when Serbs are massacred in many towns. Sara goes in hiding with half of children. She is pregnant fifteenth time. Rade keeps half the children with him, at home. Ustaša come, take him out in field, shoot him down like dog, then burn down everything he work lifetime building.

"Next morning, children are thrown on train to Jasenovac. Three survive and come back to mother four years later, but not as Serbian children, not as Orthodox children. No, they come back Croatian children, baptized Catholic. So easy for Ustaša to genocide Serbs. Just kill parents and steal children. Sara is crazy bitter and drives everyone away from her. That is why she quarrel with your mother when she makes trip home."

"And after the war," Leslie told her father. "Tito made it illegal to even talk about what happened to us. That's why nobody knows. It's as bad as it ever gets, for anybody, anywhere, and nobody knows."

Nikola nodded. "In Croatia, we are like black people here. We wear same shoes. Persecuted. When I come here, those are the people I am comfortable with. We are same. Your daughter's boyfriend, Daniel," he gestured toward the box, "he research all this. He do that for your daughter. He knows who she is. He knows who I am. He is my friend," he struck his chest with his fist, "for life."

Archie had little to say, was just quiet, very pensive. When Nikola finally announced that they needed to head home, Archie thanked them for coming, then saw them out. Of course, it would have been absurd for anyone to have expected Archie to flat out apologize or admit to being wrong about anything. When Nikola turned the engine on his car, Archie listened, then approached and gave him advice on what he should do to tune it. He told Nikola to come by that weekend and he could use his tools.

As they drove off, Leslie explained to Nikola and Bojana that offering the use of his tools was Archie-language for "Thanks. You're all right."

"Don't worry," said Nikola. "I know his language."

When Leslie checked in that week, her mom asked her if she wanted to go to the Wisconsin State Fair, the one right over the border they always went to, with them. Archie said to ask her if she wanted to go. So, Leslie took the train out to La Grange and then they drove upstate.

Leslie's poor mom was like a third wheel. Archie talked and talked and talked to Leslie, in the back seat. He talked about what he'd seen on TV, on PBS and read in the Reader's Digest, which Leslie knew he kept in the bathroom, so she always had that image to associate with whatever story he was telling. He talked about his days in the Navy and his boyhood in the Civilian Conservation Corps of the Depression Era. He talked about all the things in the world he suddenly had the free attention to notice, which he'd been saving up to tell her for days beforehand.

She realized what it was. He finally believed her. In all those debates, which were really discussions about themselves, there was really only one thing she was saying, over and over – "We're okay." He never could believe her – he wanted to hear it said – but he couldn't believe it. It wasn't till she ran that gauntlet the way she did with her relationships that he finally believed. He wasn't berating black people anymore. He wasn't even berating his own family anymore!

He'd found peace.

He even attended the event at Nikola's church, her new church, in which Leslie was baptized, right before she and Daniel got married.

The next holiday, Leslie showed up with Daniel, and she was showing. When she had the baby, she was able to present her father with exactly what he had been hating all those years --an exquisitely beautiful little Serbian boy – a replica of Miloš Roknić.

People were surprised that Daniel would have a son who looked so different from him, but he wasn't. He had an uncle on the Robeson County, NC side of the family, Dušan's side, who could pass for Archie's brother.

In the following spring, Leslie, Daniel and the baby came to visit, and Archie had something to show them. Leslie had been curious about a Mazda a neighbor was selling. Archie got it for a song. The engine needed to be rebuilt. Five dollars' worth of O rings needed to be replaced. So, all that winter he'd stood out in the cold garage disassembling that Wenkl engine. He'd thought it was a Jap engine, but no, it was a Kraut engine. He explained, at length, the physics of how it worked to Leslie.

The car was for her. As always, she knew exactly what behavior she was being rewarded for, from the man who didn't know, what he knew, all along.

* * *

Historical Note

A census following the Balkan Wars of the Nineties reveals that, out of all the purported genocides, the only people successfully genocided were the *Krajina* Serbs of Croatia. We are now deemed culturally extinct. In the 19th century we comprised as much as 40% of Croatia. There are only 4% remaining, elderly and dwindling. Survivors report that U.S. planes strafed us as we fled the land we'd defended with endless generations' blood for hundreds of years -- a land in which we had never really been citizens.

Our town names have largely been changed, or if emptied, bulldozed into oblivion. Sjeničak is now called Gvodz. Monuments, perhaps even the ossuary memorializing the victims slaughtered in the woods of Brezje, destroyed. Serb folk customs and achievements are being attributed to Croatians. (The inventor, Nikola Tesla, for example, was a *Krajina* Serb, whatever other claims may be made.) In other words, exactly the same process the United States went through following the Removal Act of the 1830's is being repeated there. That includes the erection of numerous statues of Starćević, the equivalent of Andrew Jackson. Many Americans should have little difficulty relating to or identifying with the Croats.

At the beginning of the 78 days the U.S. bombed Belgrade in 1997, the city residents heard the air raid siren. In typical Serb fashion, many ran into their homes, printed out a copy of the bullseye that had gone viral on the internet, pinned it to their chests, then ran out to the bridges. They then flipped birds at the U.S. birds flying overhead.

Not a single military target was hit by the U.S. Rather, essential infrastructure was destroyed, power plants, schools, hospitals and industrial targets, such as the thriving cigarette factory, that produced a brand popular throughout Europe. It has since been bought out by a U.S. competitor. That is typical of the 'democratization' of this 'liberated' country, rescued from its 'communist' past by the 'free' world.

A photo had been published worldwide of an emaciated looking Bosnian man, who in fact had a lung ailment in childhood that left him with a deformed chest, behind barbed wire. It was admitted by the journalists providing that photo that these men were, in fact, refugees being helped at a Serbian refugee center, who happened to be standing *in front of* barbed wire protecting a storage building. By then, the media was filled with relentless propaganda vilifying the Serbs as the fascist instigators of the war. *No one paid attention to the retraction.* Considering the enormous injury done to *Krajina* Serbs over the centuries by fascist and/or

Imperialist people it is perhaps the ultimate insult to label us fascists as we were harried into oblivion.

Twenty years later a former CIA agent, Robert Baer, admitted to spreading false rumors to Bosnian Moslems in Sarajevo about a "Serbian Supreme" plotting to invade them. It was a fiction manufactured by the CIA.

In a few more generations, the *Krajina* Serbs, who contributed so much to the freedom and culture of Europe, may be forgotten entirely, as if we never existed, while Serbia, as well, wonders if that will soon be her fate. The U.S. is, after all, quite willing to bomb us.

Pravi Crni su Srbski
Pravi Srbski su Crni.

Made in the USA
Columbia, SC
18 January 2019